Lost Cause

Ed James

1

Mark Campbell sat in the bay window, looking across the Bruntsfield rooftops towards the church dominating the street opposite. The school playground was empty in the morning sunshine. A box of light crawled along the stripped-wood floor of the living room, warming his bare feet.

A familiar view, one he enjoyed every morning, and usually with coffee. His head was thumping and he couldn't believe he'd run out of the stuff. He tugged on his socks, then his shoes.

A double Americano from the café on the corner, then into the deli next door to get some beans. The locally roasted ones. Expensive, but so worth it.

Mark got up and stretched, his back crunching as he peered down at the street. Coast seemed clear, so he grabbed his wallet, phone and keys then headed out of the flat. The stairwell had that familiar smell of cat pee. At least this block was filled with old ladies rather than students. Aye, thank God for old ladies and their cats.

He opened the door and stepped outside into the cool air, the summer breeze carrying the smell of roasting hops up from the brewery.

Coast still clear, so he stepped onto the short path to the street and let the door shut behind him.

'Mr Campbell.'

Mark stopped dead. His heart felt like someone was pulverising it with an electric wire.

Vic Hebden was leaning back against the side wall, casually checking his phone, a cigarette hanging from his lip. Sharp suit with black pinstripes, black shirt open at the neck, shiny black shoes. A big teddy boy quiff at least eight inches clear of a face criss-crossed by at least three separate knife wounds.

Trouble with a capital T.

Hell, the whole word was in capitals. Bold, italics, under-lines and a font so big each letter wouldn't even fit on a page of A0.

Mark scanned the street. Nowhere near busy enough to blend in if he ran. His car was across the road, even had his key in his pocket. Get in, lock the doors, drive off and Vic Hebden would be a distant memory.

Car doors opened and two big lumps got out of the back of a black Passat. Wearing suits and built like bouncers. A wiry one got out of the driver's side. The trio had the perfect combination of muscle and pace.

Mark was trapped.

Vic put his phone away. 'Mr Campbell, what a glorious day it is.'

Mark clenched his fists, but more out of instinct than any sudden urge to become a fighting man. 'How you doing?'

'I'm well.' Vic kicked away from the wall and squared up to Mark. 'Need a word with you, if that's okay?'

'Don't think I've got much of a choice, do I?'

'That's true, Mr Campbell. Very true.'

Despite his thumping head and his fluttering belly, Mark gave Vic a polite smile, all business. 'What can I do you for?'

'Just the small matter of you being late on the last three instal-ments of your loan.'

It was all catching up with him.

Mark swallowed down the bile rising in his throat. 'You know I'll get it to you.'

'Do I? Because that's what you told me after you'd missed the first payment. And the second.' Vic clapped Mark's arm, hard enough to hurt. 'Now, I'm a big believer in that saying, "Fool me once, shame on you. Fool me twice, shame on me".'

Mark was nodding along. Maybe charming Vic would get him out of this situation long enough to come up with a strategy. 'I know it well.'

'In that case, you can appreciate that I've been a fool once. Some might even say twice. But I can't be a fool three times, Mr Campbell. I want my money.'

Mark felt like he was going to fall over. He wished it. Begged for it. Just lie there, didn't even have to be looking up. Get whisked off to hospital with a heart attack or a stroke. Anything. Just not here, feeling like someone was digging nails into his neck. 'That might be an issue.'

Vic took a drag of his cigarette, dropped the butt on the pavement and stamped on it. 'Now that isn't what I wanted to hear.' He blew the smoke over Mark's face. 'Mr Campbell, my side of our arrangement was I gave you the capital to clear your divorce settlement. Your only duty, Mr Campbell, is to pay me on time. When I loaned you that money, you said you were good for it. But it turns out you were only good for eight payments. You've missed three now. There are another twenty-five due after that.' He reached into his pocket and pulled out a pristine box of cigarettes and a gold lighter. He put a second smoke between his lips and sparked up. 'When we got into this arrangement, I explained to you how it had to work, didn't I? Men like you, who've pissed off every reputable lending institution in this land, you've no choice but to come to me. You begged me, pleaded with me to lend you some cash. And I helped you.'

'And I'm grateful, it's just...' Mark's guts were squirming now. 'I explained to you how the nature of my business means I might go a few months without paying, but I'll be good for the balance due at the end of the quarter.'

Vic winced. 'You're a smart man, aren't you? Not many people have the brains to make it as an author. Even saw one of your books in Waterstones when I was in there with my dear old mother.'

That was a slip.

Vic having family meant there was a leverage point, not that Mark was in any position to threaten his mother.

'Would've been smart for you to set aside the money for a rainy day like this.' Vic looked up into the pristine blue sky. 'I mean, it's glorious, but you know what I mean. And I like to see the best in people, Mr Campbell. I like to help them out. But when people miss payments, it upsets me. Eight successful payments made me think you'll be good for the rest. One missed payment made me think it was a blip. Two made me think it might not be. Three? Now three makes me think it's running down the slippery slope.'

Mark froze. He needed to stay quiet. To let Vic get his soliloquy out of the way. Show he was successful in intimidating him. Then he could get some coffee in him and, with the benefit of a clear head, think through what the hell he was going to do.

Vic stood there, sucking deep on his cigarette and exhaling the dank smoke all over Mark. 'So. When can you get me the money?'

'It'll be a few weeks.'

'I need it by Friday.'

'But it's Thursday!'

Vic pressed a smelly finger to Mark's lips. 'Friday.'

'I'm serious, I—' Mark was struggling to breathe. The black spots danced around the edge of his vision. 'How much am I due you?'

The question seemed to flummox Vic. He frowned, then reached into his pocket for his phone.

The kids were let out of school for their morning break, their screaming and singing invading their conversation.

Vic checked the mobile's screen, then put it away again. 'One hundred and sixty-three grand.'

That was a really deep hole. No amount of ignoring it was

going to get Mark out of this. He had a faint glimmer of hope, though, but it wasn't going to be a quick fix. 'Okay, can I pay it all off?'

Vic laughed. 'Mr Campbell, you can't even pay off an instalment. How are you going to—'

'I'll get you it. All of it.'

'Right. Well, that's very noble of you, Mr Campbell, but let's just settle on you getting me my outstanding payments, plus the next one.'

'Look, I'm due a lump sum. It'll go a long way to clearing it all off.'

'How long are we talking?'

'Um, a couple of weeks.'

Vic took a long drag of his cigarette, deep into his lungs, then let it slowly out of his nostrils. 'I really hate this position you've put me in, Mr Campbell. You've exploited my good nature. How we've both got daughters the same age. How it'd affect Kay's degree if I didn't help you. You've let me down, Mr Campbell.' He grabbed Mark's arm like a vice. 'My job is lending people money. I really don't want to have to do this, but I have to. It's the part I really don't like. Here's the deal. You get me that payment in two weeks, or I'll have no choice but to get some friends of mine to break your legs in such a way they'll never heal.'

Mark wanted to smash Vic's face into a pulp and run away.

But a man like Vic Hebden, doing what he did, even if he got away, he'd target Mark's nearest and dearest.

He felt like he was going to throw up. 'Deal.'

'And I really hate this, Mr Campbell. I *hate* it. But you're going to think a lot of things over the next few hours, chiefly about running away. That wouldn't be a good idea. I want you to think about how I was waiting for you.'

Mark frowned. 'Excuse me?'

'Well, I called round and you could've been out. Or maybe you didn't hear the buzzer. But I was here, waiting. Think about how I knew you were here.' Vic blew smoke out of his nostrils.

'Because I know where you are at all times, Mr Campbell. You have no secrets from me.'

Mark took in the street. Any of the other cars could belong to Vic, to his goons. To whoever was staking him out. And Vic Hebden wouldn't rely on manpower alone. No, he'd have electronic means too. Probably had cameras nearby. Probably had Mark's phone hacked.

Magic.

'I'll be in touch, Mr Campbell.' Vic let go and set off down the street. 'Two weeks, otherwise...'

And Mark now knew what that would mean.

2

Mark perched on a stool and sat next to the window. Felt like he was going to be sick. He tried to drink his triple-shot Americano, but his hands were shaking, badly enough to spill dark-brown liquid through the plastic lid.

He was in deep, deep shit here.

Two weeks.

Fourteen days.

He needed *months*, not days. And he had no idea how he'd get the money.

The black dots of panic were floating around his vision.

He took off his glasses and rubbed the bridge of his nose.

Five.

Four.

Three.

Two.

One.

And Calm Mark was back, hands perfectly still. He picked up his coffee, tore off the lid and sipped the dark nectar.

Bliss.

For a few brief seconds, he wasn't facing serious physical damage.

The café was full of normal people. Two businessmen in suits talking like they were in a meeting. Three mums eating tray bakes in amongst feeding their babies. A skinny dude hammering away at a laptop, bobbing along to whatever his white headphones were playing, probably Lana Del Rey, judging from his T-shirt. The hipster behind the counter shook cocoa powder onto a pair of cappuccinos, then took them over to the businessmen.

Out of the window, though, the busy street, blocked by two passing buses.

Vic Hebden would have people there, watching Mark.

He couldn't run. They'd follow him. Trap him. Break his legs, there and then. Maybe his fingers too. He'd never be able to write again. Dictation didn't work that well with his accent, caught between at least three regions of Scotland.

Mark laughed. Even amongst it all, he was laughing.

The alternative was letting everyone see a grown man collapse into floods of tears.

He was screwed. Absolutely screwed. He'd tried to tell Vic he had a plan, but he had nothing. Nothing but morbid fear for his health and his life.

He needed to keep calm, focus on what he could do, not what he couldn't.

Well, the best thing would've been to not get into it in the first place.

Now that the impossible was out of the way, he could think a bit more clearly. Walk up to the cliff and peer over, as his therapist would say.

He could just get hammered. Sit in the pub and get shitfaced. Or buy a bottle of whisky, take it home and sink it.

All that would get him was a day closer to his deadline and a thumping hangover.

No. He needed to find the money. And he needed it now.

His flat was worth more than the outstanding capital. He could re-mortgage it. But nobody would lend to him. That was why he was in this situation in the first place. And he could barely afford the mortgage as it was.

Still, he had to try.

He took a sip of coffee and got out his phone. Took longer than it should to find his old mortgage IFA's email address, but he did. So he sent her a message.

And actually started to feel better.

A re-mortgage would give him enough to pay off the whole loan.

Okay, so what else could he do?

Well, the big elephant in the room was his book. That bastard of a novel he hadn't been able to write more than twenty-five thousand words of, that he hadn't touched in over five years. While the going had been good, he'd lived in the land of milk and honey. Then the going stopped being so good and the milk had soured and the honey turned into Marmite.

Still, he found the old contract in an email from Fiona Vickers. Long time since he'd heard from her. He didn't even know if she was still technically his literary agent and he hadn't bothered to stay in touch, just accepted the payments. Didn't ask why the flood had slowed to a trickle.

The contract was pretty simple for a publishing deal.

A third on signature. Already received, already spent.

A third on publication, but the date was four years ago. And no new one on the horizon.

But the middle third was on delivery and acceptance.

If he finished the book, got it to his editor, got him to accept it, then he'd be due...

Well, maths wasn't Mark's strong point but even he could see that it was enough to cover his debt to Vic. All of it.

When he'd taken the money from Vic, he couldn't even contemplate working for the money to get out of the hole he'd dug himself. Taking a loan was much easier. And the money coming in from his old books was still good. Now, though...

In truth, his head had been up his arse and the only thing he could write was a squiggle on a signature line.

Finish the book, then pester Hamish until he paid the cash.

That was it.

He needed it in two weeks. That was enough, right?

Mark sucked down some coffee and hit dial.

3

The restaurant door opened and Fiona Vickers peered in. Her long face with the chin tapering to a point. Hair scraped back, dressed like she was late for a session with her personal trainer. 'Mark.' She stomped over to his table. 'You okay?'

'I'm...' The weight hit Mark again, pulling him down like a falling grand piano. He pinched his nose. 'Not really.'

'Talk to me.' A smile flickered over Fiona's lips.

Mark couldn't bring himself to look at her. Outside, a heron was sitting on a rock, scanning the river, the Water of Leith. He'd never seen one in the city before, but maybe it was venturing into a new hunting ground. Now he looked at her. 'Thanks for coming. I...'

Rule number one of getting a literary agent – don't get an old university friend to do it, no matter how good they say they are.

But he had to focus on the fact Fiona was a friend. She deserved the truth here.

'You're one of my oldest friends, Fi. I'm in trouble. Deep trouble.'

'What did you do?'

'Why do you assume I did something?'

'Mark, it's you. You're always doing something.'

'Right.' And she was. Of course she was. 'I need some help.'

'As a friend or as an agent?'

'Both.'

'Mark...' Fiona's long sigh was interrupted by the waitress dropping off his pot of coffee. Fiona stared all the way through the ceremony of dotting crockery around the table, then smiled at the waitress. 'Could I get a banana and raspberry smoothie? Thank you.' The waitress left and Fiona's scowl returned. 'Mark, I'm not doing much agenting anymore. I work as a freelance editor now.'

'Magic.' Mark tipped some sugar into a cup, then poured in thick, black coffee. 'Still, you've never cancelled our arrangement and you're a co-signature to all of my deals.'

Fiona raised her eyebrows. 'That's true.'

'I need the money from Hamish. Now.'

'Right.' Fiona laughed against the backdrop of a blender going hell for leather. 'That bloody book.'

'That bloody book.'

The waitress walked over with a glass containing something that looked like it had burst from someone's veins.

'Thank you.' Fiona grabbed her smoothie and sipped through the straw. 'How long has it been now? Eighteen months?'

'Five years.'

She shut her eyes. 'You're a bloody idiot.'

Mark bit his tongue. 'That book doesn't write itself.'

'Mark, you wrote twenty-five thousand words of it six years ago. Got me to read it, then got Hamish to read it. Typical diva act from you, needing to know you were on the right path. You got a lot of praise from him.'

'I know, but... You know that Stephen King thing, where he says you should write with the door shut. Well, I opened it and I've let all the magic out.'

'Five years ago.'

'Aye, that's when we signed the deal. Before *Break the Chain*. Look, I didn't expect it to do so well. And now... Now I can't write.'

'You could've written something else instead.'

'The deal was for—'

'Mark. You should've spoken to Hamish.'

He looked away from her headlight stare. He couldn't speak.

She slurped more smoothie through her straw. 'How's the book looking?'

Mark looked away. 'Okay.'

'Okay?'

'I've got twenty-five thousand words.'

'Mark!' She slapped a hand to her forehead. 'The deal was for a hundred and fifty.'

'I know.' He still couldn't look at her for long.

'We could *maybe* get away with one-twenty. Maybe. But what the hell have you been doing with your life?'

Getting taken to the cleaners by Olivia's divorce lawyers, borrowing money from Vic Hebden. Stuff he hadn't shared with anyone.

Instead of saying it, Mark poured milk into his coffee. 'I'll get down to the National Library. I'm hoping to close out the research phase today.'

Her mouth hung open. 'The *research phase*?'

'You know me. My process is a bit organic and—'

'When you use words like that, it just sounds like bullshit, Mark. Tell me straight.'

'I'm serious. It's mostly written in my head, at least, but I just need to back up a few things and straighten out some logic, then I'll get at it. And I can get paid for it. But...'

She narrowed her eyes. 'What?'

'I really need a chunk of the money now.'

Fiona slammed her smoothie down. 'You need to take this up with Hamish. You. Not me.'

Mark felt that surge of pressure on his shoulders, squashing him like all of the millions of words he'd written in his career each weighed a ton. 'Fi, I'm desperate.'

'So you say.' She shook her head. 'I'm out of that game. It's just not worth the hassle of dealing with people like you. And Hamish isn't going to give you money for nothing. I mean, aye, he did when you signed the deal, based on healthy pre-orders and a film deal, but you need to *finish* the book to get the money.'

Magic...

Mark slumped back in the chair. 'I've got like ten ideas for the next book and I can send you—'

'*Mark.*' She sucked up smoothie again, blasting the straw. 'Focus on this one. Get it done. And *speak to Hamish.* He's a good guy.'

Mark took a sip of coffee. His headache had gone, but everything else ached. 'If you can get me some cash until—'

'Mark, what's really going on?'

He looked away again. His eyes hurt, like he'd been staring into the sun. 'Fi, I'm in debt to some bad people.'

'How bad?'

'Bad. And very badly. I need that money in two weeks.'

'Mark!'

'I'm serious. I'm fucked.'

'How much debt are you in?'

Mark felt tears forming behind his nose. The first stages of a panic attack gripping him by the eyeballs.

Fiona reached over and touched his hand. 'I'm your friend, okay? If you need my help, then I need you to be honest with me.'

'Okay.' He sighed. 'All that stuff with...' He couldn't bring himself to say her name. 'Well, my divorce cleared me out. And to get away from that situation, I had to pay her a lot of money. Thing is, I had to borrow that cash from... Well, someone you don't want to know about.'

'You're in debt to a loan shark?'

'Right. I thought he was okay, but he's been threatening me.'

'You should go to the cops.'

'It's not that simple.'

'Nothing ever is with you.'

She was right. But he really couldn't go to the cops. Half of them might be on Hebden's payroll.

'Is it Vic Hebden?'

'I'm not saying.'

'Mark, you really are a bloody idiot.'

'Aye, I am.'

She dumped the straw on the table and slurped smoothie straight from the glass. Then sat there, arms folded, shaking her head. 'Mark, I wish you'd just write about police officers or middle-class people with missing kids.'

'Right.' He smiled, but he was beyond humour. 'Thing is, this book'll sell itself. Hamish knows that.'

'Remind me what the book is?'

'Way to make an author feel important.' Mark laughed. 'It's a real-life tale of Romeo and Juliet set in the Highland Clearances. She's the daughter of two crofters, he's the son and heir of the landowner.'

'Right. I remember it now.' Fiona pouted at him. 'I told you. I'm not an agent anymore. I can't do this.'

'Fi, I'm serious. I have been working on it again. Kay's up in the Highlands for a couple of weeks doing research for me.'

'Wee Kay?'

'Aye. She's studying history at Glasgow.'

Fiona snorted. 'Christ, last time I saw her she asked me about bras but she was years away from wearing one.'

Mark felt a tug of sadness and regret in his stomach.

Fiona had been the first person he'd told when Cath was pregnant.

She'd visited them in hospital after she gave birth.

Hell, if they'd been religious, she'd have been her godmother.

'Kay's sniffing around the glen the book's set in, asking questions of the locals, trying to find the landowner's descendants. I'm meeting her next week for a few days of father-daughter time. Supposed to be a working holiday. Like I said, I've already got the scaffolding of the story up here.' He tapped his temple. 'The plan was to get her to make some notes, then show me the landscape, then I'd edit some of her notes so it read like me and just insert it into the manuscript. Done. Simple. Thirty, forty thousand words of description mostly for free. Well, her hotel bill and petrol. And phone bill. And food.'

'But?'

'I still need a few weeks to do all that work. And if it's another hundred thousand words? I can't do that. And I need the money now. The cash Hamish is due me will clear the debt.'

'Mark, you won't get the full amount without the full book.'

'I just need to cover the overdue payments. Then I can meet up with Kay and I'm on the home straight. All I need is for you to rep me one last time. Okay?'

She looked away, shaking her head, then her gaze drilled into him. 'You better be on the level here.'

'Of course I am.'

She drank more smoothie, thinking it all through. She screwed up her face, then grabbed his hand and squeezed it. 'Let me give you some advice. Once you've finished this book, you need to stop being such a bloody idiot. This amount of debt and hassle isn't cool. And this is the last time I'm helping you. Ever.'

Mark sipped his coffee. 'What about selling some foreign deals?'

'*Mark*. You've not changed since uni, have you? In all that time. Your attitude to money and people stinks. It has to change.'

'Come on, that's not fair.'

'No? I gave you half my student loan because you'd bought a fancy laptop and didn't have money to even eat. And twenty years later, I'm still the person you're asking for financial help.'

'You are my agent.'

'Aye, and how many birthdays or Christmases have you not bothered to get in touch? How many royalty payments? I even missed off the remittance advice a few times in case your accountant needed it, just so you'd talk to me.'

He took off his glasses and blew on the lenses. Truth was, he felt so small the cloth could suffocate him. 'You know it's all because—'

'Some bollocks to do with your dad, aye. I know, Mark. But most people get therapy for childhood trauma, rather than repeat their father's mistakes in record time. Stop treating people as a means to an end. Like I am to you just now. It's why I can't work with you anymore.'

'Okay, I get that. It's something I need to work on. Something I'll fix.'

She stared out of the window, now spattered with rain. One thing about Edinburgh was a clear sky meant you were probably getting rain later. She looked back at him. 'Fine. Okay.'

Mark could've punched the air. 'You'll do it?'

'Aye.' She pushed her empty glass away. 'And I could say it's because we're old friends, but I need my fifteen percent of that money. And you're lucky that Hamish is one of my current clients.'

4

Hamish Archibald.

Raven-haired little sod called himself an editor, but the only reason he got to impose deadlines on anyone was because his father was the guy who signed the cheques at Castle Street Press. Or actioned the bank transfers.

Barely thirty, but he dressed like an old man. Fancy shirt, tweed jacket, jeans, pointy brown shoes. Stubble and a voice artificially lowered. 'Fiona...' He placed his arms on her shoulders and did the *mwa mwa*. '*So* lovely to see you.'

'Mark Campbell?' Hamish looked at him with a sneering expression on his face. It softened a bit and he held out a hand. 'How's it going, my friend?'

No cheek-kissing, but Mark didn't mind. He shook the hand and squeezed, trying to assert dominance, but Hamish had a ferocious grip. A score draw, maybe. 'Good to see you, Hamish.'

'Always.' Hamish let go and sat behind his desk. A vintage oak thing, polished to a shine. Aside from a pile of books, it had a MacBook and a Dell laptop, like Hamish couldn't decide which side of the fence to sit on. 'Please, have a seat.'

Mark let Fiona go first. The office hadn't changed much in the five years since Mark had last been in the place. Since Fiona had wrung a six-figure deal out of him. A new bookshelf was filled with hardbacks, which looked to be first editions of Ian Rankin's back catalogue, probably signed. A few others Mark didn't recognise.

Mark took the free chair, closer to the window. While it was on Castle Street, it looked out on the back lane behind Thistle Street. Mark couldn't remember if it was still called that this far along. Maybe Young Street. Felt like the long road was trying to trip up tourists by changing name every block, whereas Rose Street—its parallel cousin—ran from square to square on the other side of George Street. Easy.

'Now.' Hamish rested on his tweed jacket's elbow patches. 'Normally I'd book a table at the Witchery or the Kitchin, but you've kind of swarmed me here. What can I do for you both?'

Fiona kept her gaze locked on Hamish. 'Mark's wondering if he could receive a further drawdown on the advance.'

Twitches ran across Hamish's forehead. He shifted his focus between them, eyes flickering with confusion, then with humour. He laughed, then sucked in a few breaths, then laughed again.

Mark and Fiona didn't join in.

'Are you *serious?*' Hamish was looking right at Mark now.

He gripped the chair arms. Warm plastic and cold metal. 'I am.'

Hamish ran a hand over his mouth. 'Mark, you were supposed to deliver that book to me *five years ago.*'

'I know and I'm sorry.'

'Not sorry enough to pick up the phone or answer my emails. You know, I thought you'd *died*, but I saw you in Teuchter's one night. And you blanked me.'

Mark wanted to crawl into a corner and curl up in a ball. If it wasn't for the threats against his health, he wouldn't have gone anywhere near the New Town, let alone into Hamish's office. But he was desperate and he needed that money. 'I don't remember that, but I'm truly sorry. Thing is, I'm making good progress with the book.'

Hamish smoothed down his stubble, eyes tight. 'How good are we talking?'

'Very.' Mark cleared his throat. 'My daughter's doing some research for me up in—'

'Strathruthven.' Hamish smiled. 'Ah yes, I remember it well from the words you sent me *five years ago*. How many more are there now?'

'Not that many, but I've had personal stuff to contend with.'

'A drinking problem?'

Fiona snorted. 'A marriage and a divorce.'

'Oh?' Hamish seemed interested now. The whiff of gossip and scandal. He wheeled around in his chair. 'What's the ask?'

Mark was due a good six figures, more than enough to wipe out the debt to Vic Hebden, but that was all dependent on Hamish accepting the work and it being published. He just needed enough to get Vic off his back for now and the next few months. 'Thirty grand would do.'

Hamish got up and walked over to the window, lips pursed. 'Well, you've got a flair for the dramatic, I'll give you that.' He looked over at Fiona. 'What's your thinking on this?'

'I...' Fiona paused, then brushed her trousers. 'I don't know, to be honest. Thing is, Mark's way overdue on his delivery schedule. *Break The Chain* has stopped selling, certainly nothing like it was when we inked this deal. And the film has stalled.'

As much as Mark liked having his Ms Fifteen Percent to act as a bridge between him and his publisher, when his agent and his editor ganged up on him...

Fiona raised her shoulder. 'But you were generous enough to give us a comfortable six figures to secure your biggest author's next book, sight unseen, and you've already paid us a big chunk of the advance. Now, you could say that's a sunk cost and write it off, but Mark is giving you the opportunity to make good on that deal. He's made solid progress on the rest of the book and it's a very commercial project right now. I've had interest from Netflix and Apple.'

Mark almost believed her himself. Truth and he had become strangers.

Hamish slumped back in his chair and crossed his legs. 'Thirty thousand?' He blew air up his face. He picked up a black notebook and scrawled in it with a fancy fountain pen. Seemed like he circled something. 'The money could be found,' he raised a finger, 'providing we can knock, say, twenty percent off the overall figure?'

Fiona looked at Mark, who was nodding like a dog in the back of a car. 'That's not an issue.'

'Fine.'

'I need the cash in my account two weeks today.'

Hamish looked up at the wall. 'You're in luck. We're doing our banking that day.'

'That's fine.' Mark was almost crying. 'Thank you.'

'Don't get too excited. Before I draw down the funds, I need the next thirty thousand words by a week on Monday.'

'Deal.' Mark shot to his feet and held out his hand. 'Thank you.'

Hamish frowned at him. 'Feels like I've stepped into a trap here.'

'No, I'm just really grateful for your help.' Mark gave him a tight nod. 'Thank you, Hamish. I really appreciate it.'

'The final condition is it needs to be *at least* as good as the first section. If it's not, I won't give you the money.'

5

Mark held the café door for Fiona. 'I mean, at least as good? That's a tall order.'

Fiona elbowed Mark out of the way of the counter. 'I'll fetch the coffees, you find your work on your laptop.'

'Sure.' Mark shuffled through the café and rested his laptop bag on the table. He was sweating and stank pretty badly.

The couple at the nearest table seemed to be in the middle of breaking up and were giving him hostile stares for daring to sit that close to them.

Mark ignored them.

He'd gone from shaking from fear to shaking from adrenaline in two hours. Less than that. It was only eleven o'clock on Thursday. He had ten days to write and edit thirty thousand words, then hope that Hamish gave him the money. Deposit it in the bank, then take it out and—

Shit.

Didn't they limit cash withdrawals to ten grand? Something to do with money laundering. Maybe.

Vic Hebden must've had that problem before. Must be ways around it. Maybe Mark just had to give him ten thousand one day, then do the rest over the weekend.

He'd be on a roll with the book. Wouldn't be able to keep up that pace, obviously, but he'd be able to finish the thing in a couple of months. Then get his money and finally settle his total debt with Vic.

Another big chunk when the book was published. Probably even have a flurry of sales of *Break the Chain* before that.

Aye, things were looking up.

'Here.' Fiona put the tray between them. Two coffees, two Diet Cokes, and two slices of something very chocolatey. 'You'll need this for your energy.'

'Cheers.' Mark reached for a can and took a deep drink. 'Okay. I wanted to thank you for—'

'Shut up. No time for that. Just show me what you've got.'

'Here.' He swivelled his laptop around for her to look at.

She stared at the screen for a few seconds, then got out her phone and fiddled about with it. Her lips twisted, her forehead creased. Then she looked up at the ceiling. 'You've written a hundred words in five years.'

'It's more than that. Isn't it?' He took the computer back and looked at it. But the chunk of text she'd highlighted... Word told him it was a hundred and nine words. 'I mean, it's *technically* more, but...'

'Tell me you've got some stuff elsewhere.'

Mark scratched at his neck. 'There's an outline.'

'Show me.'

Mark sifted through the pigsty of his folders, then pulled it up and let her look at it.

She read, but her frown just deepened. 'Mark, you've got "something cool with a horse" here. How the hell are you going to—?'

'Relax. I'll just go home and get my head down.'

'It's possible for someone to write thirty thousand words in ten days, but you? Hardly.'

'It's just three thousand a day. I know this mad bastard who does ten thousand a day.'

'What does he write?'

'Police procedurals. Daft cops doing daft things. Why?'

'Well, I know who you're talking about and his books aren't pretty. Remember, you need these words to be good. Hamish needs to approve it.'

Thirty really was pushing things, especially as, despite all his protestations, he'd no idea what happened next. Other than a maritime disaster at the end, the rest of it was yet to be discovered.

But he had to at least try.

'Look, I'll get rocket-fuelled on coffee and just let my fingers dance. I'll get it done.'

'Don't mess Hamish about, Mark. This is *my* reputation on the line as well as yours. I work with Hamish on a weekly basis. He pays me, decently. And publishers speak to each other. If you dick him around, it'll reflect badly on *me*. And I need the work.'

'Okay, I'll keep you out of it.'

And he realised Hamish agreed to the preposterous deal so he could get them out of his office. Being ambushed like that, the first thing you'd do is clear them out. What was it Mark's old therapist said? It's not just fight or flight, you've got freeze and fawn. And Hamish had been fawning to get rid of them.

Nothing was written down. Hamish could change his mind.

Mark had fallen for it. So had Fiona. 'If I'm going to hand in my thirty thousand words, I need to know I'll get the cash on that Friday. Otherwise I'll be waiting another month. And I don't have another month. And Hamish could just say it wasn't as good as the first thirty. Keep dangling that carrot until the whole thing's done.'

'Well, make it good. You have to trust Hamish, Mark. It's the only hope you've got.'

'Can you get something in writing, please?'

'*Fine.*' She narrowed her eyes and flared her nostrils. 'You're such a dickhead.'

'That's true.' Mark smiled. 'Look, I'll get home, shut the door, make a pot of coffee and get hold of Kay, then weave her notes in. Locations, family trees, all the detailed stuff my readers love. The stuff Hamish wants. That'll be at least ten thousand. I'll be writing by noon. Worst case, I'll leave out most of the location stuff, then I'll wedge in Kay's material later. Hamish will see the story and how good it is.'

She didn't look like she believed him.

'But that "something cool with a horse" will be a tense horse-back chase across the glen, with ten armed shepherds shooting muskets at my hero. You'll love it. Hamish will *adore* it.' He smiled at her, trying to get her to buy into it. 'Then I'll meet up with Kay in Inverness and see it all for myself. She's doing research for the end of the book, but I'll get her focusing on this section. Trust me, it'll all take care of itself. We'll get this book published, you'll get your cut. Then you won't have to deal with me.'

Fiona drank a sip of her coffee, eyes shut. 'Fine.'

Mark pushed his chair back. All he could do now was speak to his daughter, find out how much work she'd done. 'Thanks for doing this. I really, really appreciate it.'

'Just don't let me down, Mark.'

6

Mark sat at his desk and plugged his laptop back into his monitor. The screen was black and he couldn't bring himself to wake it up. He got out his phone and checked his message to Kay. Still unread.

Magic.

He sent another:

Kay, can you give me a call? Cheers.

Maybe he should be more explicit, tell her he needed her research now.

No.

That'd be desperate. He needed to focus on this book. Get those words done. Turn words into sentences, then sentences into pages. Make something cool on a horse happen. Soon enough, he'd have enough for Hamish. He'd have his money and Vic Hebden would be off his case.

He stabbed at his keyboard and the thing didn't wake the laptop.

Magic. Just magic.

His phone blared out.

Kay wants to FaceTime

Mark answered the call.

Her almond-shaped face filled the screen, though she was more tanned than he'd seen her in years. All that outside air and sun. Her red hair was in a ponytail, blown about by the wind, but nothing could tame the curls she got from her mother. Deep blue sea behind her and the call of seagulls. Those daft white buds stuck out of her ears, like she had an ear infection on both sides. 'Hey, what's up, Dad?'

Mark settled back in his chair, trying to act calm as he held his phone in front of his face. 'How are you doing, kiddo?'

'Good.' She popped a button of gum into her mouth. 'What's up?'

'Just wondering how you're getting on up there?'

'Good fun.' She was on an empty beach somewhere, deep blue sea and glorious sand, kicked up by the strong wind. 'Thank you for letting me help with this.'

'It's all good, Kay. Thing is, I was wondering when I could get some of the research?'

She frowned. 'Why?'

Always questioning him. Always. 'I've just... Look, I need to get a chunk of the book to my editor earlier than scheduled.'

'And you need my stuff, why?'

Mark held up his free hand. 'Not all of it, okay, just the stuff we talked about around Strathruthven.'

'Are you in trouble or something?'

'No. What makes you think that?'

'Well, it's just you said, "take as long as you want", and now it's "give me it all now". What's up?'

'Nothing's up and it's not all.'

'This anything to do with Olivia?'

Even hearing the name made Mark jerk forward. Feel sick. 'What do you mean?'

'You know how it is. We talk, Dad. She said she's worried you

27

might be in some kind of money trouble. Is it anything to do with that?'

'Of course not.' And Mark had just lied to his kid. Magic. 'Look, it's nothing to do with her, but yes, I'm in a bit of debt. I've agreed with my editor to get some more of the money due to me if I can deliver a percentage of the book. Nothing to worry about.'

Aye, keep telling yourself that.

'How much debt?'

'Nothing. It's a small amount.'

'Dad, please tell me. How much do you owe?'

'Like I said, it's not much. Just send me the research, please. That's all I need.'

'Come on, Dad, you look so stressed. Have you been sleeping?'

'My sleep's fine.'

'Dad...'

'Kay, I'm fine. Really. My advance will cover it.'

'Well.' The wind whipped her ponytail around her face and her lips moved but he didn't catch what she said.

'Sorry, I didn't—'

'I said, I'll get you some stuff tonight, but there's a *lot* I haven't done.'

'Kay, tell me you've—'

'Dad, it's just growing arms and legs, that's all. But it'll be amazing stuff. Just you wait to see it.'

'Okay, sounds great. But get me that stuff tonight. Alright?' He grimaced. 'I know I was going to come up next week, but—'

'You've got writing to do. Yeah, yeah, I get it.'

'Oh, okay.' Mark scratched his neck. 'But in two weeks' time?'

'Cool.' She looked away from her phone. 'I'll look forward to it. Might go back to Glasgow for a couple of days.' She said something but it was lost to the wind. '—more money, if that's okay?'

Mark shut his eyes. 'How much?'

'Two hundred?'

'Kay, I gave you five hundred last week?'

'Dad, I'm in the Highlands... It's *so* expensive here.'

'Fine.' Mark sighed. Then put on a smile. 'I'll send it soon. Once I've got your notes.'

She huffed like she was thirteen again. 'Fine.'

'I love you, okay?'

'Dad, have you gone mad?'

'No, I just... I don't tell you it enough. That's all.'

'Well, I love you too.' And she was gone.

Mark put his phone down and leaned forward to shake his mouse. Finally, the screen lit up.

Now, he just needed to write this bastard of a book.

He rested his wrists on the keyboard, his fingers in position. He read the last paragraph he'd written, years before.

He'd written books before.

This should be easy.

One week later

The giant monster with huge teeth loomed over him, twenty feet tall. Strong, powerful, and one swipe of those giant fists would squash him. 'Give me my money!' the monster's breath reeked of death, acrid and sharp. Tangy. Its voice was deep, making the ground rumble.

'I don't have it!' Mark's own voice was quiet, lost to the thumping rhythm of his stomping feet as he tried to back away. 'I'll get it, but—'

'No more time!' The giant grabbed Mark and picked him up off the ground, then started squeezing him tighter and tighter until—

'No!' Mark opened his eyes and jerked upright.

He was in his flat. Alone. Just him, an empty cafetière and his laptop.

He'd fallen asleep.

Magic.

He looked at his screen, blinking hard. Seventeen thousand words in a week. Normally he'd kill for that kind of rate, but now? He still had so much more to do. Call it another eight, then his editing should push it over the line.

Trouble was, though, he really needed to think as he was

working. This wasn't just dictation. He needed to think through what was happening in each of the four plot strands he had going simultaneously.

Though Hamish didn't say Mark needed the words to be consecutive...

He could focus on Jamie's story. Right?

No. He needed to do it the right way.

And he really needed to go to the toilet. Then more coffee. He picked up the cafetière and headed through to the kitchen, filled the kettle, set it to boil and started to panic.

Shite.

He was screwed. It hit him like a musket shot in the back from a shepherd on horseback.

He checked his phone. No messages. Great being alone in the universe, wasn't it?

He went into his emails and *still* nothing from Fiona. What was going on? So he sent another one:

Fi,
Let me know that you've got the contract revision agreed with Hamish, please. Need to know.

The worst bit was still nothing from Kay. Typical. At his hour of greatest need, she was avoiding him. Usually she lived online, her phone never out of her hands, but it was days since he'd seen an online status in any of her many messaging apps.

Sod it, he'd given the little madam enough slack.

Mark tried her mobile.

'This is Kay, I can't take your call just now. Leave a message and I'll get back to you.'

'Kay, it's Dad. Give me a call, would you? Cheers.' He killed it and hit dial again.

'This is Kay, I can't—'

Magic.

He chucked the phone back on the counter, scooped some of his freshly ground coffee into the cafetière, then filled it right up.

Now he had to wait. He could write, but the coffee would grow cold by the time he surfaced. And he was yawning big time now. He couldn't face another of those nightmares, the ones that had plagued him for a week now. Sleep each night was just lying there, then his body wanted to catch up while he needed to work.

He really needed those words from Kay. He tried to think back to the last time he'd heard from her. Four days ago, still promising to email stuff through. Maybe she had and it was in his spam folder.

Nope, nothing from her anywhere. He searched for Kay Campbell. Nothing since he'd sent her some cash for petrol and food. His spam folder was just offers to increase his penis size or have sex with beautiful women who couldn't spell and used way too many emojis.

Magic.

A notification popped up, a text from an unknown number:

Time's running out. One week, my friend.

No prizes for guessing who that was from.

Then an email from Fiona. His heart raced as he read it:

Mark,

Further to your message, I've chatted with Hamish, who put me on to Shona in his contracts department. They won't offer a formal revision to the signed contract, but I have a written agreement that they will pay a proportion of the cash on delivery, providing the quality is sufficient. It needs to be thirty thousand words and it needs to be, in his words, the very best.

And payment will be due a week today.

Let me know if there's anything else.

Regards,

Fiona

Well, that was something, though the formal wording jarred a bit. Regards, eh?

Another few days until he got the rough shape of it, then some solid editing and it'd be more than good.

He just needed that stuff from Kay.

He tapped out another message and sent it:

Kay, give me a ring. Or text me. Dad

He copied it and pasted it into the other services he knew she was using. WhatsApp, Instagram, Twitter, Schoolbook, even Facebook Messenger. The Lord alone knew what else she was on. Could you send direct messages on TikTok?

Maybe the phone reception was crap up there.

Then again, the last time he'd been to the Highlands was three years ago and it was full bars of 4G everywhere. Even in the deepest glens. No, she had no excuse.

Sod it, he pulled out the hotel booking he'd made. Two rooms, hers for four weeks, his for three nights. Still staggered him how much it cost to stay in Inverness of all places. He hit dial.

They answered straight away. 'Lamb's Hotel. Simon speaking.' Nasal voice, lowlands accent. 'How may I help?'

'Hi, I've got a reservation and my—'

'What's the name, sir?'

'Mark Campbell.'

'Just one second.' Sounded like he was typing. 'Ah yes, I see that you've got two rooms, one of which is presently occupied?'

'That's right. It's for my daughter—'

'Oh, hang on a bloody minute. You've got a cheek.'

'Excuse me?'

'Well, the little madam ran off, didn't she? Without paying! And I'll tell you now, she completely took the piss on the minibar. Emptied it every night she was here. Two meals in the restaurant, including drinks. She owes me six hundred quid!'

Six hundred quid Mark didn't have.

'Is she definitely not there?'

'No, not since,' he blew air across his lips, 'Tuesday morning? Now, when can I expect payment on that room? The credit card she gave me has bounced.'

'I'll have to ring you back.' Mark ended the call and collapsed against the wall.

What the hell was going on?

Had Kay run off? Really?

She did it once was she was six, thinking she wasn't wanted by her mum and dad. Took *years* for her to get over it. Not that it held their marriage together.

Six hundred quid... How the hell do you spend that on a mini-bar? And every night?

He redialled Kay's number and it rang, at least. Then it was answered.

'Hello?' A male voice.

Mark tightened his grip on his phone. 'Who is this?'

'No, pal, who's *this*?' The voice sounded familiar, but Mark couldn't quite place it. 'Hang on.' A pause. 'Are you her dad again?'

'No, I'm her dad only once.'

'Don't get funny with me, pal. You owe me six hundred quid plus twelve hundred for the room!'

The hotel owner. Mark felt his hope deflate. 'She's really not there?'

'No, pal. I let myself into her room. Far as I'm concerned, I can just chuck her stuff out. Might sell it to recoup my money.'

'I'll pay it.'

'That's very kind of you. I'll send you the invoice in the post.' Click and he was gone.

Mark was sweating again. He needed to think, but his brain was like a soggy tuna melt. Kay leaving her phone in a hotel room... Thing was practically glued to her fingers.

She'd *never* leave it.

Where the hell was she?

8

Mark should never have agreed to let her go up there on her own.

Why the hell had she run off? Where was she?

He picked up his phone and hit dial.

'Eight five three seven one seven?' That warm deep voice, from far too many cigars and too many glasses of port in the golf club bar.

Mark paced around his living room. 'Charlie, it's Mark.'

'Mark. How's you?'

'I'm fine.' Mark paused, trying to figure out the words. 'It's... Is Kay there?'

'Kay? No, she's up in Inverness, I think.'

'You *think*? She's your stepdaughter, Charlie, you should know.'

'Listen to me, Mark. You don't get to—'

'Have you heard from her recently?'

'Well, aye. I mean... Aye. It's just... Not sure.'

'Not sure. Magic.'

'Is she all right?'

'Well, that's the thing. You know she's working for me in the Highlands and—'

'Cath! Phone!' The noise battered Mark's ear. Must be the landline receiver clunking off the side table. Mark had been inside their house once, to collect Kay. Could still picture the place. Not his taste, that was an understatement.

'Mark!' Cath had that flush of happiness she got from company. Or too much wine. At half twelve. She sounded like she was a hundred miles from the phone. 'Everything okay?'

'Hope so. Have you heard—'

'Is this working?'

'You've got it the wrong way up.' Charlie sounded like he was inside the phone.

'Mark?' Cath sounded clearer now. 'What's going on?'

He scratched his chin, trying to find the right words. 'I'm trying to get hold of Kay.'

'Kay? Why?'

'You know how she's doing this work for me?'

'Up in Inverness, aye. Is it going well?'

'I'd love to know. I haven't heard from her in a few days. And she's left her hotel and cleared out the minibar, leaving a bill the size of a mortgage payment.'

'Sounds like our Kay, Mark. She's a flighty soul. Just like you.' Cath laughed. 'And she's been out of touch before. Like when she was working in Spain last summer, before uni.'

Mark remembered her going, but she was on Skype to him every other day. Having fun, but she seemed a bit lonely. The more he dug into it, the more the realisation grew that he was the parent closest to Kay, despite living with her mother and Charlie since their divorce.

'When she was wee, after we divorced, she used to run off.' Icy Cath was back. The woman who left Mark. The woman who divorced him. 'I used to skelp her behind when she'd get back, but it had no effect on her. Are you worried?'

Mark let out a deep breath. Truth was, he was worried. Maybe not worried, but concerned. And not just for his own selfish reasons. Needing her words to save his arse. 'Cath, the thing is, she's left her phone behind in the hotel room.'

'Her *phone*? Thing's practically part of her.'

'I know, which is why I'm a bit worried.'

'With good reason.'

'She's just run off, but I'm going to find her, okay? I'd really appreciate it if you had any idea where I should look first.'

'You could speak to her flatmates.'

Mark had that squirming in his guts. 'A flat?'

'Do you actually speak to her, Mark?'

'Aye, of course I do, it's just I've been paying for halls of residence, which is a lot more than a flat.'

'Aye, it's the same kind of thing. Self-catering, six of them to a flat. Wee place just off Byres Road.'

Mark was realising how much of a stranger his daughter was.

9

The flat was pretty far off Byres Road, as it happened.

Mark walked through the pissing Glasgow rain, forty miles away from his Edinburgh flat and the work that'd save his legs, but here he was, trying to find out where his daughter was.

Buggering off like that...

A bus passed, spraying most of a puddle over his legs.

He tried to shake the water off, but he was soaked through, down to his shoes. Fuck's sake!

The address Cath had given him was one of those modern blocks you'd see everywhere in central Edinburgh. Student accommodation was big business now.

He tried the Entrycom but didn't hold out much hope for anyone to be in during the summer holidays.

'Aye?' The voice was distorted and harsh. He couldn't tell if it was Kay or literally any other human being.

'Looking for Kay?'

The buzzer sounded and the door clunked.

Mark stepped inside, acting like a man whose daughter lived there and wanted to see him. Like dropping by was the norm.

The stairwell was actually cleaner than his one through in

Edinburgh. Plants draped over the banisters, crawling up. Smelled like someone was baking a loaf of sourdough. More a hippie commune than student halls.

He set off up the stairs, heading right to the top. Flat eighteen had a door tag:

Stacy
Brianna
Kay

Mark didn't need to read the other three names. He knocked. The bread smell was making him hungry.

The door crept open and a pale girl looked out. Dark eye makeup. Darker hair. Skinny. Chewing gum. Looking him up and down. 'Can I help you?' Dundonian accent.

'I'm Kay's dad. Is she here?'

That look again, the up and down. Her bottom lip stuck out, showing a couple of piercings. A third in her tongue. She rolled her eyes. 'She's up in the Highlands.'

Mark smiled at her. 'Won't mind if I see her room, then?'

'How am I supposed to know you're her dad, eh?'

'Oh, I'm him.' Mark widened his grin. 'Best way to check is to get one of my books and compare the author photo.' Though he hadn't published anything in five years and those photos were ten years earlier and three stone lighter. He put his foot in the door, pre-emptively. 'Please, I just need to speak to her.'

'Why would she be here?'

'She told me she might head back here.'

'Well, she's not.'

'Look, she's run off from the hotel I'm supposed to meet her at, leaving a massive bill. And... I just need to see her.'

She folded her arms. 'I'm here on my own, so there's no—'

'I'm not in the mood for this. She's run off, so I really need to see if she's here or not.'

Another sassy look, mouth hanging open, then she stepped aside. 'At the end, by the toilet.'

'Thank you.' Mark entered the flat. One of those huge halls that must limit the bedroom sizes. Place was sweltering despite the Glaswegian weather outside. 'You staying here for the summer?'

'Me and Stacy are. The other rooms are empty until September.'

'So you're Brianna?'

'Right. Kay's working for you, right?'

'Supposedly.' Mark opened the door and it was full of his kid's crap. Her books on the desk. Her posters filling the walls. Her clothes all over the floor. Just like her mother.

And aye, she wasn't here.

Mark stormed through the flat, opening doors and checking in rooms. Not hiding in the bathroom. Nor the other bedroom, tidy as a nun's in a convent. Three empties and the final bedroom was stuffed full of boxes, but Kay wasn't hiding behind them or inside them. The kitchen was empty, just two mismatched sofas, a joint burning away on the scarred coffee table.

A wall was stuffed full of Polaroid shots, any combination of six smiling female faces and the occasional lad. Old school, just like what Mark, Fiona and Cath had in their student flat.

Mark felt his shoulders slouch. He'd hoped she was here, hiding out. Maybe with a boyfriend. Or on her own. Just here. With a few thousand words for him. Words he could run through and use as the basis for his bloody book.

He needed to find her.

And he had no idea where she was.

He looked around at Brianna. 'Here's the thing, Kay's run off and I haven't heard from her in a while. She's disappeared from the hotel she's staying at in Inverness. Left a massive bill and her phone.'

Brianna's eyes bulged. 'Her *phone*?'

'Right. So I know it's serious.'

'Well, I haven't heard from Kay in a couple of weeks. Like I said. Since she went up to Inverness.'

'Did she get the train or bus?'

'Kay?' Brianna laughed. 'She wouldn't go to the *shops* in anything but her car, dude.'

'You got the number plate?'

'Can't even remember my own.'

This was hopeless. Kay could be anywhere.

'Okay, I'm going to need a list of friends and their phone numbers. People like Stacy.' He pointed at the wall. 'All the people on there.'

'Dude, you're not a cop.'

'No, but I'd hope you'd want to know she was okay.'

'I do, but...' Brianna picked up her phone, almost bigger than her head. 'Like, there's a lot?'

'I can deal with a lot. I just want to find her.'

Brianna thumbed through her phone. 'Did you speak to her mother?'

'Aye. Cath hasn't—'

'What?' Brianna screwed up her face. 'No, her mum's called Olivia.'

Oh bloody hell.

Mark felt everything in him tighten and clench. As if this couldn't get any worse. 'Olivia was here?'

'Aye. She used to come here for a coffee every week. Good laugh, you know?'

'Sure she is.' Mark nodded. 'I'll get out of your hair, then.' He set off towards the door.

'Don't you want those numbers?'

'I'll come back to you if I need them.'

She lifted a shoulder. 'Suit yourself.'

'And thanks.' Mark left the flat and shuttled down the staircase. Bloody hell. He got out his phone and sifted through his contacts, hoping to hell Olivia hadn't blocked his number. He found it and hit dial, then put his phone to his ear, listening to the ringing tone as he walked back out into the rain.

Ringing. At least she hadn't been that petty.

He had.

'Well, there's a Deacon Blue song I don't need to listen to

when I finish work.' Olivia's voice was cold. She was in an office, surrounded by the rumble of chatter and the hammering of keyboards.

Mark stopped in the rain. 'What, *Dignity?*'

'No, *When Will You (Make My Telephone Ring)?*'

Always a song for everything...

'Right, okay. Thing is, I'm ringing you right now, Liv,' every word felt like it cost more than one of Vic Hebden's instalments, 'because I need your help.'

'*You* need *my* help?' Olivia laughed down the line. 'That's brilliant.'

'I'm desperate. Kay's run off.'

The laughter died. 'What's happened?'

'Long story. You heard from her?'

'No, but I'm at work and I can spare a few minutes.'

10

'In here.' Olivia showed Mark into a meeting room, then shut the door behind her. 'You've got a bloody cheek.'

Mark couldn't get over how well she looked. Healthy. Recovered. The bags under her eyes had gone. Her hair seemed to have lost the couple of streaks of grey she'd blamed on him. 'You're looking well.'

'Shut up. Sit down.'

Mark knew when to comply, so he did. At the end of the table, looking out onto the office space. Busy today, barely any free desks that he could see. And the Glasgow rain hit the window. The sooner he was away from this infernal city, the better. 'Like I said on the phone, I think Kay's run away.'

Olivia sat next to him. 'Why do you think that?'

'Because she's gone missing?'

She shut her eyes like she was dealing with a child. 'Why do you think she's run away?'

'Well, she left a hotel with an unpaid bill. Six hundred quid of minibar on top of... A lot of money for the room.'

'She's not just larking around?'

'No, Liv. She's—'

'When did you last hear from her?'

'Few days ago.'

'When, Mark?'

He got out his phone. He'd completely forgotten how tough Liv could be. Insistent. Thorough. Forensic. 'Monday.'

'Morning? Night?'

'Lunchtime. Phone call.'

'How was she?'

Mark tried to think back. He'd thought about little else on the way through. All he had for Olivia was a shrug. 'She didn't sound like someone who was on the verge of running away.'

'Who does?'

Mark threw his hands in the air. 'Liv, I'm here asking for your help, not the Spanish Inquisition.'

She folded her arms. 'Mark.'

'I'm sorry. I've been to her flat and I spoke to one of her flatmates. She hasn't seen or heard from her. You didn't think to tell me you were having tea and scones with her every week?'

'Why would I? It's none of your business.'

'What, my daughter and my ex-wife having—'

'Aye, Mark. Exactly. It's none of your business what I do. Not anymore.'

Mark knew he was losing this, but he couldn't stop himself reverting to old habits. He rested on his elbows and dug the heels of his hands into his eyes. 'Liv, all I'm saying is, if you got close to her, maybe you know where she is.'

'I don't.'

'Okay. When was the last time *you* heard from her?'

'WhatsApped her on Tuesday.'

'You get a reply?'

Olivia took out her mobile and checked it. 'Nope.'

'You get a read receipt?'

'Not been read, no.'

Mark rocked back in his seat. 'Magic...'

'Are you really that worried about her?'

'Would I be here if I wasn't?' Mark raised his hands. 'Sorry. Old habits die hard.'

'I spoke to her on Monday night. She seemed fine, but she was asking about your money problems?'

'There's nothing there.'

'Well, she seemed to think there was.'

Mark sighed. 'She left her phone in her hotel room.'

Olivia's eyes were wide.

'Aye. So I need your help, Liv.'

'Oh god... You want to drive up there and search for her, don't you?'

'Damn right.' Mark didn't have a choice – a pressing book deadline and all the research in the world still to do. A physical threat from a loan shark.

But Kay was missing. His wee girl. Gone.

The impossible choice between his daughter and his health, well it wasn't that impossible.

'I've got to do this, Liv.' Mark took another deep breath. 'She's my daughter. I need her to be okay.'

'Mark, what are you holding back from me?'

The paperweight on the desk just outside the office was just like one his gran used to have. Like a planet's surface and lower atmosphere, or at least that's what he told himself.

'Mark. Look at me.'

He did and wished he hadn't.

'I know you, Mark William Campbell.' Her eyes were full of fire and rage, just like they'd been during the last two years of their marriage. He'd hidden away from her, down deep in his cave. Under the water. 'What are you hiding, Mark?'

Mark swallowed down a lie. 'This is happening at a bad time for me, that's all. I've got to get this book to my editor and... And I need the money.' He half-expected to blurt out about Vic Hebden, but no, he'd managed to avoid that disaster. 'Liv, I just need your help.'

'What, you think knowing a cop will help speed up the process?'

'I'm desperate, Liv.'

'Christ.' She looked like she wanted to kick him. 'What did I ever see in you?'

'Some shite about opposites attracting?'

She laughed at that. 'It ain't fiction, it's a natural fact...' She went over to the side and pulled some forms out of a pigeonhole, then slapped them on the table in front of him. She clicked out her pen and scribbled in the corner. 'Here, fill this out.'

A missing person's case form. 'Liv, I need to get up there and—'

'Mark. If you want my help, you do this by the book. Fill that out. I'll speak to my boss about it. Obviously I can't be the investigating officer, but I want to help.'

11

'You have arrived at your destination.'

And it didn't look like the right place.

Through the rain-speckled windscreen, Inverness buzzed with life, a much busier city than Mark remembered. Standard high street stores, though barely any had shut down and replaced with charity shops. Place was still thriving.

The architecture reminded him of George IV Bridge in Edinburgh, that little glimpse of home from hundreds of miles away. Well, about a hundred and fifty.

Mark blinked away the fatigue of driving four hours straight, and most of that up the A9. Still nowhere near enough sections of dual carriageway and way too many roadworks. He cradled the can of WakeyWakey energy drink and finished it off. The stuff was tolerable when chilled, but at the temperature of a car with broken air conditioning and with Scottish humidity? Vile. And who thought passionfruit and vanilla was a flavour?

Maybe he should've caught the train and spent the four hours hammering the keyboard, writing that bastard book. He tossed the can onto the back floor, then got out into the cool afternoon. Nothing like the Highland air to reconnect him with reality and it was much drier than Glasgow. He took out his phone and called Olivia. 'Well, I'm in the city of your birth.'

'I'm waiting outside.'

Mark spotted it. The Turncoat's Arms. Charming name for a grotty modern boozer. Had the signage of an old pub, but the building was mid-Nineties at the earliest.

Olivia was shaking off her brolly. 'What kept you?'

Mark almost tripped on the steps. 'Thought I lost you at Perth, but it seems like you lost me. What speed were you doing?'

'And I stopped for a sandwich.'

'What? How?'

'It's called Advanced Driving Training.' She lifted an eyebrow. 'And you drive like my dad before his cataract surgery.'

'I'm not that bad, am I?'

'No, but you're not that good.'

Mark let her enter first.

The pub was empty, except for a bored-looking woman behind the bar, messing about on her phone.

Just one drinker in there, sitting in the corner away from the bar, back to the wall, watching the door. The erect posture and sharp gaze of a cop. Shaved head, and thick stubble starting halfway down his ears. And that lime shirt was seriously out of place in a pub like this.

Olivia made a beeline for him and got a tight hug.

'Good to see you, Libby.'

Libby? Nobody called her that. Liv, aye. Olivia if you didn't know her or you were her father.

Aye, there was a story there. Not that it was any of Mark's business.

He followed her over, smiling.

'This is Mark Campbell.' Olivia gave an offhand wave. 'The girl's father.'

That was it? That was how she described him?

'DS Adam Mathieson.' He shook Mark's hand, firm but not tight. 'I'm an old mate of Libby's from school.' He sipped from a cup of tea, but he only had eyes for Olivia. He gestured over to the bar. 'Can I get you two anything?'

Mark's belly rumbled, as if on cue. 'Could I—'

'Much as I'd love to sit and chat,' Olivia said, 'we really need to get on.'

'Aye, aye, but you've just driven up from the lowlands. Aren't you thirsty? Hungry?'

'I'm fine.' Olivia smiled. 'We're fine.'

Mark swallowed down his impatience. But that was all he was going to swallow down.

Adam tilted his head to the side. 'How are you coping, Mark?'

'With what?'

'Your kid being missing.'

'Fine.' Mark took the seat opposite. 'My daughter's just run off.' But he had that fluttering in his chest.

Adam took a good look at Mark. 'Obviously Libby here can't be officially attached, but our bosses have let her work it as a liaison to the family. So, you. And my team has picked this up as a missing person's case. And we're kind of stretched, so I'll help but the reality is we'll all work together. Us three.'

'Thank you.'

Adam narrowed his eyes at Mark. 'Libby says Kay's here doing some work on a book for you?'

'That's right.'

'You're an author?'

'It's my job, so aye.'

'What's this book about?'

'The Highland Clearances.'

'Oh.' Adam laughed. 'Right.'

'Tell me you've heard of—'

'Of course I've heard of the Highland Clearances.' Adam took a sip of tea. 'Takes a brave man to tackle that topic.' He pushed the cup and saucer away from him, then stood and nodded at the barmaid. 'Sheena, good as ever.'

She looked up from her phone and her shoulders slumped. 'Cheers, boss.'

Mark frowned at him. 'Boss?'

'Afraid so.' Adam hauled on a navy suit jacket that didn't match his charcoal trousers or that lime shirt that seemed to get brighter and brighter. 'My old man left us this place when he popped his clogs. Runs itself, or Sheena does.' He held the door open for Olivia. Before Mark could get out, an old man waddled inside. Adam said, 'Afternoon, Archie.'

'Aye, son. Braw day.' The old boy almost knocked Mark off his feet as he barged past.

Adam walked off, sucking on a vape stick, exhaling a cloud that caught the wind. 'Follow me.'

Mark struggled to keep pace with him. 'Adam, I'm not sure what you—'

'Mark.' Adam gripped his arm, tight enough to hurt. 'Just so we're clear, I'm not doing this for you. I'm doing it for her.' He nodded over at Olivia. 'I owe her.'

Olivia was talking on the phone, avoiding Mark's gaze.

Mark laughed. 'I think you're overstating the help I need.'

'Let's hope that's the case. I'm a detective in the Highlands and that's exactly what you need.'

Olivia slowed down. 'Cath, it's Liv. What kind of car does Kay drive?'

His two exes on the phone. Magic...

Adam was lurking around, smiling at Mark.

'A Ford Fiesta, got it.' Olivia repeated the registration number, though Mark doubted that there were that many purple S-reg Fiestas left in Scotland, let alone Inverness.

'Thanks for that, Cath.' Olivia killed the call and tapped something into her phone. 'Don't leave me hanging on the telephone...' She nodded at Adam. 'Can you run her plates for me? Just texted you them.'

'Sure thing.' Adam checked his mobile. 'While they're doing that, let's go and see this hotel.'

12

L amb's Hotel was an ancient staging inn with a large sheep stuck out of the front of the building.

Mark waited for a bus to pass, then darted across the road and into the hotel. It smelled of wood smoke and fried bacon.

Adam's warrant card opened doors Mark could never hope to. Going to Olivia was definitely the right thing, even if it meant being stuck with him.

Olivia smiled at Mark. A weird sensation, something he hadn't seen from her in a long time. 'Mark, Mr Lamb's going to show us her room.'

Behind the desk was a squat man with a long face, looking as happy as a wet fortnight in Montrose. 'Call me Simon.' He turned around and lumbered up the carpeted stairs.

Olivia followed Adam up on the inside, leaving Mark to climb up behind.

Lamb unlocked the door with a massive set of keys. He nudged it open, eyes dancing back to the corridor, like he was fearful that Kay might return any moment. 'We let her the room for two weeks, as you know. Wish I'd insisted she paid in advance, but hey ho.'

Adam waved inside the door. 'Mind if I go in?'

Lamb grimaced. 'Sure thing.'

'Thanks, man.'

Kay's room was small but overlooked the street. Her suitcase lay open on the luggage rack, half full of dirty clothes, the remainder hanging up in her wardrobe.

Mark couldn't understand when anyone would find enough time or motivation to hang up clothes in a hotel room, least of all his daughter.

The long desk was tidier than his ever would be. Her phone sat in the middle, next to a book.

Break The Chain by Mark Campbell.

What the hell?

Had she finally got around to reading it?

Adam picked it up with his blue plasticky-gloves. 'The spine's flawless. Fresh from the bookshop. Doesn't look like she's opened it, let alone read it.'

Mark shrugged. 'She was a very careful reader. Never dented the spine. Sold them on eBay after she'd read them.'

'Selling her dad's book? That's *cold*.'

'Not mine. I don't want her reading my stuff.'

'And yet it looks like she probably has.' Adam read the back cover. 'Talk to me about this book.' He looked up at Mark. 'Bet you're good at that.'

Cheeky sod.

Still, he was helping them.

'Well, what's there to say? That's my breakthrough hit.'

Adam was looking inside the book. 'Published in 2015. No later ones?'

Mark had to look away. 'There aren't any.'

'Writer's block?'

Mark could deny it, suggest writer's block wasn't a thing. But he didn't have the energy. And it wasn't exactly far off the truth. 'Something like that.'

Adam tossed the book back on the table. 'Been on the telly yet?'

Mark winced. Another sore point. 'If you're half as good at

finding missing students as picking holes in my career... We sold the film rights, but it's not been made.'

'Yet or never?'

'Yet.'

'Right, right. I'd give your books a go, but if it's not got mutants or pirates in it, I'm not interested.' Adam put the book in a bag. 'Might get prints off it, though.' He got out another bag and put the phone inside. 'This, though... A teenager leaving their phone is like us leaving a hand or a foot.'

Olivia side-eyed Mark. 'That doesn't apply to *everyone* our age, eh?'

He blushed. 'I'm not that bad.'

'No, you really are.' Olivia smiled at Adam. 'Your lot got capacity to run that?'

'Just because it's the Highlands doesn't mean we're standing around with our thumbs up our—' Adam coughed, looking at Lamb. 'Aye, I've got people who can process it, but she's a runaway, right?' He sniffed. 'Thing I'm wondering is why she's left it?' He looked at Mark. 'You or her mum pay for the contract?'

'Me.'

'Well, there you go. You can snoop on her, right?'

'Can I?'

Olivia rolled her eyes. 'Aye, not for ages, eh?'

Mark sighed. 'Look, she told me she was getting hassled by this boy. But didn't tell me who. So I looked at her phone when she was in the shower, then I spoke to his parents about it, but Kay didn't see the funny side.'

'Well, there you go.' Adam pocketed the phone and book. 'Leaving the book behind too. Like she's sending you a message, Mark. She's running away from *you.*'

That hit Mark in the gut like a punch.

'I'll go and chase forensics up.' Adam patted his pocket and scooted off out of there.

Olivia had cornered Lamb over by the window. 'When did you say you last saw her?'

'Tuesday.' Lamb checked his watch, like that would list the times. 'Ten o'clock in the morning.'

'That's quite precise.'

'Aye, well, she asked for a late breakfast, so of course I let her have it, like a mug.' He scowled at Mark, nostrils flaring. 'Twenty quid a day on top of the bill, mind.'

Olivia frowned at Lamb. 'Did she have her breakfast?'

'Aye, had to get vegan bacon in and everything. Stuff's not cheap. Working on her computer while she ate.'

Something fluttered in Mark's stomach. Hope? He didn't know. He scanned the room for the MacBook he'd bought her for Christmas, back when he had some cash and he didn't mind being ripped off by Californian tech giants. 'Did she have the laptop with her when she went?'

Lamb scratched at his chin, frowning. 'I'm buggered if I know, sorry.'

Olivia folded her arms. 'Did she meet anyone while she was here?'

'We have strict rules on fraternisation.'

'Understandable.' Oliva smiled. 'No cups of coffee with anyone?'

'Not that I recall.'

'See her with anyone?'

'Well, once or twice. She dropped her key off on Sunday morning, there was someone outside... Whether he was here to pick her up, I can't say.'

'He?'

'I think so.'

'You get a look at him?'

'Sadly not.'

'Did they take her car or his?'

'Not her Fiesta, that's for sure.' Aye, Simon Lamb was the type to keep a log of everybody's comings and goings. 'What do you want me to do with her stuff?'

'I'll pack it up.'

'Suit yourself.' Lamb sniffed. 'Now, about that bill?'

Mark reached into his pocket for his credit card. 'Better stick it on this.'

Lamb snatched it out of his hand and shot off out of there.

Mark scurried down the stairs after him, down to the smoky entrance, engulfed with the smell of roasting meat.

Lamb had the machine all ready. 'There you go, sir.'

Eighteen hundred quid, just like that. 'Can I get this all itemised, please.'

'Aye, aye.' Lamb pushed the machine at him again.

Mark slotted his card in and tapped in the PIN. 'Thanks.'

'Don't mention it.'

Mark took his card back. 'Okay, well, thanks for showing us her room.'

'I hope you find her.'

'Thanks.' Mark pushed out into fresh air and stomped across the tarmac towards their cars.

'Panic on the streets of Inverness.' Olivia was wheeling Kay's luggage out. 'You left this!'

Mark stopped dead on the pavement. 'Right. Sorry.' He took the case. 'How does this look to you? Be honest.'

Olivia had her mobile out, smiling at something. A text, maybe? 'She's probably run off, Mark.'

But she swallowed. She was lying.

'Liv, I said "be honest".'

She sighed. 'Look, the truth is we just don't know. Parents and loved ones never assume "she's run off". But whether something has happened to her? I don't know. Given she's left her phone, I think there's a possibility that... I don't know. Some kind of foul play. Maybe had an accident.'

Mark leaned back against a lamppost. Took everything he had not to collapse.

Olivia rested a hand on his shoulder. 'But that doesn't mean she's not run off. Good cops think dirty and prove otherwise. While we were driving, Adam conducted a "search urgency" assessment. The fact she has no money and left her phone behind is suspicious enough. But Adam isn't just a good cop, he's a great one. Adam will run her phone records and find out who's been calling. He's got people scouring the Highlands for her.'

Mark stood up tall and tried to see it as good news. As a positive. He had to believe she was okay. Just had to. 'Thanks for helping.'

'I mean it when I say she was like a daughter to me.'

'So I gather.'

'What's that supposed to mean?'

'You were close to her. That's cool.'

'Alright.' It didn't look like it, not by the way her eyebrows rose. A reaction he hadn't seen in her before.

'I doubt it's a private plate. Aye.' Adam was leaning against Mark's car. His voice was all soft, like butter at room temperature for an hour. 'Okay, cool. Cheers. Aye.' He ended the call and paused, staring into space. 'Well, my guy's just run the plates through the system and got a ton of sightings of Kay's car.'

13

Mark finished chewing his sandwich, which tasted of mealy tomato, all sickly sweet and sour, and took in the street. A charity shop. A café. A computer repair shop. Nothing seemed to stick out. 'So, where's her car now?'

'Now that's something I can't answer.' Adam gave him the hard inspection of a cop. 'But the CCTV caught her.' He waved at a car two spaces up from Mark's. 'She was in that exact space on Saturday afternoon.'

And unless it was some kind of Transformer, her car had driven off rather than morphing into an Audi SUV.

'After is a bit trickier. The system's a bit patchy up here. You're lucky to get those hits, to be honest.' Adam pointed over the road. 'Drug dealer stayed in a flat up there, so we got approval to mount these cameras. Big Tom's been doing twenty at Her Majesty's Pleasure since February, but we're not in any rush to take the camera down. But I've got something else.' He led them into a Victorian shopping arcade.

Two health food clones seemed to be in a price war, a couple of cafés Mark didn't fancy the look of, then a tempting bookshop. Sometimes Mark couldn't stop himself finding copies of his books and announcing the news to the owner. More often than not, he'd be asked to sign them. Other than signed stock being ineligible for returns according to his contract, having a bookseller eager to shift the copies and order in new stock could only be a good thing.

Adam stopped outside a barber doing a brisk afternoon trade and pointed along the way. 'She went in there.'

A strange-looking shop sat a few doors in from the exit to another street, *Avartagh's Esoterica* written above the door in an arcane typeface, like something out of the first edition of the Bible. The windows were obscured by bookcases, letting in very little light and giving even less of a clue as to what was inside. Books and New Age malarkey.

Olivia frowned. 'Is esoterica porn?'

'And you're trying to paint *me* as the country bumpkin, eh?' Adam laughed. 'It covers a multitude of sins. Literally. Supernatural things. Weird stuff. The owner's a good lad, though. He sells books and crystals and homeopathic remedies and God knows what else. Actually, I think even God might not know half of it.'

Mark didn't think Kay would be interested in a place like that. Then again, he didn't seem to know her at all well. 'How do you know Kay was in here?'

'I don't just sit in the pub all day, you know.' Adam walked over to the window. 'Got her on a camera walking along here.'

Mark caught sight of the camera above the door to a café. 'Thing is, my book's about the Clearances, so I'm struggling to see why she'd be hanging around this place.' He turned to Olivia. 'She's not into that nonsense, is she?'

'No, she is and it's not nonsense.' Olivia stood next to Adam. 'Has a crystal in her bag all the time. Thinks it brings good luck from the universe.'

Mark felt like a total loser who didn't know his own daughter.

'Well, whatever luck the universe brought her, she's been in here.' Adam opened the door and the bell rattled as he stepped inside.

Mark followed and took in the strange store. Two or three times the size of Adam's pub and rammed with bookshelves, the nearest ones stuffed full of old-style hardcovers. A quarter of the shop was taken up by a large table in the corner, artfully displaying some Viking paraphernalia. He scowled at Adam. 'Don't tell me you're into all this mumbo jumbo?'

'Aye, well, it's a grey area, isn't it? Best to hedge your bets.' Adam rapped his knuckles on the scarred wooden counter. 'Séan, you in?' he shouted. 'Some of the things he's told me would make your hair stand up.' He rubbed his bald head. 'Mine too, if I had any left.'

Mark ignored the joke. 'There's a big business in scaring people. Doesn't mean it's true.'

'Doesn't mean it's not.' Adam stood on his tiptoes, as if that would attract anyone. 'Introducing wolves to cover up vampires and werewolves living in the Highlands.'

Mark wasn't easily spooked, but with his daughter missing... 'That's rubbish.'

Adam laughed. 'It is, aye.' He passed Mark a book. 'Have a look at that, though.'

The cover was a spooky field emerging out of the mist. *The Bloody Glen* by Brad Overton.

Séan is a vampire, sworn to protect the Highlands of Scotland from other supernatural beings.

When an invading force of vampires from continental Europe starts decimating cattle in the Highlands, Séan and his team are dispatched to hunt them down.

The trouble is, Séan soon questions who the real monsters are and who he can trust.

'What a load of shite.' Mark handed it back. 'A self-published novel?'

'The owner wrote it under a pen name. Got a thousand copies printed. Sold two, I think.'

Beads rattled as a curtain crawled aside and a wraith-like man appeared from the kitchen at the back. Bright red hair tugged back in a tight ponytail, wild fronds escaping all over. The pallid skin of an IT worker. Victorian-era clothes: white collarless shirt with a neckerchief; brown leather waistcoat with pocket watch; dark-brown trousers tucked into deep-green Chelsea boots. 'Morning, sergeant.' His voice sent a shiver down Mark's spine. A whispered rasp, with an accent trapped somewhere in pre-Revolutionary America.

Aye, this guy had serial killer written all over him.

Probably had someone tied up in the back.

He could have Kay through there.

'It's afternoon, Séan.' Adam gestured to his side. 'This is Mark Campbell. And an old friend, Olivia Blackman.'

'Pleased to meet you both.' Séan offered a hand, with the sort of fingernails that usually went with fingerpicking an acoustic guitar, or a serious cocaine habit. 'Any friend of Adam's is a friend of mine.'

Mark shook his hand and it felt like he could crush it in one decent squeeze.

Adam held out his phone, showing a photo of Kay that Mark had never seen. Olivia must've taken it and sent it to him. 'Séan, I gather this woman visited you on Saturday?'

Séan craned his neck to inspect it. 'Why do you ask?'

Adam pointed at Mark. 'Because she's gone missing. You recognise her?'

'Ah, yes. Kay, isn't it?' Séan waited for Adam's nod, head tilted to one side. He patted down the fine hair on the top. 'Came in a few times. Kept coming in to look at a book. Follow me.' He led them deep into the bowels of the shop and ran his fragile fingers along an overflowing bookshelf, dislodging dust in the process. He picked up an old-style hardback with an ornate hand-stitched cover, and flicked through the pages. 'Here you go.' He held it out.

Satanism in the Highlands

What the hell?

Mark let the book rest on a table. 'She was interested in Satanism?'

Séan shrugged. 'She came in a few times and kept going to that section.'

Mark took the book and skimmed the chapter Séan had opened it to. It seemed to cover a cult operating in Strathruthven, the area around Ruthven and Kinbrace.

Where his book was set.

Kinbrace was a stop on the Far North train line up to Wick and Thurso. Ruthven was a small village, at the bottom of the glen, next to a system of lochs. Home of one of the worst atrocities in the Highland Clearances, hence Mark setting his book there.

Okay, so maybe it was useful. But the Satanism?

Mark felt that fire in his belly, long since diminished. A flame, flickering away, hungry to explore and share with the world.

His eye picked out dates like an eagle spotting rabbits in a field. The Second World War was as late as the chapter went, with nothing before 1819, which was after his novel's timeline. 'Did she say why she was looking at this?'

'Nope.' Séan reached over and turned the page. 'This was the other matter she seemed interested in.'

The Laird of Wedale Disaster

In May 1822, a clipper called the Laird of Wedale set off from Helmsdale Harbour, bound for Leith, now part of Edinburgh. Two hundred ex-crofters aboard, evicted from their lands and homes, heading for a new life in the country's central belt. Edinburgh's or Glasgow's factories, the shipyards of Leith and Govan, the mines of the Lothians and Lanarkshire, fishing from the coastal villages and towns, or maybe familiar work in the Borders, in the farms and mills lining the Tweed from Peebles to Berwick.

A tale Mark had read so many times, though this one had an even-more tragic twist – all souls lost at sea in a storm.

Adam took the book. 'You know about that?'

'It's a part of my story. Something for the culmination. Capturing the personal tragedy, like in *Titanic*. The lovers' plan is to escape to the lowlands to live a new life, only to die in a maritime disaster.'

Adam barked out a laugh. 'And people want to read that?'

Mark ignored him and grabbed the book back. The chapter ran for pages and pages, grief-stricken accounts from family and friends still to travel south and those who'd already made the journey. A true account of the personal cost of the Clearances on real people would be useful for his book. And it could be a clue as to what the hell Kay had been up to, certainly. 'She definitely looked at this?'

'Indeed. Also asked me about Helmsdale Harbour, which is a place I could satisfy her curiosity for a much more manageable price.' Séan led over to a shelf where he seemed to have rescued an entire print run of a thin volume.

Helmsdale and Strathruthven Through the Ages

Mark handed it back. 'I'll take it.' He grabbed the other book. 'And this.'

'Always good to make a sale to a first-time customer.' Séan opened the front page and examined the price. 'Bargain, too.' He headed back to the counter and stood by the till, raising his eyebrow at Mark. 'Is there anything else?'

'I'm good.' Mark looked around the place while the till rattled and clanked.

Adam was over by the Viking display.

Olivia walked over to Mark. 'You look like you've seen a ghost?'

'If Kay's definitely been here, running through the books on the shelves and finding that one... Maybe she's headed to Helmsdale to see where the disaster happened.'

'Why didn't she stay up that way instead of down here in Inverness?'

'I suggested that, but I think she quite liked the idea of staying in the city.'

Behind the till, Séan was smiling, impatient like he wanted to get back to his victim in the back. He pointed at a stack of his paperbacks on the counter. 'Can I interest you in a copy of this novel?'

The number of times some wannabe had tried to push their book on Mark... 'I'm good. Thanks.'

'Adam's a big fan.'

Mark frowned at him. 'Thought you only read stuff with pirates and mutants?'

'A load of both in that.' Adam walked over. 'Sometimes at the same time.'

Séan clasped his hands together. 'Sixty-three pounds.'

Mark swallowed down his anger. This infernal city was determined to rip him off. Instead of complaining, he handed over his card. 'Need a receipt, thanks.'

Séan hand-wrote one like it was still the Sixties, and produced it with a flourish, but it was so elaborately scrawled that Mark doubted his accountant would accept it. 'Thanks for your business.'

'Cheers.' Mark frowned. 'Do you have any idea where else Kay might've been?'

Séan was inspecting his long fingernail. 'Well, I sold her another tome, but I can't show you it as it's in her possession.'

'What was it?'

'A history of Boleskine House.'

Felt like someone had slid an icicle up Mark's spine. He knew all about that place and its history. More than most. Why the hell was Kay interested in *there*?

'Let's go.' Adam bundled them out of the shop and held the door as it swung shut. 'You find what you were looking for?'

'Maybe.' Mark winced at the weighty bag he was carrying. 'Though I think he saw me coming.'

'He's a wily sod, that's for sure.' Adam sucked in a deep

breath. 'If she's been looking into this boat, you should maybe head up there.'

'Maybe.' Mark grabbed the bag's handle tight. Felt heavier than it should. 'Still nothing on her car?'

Adam checked his phone. 'There's a search running, so if she drives south, we'll find her.'

'What about north?'

'Aye, good luck. No cameras.' Adam clapped a hand on Mark's arm. 'There's a BOLO on her. That's "Be On the Look Out". If she's seen, we'll get her.'

'But you think Helmsdale's a dead end?'

'No.' Adam tapped Mark's bag with his shoe. 'Could've easily got there without flagging on the system. Nothing north of the city. But it's funny he mentioned that book, because I do have a hit for her leaving Inverness on Monday morning. She took the road on the south bank of Loch Ness.'

Mark felt that tightening in his guts. 'Heading for Boleskine House.'

14

During the ten years Mark was involved with Olivia - five years as a couple, five years married, now a year divorced - he'd been up here a lot and a lot of work had been done to the A9, upgrading that infernal road into something close to resembling a modern highway. Still, you were always just one turn away from a single-track road. Like this one, pockmarked with passing places that people seemed to actually respect, unlike in the lowlands.

Mark trundled along the carriageway, his gaze shooting between the road ahead, the satnav, and the scenery. The loch was supposedly somewhere on the right, but it was obscured by the thick wall of beech trees in full bloom.

The satnav display occasionally read 'General Wade's Military Road', like it was some cute Tartan-shortbread-tin path through the Highlands and not a network of paths used by the British army to tame the fierce locals.

God, there was so much history up here. And not all of it personal.

'You have arrived at your destination.'

Mark pulled into a parking bay and let a camper van rip past. He got out into the now-humid afternoon and took a deep breath of the fresh air. The old gatehouse basked in the sun. A tiny wee place with an over-sized porch almost bigger than the rest of it.

Up on the hill behind stood what was left of Boleskine House. A long, flat, white building almost swallowed up by trees. Seemed to be in the middle of restoration, currently held in place by scaffolding and fences. The drone of pop music blasted out of portable radios.

Mark had that churning deep in his bowels. They shouldn't bother rebuilding it after the fire.

An old hunting lodge bought by Aleister Crowley at the turn of the last century. Crowley, the occultist who'd invented modern Satanism.

Do what thou wilt shall be the whole of the law.

The man who had invoked a demon from hell inside, only to be interrupted partway through the ritual, leaving the demon in residence, along with the Twelve Lords of Hell.

If you believed that.

Jimmy Page of Led Zeppelin certainly did and bought the place for its Satanist history. Never lived here and sold it in the early Eighties. It burnt down five years ago, though no Lords of Hell were responsible. And it was human beings who were to blame for the torment between Page's sale and the fire.

Mark did a quick google. Rumours that James McNab bought it recently. Another idiotic rock star who dabbled in the occult. Maybe just rumours, but someone was restoring the place, that's for sure.

Being back here, feeling the chill wind from the loch, even in midsummer, Mark started to wonder what on earth his daughter was doing here. Who'd told her about what happened.

And where the hell were Adam and Olivia?

A bashed-up car pulled in outside the gatehouse and an old man got out, tall and gaunt. 'Can I help you, sir?'

There were a few ways Mark could play this. Waiting on either serving detective sergeant was the smartest. Blundering in was the most stupid.

He nodded up at the house. 'Nice place up there.'

The man didn't even look at the house. 'Nice would be stretching it.'

'You live here?'

'Aye, son. In the gatehouse.' The man nudged his car door shut. 'You one of those Led Zep fans doing the pilgrimage?'

'Not me, no.' Mark held out his phone, showing the most-recent photo of his daughter. Quite a pretty one, the light capturing her mother's eyes. 'Wondering if you'd seen this woman?'

He didn't look at the phone. 'Are you a police officer?'

'No. She's my daughter. Been missing since Tuesday.'

'Well.' The man opened the gate then finally looked at the photo. 'Well, she did visit, aye. A bonny lassie.'

Something in the way he said it. That curl of his lip, or the spark in his eye... It really got Mark, jabbed him in the kidneys.

'What's that supposed to mean?'

'What's what supposed to mean?'

Mark cast his eye up to the ruined building. 'Are you keeping her here or something?'

'Am I *what*?'

'You heard me.' Mark squared up to him, going forehead to forehead. 'Have you got her tied up in there?'

He stepped away from Mark. 'Mate, you need to bugger off.' He pointed at Mark's car. 'Get out of here. Now, or I'll call the police.'

'I'm working with them. I need to—'

'Are you hell with the cops. Get out of here!'

Mark felt that volcanic rage burning away. But he knew why too, and he tried to control it. 'I'm sorry. I'm not a police officer but I am working *with* them.'

'I don't have to say anything to you.'

'I know.' Mark swallowed. 'But Kay's my daughter. Please. Help me find her.'

'I don't know what you want me to say?'

'I know why she might've been here. There was a cult based here.'

'Aye, back in the Eighties after Jimmy Page sold it.'

'Did she ask you about it?'

He fixed Mark with a hard stare, then it softened into a chuckle. 'Bright as a button, she was. Asked me a couple of questions about the place, much like you're doing now, then I invited her in for a cup of tea and a scone.' He looked away. 'Inside, she started asking about the left-hand path, if you catch my drift.'

Satanism.

Black magic.

Well, invoking Beelzebub was the lesser evil that occurred here.

'Trouble is, I don't know much about what happened. Just looking after the place for a friend, while he organises the renovations.'

'Is that friend James McNab, by any chance?'

'I can neither confirm nor deny it.' He tapped his nose with the sort of gleam in his eyes that was closer to the former. 'She did talk a lot about this famous father of hers.'

'Hardly famous.'

He grinned. 'Thing is, I do know about Satanism. Not just the daft sort that was practised here, where numpty hippies tried to invoke diabolic forces to guide them through a libertarian lifestyle.' He looked away, over towards the loch. 'But also the sort that was practised further north of here. The truly evil kind.'

'What do you mean?'

'Actual devil worship. Child abuse. Ritual murder.'

'Isn't that a myth?'

'Define a myth.' He stepped into his garden, his foot crunching on the path. 'A myth is a story. There's usually a kernel of truth to it. I suggested she ask at a certain bookshop in town, but she'd already been. So I pointed her to a few sites up north.' His head jerked to the side and he watched a black sports car pull into the space behind Mark's. 'Now, son, that's all I can offer. I hope you find young Kay. She's a good lass.' He gave a dark look at the car, then jogged up the steps into the house.

Olivia got out and leaned against the door. 'Sorry, got held up back there.'

'Well, she was here on Monday.' Mark nodded at the house. 'Spoke to him about Satanism and black magic.'

'Got a black magic woman...' Olivia laughed, but she looked up the hill at the building. Construction work clattered away. The tinny music was chart pop rather than the thump of hard blues rock. 'This isn't the first time I've been here.'

'Nor me.'

She frowned at him.

Mark spotted Adam in the car, talking to someone on the phone. No way was he going to talk to her about it, not with him about. 'Go on?'

'One night, we drove here from town. Me, Adam and an old friend. Craig Gillespie. He was massively into Led Zep at the time. Played us *Stairway to Heaven* backwards. You ever heard it?'

A horde of spiders crawled up Mark's spine. 'There was a little tool shed where he made us suffer.'

She raised her eyebrows. 'You know it well enough to quote it?'

'I'm a fan.'

'Well, you never listened to Led Zep when we lived together.'

'Not while you were in.' Mark gave a smile. 'It's all bollocks, though. Why would anyone waste so much time writing lyrics that read a message when played backwards?'

'If you give bored rock stars with drug habits and an interest in the occult a ton of free time in recording studios, you don't think they'd get around to it?'

'Okay, if you're going to do it, why not have it make sense? How scary is a little tool shed?'

'Depends what tools he's got in there.' Olivia was looking around like one of Satan's Lords of Hell was near.

Mark shook his head. 'The mind hears what it wants to hear.'

'Okay, so you don't believe it.' Olivia folded her arms. 'Or don't you want to believe it?'

'I just don't buy the occult side of it, that's all.'

69

'Suit yourself. But all that stuff about rock bands selling their souls to the devil. Oh, it makes me wonder...'

Like Robert Plant sang in *Stairway to Heaven*, forwards.

And she was giving him that look. 'Something you want to talk about?'

'Me? No. Other than my daughter being missing, I'm peachy.'

That house, though. So much torment in there. Not so much in those four walls, but... At least all the cabins behind had been torched and their very existence lost to the mists of time.

Olivia's look became one of concern. 'Mark, if you want to talk about it, I'm here for you.'

'Thanks.'

'I'm serious. You can talk to me.'

'Thank you.' *Now shut up, Liv, please.*

'Cool, cheers.' Adam got out of his car and tossed his phone in the air then caught it. 'My guy has a hit on her mobile number in Helmsdale on Monday evening. Before she went missing.'

Mark pointed at the house. 'He reckoned Kay was heading up north to check out some sites related to bloody devil worship.'

'Well, let's see if she found her bloody devil worshippers.'

15

Led Zeppelin played through Mark's car stereo, though at least it had moved on from *Stairway to Heaven*'s folk-metal stomp to some of the darker meat on their next album. Somehow *Over the Hills and Far Away* was a fitting soundtrack to driving through Inverness. The view across the Moray Firth was something else, though.

Still made his hair stand up. The land beyond had that draw of the unknown, the mystical hills in the distance, shouting at him to come and climb them.

There be dragons.

Or maybe just his daughter.

Helmsdale was sixty-three miles north, according to his satnav. Where the *Laird of Wedale* had sailed from, carrying the local crofters who had been turfed from their Strathruthven homes to a new life in the lowlands.

Mark followed Olivia's car onto the Kessock Bridge, the thumping rhythm rumbling through his legs and up his spine. The gradual climb up to the Black Isle, with the industrial side of Inverness sprawling below, the Moray Firth widening out on the other side as it flowed into the North Sea.

He checked the wing mirror and slowed as he got to the halfway point.

Right. Fucking. There.

Where it happened.

That strut climbing up into the blue sky, the giant cables running north and south the only things suspending the carriageways above the water. A narrow walkway ran alongside, with a man and his dog jogging along.

An oil tanker rumbled past him, giving him a blast of the horn for good measure.

His mobile rang, cutting Robert Plant's moan dead.

Olivia calling...

Mark sped up away from the strut and answered the phone. 'Hey, what's up?'

'You got a flat tyre, or something?'

'No.' Mark swallowed down years of sadness. 'Just wondering how many more times I have to play *Stairway to Heaven* forwards to counteract the possibility of luring a stray demon.'

'You daft sod.'

'Truth is, I just had a call from Cath, so had to take it slow.'

'Say no more. We'll see you in Helmsdale.'

16

Some little sods had turned the road sign so it pointed away from the harbour.

Mark only realised when he heard Olivia's honking and caught her flashing lights in the rear-view. He pulled a quick three-pointer and followed her down to the shore.

At least there was plenty of parking.

Nothing else to write home about. Down in Fife or Ayrshire, the place would be full of cafés, ice cream parlours, arcades, shops selling crap to tourists. Here, there were just houses. Maybe a café but it didn't look open. And wasn't clear if that's what it actually was.

Mark got out into the stiff breeze, but from down here, he couldn't make out the distant hills that had been an almost-constant companion on the journey up, following in the slip-stream of Olivia's high-tech sports car.

A car the divorce paid for. Meaning he'd paid for it.

Hard not to resent it. Or her.

'Gorgeous smell.' Olivia furrowed her brow. 'I can almost see why you write. You get to travel all over the place and see lots of cool stuff.'

'Something like that. But you get to travel in your job, right?'

'Speaking to a victim of domestic abuse in Paisley isn't exactly exotic.' She sniffed.

Adam's car rolled to a stop and he got out.

Olivia patted Mark's arm. 'We'll have a little poke around in that café. You make yourself useful.' She led Adam off towards a row of houses with flags flapping in the breeze and flowers in full bloom.

Mark closed his eyes. That familiar tang of decaying seaweed, the kelp that would sustain the crofters back in the past. He felt so alone. His whole world had been built around Olivia and then he'd made such a mess of it. He was left with his daughter, but she wasn't his wee girl anymore. Almost an adult and much wiser than him.

He reopened his eyes and scanned around the town. The village. The rapid clinking of sails from the boats in the harbour, located in the only tame section of a wild and rugged coast, a small gap where tall sea cliffs descended to a pebble beach. The harbour itself arched around under the huge blue sky, beyond it just the emptiness of the North Sea. Probably not a soul between here and Norway. Or Denmark. He tried to trace the line of the coast south. The A9 bridged the River Helmsdale, rustling with traffic, though nothing that could be described as heavy. He was probably looking at the Black Isle from the opposite side, but he couldn't decide.

The small sections of beach would be difficult to access, with no sign of any steps down. While the hills inland hadn't changed at all, Mark wondered how much the cliffs had eroded since the resettled crofters moved here. He'd read all too many accounts of their harsh lives, staying in makeshift tents that would struggle in the south of France, let alone the north of Scotland. Then they built stone cottages that hadn't lasted. Living off kelp and whatever they could scavenge. Some cattle, some poultry, but not much else.

Crofting would've been a tough life, but it would've been a life. Living here, though, would more likely mean dying. Starvation, thirst, injury, take your pick. Then to be shunted aboard boats heading south, all against their wills. Pawns in a game they didn't understand they were playing.

Kay was researching the lives of the folk who'd suffered that ordeal. The *Laird of Wedale* had set sail from this very point. Didn't get very far out to sea, by all accounts, before it sank. It would still be lying in the surprisingly deep waters, its ghastly cargo long since decayed and eaten by fish.

Didn't bear thinking about.

A gruesome ending to his novel, the kind of cruel tragedy that people kept thinking about long after.

And the material Mark didn't need for months.

Magic.

Olivia stomped back over. No sign of Adam. 'Well, a woman who might've matched Kay's description might've had a vegan salad on Monday afternoon, but they couldn't definitively say if it was her.' She thumbed behind her. 'Adam's taking a statement.'

'Thanks.' The boats all seemed empty. 'What now?'

'Adam's guy is still pulling her earlier phone records.'

'Shouldn't he have got the whole lot?'

'You'd think so, but no. Probably because it's a favour to me, he's... Well, there was a mistake.'

'A *mistake*?'

'One of his guys got the wrong month range.'

'How? How the hell is that possible?'

'Because they're looking at historic crimes, probably. Not used to live missing persons like this. I don't know, Mark. I'm sorry.' Olivia scanned the harbour. 'Still, her phone *was* here. And that sighting, let's assume for now that it was her here on Monday.' Her phone chirped, but she didn't check it. 'What happened back at the bridge?'

'Bridge?'

'Kessock Bridge.'

'Nothing.' Mark walked off back to the car.

Olivia grabbed his arm and stopped him. 'Come on, Mark. You pulled in back there. Why?'

Mark shook free and walked away.

'Sure, run away from your problems, Mark. Just like you always do.'

He stopped. She was right. He always ran. And where had that got him? Two divorces and a missing child. Debt and a threat from a loan shark. 'I think Kay was at Boleskine House because she found out about my past.' He looked her right in the eye. 'I used to live there.'

'You grew up there?'

He could only nod.

'Mark, we were married for five years and this is the first I've heard of it. We visited my folks in Inverness like three times a year and you didn't think to say?'

'I don't have an answer for it, Liv.'

'If you need to talk, I'm listening.'

'My parents joined this cult when I was seven. This hippie thing, based at Boleskine House. We stayed in these cabins out the back. Everybody mucked in. School was a couple of the women teaching us folk histories and stuff.'

'Sounds idyllic.'

'Sounds it, maybe.'

'She never talked to you about it?'

'Never really talked to her.'

'I know, Mark.'

'Come on, Liv. She never wanted daddy time. Trouble with the group we were in... It was a religious sect.'

She frowned. 'Like in your book?'

'Right. And one morning, the cops and social workers raided the place. Said we were Satan worshippers. How the parents were abusing the children. We were all taken to this safe house down in Perth.'

'Were the allegations true?'

'Of course not. Some arsehole in the council got it in his head that there was stuff going on. His church wasn't happy with us. I mean, our life was fine, a bit cold and dark but it was fine. The worst bit was the investigation meant I was separated from my parents.'

'You never talked about your parents.'

'With good reason.' He sighed. 'If my parents hadn't been involved, they wouldn't have been accused of the abuse. And my dad might not have died.'

'You mean he didn't die of stomach cancer like you told me?'

He couldn't look at her. 'Sorry. I shouldn't have lied, but...'

'But the truth was too much to deal with?'

'Right. They were all trying to fight the case, trying to get their kids back. But it wasn't looking good for them. One morning, my old man left and they never saw him again. Turned out he was so indebted to the cult he couldn't afford to pay a good lawyer to fight it and get me back. He ran out of cash, and he couldn't face being convicted of child abuse, so he took a header off the Kessock Bridge.'

Olivia wrapped him in a hug. 'Mark, you could've told me.'

'I'm sorry, Liv. You're the first person I've talked to about this in like twenty-five years.'

'Not Cath?'

'Hell no. Not even my therapist.' Mark broke free. 'You see why I had to write that book? Why it cost me so much. Why I haven't been able to write much since.'

'And I can see why you were so difficult when you were writing it. Mark, you really should've talked to someone. If not me, then your therapist.'

'I tried, but...'

'Thought you two were divorced?' Adam was striding over, hands in pockets. 'They've got a room upstairs if you need it?'

Olivia broke off from their clinch. 'You get anything?'

He frowned. 'Does Badbea mean anything to you two?'

Mark knew the name, just where from? Then he got it. 'It's a Clearances site. Halfway between here and John O'Groats. Why?'

'Well, Kay's phone records show she was here, so that was her eating the vegan salad. But she was at Badbea before that.'

17

Mark followed Olivia and Adam along the rough path, heather and gorse running wild on both sides, with no sign of any grass. The bright blue sky and beating sun still didn't cut through, giving him a chill.

The path wound round in a tight bend. Mark planted his foot but slipped and went down. He caught his arm on the spines of a gorse bush. 'Ah, you bastard!'

Adam held out a hand. 'You okay?'

'Am I hell.' Mark sat there, inspecting the damage. He'd cut his hand right open, so he licked the wound, then took Adam's hand and let him winch him back up to standing. 'Cheers.'

Adam powered down the path towards the glistening blue sea, trying to catch Olivia.

Mark followed, but even slower than before. Once slashed by gorse, twice shy.

A square monument rose out of the ground, maybe twenty feet tall and with a crow-step roof.

Mark almost lost his footing again as he descended towards it.

Plaques mounted on all four sides, commemorating tragic lives in the Clearances. Nobody who featured in Mark's book, thankfully.

The path led on through a large path of grass, different to the rough ground either side.

Mark gestured at it. 'See where there's no heather? This land would've been cleared by the crofters to live and raise their cattle.'

Adam stopped, frowning. 'This was a croft?'

'No, it was a whole village. Something like a hundred and sixty people lived here.'

Adam exhaled. 'Doesn't bear thinking about, does it?'

'After they'd been cleared from their lands in the glens, the landowners shoved them out to the coast, forcing them to retrain as fishermen. The land here would've been much worse than over in, say, Strathruthven. They had to start again from nothing. Well, maybe each family would have a cow and some hens. Some seeds for kale, oats and some potatoes. But that's it. The rest would come from fishing and that water is as still as it gets today.'

Adam watched the tall waves crashing to the cliffs. 'Brutal.'

'That's the word for it.' Mark walked off along the path and stopped by a box of broken stone walls. Eight foot by sixteen and overtaken by grasses. 'The last people only moved out of here a hundred years ago, but it feels like they left before the Romans.'

'Really does.' Olivia was scouring the place. 'Was this where they kept the cattle?'

'No, this was a house.' Mark shielded his eyes from the sun and scanned the deadly hillside, which lead down to severe cliffs. 'It's fine on a day like this, but in November or February? They'd have to tether their livestock and their children in case they blew away.'

'My god.' Adam rubbed at his throat. 'Is this in your book?'

'Not yet. I was going to have them board the boat the night after they were cleared from the glen, but maybe living on the coast would increase their suffering and motivate their desperate need to move south.'

Aye, and Jamie would have to return to Strathruthven to face his father, disgusted at the betrayal.

God, feeling that embroiled in a book was something he hadn't experienced in years.

Adam picked something up from the corner of the room. A white plastic bag. 'I wish people would take their shite home with them. Bloody hell.'

Mark crept through the ruined house, careful not to stir the dead or their ghosts. 'What's up?'

Adam held the bag out. *Avartagh's Esoterica*, the logo etched in the same arcane script as the shop signage. 'Kay might've left it.'

Mark's heart was fluttering. 'What's in there?'

Adam opened the bag with gloved hands and pulled out a partly read copy of *The Bloody Glen* by Brad Overton. 'Signed by the author. To Kay. Hope this thrills you. Séan.' He sighed. 'Thought the point in a pen name was nobody knew who you were.'

Mark inspected it. The handwriting was a long scrawl. But nothing else of note.

'Oh, what's this?' Adam pulled out a notebook, stuffed full of papers. Navy with an inscription:

Almost Family.

Olivia gasped. 'I gave her that.' She snatched it out of his hand. 'Property of Kay Campbell. No contact information, obviously, but it's hers. Her notes.' She looked at Mark. 'Kay was here.'

The bag was slightly weathered and the book damp, so Mark didn't know how long. Presumably Monday.

Olivia pored through the rest of her notes, letting Mark see over her shoulder. Seemed to be prints from newspapers, rather than the interviews she'd written up.

Which must be on her laptop.

Magic.

It was all in chronological order, at least. The last few pages outlined her movements over the previous few days. A lot on Boleskine House, but more about the Crowley mythology and nothing on what the hell she was so interested in down there.

Some names of people to interview, though. William Turnbull, Elizabeth Ruthven, James McNab.

Olivia tapped the page. 'You know these people?'

'Maybe.' The wind caught the pages so Olivia had to grip tighter for Mark to see. 'James McNab owns Boleskine House.'

'You want to head back there?'

'Hardly. He lives in Sussex, so it's a bit of a stretch. Besides, his name's crossed out.'

'So she's spoken to him?'

'Or there's no point. No idea who the others are, but Ruthven... Well, that's probably someone from the Strathruthven area.'

Olivia pulled out a folded-up page and opened it out, almost losing it to the wind. She folded it the other way and showed it to Mark.

A map covering the top wedge of Scotland north of Inverness. Sutherland and Caithness. A tourist information job, but a few spots up the east coast were marked, including Helmsdale and Badbea. Another couple running inland, looking like Kinbrace and Ruthven. Then a triple-circle around Wick in the far north-east.

Olivia refolded it, passed it to Adam.

He stuffed it into the notebook, then put them both into the bag. 'What's this?' He held up a business card for the shop.

On the flipside was a neat note in the same exquisite hand-writing as the book's dedication:

Mhairi, barmaid, Crossed Arms.

'That lying sod.' Adam shook his head. 'Slipped his mind that he'd told Kay about this Mhairi, eh?'

Mark frowned. 'Have you heard of this place?'

Olivia clapped his arm. 'Buckle up. They do a cracking steak pie.'

18

The Crossed Arms was one of those pubs where incomers bought up a failing business, installed a pizza oven and some beer taps, then kept it in a state of shabby chic. Pale-blue tables with scuffed edges, hipster IPAs with in-joke names: Dip Your Wick; Highland Coffee; Orcadian Incest.

And no steak pie.

No food in front of Mark yet.

And no Olivia.

Mark sat there, doing everything he could to ignore the hunger gnawing at his stomach. Yet another hour driving. Yet another twenty minutes finding parking.

The pub was busy with Friday evening trade. So busy he had to settle for a seat outside, the sort of bench that most parks used to have, where everything was screwed together, which nobody over the age of fifteen could comfortably sit on.

The evening was reasonably calm, only the lightest breeze in the air – the sky had cleared of its few clouds, giving that true rarity of a Scottish summer's day.

Mark pored through the photos of Kay's notebook he'd taken, but he could barely focus on it. Where the hell was she? Why come here? Who was Mhairi?

'How could I dance with another?' Olivia stood over him. 'Want the good news or the bad?'

'You know me, Liv. Start with the bad.'

'Okay, Adam's still in the station. He's got nobody to run the detailed phone records for us. And his BOLO has been quite the talk of the town. His guys up here have been asking all over for her. Tourist information, library, the museums, a few local lawyers. Trawled the hospitals and health centres from Thurso down to Oban and Perth. And nobody matches her description.'

Mark blew out a deep breath. At least his worst fears hadn't come to pass yet. Still, they were no further forward. 'And what's the good news?'

'That's it.'

'Oh. Right.'

'His DI's approved his time on this.'

'That's it?'

'Well, aye.' She seemed a bit disappointed, but he didn't know why. 'Mark, you've got the pleasure of Adam's company for another day.'

'Still find it weird that his boss is devoting a DS to a missing person's case.'

'They treat it very seriously up here. Besides, it's a personal favour to me.'

The waiter returned with their plates of food, placing Mark's burger in front of him first.

A thick lump of grilled beef, coleslaw dripping all over the chips, onion rings and salad.

His mouth watered now. 'Magic, thanks.'

'Can I get you any sauces?'

Mark shook his head. 'No, I'm good.'

Olivia looked up from her large piece of battered haddock, its golden shell covering a mound of chips underneath. 'Is Mhairi on tonight?'

The waiter checked his watch. 'Aye, starts in five minutes. Why?'

'Just need to speak to her about something. You know how it is.'

The waiter rolled his eyes. '*Something*, aye?' He laughed. 'Right. Heard that before. Will do.' And he shot off.

Mark snatched a handful of chips and swallowed them down. 'What was that about?'

'Drugs, probably.' Olivia raised her chinking glass of cola. 'Never spent as much time up here as I'd like.' She sliced into her fish. 'Beautiful, isn't it?'

'Know what they say about any holiday in Scotland. It's fine if you get the weather.' Mark bit into his burger and chewed, the lumps of gristle sticking to his teeth. 'Just shove on a cagoule and you'll be fine. But it's the wind that gets you.' He took another bite from his burger.

'The wind's nothing. A fleece will sort you out.'

'You need to show me where to buy a fleece then, because every one I've ever bought has been rubbish.'

'Literally.'

'Eh?'

'Mark, they're made from recycled plastic bottles.'

'Never knew that.' Mark picked up a chip. His stomach was starting to cramp up, which always happened when he tried to eat too quickly.

She took her time finishing chewing, blowing out from the hot food. 'I just don't get why she was so obsessed with a boat that sank in Helmsdale way back when.'

'My book's about the betrayal of the crofters by the landowners. Sheep being a better income than people.'

'Your books are way too brutal for me.'

'Hey, it's Scotland. Can't buy a fleece that shields you from our history.'

'Ain't that the truth.'

Mark ate an onion ring and fat dribbled down his chin. He wiped it away. 'Don't know if you noticed when we were driving up, when it shifted from Sutherland to Caithness?'

'Go on?'

'Well, further south there were a few wee towns. Helmsdale, Golspie, Brora. Tiny wee places, but that was pretty much it north of Tain. Soon as we hit the border with Caithness, it was a long row of wee houses lining the road. One every hundred yards for about fifteen miles. If they were all together, that'd be a big town.'

She crunched her fish. 'Why is that?'

'Well, I think it's because the crofts weren't cleared in Caithness. Or at least nowhere near as badly. I mean, it's not like they didn't do it up here, but it was a lot less prevalent and much less savage than in Sutherland.'

Olivia was staring at her phone, like the BBC News app was more interesting than anything Mark had to say.

Mark took another bite of burger.

'Were you after me?' A young woman in black Goth makeup was frowning over at them.

Olivia smiled at her. 'Mhairi?'

She nodded. 'Chunter said to come and speak to you.'

'Thank you. I'm a police officer. DS Olivia Blackman.' Olivia reached over for her phone and held it up to her. 'Just wondering if you recognised this woman?'

Mhairi shook her head.

Olivia put the phone down again. 'She never came here?'

'Not that I know of. Who is she?'

'My daughter,' said Mark. 'She's been missing since Tuesday. Her name's Kay.'

'Ah, right. Well, I got a message on Facebook through my page from a Kay Campbell. That's her, eh?'

Olivia nodded. 'What's this page of yours about?'

Mhairi ran a hand through her hair. 'Black magic and stuff? Bit of local history. The dark stuff, though. I *think* Kay was interested the *Laird of Wedale* disaster.'

'She say why?' asked Olivia.

'Just that she wanted to talk. I'd written an article, based on stuff I got from a book. How they were all witches and that, and this was a mass drowning. She wanted to chat about it, so I said to

85

come here. Said she'd be here on Tuesday, but she never showed up.'

Which didn't add anything to their timeline of her movements.

'Thank you.' Olivia passed a business card to Mhairi. 'Give me a ring if she gets in touch again, aye?'

'Will do. Hope you find your daughter.' Mhairi gathered up their plates and headed inside.

'Libby!' Adam was charging towards them, waving his arms.

Olivia got up and ran over. 'Have you found her?'

Mark felt his heart thudding in his chest. He struggled out of the bench, almost falling over. At least they didn't see him, though the rest of the customers did.

'Afraid not.' Adam dipped his head. 'But we've found her car.'

19

Mark pulled into the car park at Kinbrace just as the train trundled off down the single tracks, heading south towards civilisation. The ninety minutes from Wick felt like weeks. No more driving for a bit. He hoped.

No messages on his phone.

Mark got out to look around. Kinbrace was barely even a village, just a single-track road weaving through boxy houses, a train platform and a level crossing. Far from the sea in all directions, just some hills visible on the horizon. The weather was like a different season than the coast, overcast with a heavy threat of rain. Trees hid some other houses.

He couldn't imagine being any further away from home, though the smell of barbecuing meat on the breeze at least made him feel like he was near people.

The only place Mark recognised on the road sign was Ruthven, seven miles distant.

Adam's car pulled up next to them and he got out, glowering. 'Knew I shouldn't have left my car in Helmsdale. Some wee toerag's battered the wing mirror.' He joined Mark. 'Where is he?'

'Who?'

'Edgar.' Adam looked around. 'The nearest staffed station is in

Brora.' He pointed down the train line. 'It's *miles* that away.' He squinted, said 'Aha,' then set off down the road, away from the station.

Olivia got out and followed him.

Mark jogged to catch up with her, passing a row of farm machinery. Red lorry cabs with the backs all bare and open. Maybe it was for forestry work.

Two cops stood at the end, hands in pockets.

Adam waved them down. 'Edgar?'

The older was a heavyset man in his forties, bushy eyebrows sprouting out from thick curly locks. He pulled his cap on. 'Well, if it isn't Adam Mathieson.' He clapped his arm. 'How the devil are you?'

'I'm fine. This is DS Olivia Blackman.'

She held out a hand. 'Based in Glasgow.'

Edgar snorted. 'Long way from home, aren't you?' He shook her hand, then offered his to Mark. 'Who's your bonnie lad here?'

'Mark Campbell.' He took the hand. 'Nice to meet you.'

'Well, here's the offending article.' Edgar stepped aside to reveal a purple Fiesta, catching the evening sun.

Kay's car.

Mark felt something like relief swimming around his veins.

Edgar's colleague, a constable a good fifteen years younger, was shining a torch inside the vehicle. 'Doesn't look like anybody's been inside for a couple days, like.'

Olivia frowned at him. 'What makes you say that?'

The constable pointed with his free hand. 'Yon big spider's set up home.'

Edgar rested his hand on the bonnet. 'We've been on to Scot-Rail and spoken to the manager of the car parks. Sends a lad out once a week to check for this kind of thing. Noted it down on Tuesday afternoon.'

A frown etched into Olivia's forehead. 'But he didn't call it in?'

'Hardly.' Edgar laughed. 'Your BOLO was what made us think twice, hence us finding it. The lad didn't see her, but we've asked around. Nobody saw the car arrive. But then, nobody sees anything around here.' He gave a deep sigh. 'Car found near a railway station. Makes me think that the owner of the car got on a train. That line's miles better than it used to be. Four a day now. Mind when it was just one each way. Running the video now.'

The train station didn't even have a car park, but there were CCTV cameras on the platform. South was back to Inverness, north was Wick or Thurso. Neither of those particularly made sense, especially if she was leaving her car here.

Adam gave a broad smile. 'Any chance you could go chase that up for me?'

'Aye, sure.' Edgar slouched off with his wee pal.

Mark peered inside the car. Fast food wrappers and crushed cans of energy drink, just like in his. 'Kay was staying in Inverness. Two hours away. Think she caught the train back there?'

Olivia was over the other side, hands cupped on the driver window. 'We need to ask her.'

Mark joined her on that side. 'Is that supposed to be helpful?'

'No, but... Missing persons cases are the hardest, Mark. Murders and assaults you get clues from the bodies. Forensics, you name it. Missing persons, you've got something happening, but it only makes sense to the person who's gone missing. And usually you only find out in hindsight.'

Adam craned his neck to look around. Edgar and his pal were both on phone calls. 'Lazy bastards.' He charged off after them.

Sod it.

Mark tried the car door and it clicked open. He got behind the wheel and tried all the usual spots. No keys tumbled out from behind either sun visor. Door pockets on both sides were empty. The glove box was open, though.

Bingo.

A mobile phone sat in there. A cheap model, years out of date.

Mark pressed the power button. Nothing. Thing was dead. Needed one of those charger cables he didn't know the name of, different to his phone, but common enough. Anyone with a Kindle or most Android phones would have one that fitted.

Mark pocketed it and stepped out. 'Have you still got an iPhone?'

Olivia nudged the boot shut. 'No, I got a Samsung last year. Why?'

Mark showed her the phone, palmed. 'Need a charger for this.'

'Car's open, I'll keep those two occupied.'

'Cheers.' Mark walked over, keeping his hand wrapped around the phone.

Adam spotted him. 'You okay, Mark?'

'Just need to make a call.'

'Oh. Okay.'

Mark passed them, then spun around. 'Anything on the CCTV?'

Edgar smiled. 'That's a police matter, sir.'

'Of course.' Mark slipped into the passenger side of Olivia's Toyota, the seat still warm from Adam's bum. The charger cable was all mangled and frayed, but at least it fit the slot. Magic.

He plugged Kay's phone in and waited.

Nothing happened.

He thumbed the ignition, enough to get the power on. And the phone's screen started glowing. He was in.

Except it had a fingerprint scanner, blocking access.

Maybe not that old, then.

Still, the phone buzzed. A few text messages popped up, their contents and senders hidden.

The driver door opened and Olivia got behind the wheel. 'Any joy?'

'Locked. Would yours or Adam's guys be able to get into it?'

She inspected the device. 'I'd want to send it down to my forensics guys in Glasgow. Same story as the one we found in her room. Take a few days to get there in the internal mail, then another few for them to get started on it. And there's no guarantee they could get in.' She handed the phone back. 'Sorry.'

'Surely they've got someone here who can—'

'Aye, they do. One, you bought her a phone that's really hard to crack. Two, I kind of don't trust them.'

'But you're adding a few days on—'

'He tried, he failed. That's it.'

'Right.' Mark stared at the phone.

It buzzed. A missed call notification. Just a number. And no text message for a voicemail.

'A missed call from someone.' Mark held up the phone. 'Should I call it back?'

She shook her head. 'Never leave a trail, Mark.'

'But someone's called her, Liv. It could be important.'

She squinted at the screen, then tapped something into her own phone, then put it to her ear. 'Hi, I'm looking for a Kay Campbell.' Pause. 'It's Detective Sergeant Olivia Blackman of Police Scotland, sir.' Another pause, longer. 'That sounds like a good idea. Be there in ten minutes.' She ended the call, pocketed the phone and turned on the ignition. 'Better if you follow me, Mark. And get Adam to come over too.'

He opened the door and put his foot on the ground. 'Who was that?'

'Someone who Kay was supposed to meet on Tuesday afternoon.'

20

Mark hauled the wheel left and right, trying to keep on the single-track road and not tip his car into the hard ditch or the harder stone wall on the other side. He steered onto a long straight, nothing but sheep and the occasional tree. Barren, mountains looming behind smaller hills, but Mark had always felt a close affinity with the Highlands, stark and hostile as it was.

A quarry gouged a hole out of a hill, with a trail of lorries transporting rocks south. The rest of the hillside was a serious forestry operation, covering miles and miles, leaving a trail of felled trees that looked like ribs made from toppled gravestones.

Still bright daylight despite the late hour. This time of year, only a couple of days away from the summer solstice, they were so far north that it wouldn't get dark all night.

Red lights up ahead. Olivia's Toyota, trying and failing to navigate an immobile flock of sheep filling the single track. Adam's car was nowhere to be seen. Typical.

Mark slowed to a halt right behind her, then followed through the flock.

Olivia cleared the sheep and floored it, shooting off along the road.

Mark's car didn't have the same power, instead sticking to a steady thirty, which still felt too fast.

A thick plantation curved down to meet him, a tidy regiment of native trees incongruous with the landscape's bare brutality.

Olivia was waiting up ahead, indicating a fork from the main road, heading for Ruthven and a brown sign for Ruthven Castle. She shot off again.

Mark followed as quick as he could, rounding a bend. A large loch appeared, shimmering in the late evening sun. What he wouldn't give for another lane, not that there was anything to overtake. He passed the sign for Ruthven:

Twinned with Tutzing, Bavaria.
Ullaich thu fhèin.

Yet another Gaelic term Mark didn't know.

He slid into Ruthven, a typical small Scottish village, rows of houses either side of a long main street, a mixture of Victorian villas and modern white-harled semis.

Mark pulled in behind Olivia and got out. No sign of Adam's car.

A shop, a tearoom and a baronial hotel in the middle of a market square, opposite a grand church of post-war construction, dirty concrete rather than pristine stone. Sounded like a choir was practising inside. He didn't recognise the hymn.

Another sign pointed to the Catholic church at the loch end of the village; seemed strange for such a small place to have two churches. Then again, Mark wouldn't be surprised to find a sprawling Free Church lurking somewhere, with a growing congregation.

Maybe a mile away, a castle perched on an island halfway round the loch, separated from the mainland by a narrow stretch of water. Lights shone in a tower, but the rest of the building was shrouded in mist.

Mark pointed at it. 'Is that Ruthven Castle?'

'Could make a detective of you.' She plipped her locks and walked inside the Ruthven Arms Hotel. 'Adam should be inside.'

The hotel was a big thing occupying the plot of six houses, with twice as many turrets jutting out. Ornate mason-work above the door, possibly reading 'Be Ready for Tomorrow', but it was too weathered to know for sure. Either way, that was a motto to live by.

Mark struggled to open the heavy door, then entered the hotel.

Olivia was leaning against the reception desk, the ring from the bell still rattling around the open space.

Coffee tables and armchairs tastefully spread out. A spiral staircase leading up. And no sign of anyone. Quite a fancy place, then, but it had seen better days. A wonder somewhere this size could survive in a town like this. Tourists would mostly stick to the North Coast 500 route, miles away on the coast.

Mark joined her by the desk. 'Who are we meeting here?'

'Adam!' Olivia set off again, hands in pockets, heading for the lounge.

Mark followed her and, to his surprise, the lounge was busy.

A long wooden bar, but no sign of any staff. A large open fire burned away, even though it shouldn't on a warm evening like this. Two settees in front of the fire, hosting two couples who looked early twenties, red-headed and ignoring the arrival of two strangers.

A large TV sat in the corner, showing the aftermath of a football match. Mark had no idea who was playing and didn't care, but it had its hooks into Adam, who was propping up the bar.

A grizzled man sat at a table in the middle of the bar's lounge area, sipping from a pint of some heavy Highland ale, then beasting a cheese and pickle sandwich. The classic Scottish half-pound of grated orange cheddar, an inch of butter and a scraping of pickle, all on white bread.

Olivia waved at him. 'John?'

He licked at his teeth. 'What makes you think that?'

She took a seat opposite him. 'You've got the look of a John.'

He laughed and held out his hand. 'John Rennie. Pleasure.'

'DS Olivia Blackman.' She gave a flash of her warrant card and shook the offered hand. 'This is DS Adam Mathieson.'

Just as he took the seat between them.

'Two detective sergeants?' Rennie laughed, spraying beer foam onto his plate. 'You must think I'm a very naughty boy.'

'That a guilty conscience there?' Adam's grin faded to a sneer. 'Anyway, this is Mark Campbell, who employs our mutual acquaintance.'

'Ooh.' Rennie winked at him. 'A Campbell. You'll not be popular in these parts.'

'I've not massacred anyone. Yet.'

'Don't worry, son.' Rennie took another bite of his sandwich. 'I'll not judge you for it. Others might, but not me.'

The barman appeared behind the bar, draping a towel over his shoulder, then pulled a pint pump until it stopped hissing and started pouring beer.

Olivia stood up. 'Can I get you anything?'

'Fresh orange and lemonade. Pint, please.' Mark was gasping from all that incessant driving.

Adam nodded. 'Same.'

'Coming right up.' She patted down her pockets. 'Get you a refill, John?'

It earned a raised glass of beer. 'And a wee dram, darling, if you're feeling generous.'

She slouched off to the bar with the grudging smile she usually reserved for her ex-husband.

Mark grabbed a seat from an adjacent table and sat next to Rennie. 'I'm looking for my daughter. Gather she was meeting you?'

'Young Kay, aye. She was a game lass and no mistake. I saw her getting stuck into the guests in here a couple of times.'

'Getting stuck into?'

Rennie laughed. 'Chatty sort, if you catch my drift.'

'Flirting?'

'Maybe.'

'Well.' Adam leaned forward, blocking Mark's line of sight. 'John, I don't know what Libby told you, but Kay's missing. You were supposed to meet her on Tuesday afternoon. That right?'

'Well, aye. But I've seen her in here before. And she didn't show. Saw her in the tearoom once before my work.'

'What do you do?'

'I'm a ghillie.'

Mark frowned. 'Didn't know you still had them up here.'

'Impressed a lowlander knows what one is.'

'Leading hunts and fishing expeditions. That kind of thing, aye?'

Rennie swirled his beer around the glass and finished it, his thirsty eyes scouring the bar, urging Olivia back with more. 'Some of the old ways persist.'

'What's a ghillie do in this day and age?'

'I'm basically a golf caddie, but for shooting. Plenty of hunting parties these days that need a guide out on the moors and glens. I just take them out, load their rifles, tell the toffee-nosed idiots where to point them. Half the time, I'm stopping the daft buggers shooting each other instead of the pheasants.'

Aye, John Rennie was a Class-A patter merchant.

Maybe there would be something useful among the noise.

Adam leaned forward. 'Did she give you any kind of a reason to explain why she might run away?'

'Like I said, hardly spoke to the lassie.' Rennie collected two fresh glasses from Olivia, one of beer, the other amber nectar. 'Cheers, hen.' He took a sip of whisky. 'Aye, that's the ticket.'

Olivia sat back down and distributed the three glasses between her, Adam and Mark.

Rennie raised his whisky. '*Slainte.*' He took a deep drink. 'Notice I'm the only one drinking, though.'

'Cheers.' Mark held up his pint glass, wishing it was something a lot stronger than orange and lemonade. 'What was Kay asking about?'

'Something to do with a book she was doing research for.'

Olivia groaned – her phone was ringing. 'Sorry.' She got up and walked off.

Rennie pointed down at Mark's nearly empty glass. 'Fresh orange and lemonade.' He chuckled. 'You boys. Nowhere else in the civilised world would orange juice be described as "fresh orange". You're not going to join me in a dram now she's gone?'

Mark thought about it long and hard. 'No, I'm driving.' And he might have to drive all the way back to Edinburgh.

'Suit yourself.' Rennie stormed over to the bar like a man who hadn't touched a drop in years, rather than someone who'd just sank four units in ten minutes.

Adam exhaled deeply. 'I hope Libby knows what she's doing with this arsehole.'

Both couples were staring at them but shifted their gazes as soon as Mark noticed.

The outside door opened and a man stepped in from the patio, red face, clutching an empty bottle of wine.

Behind him, a woman with red hair in ringlets stood on the lawn, facing away, talking on her phone.

Kay!

21

Mark charged across the bar, past the wine-bottle-toting man, and out onto the back patio. The air was cooling, but still warm enough. A group of five sat around a table, giving him a look as he charged past.

Mark hopped down the steps to the lawn. 'Kay!'

She was walking away, heading for a gate to a lane running along the back of the village.

'Kay!' Mark started to run. She wasn't getting out of his sight now. 'Kay!'

She turned around, frowning at him.

And it wasn't her.

About fifteen years too old, with a lantern jaw instead of Kay's pointy face. 'Can I help you?' Northern Irish accent.

Mark raised his hands. 'Sorry. Thought you were someone else.'

'Okay?' She looked at him like he'd just escaped from prison.

'Are you a guest here?' he asked.

'What of it?'

'Just wondering if you could help me.' Mark got out his phone and found the photo of Kay. 'Have you seen her?'

She squinted at the screen. 'I mean, she could be my daughter, but I haven't got one. And I haven't seen her, no.'

'Okay. Thanks.'

She turned back to her phone call. 'Aye, just some random guy. So, what's up with Jenny?'

Mark caught his breath, then set off back to the hotel. The courtyard was lit up with fairy lights hanging from a weeping willow spiralling up the back of the building. He checked his phone as he walked, as much to see if there was anything from anyone, his first ex-wife or Kay even, as saving face at the people laughing at him. He went back into the heat of the bar.

Rennie was leaning against his chair, cradling a fresh whisky in his free hand, a claw hooked around to protect the nectar. He sank the glass, rolled the empty over the table like he wanted nothing more to do with it, then clapped his hands. 'Right, I'm off.' He patted Mark's shoulder and made to leave. 'Good luck finding her.'

No sign of Adam. Magic. Two cops and Mark was the one having to do the police work.

'Just a sec.' Mark caught his arm. 'Sure I can't get you another?'

Rennie stuck his tongue in his cheek. 'Son, I've a loaf of bread to bake when I get in. My sourdough will be over-proved as it is.' He frowned. 'Or is it over-proofed?' He scowled. 'Good luck with finding her, son.'

'It'll just take a second. Please.'

'This better be quick.' Rennie caught the barman's eye and pointed at Mark, then got a thumb's up. He sat down again and leaned forward onto his elbows. 'Go on?'

'I'm writing a book set around here. A doomed romance set during the Highland Clearances.'

'Brave man.'

A couple of the women glanced over their way.

'Did Kay mention the *Laird of Wedale* disaster?'

Rennie leaned in, all conspiratorial. 'The boat?' He sniffed.

'Be very careful, son. The people up here are like the hills, they have very long memories.'

'So you know about it?'

'When I spoke to her on Monday, I couldn't speak freely at the time. That ship...' Rennie lowered his voice, almost to a whisper. 'Kay was asking me some questions. Pointed ones, like she didn't think it had really sunk.'

'Seriously?'

'She'd found something suggesting the crofters were killed and buried somewhere around here.'

'Did she have any evidence?'

'Not that I saw. Ask me, it's a load of old nonsense. That boat sinking was a tragedy. Nothing more, nothing less.'

Mark sat back and swirled ice cubes around his glass. 'Any idea if she'd been speaking to anyone else about it?'

'Nope. Sorry. Told you to ask at the tearoom. Opens at eight tomorrow.'

'You said she'd been in here, though. Getting stuck into the guests, right?'

'Well, aye, but I don't know who.'

'She found you, though. How did she know to speak to you?'

'Everybody in this town knows me.' Rennie stared up at the ceiling. 'If you must know, she collared me in Maggie's on Monday morning while I was getting my scones and tea for a shoot over the glen.'

'You didn't see her chatting to anyone?'

'Sorry. Kay was on her own and I was in a hurry to get out of there with my tea and my scones. Besides, I didn't want anyone overhearing us. So I arranged to meet her in my cottage, only place I could guarantee privacy.'

And that didn't sound seedy...

'But Kay never showed. I called her, but she didn't answer.'

Olivia sat back down again and tossed her phone into the middle of the table, her daggers look shutting up Mark. 'Mr Rennie, Kay's been missing since Tuesday morning. She was supposed to turn up in *your cottage?*'

'Aye, well.' Rennie evaded her gaze. 'Now you say it like that...'

'She's missing. You seem to have been the last person to see her.'

'Come on...' A bead of sweat ran down Rennie's forehead. 'You can't think I've anything to do with this, can you?'

'I don't know what to think.'

'If you want my take on it?' Rennie leaned in close. 'People around here like to protect their legacies. Could be her asking a load of questions about the distant past put someone's nose out of joint.' He spoke in an undertone: 'But I'd be focusing on Bill Turnbull and Liz Ruthven, if I was you.'

Names from Kay's notebook. Maybe people with a legacy to lose. Or just red herrings distracting them from whatever Rennie himself had done.

Olivia had her own notebook out, scribbling away. 'Did she mention them?'

'Not to me. But if she's asking me, she'll surely have been asking them.' Rennie stood up. 'Lady Ruthven lives in the castle over by the loch. William Turnbull owns all the land for miles around. Acres and acres of bugger all.'

A lot of space to bury a body. Or store them in a remote outbuilding.

'And Bill's my boss. Let me know if you want a word with him.'

'That'd be good.' Mark handed him a business card.

'Mark Campbell. Historian. Lover. Fighter.' Rennie grinned. 'I'll let you know how it goes with Bill. Sweet dreams.' And he set off towards the door like he was charging across a glen after a downed pheasant.

Mark slouched back in his chair. The card felt like a harmless joke when he got them done, but now... Searching for his missing daughter? Aye, it felt crass. Hardly the look of a professional.

Olivia slumped back in her chair and watched Rennie march out of the room. 'Do you honestly think Kay asking people about some maritime disaster has stirred up a hornet's nest?' She finished her drink, shaking her head. 'Knowing her, she could be at a party over in Ullapool. Or she's on a boat to Benbecula or Lewis. Anywhere. Hell, she could be tucked up in bed with a stinking cold. Could be she's absconded with that guy picking her up from the B&B.'

Mark thought it through. It didn't sit right that her trail went cold like that, with no further clues. Leaving her phone in her hotel. Or a burner in the glovebox.

She stood up. 'I'll dig into Rennie's background. See if he's got previous.'

Christ, his head was throbbing. He gestured at the phone Olivia was staring deep into. 'Everything okay?'

'Aye, it's all fine.' She finished her glass and left a pile of ice cubes at the bottom. 'Got some work calls to catch up on.' She looked around. 'Where the hell is Adam?'

'Sure you can afford the time to help me?'

'Of course.' She was on her feet now. 'Kay's kind of like a daughter to me. Let's meet up for breakfast, then see what's what.'

Mark got up and followed her through to reception. 'You want to stay here?'

'No, I'm going to stay with my folks in Inverness, but you should. If Kay's been spending her time here, not far from Kinbrace, where she left her car.'

22

Mark rang the bell on the reception desk again and stepped back, looking for anyone to help.

The curtain swooshed to the side and a sprightly man strolled out, hands on hips. Late forties, the chandelier's light bouncing off his bald head, shaved to the bone. Full Highland dress – kilt, jacket, sporran, the lot – with a brass name badge attached to his jacket: Mr Harris. 'Can I help you, sir?'

Mark stood up tall. 'Well, I'm wondering if you've had a Kay Campbell staying here recently?'

'Let me see.' Harris picked up the large ledger and flicked through the pages, finally settling on one. He wetted his finger and ran it down the page. 'No, I'm afraid not.'

She could be staying under an assumed name, maybe. Or this mystery boyfriend. Assuming he was a boyfriend, of course.

Olivia got out her phone and showed the photo. 'Do you recognise her?'

Harris pinched his lips as he inspected it. He glanced between them. 'If you don't mind me asking, who is the young woman?'

'My daughter. She's missing.' Mark let out a hollow sigh. 'We believe she's been in the village. I gather she's been here.'

'Well, I'm afraid I don't recognise her. If she's been here, it'll have been on a colleague's shift.'

Mark asked, 'Do you have any rooms for the night?'

Harris licked his lips. 'How long are you looking for?'

'At least tonight.' Mark glanced at Olivia. 'Maybe a couple of nights extra?'

Harris went back to his ledger. 'Ah.'

'Is that a good "ah" or a bad one?'

'Well. The village's annual ceilidh is on Saturday night, so it'll get busy this weekend, but we do have some capacity now. Depending on the facilities you require, we have rooms ranging from fifty to eighty pounds a night.'

'Is there anywhere else to stay in the area?'

Harris jutted out his jaw. 'There are a couple of B&Bs down in Helmsdale if this isn't suitable.'

'No, this is fine,' said Mark. 'Just wondered, that's all. I'll need one with a desk, if that's possible.'

'I see.' Harris ran his finger down the ledger. 'In that case, I'm afraid it will be the eighty pounds tariff.'

'Thank you.' Mark handed over his credit card. 'Please can you keep it open for extras?'

'Sure thing.' Harris swiped the card, then handed Olivia a brass key. 'Room 106.'

Olivia shivered with revulsion. 'We're not together.'

'Ah, I see.' Harris laughed. 'My mistake.' He handed the key to Mark. 'Do you require a room, madam?'

She smiled. 'I'm good, thank you.'

'Breakfast is served until half past nine. Enjoy your stay.'

Mark grabbed his bag and key, then set off towards the stairs.

'One final thing.' Harris pushed a flyer across the dark oak desk. 'Can I interest you in Saturday's midsummer ceilidh?'

Olivia took the flyer. 'Thanks, but I hope to be back in Glasgow by then.' She set off away from the desk.

'Very well.'

Mark followed her outside towards his car. 'Do you want to get something to eat or—'

'I'll need to get to Mum's.'

'Oh. Okay.'

She frowned. 'Ah, there's Adam.'

He was marching out of the hotel, doing up his flies and drying his hands on his trousers.

Olivia leaned in close. 'Mark, I'm doing this for Kay, alright? Not you. Please remember that. We're not going to rekindle anything.'

23

'Mark, I'm sorry.' Cath yawned down the line. 'I'm just *really* tired and I need to go to bed.'

Nothing to do with her hitting the wine a few hours early on a Thursday...

'Right.' Mark lay back on the spongy bed, staring up at the nicotine stuck to the ceiling's swirling design. No duvet, just layers of blankets covered with a pattern that'd probably give him nightmares. 'Any news from your end?'

Cath sighed down the line. 'I've not heard from her, no. I'd tell you if I had.'

'Okay, I just wanted to check.'

'Aye. Thanks. Call me when you get some news, aye?' Click, and she was gone.

Mark dropped his phone on the pillow. Two ex-Mrs Campbells, two women who didn't so much hate him as seem oblivious to him.

Never work with family, no matter how much they beg and plead and guilt you into it.

Trying to help out his daughter, get her some experience doing something real. And whatever had happened, wherever she was, hard not to think that was all on him.

What Adam said back in her hotel room stung him. Leaving his book. Leaving her phone, the one he paid for. Meant she was running from him.

Magic...

His lonely hotel room was small, a huge desk taking up the entire wall opposite the bed. Mark had managed to fit all of his stuff on it with plenty of space left to work. Already a pigsty, full of his papers and other odds and sods, including the books from Inverness.

The biggest weight on the desk was the unwritten words.

Five years avoiding this book and the money was gone, nowhere near being adequately replaced by the trickle of royalties from his other books. And he was *weeks* from the delivery of this, let alone the delivery and acceptance payment.

A weekend to finish it.

Vic Hebden's deadline hammered down on his shoulders like ten-inch nails.

Mark hauled himself up and walked over to the sink. He sucked down a glass of tap water and tried to clear his head. Felt like he was drowning.

Kay going missing just added to the perfect storm. Maybe he should be more like Cath, focus on what he could do to save himself, not try to find their daughter.

But she'd been in some weird places. Boleskine House, for one. Unearthing his own past, the truth he hadn't shared with her.

And that bloody boat...

Why?

He needed to find her, but that was tomorrow. Right now, his priority was getting the words down.

He reached into his bag for a tin of mango and spearmint energy drink. Maybe it would be more tolerable at room temperature. He opened the can and took a sip.

Here goes.

24

Mark woke up with a jolt, his head thudding, heart thumping.

The wind rattled the windows, hard, like the glass was about to tumble into his room. The bedside clock read 1.03.

He'd fallen asleep on his laptop. His neck ached.

He woke the laptop and saw that at least he'd managed over two thousand words today. A quick skim and it seemed decent. Hamish knew good writing from bad, but Mark felt he was going to pass the test. And that was without editing.

It felt good to get at the book. To add to it. The characters were walking around his head again, he just wished he had more time to enjoy their company.

He padded over to the small bathroom, poured a glass of water, lukewarm, then sat on the toilet to drink it down while he drained his bladder. He refilled the glass and headed back to the desk, stumbling as he left the bathroom.

He felt absolutely hammered and yet he'd not touched a drop of booze in weeks.

The window frame was shaking like a demon was trying to get

into his room. He hadn't noticed the wind when he'd arrived in the village, but it was howling now.

He got up and pulled open the curtains.

Twilight outside, the full moon and the midsummer solstice combining to light up the garden at the back of the hotel in a dark blue, like a permanent dusk.

Crows swept around the garden, some pecking at the ground.

Hidden under the branches of a tree, green eyes peered out at him. *Human* eyes. Full of fear and despair. Someone was looking at him. A human shape, hidden by a tree.

Then they disappeared.

He cleaned his glasses, then put them back on.

A dog stood on the lawn, staring up at him, its green eyes glowing.

Goose flesh rode up his arm, like a wave.

Mark put his head right against the window, pressing his lenses against the glass. It was dark out there and he screwed up his eyes, trying to focus.

The dog ran away from the tree, heading for the lane at the back, leading to fields and the loch.

Mark tugged the curtains together then lay down on his bed.

That was just his mind playing tricks with him.

Right?

25

Mark jolted out of his sleep. He opened his eyes, and the room was practically glowing, the blue light bursting through the curtains.

He was on the bed, fully dressed and had no memory of lying down.

He got up and walked over to the window.

The garden was empty, save for a waiter clearing tables on the patio.

He had the faint embers of a dream but couldn't quite remember it. Definitely involved dogs and...

He checked his phone. Nothing from Cathy or Kay. Though, aye, both of her phones were in police evidence.

Three missed calls from Olivia. And a text:

Guess we're not having breakfast then?

The clock read 09:50.

He'd slept in and missed breakfast.

Magic.

He was starving and his body needed a jumpstart. Just his

luck to stay at the only hotel in Scotland without a tea-making facility in the room, even with a massive desk. He could ask reception to send up a strong coffee. Maybe the shop had some of that energy drink, but hopefully not whatever the last can had been, pineapple and shiitake mushroom or whatever it was. The sickly-sweet smell haunted the room like a ghost.

A thump on the door.

Mark padded over, hooked on the chain and opened the door to a crack. 'Who is it?' But it came out as 'Woo-blub.' He swallowed what was left of his water. 'Who is it?'

A woman stood there, head tilted to the side. She seemed familiar, tall and stern. He got it – one of the couples in the bar last night. 'Time to clean your room, sir.'

'Okay.' Mark stood there in his underwear. 'Just a sec.' He shut the door and scanned the room.

Where the hell were his clothes? Where was his bag?

A cold trickle of sweat ran down his spine. He felt hungover but hadn't drunk anything except a glass of orange and some water. Oh and the two cans of that infernal drink.

The phone on the desk rang.

He picked it up. 'Hello?'

Harris, the phone line crackling despite it only being a few metres' distance. 'Mr Campbell, there's someone here to see you.'

Mark took a deep breath. 'I'll be down in a sec.' He pulled on a t-shirt and hauled on his jeans, then put his feet into his trainers and laced them up. He stepped out into the corridor, making sure that he had his key, then raced down the stairs to the empty reception area.

A radio played somewhere, deep voices discussing football.

Mark hit the bell and yawned. He looked around the deserted reception hall. If he'd joined John Rennie in a vat of whisky, he surely wouldn't have felt any worse than this. He caught a glimpse of himself in the mirror behind the desk. Dark rings under his eyes, stubble on the verge of a beard, like he hadn't slept in days. And the mad stare of someone who had lost his mind.

Mark closed his eyes as he waited, tossing his glasses onto the desk. He was exhausted, using energy drinks and strong coffee to power through. He needed sleep, but he needed his legs more.

Harris stepped through the curtain, grinning from ear to ear. He clocked Mark approaching and straightened up his tie. 'Mr Campbell.'

'Morning.' Mark frowned at the absence of anyone else. 'Where is—'

'Ah, yes.' Harris was beaming. 'He had to step out to take a call. A man in his position is certainly lucky they installed the mobile mast recently!'

'Indeed. Thanks.' Mark walked away from the desk towards the front door.

Adam was outside the hotel on his phone, and Mark got a casual raised hand but no eye contact. 'Well, thanks anyway.'

Mark joined Adam by his car. 'Morning.'

'Bloody nightmare last night. Up till four.' Adam seemed fresh, like he'd just got back from a particularly restful holiday, compared to Mark's death cooled down. 'But you look like you've been up all night partying.'

'Barely slept?'

'Few drinks with Libby?'

'Hardly. She's staying with her parents.'

'Huh. Could've given her a lift.'

'Got a few missed calls from her.'

'Aye, she's in the tearoom.'

A dog walked along the high street, stopping to get patted by an old man. Ginger fur and pointy ears putting it at the opposite end of the canine spectrum from a labradoodle or a pug. Could be a distant ancestor of a greyhound, but it was too chunky. It clocked him and scurried off along the high street, slipping down the lane towards the loch and the castle.

'You okay there, chief?' asked Adam.

'I'm fine.'

'Seem a bit freaked out by that pooch.'

'I saw a dog outside my room last night, that's all.'

Adam laughed, then clapped his arm. 'Libby's waiting in that tearoom. Your kid collared Rennie in there, right? Get yourself dressed. And you can maybe get some coffee in you, eh?'

26

The rain thundered down, smacking off the pavement like someone was chucking eggs at them.

Mark jogged ahead and tore open the door to Maggie's Tea Room. He held it open for Adam, who was walking slowly, talking on his phone, hood up and unhindered by the rain.

June and he needed a coat. Welcome to Scotland.

Sod him, then.

Mark left Adam outside and walked over to the counter. No signs of anyone, other than the blaring radio and the smell of scones baking in the oven.

No Olivia. Great.

Mark rang the bell.

An elderly lady hurried through from the kitchen, blowing air up her face. 'Roasting in here.' Glasses hung round her neck on a cord. Name badge read 'Maggie', so she must have been the owner. 'Hi, son. What can I get you?'

'Eh, supposed to be meeting someone.'

'Well, there's nobody here.'

Mark looked outside. Adam was still talking to someone. 'Can I get a coffee and a roll?'

'What do you want on it?'

'Eh, bacon, haggis and egg?'

'Tattie scone on that?'

'Oh, please.'

Maggie wrote it down and stuck it to a board, but there didn't seem to be anyone else to make the order. 'It'll be two fifty.'

'I could barely get a teabag for that in Edinburgh.'

She laughed. 'Pay when you leave, son. You up here for a wee holiday?'

'Not really.' Mark took out his mobile and showed her Kay's photo. 'Do you recognise her?'

Maggie put on her glasses, but it didn't seem to stop her squinting. 'Oh aye. I know her face. Lassie was asking about her this morning too.'

'That'll be my...' Ex-wife. 'My friend. Olivia. Olivia Blackman.'

'Right, aye. That's her.'

'She here?'

'No, she left. This is Kay, right? She came in a couple of mornings this week.' She clicked her fingers. 'Had a coffee and a sourdough with avocado like they all want these days.'

'Remember which mornings?'

'Mm.' Maggie eased off her glasses and let them dangle free. 'Monday?'

'You're sure?'

She clicked her fingers again. 'Aye, that's when the laddie brings my flour.' She poured coffee into a mug from a steaming pot and placed it on a tray next to a jug with barely enough milk.

Mark pulled the tray over his side of the counter. 'Was she with anyone?'

The scowl deepened. 'Don't think so. You should try the paper shop. They're the only other place in the village. Other than the kirk and the hotel.'

'Thanks.' Mark looked outside. Adam was *still* on the phone.

'Now, I'll just make your breakfast.' She scurried off into the kitchen, snatching up the ticket and leaving him on his own.

Mark took the tray over to the table in the corner, looking

along the high street. Generic Scottish architecture. He could have been in Fife, Ayrshire, Angus, the Borders.

And he got that tickling at the back of his head, suggesting he'd already thought that. He noted it down, anyway. Maybe the lowlands police officer character could think it in the book.

It was good.

Well, no, but he could stretch it out to thirty words, fill out the book a bit.

God knows he needed to.

Christ, he should've brought his laptop. Get some work done while he was eating. He got out his phone and texted Olivia:

In cafe. Where are you?

He rested it on the table, then poured the milk into his coffee. Sure enough, it swallowed up all the milk but barely changed colour. He chewed through the coffee and a draught of air from the door breathed across his face. 'Sure you shouldn't be back in Inverness?'

'But I'm so happy here.' A man stood there, dressed like a Dickensian chimney sweep but built like a Mexican wrestler. He was that big he probably had to take the door off to get inside. But he had the upper-class English accent you only got from a very expensive education. 'So very, very happy here.'

Adam was still outside, wheeling around in a tight circle as he talked.

Sod it, Mark decided to engage the weirdo. 'Why are you so happy?'

'Well, because the end of days are coming, my friend.'

Mark sat back and took off his glasses. 'Really. And why does that make you happy?'

'We're into the last few hours. It'll be so fulfilling to know my life's work is done, that I've saved so many souls. Can I interest you—'

'Cosmo, Cosmo, Cosmo.' Another man grabbed his arm, glowering. Not as tall and his goatee was more of a mane than a beard, hanging down to cover the logo on his faded T-shirt. Looked mid-thirties, but he could be younger. His pale baseball cap was curved at the front and soaked with sweat. 'Told you not to upset the tourists. Go and sit down.'

But Cosmo wouldn't be dissuaded. He handed Mark a leaflet. 'Read this, it'll change your life.' Now he walked over to the table.

His friend watched Cosmo go, then his fierce look softened to a smile and he held out a fist. 'Josh Urquhart.' The posh Scottish surname clashed with the accent. Kent or Surrey.

'Mark.' He bumped it. 'Sorry, I thought he was someone else.'

'I wish he was someone else.' Urquhart smoothed down his beard, then flipped the chair around to sit backwards. 'You can't choose your messiah, I guess.' He sighed. 'What brings you here?'

A group of people dressed similarly to Cosmo filed in and sat around a large table, laughing and jostling with each other. Seven of them, three men and four women. Twenties, maybe, with the look of people living off the land. Heavy tans and hair bleached by the sun, even this far north.

Mark picked up his phone and held it up. 'Do you recognise her?'

'She's cute.' Urquhart was inspecting the photo with great care. 'But no, I don't. Why? She a friend of yours?'

'My daughter. I'm really worried about her.' Mark caught Adam outside and got a snapping pain in his neck. 'The police think she could've run away.'

'I see. My deepest condolences. The cops know?'

Mark nodded out of the door. 'Working with a couple of them just now.'

'Well, I hope you find her.' Urquhart drummed the chair back with his thumbs, then got to his feet. 'What's she doing up here, if you don't mind me asking?'

'I'm writing a book about the Highland Clearances and she's doing some research for me.'

'Tough topic.'

'Someone's got to tell the truth.'

'Sure. I hear you. The truth is what it's aaaaaaall about. Enlightenment. Knowledge.'

Mark sat back and sipped his coffee. 'That what you're selling?'

'Selling? No, man.' Urquhart hoisted his beard up enough to reveal the T-shirt's logo. BE PREPARED, above a cartoon drawing of a demon. 'That's what I'm *offering*. Free of charge. If you're interested, then you can have it. But only if you're willing.'

'Not my scene.'

'It's a shame to hear that.' Urquhart smirked. 'Let me know when you're ready.'

'You expect me to ever become ready?'

'Everyone comes round, just depends how long it takes them. And time's running out.' Urquhart tapped his cap and got up, then walked over to join his friends.

Enlightenment. Funny how that always needed to be sold to the lost and lonely.

But it got Mark thinking back to the book in Séan Avartagh's shop, with the section on Satanism in the Highlands, the one that had so entranced Kay. What if that's what drew her to this village?

Maggie stepped back through into the café and groaned. 'Josh, I told you to call in advance.'

'Well, we just fancied a cuppa and a scone.' And Urquhart had been trained well, saying it so it rhymed with gone rather than cone. 'Usual, all round.'

'Sure.' Maggie headed over to Mark and placed his roll in front of him. 'Can I get you anything else, son?'

'I'm good.' Mark waved towards the group in the corner. 'Who are they?'

She glanced around and then leaned in close. 'They're from the *centre*.'

'The centre?'

'Don't ask...' She returned to the till, allowing Mark to chew through his roll.

Adam came in at last, giving the group a wide berth, then righted the chair and sat opposite Mark. He caught Maggie's attention, pointed at Mark's cup and got a smile from her. Then he frowned at Mark like he was dealing with a victim of crime. 'You okay there?'

'Peachy.' Mark rested his roll back on the plate. 'Anything on Kay?'

Adam ran his hand down his face. 'Nothing, sorry. Super busy just now.'

'What else are you working on?'

Adam looked around the other tables. 'Like I can just tell you that.'

'Come on. I know the drill.'

Adam glanced over to the counter, but Maggie was missing. 'If you must know, I'm working a series of robberies all the way up the A9. Over the last three years, someone's stopped six delivery vans and cleared them out. They get a few four-by-fours to box them in down a country lane, then steal whatever's in them and let the driver go. Robbed a few mills too. Tons and tons of flour, oats, barley. So if someone's building the world's biggest flapjack, then I'm onto them. Otherwise... Why steal *flour*?'

'Seems strange.'

'Aye, that's what's had me scratching my head about it. How weird it is.' Adam let out a slow breath. 'Can you believe it?'

'Why hasn't this been on the news?'

'Search me.' Adam scowled. 'I mean, we don't get a lot of murders up this way. Don't get a lot of anything. And tight-knit communities don't spill the beans. Last night, someone pulled over an articulated lorry at gunpoint just north of bloody Dornoch...' He sighed, a kind of 'why me?' thing. 'Cleared the whole thing out. We're seeing if we can pull satellite images, but someone set off fires that obscured the area with smoke. Going to be a nightmare.'

'Sure you shouldn't be focused on that instead of being here with me?'

'That's a waiting game. Besides, I've got my team out and about.' Adam winced. 'And I still owe Libby, so here I am.'

'You must owe Liv something big.'

'Very big.' Adam took his coffee from Maggie and tested it, then sank it one go.

'Wow.' Maggie laughed. 'Can I get you refills?'

They both nodded.

Adam waited for her to shuffle over with their mugs. 'Wee Jim's going through Kay's phone records today. Both her phone and that burner. We'll see who she's been speaking to.'

'Right, good.'

'Take it you've heard nothing from her?'

'Still radio silence.' Mark winced. 'Spoke to her mother last night and she's still not heard either.'

'Isn't she worried?'

'Hard to tell with Cath. She's always angry with me.'

'Making a bit of a habit of that, aren't you?'

Mark ignored him. 'I've been thinking about what you were saying. About how she was running from me because—'

Maggie came back over with fresh mugs for them both. 'Wednesday.'

Mark frowned at her. 'Wednesday?'

'That lassie. Kay. She was in here on Wednesday.'

Mark got a stab of excitement. That would update the time-line. 'You're sure of that?'

'Definitely. The coffee roaster from Cromarty pops in on a Wednesday with another bag of his beans. Aye, definitely Wednesday.' She sauntered back to the till, then came back with a sheet of paper. 'Here's the delivery note. See?'

Sure enough, the delivery from Al's Beans was timestamped on Wednesday. Eleven fifty-three.

Progress.

Kay was definitely in the village after she'd left Inverness.

Why leave her stuff back there? Why the two phones?

And why stand up John Rennie? Where had she stayed on Tuesday night? And who with?

'Thanks.' Adam took the delivery slip. 'Might need a wee statement from you.'

'Sure thing. Whenever.' Maggie walked back to her counter.

Mark took a final bite of his breakfast, eager to get moving. 'So, where's Liv?'

'Libby?' Adam was staring at his phone. 'No idea.'

'Well, let's find her.' Mark got up and left a fiver and some coins on the counter.

'Cheers, son.' Maggie gave him a smile. 'Oh, I think your lassie was talking to the blacksmith.'

'Kay?'

'Aye, both times I saw her in here, actually. Ray's always in at the same time every morning for his breakfast. Could make porridge himself, I suppose, but I need the money and quite enjoy the company. Of course, you've missed him today. He lives at the end of the village past the Catholic church.'

27

Adam was powering along the street, talking on his phone. Again. He looked back at Mark, then away again. 'Aye, aye, well, Davie, if you could get him to do it, I'd appreciate it. Cheers.' He ended the call and pocketed the phone. 'Feel more human after that?'

'Just a bit.' Mark zipped up his coat. A thick mist hung in the air, making him shiver. This far from the sea, it couldn't be haar but he'd no idea what it was. At least it had stopped raining. 'You getting hassle from the boss?'

'Aye, Emery's giving me grief for helping you. So I'm giving my guys grief so they can pull their finger out.' Adam rubbed at his neck. 'Bit weird how a blacksmith's based here, on the road to nowhere with no passing trade. Besides, you'd think he'd advertise, wouldn't you? And in the grounds of the old Catholic church. Catholics up here?'

Mark followed the signs away from the village, hugging the side of the main road, though no cars passed them. 'It was the main religion until the Clearances.'

'Huh, I never knew that.'

'Aren't you local?'

'Didn't pay attention in RE at school.'

122

'It's something I cover in the bits of the book I've actually written. Some crofters were still clinging to their Irish ancestry and the Catholic faith. One of my characters, Margaret, her father is a crofter. His theory was the Clearances were an anti-Catholic act undertaken by Protestant landowners.'

'Don't say that too loudly around here, Mark. The locals like to think they sprang out of the ground thousands of years ago or were put here by God. No such thing as population migration.'

Mark followed the sign down a lane by the last house, through a shabby row of cherry trees, tiny buds on the branches. He stopped by a thick hedge, which swallowed up a sign.

Rings by Raymond

Mark opened a gate and walked down an overgrown path leading to a stone cottage hidden between two oaks. White walls, with dormer windows upstairs. The garden was in full bloom, wildflowers all doing their thing and mercifully few thistles and nettles.

Mark rattled the door knocker. No signs of life inside, but a burning smell hung on the air. Could be toast, could be from the blacksmithing.

Blacksmithery?

Mark didn't know – usually he left that kind of thing to a spellchecker or an editor.

The door opened and a stout old man peered out. A barrel on thin legs, with a rugged beard and greying hair. 'Can I help you?'

'We're looking for the blacksmith.'

'Well, you've found him. Raymond's the name. Melting metal and forging rings is my game.' The blacksmith looked at Mark, then Adam, then back. 'You boys want to see my forge?'

'You've got a forge?' asked Adam.

'In the back garden. How else do you think Raymond Shearer makes perfect rings?' He bellowed out a laugh. 'You lads looking for a wedding ring?'

Mark held up a hand. 'No.'

'Takes all sorts these days. Wait, you're already married to each other, right?'

'To *him*?' Mark raised his hands. 'No, I'm recently divorced.'

'Aye, aye.' Shearer winked. 'What about for your next marriage?'

'Not planning on remarrying anytime soon.'

'You've got a glint in your eye, laddie. That's for sure. And who am I to judge?'

'We don't want to see your forge, thank you very much. DS Adam Mathieson.' He held out his warrant card, a frosty look on his face, then held up a printed photo of Kay. 'We're looking for Kay Campbell.'

Shearer tugged at his beard, then whistled. 'Oh aye.' He opened the door wide. 'Come away through, lads.' He disappeared inside.

Mark stepped through into a tiny kitchen.

Olivia was sitting at a large table, scowling at Mark. 'There you are.'

Shearer started pottering around, clattering things around the kitchen.

Mark sat next to Olivia. 'We were in the tearoom.'

'Aye, well, I've been busy.' She nodded towards Shearer, whistling away as he did God knows what. 'The woman in the tearoom said he'd been speaking to Kay.'

'On Wednesday.'

Olivia frowned. 'Sure about that?'

'The coffee boy from Cromarty was in.'

'Now.' Shearer opened the back door and brushed his hands together. The smell of burning filled the room. 'Forge is just about up to heat.' He held up a tray laden with metal cups, a metal jug and a metal teapot with a wooden handle. 'Forged all these myself.' He grinned wide. 'Now, are you sure I can't make you a ring?'

Olivia shook her head. 'You were saying you talked to Kay in the tearoom?'

'Oh aye, aye. Spoke to her a couple of times as I was having my breakfast. Very smart young lassie, indeed. She was just sitting at a table, keeping herself to herself, working on her MacBook Pro, but I couldn't tell if it was one of the M1 models or an older Intel one.'

Raymond Shearer was an Apple fanboy. Wow.

'Did you see her speaking to anyone?' asked Olivia.

'Just me in there.'

Mark took another sip. 'And this was on Wednesday?'

'Think so, aye.' Shearer eyed Olivia. 'Told me she's working for some lunatic writing a book on the Highland Clearances.'

'That's me.'

'You're *the* Mark Campbell?' Shearer whistled. 'I'll say this for you, son, you're either very daft, or you've got balls like a Highland bull. Especially with a name like that.'

'The Clan Campbell wasn't a key perpetrator in the Clearances.'

Shearer grinned. 'Aye, and next you'll be exonerating them for Glencoe?'

Down in Edinburgh and Glasgow, it was hard keeping up with yesterday. Up here, they still talked about events hundreds of years ago like they'd happened to them that morning.

Olivia asked, 'Was Kay asking you about anything in particular?'

'Just the Clearances around here. Nasty business, driven by greed. See, the chieftains were supposed to protect their clans, not betray them. When they became lords and ladies they forgot where they came from. Thought they were special, put there by God and allowed to do what they wanted. But they were just stupid men, blighted by greed and ignorance. Pushing crofters from their ancient homes and replacing them with sheep. It was butchery.'

'But Kay must've asked you something specific?'

'Well, about Ruthven village, mainly. She was fascinated by the place. Like how it's still here and thriving, despite the area being brutalised back then. Wondered how it'd escaped. How my ancestors escaped.' Shearer reached over for a shiny MacBook, a pro model, the kind Mark would never have the money for. He opened it and clicked away at something. 'Way I see it, if you worked the land, you weren't worth anything to the clan chieftains. But if you provided a valuable service to them, they kept you on.' He showed the screen, with a family tree growing like an upside-down fern. 'And mine's an ancient craft, passed down from father to son through the centuries. It's what kept us here, kept us useful. Despite the name, us Shearers have been doing metallurgy here for a long time.'

Adam's eyes were glazing over. 'That was all Kay asked you?'

'Well, she was asking us about the *Laird of Wedale*. I mean, maybe the lassie's cracked in the head, but she'd bought into some conspiracy theory.' Shearer scratched at his beard. 'Heard it a few times myself. Load of crap, if you ask me... Those crofters were lost at sea. It's a historical fact.'

'What does this conspiracy theory say?' asked Mark.

'The Turnbulls or the Ruthvens killed them and faked the whole thing. I mean... Load of nonsense!'

'The Ruthvens, who—'

'Aye, the village is named after them. And the family after the castle. And the clan. Lady Ruthven lives there, but good luck getting her to speak. That's what I told young Kay.'

'She was asking about her?'

'Course she was.' Shearer beamed. 'We used to have songs as kids about that family, you know? Like *Ring-a-ring-o'-roses*, children's songs that actually tell a very interesting adult story. *Ruthven, Ruthven, head's on fire. Ruthven, Ruthven, family of liars. Highland wolves, gut you at night. Clear the lands, clear the blight. Ruthven, Ruthven, drown you at night.*' He grabbed Mark's nose and did the stealing trick.

'Get off!' Mark pushed him away.

Adam and Olivia were laughing along with Shearer.

Mark got out his notebook and jotted it all down while his rage subsided. Seemed wild, but folk history very often contained truth hidden behind all the layers. 'What about the Turnbull family?'

'Och, I wouldn't pay them too much mind. In those days, the Ruthvens owned all the land around here.'

'But it's in William Turnbull's hands now?'

'Aye, aye. Nasty piece of work, him.' Shearer laughed. 'Thing is, your lassie was asking if there was any possibility of an anti-Catholic motivation to the Clearances. Where would she get such an idea from?'

'Wonder.' Adam was raising his eyebrows at Mark. 'So what did you tell her?'

'Well. The Ruthvens and Turnbulls were Protestants and had private chapels in their homes. The parish church, though, was Catholic. It burnt down and went to ruin. Nobody rebuilt it. The Presbyterian church on the high street was only built just after the First World War.'

'Nobody wanted to rebuild the Catholic church?'

'Nobody left to do it, son. All cleared out.' Shearer walked over to the door and peered out. 'I'm just about to smelt some rings if you want to watch?'

Olivia smiled. 'No, we need to get on.'

'Well, suit yourselves.' Shearer stopped in the doorway. 'Thing is, young Kay was asking me about the Satanists.'

Adam laughed. 'Satanists?'

'Asking if the folk around here were killed because they worshipped the devil.' Shearer crossed himself. 'I was raised Catholic and my father, God rest his soul, used to talk about Sa— that kind of thing a fair amount, especially once he had a nip in him. All this talk of how the devil roamed these parts and...'

Olivia was frowning. 'You seem to believe it?'

'Well, I showed young Kay the ruins. How about I show you and you make up your own minds?'

28

Shearer pointed into a wild field behind his walled garden. 'There it is.'

Hidden by the thick fog, a narrow path was beaten through the tall grasses and the mustard rash of gorse. Two walls of a building stood alone, ancient stone scorched black and overgrown with moss and lichen. Buddleia grew between them, adding a splash of purple. Ash, oak and birch trees had grown up as the building had crumbled away, and now cast a long shadow inside. The heavy front door was still upright in one of the walls, the scarred oak wedged in place by rubble.

'I can see exactly what you mean.' Olivia looked over at Shearer. 'Wonder what they did to anger God.'

Shearer fixed a hard stare on her. 'That's not something to joke about, lass.'

Maybe it was true and the devil worship led to sick behaviour that the landowner used to justify mass murder. Either way, the ruined building would be a good metaphor to use in one of Mark's many unwritten chapters. Maybe he could even fictionalise its burning. Aye, that'd fit as a metaphor for the tensions between the characters and the unquenched passion.

He got out his notebook and scribbled some ideas down, how

the Catholic locals and their religion had been battered down and erased, much like the church. He pocketed it. 'Did Kay go inside?'

Shearer was still standing by the gate, fingers gripping the wood tight. 'Aye, but I warned her it might be dangerous in there.'

'We promise not to sue if anything falls on us.'

Shearer folded his bulky arms across his chest, like he could ward off the spirits that had claimed the church. 'On you go, then.' He stayed by the gate.

Mark led her over to the door. 'What's got him so scared?'

Olivia raised an eyebrow. 'This isn't spooking you?'

'No.' Mark tried the door handle but it wouldn't budge. The lintel was cracked in several places and the door was probably the only thing keeping the whole thing standing. He traced the wall around to a metre-wide break and peered through.

Nature hadn't managed to reclaim as much as he'd expected. The slate roof and the far wall had collapsed, crushing the pews and the altar.

Bees and butterflies populated the space, indifferent to human presence.

Adam stepped through the wall and walked across the debris.

Mark followed over the crumbling flagstones. Generations of local kids had probably used this place as a den, shaded from the sun by the trees.

Standing there, Mark could believe in the supernatural, either the idea of a benevolent God the church pushed, or otherwise. The architecture seemed to encourage fear of a higher power, rather than joy at their love.

Still, it was hard to shake the feeling that something bad happened here.

A large window frame sat in the other standing wall, the shards of stained glass still in the bottom left quadrant, mired under years of dirt and decay.

Mark rubbed at the glass with his sleeve, slowly revealing some dulled colours. The sun would've probably shone directly through the window at this time of year, but the trees now obscured it.

The art was exquisite, a group of crofters in drab clothes hiding in the shadows of the church. In the foreground, a monk wore brown robes, his head shaved into a tonsure, holding up a Bible and a cross, warding off a demonic figure, most of its head missing, replaced by fire coming from the skull.

'Mark.'

He jolted out of his reverie.

Olivia was crouching on a fallen pillar, rubbing away at another window. 'Check this out.'

Mark traced a path through the ruins, past a large bramble bush. The window was darker on this side and covered in much more dirt.

Olivia rubbed her hand against the glass then jerked her arm back, instinctively sucking at the cut on the pinkie of her left hand. 'Christ, I didn't expect the glass to be sharp.'

'You want to watch that.'

'Infection, right?'

Mark looked around. 'More like the vampires around here.'

'Aye, funny.' She'd cleared most of the mud, though, leaving a bloody smear across the glass.

Other than the corner, this window was pretty much intact. The same demonic figure was here, kneeling in front of a much larger being, twice its size, and engulfed in flame. The monk faced off against them, clutching a Bible and raising a crucifix, but he seemed to be losing his fight.

Olivia pointed at it. 'Think that's supposed to be Satan?'

Mark noticed a detail in the background. A group of figures carrying pitchforks and flaming torches, leading a pack of snarling dogs as they laid into people in elaborate suits. Landowners? He examined it closer.

He retraced his steps back out of the ruined church.

Over by the gate, Shearer was mouthing incantations. 'See what I mean?'

Mark pointed back at the window. 'That window, that's—'

'*Him.*' Shearer crossed himself and muttered some prayers, struggling to breathe. 'That's why the building burnt down.'

'You're saying the building burnt down because of a monk fighting the devil?'

'Don't be daft! No, I mean the church was fighting a battle with the forces of darkness. Which they lost.' Shearer shook his head. 'The church was overtaken by the... by people who had differing views. They forced the Catholics out or converted them, then used that place for their own ceremonies. They replaced the glass, telling their own story. My great-great-great-grandfather took matters into his own hands and burnt the place down.'

'Wow.' Mark frowned. 'Have you got anything written down about this?'

'Exactly what young Kay asked.' Shearer pointed at the church. 'Those windows? That's pretty much all we have.' He turned away from the building but didn't walk off. 'Seriously, son. You shouldn't mess with forces you don't understand.'

'You don't believe any of that, do you?'

'One thing I've learnt is that the evil in men is way worse than any supernatural evil you can imagine. And those laddies are doing a lot of imagining.'

'What laddies?'

Shearer looked over at him like he'd lost his mind. 'The Satanists!'

'I thought they were all killed on the boat?'

'Son, they're still here!'

'You're saying there are devil worshippers around here?'

'Aye, son. Blatant about it. *Blatant.*' A gob of spit flew from his mouth. 'And Kay was going to speak to them! I told her not to, but she wouldn't listen!'

29

Mark walked along the pavement, ignoring Adam's attempts at eye contact. 'If Kay was speaking to these Satanists, we need to as well.'

'Don't disagree.' Adam stopped on the high street. 'But… Good luck with that.' He checked his phone. 'Oh crap. I've got to get back.' He took some shades out of his pocket and popped them on. Two unflattering images of Mark reflected back at him. 'Catch you guys later.'

Olivia blocked him. 'Where are you going?'

'Confidential.'

'Come on, Adam. What's going on?'

'Another possible robbery down in Lairg.' He shuffled past Olivia. 'I'll be in touch.'

Olivia laughed, harsh and strong. 'No, you don't. You're the investigating officer here, not me.'

'Look, I'll cover for you, okay? You find her. I've got your back.'

Her mouth twisted up. 'That's not how I do things.'

'No, but I just need a wee bit of leeway.'

'I'm not happy with that. The deal was to—'

'Aye, okay. Look, I do need to make some calls first. Okay?'

She smiled. 'Thank you.'

Mark blocked his path this time. 'I spoke to these guys inside the tearoom. One called Cosmo, another called Josh. You know them?'

Adam looked away. 'Aye, I do.'

Mark found the leaflet in his pocket. '"Take the Left-hand Path". Are they on your radar?'

'Bunch of clowns.' Adam was cleaning his shades and ignoring the leaflet. 'Most of them came up from London, bought a chunk of land. Get drunk every so often and come into the village to wreak havoc. Not very popular with the locals.'

'They're some kind of end-of-days cult, right?'

'Right. That Cosmo guy thinks he's the Third Coming.'

'The *third*?' asked Olivia.

'You don't want to know who the second was. Anyway. Aside from the drinking, they get into the occasional fight. Trouble is, there are just as many crimes committed *against* them as by them.'

'These are the Satanists, right? We need to speak to them.'

'That's them, aye.' Adam looked over at Olivia, then shook his head. 'I'll catch up with you there, okay?'

'Fine.' Olivia frowned as he walked up to her, then let him hug her. Mark couldn't see or hear what Adam said, but she said, 'Don't mess me about, okay?'

Adam gave Mark a mock salute, then charged off along the high street towards his car.

Olivia's eyes followed him, but she stayed where she was. Then shot Mark a glare. 'I waited for you in the hotel while you were sleeping.'

Mark couldn't look at her, instead glancing over at the church and its 'TRY PRAYING' posters on both sides of the door. 'Sorry. I slept in. Didn't get much sleep last night.'

'I'm used to it. You're a night owl. I'm not.' She sighed. 'Didn't find anything about her, though. Asked the guests at breakfast, but nobody recognised her. Same with the paper shop. Strange place.

The local papers are today's, but the nationals are yesterday's. Worse than when you're on holiday in Spain.'

Mark smiled. 'All we're doing is chasing a two-day-old shadow, Liv. Where is she?'

'I don't know, but let's visit some real-life Satanists, eh?'

30

Olivia hurtled down the lane through the glen behind Ruthven village, shooting along the single-track road like she *knew* there were no cars coming for miles and miles. Out of the window, the ominous hills in the distance inching closer. The mist disappeared the further they went from the loch.

Just up ahead, a sign at the side of the road read 'Left-hand Path Healing Centre, Next Left-hand!'.

Mark found the flyer in his pocket, the one Cosmo had given him in the tearoom.

TAKE THE LEFT-HAND PATH

Lots of dense text, the kind that made people seem crazy, and he couldn't read it for fear of getting carsick. Especially with Olivia's wild driving.

Why the hell had Kay wanted to visit them? Was she with them?

She slammed on the brakes.

Mark shot forward, his seatbelt biting into his chest.

Two wild ducks waddled across the road, followed by a trail of fluffy ducklings.

She drove on, much slower though. 'What on earth is the right-hand path?'

Mark searched around for any other signs. 'Magic.'

'You keep using that word.'

'Do I?'

'One of those ones you don't notice, clearly.'

'Right, sorry I'm so annoying.' Mark scratched his temple. 'Kind of like you and your song lyrics.'

'Eh?'

'Never mind. There are two types of magic. Left-hand path and right. Right is white magic, benevolent stuff. Kind of like Buddhism, really.'

She slowed the car. 'And left is Satanism?'

'Black magic, aye. Sex magic. Personal anarchy. Rejecting the status quo.'

'Down, down, deeper and down.' Olivia pulled off the road and parked the car on the verge just past the entrance, leaving enough room for someone to pass.

'See, there you go again.' Mark got out first into the hot air. 'Well, that's an inviting place.'

A wooden fortress lurked behind giant steel gates, surrounded by a metal fence maybe eighteen feet tall. Acres of land too, enough to house hundreds of people.

For a healing centre, it was more like they were trapping you inside and was a lot less appealing in person than in print

'Okay, Mark. I'm in charge here. We do things my way. You do what I say. No nonsense like back at Boleskine.'

'That wasn't nonsense.'

'I saw you square up to him. My way or the single-lane highway with very infrequent crawler lanes.' Olivia raised her eyebrows. 'Any nonsense, malarkey or shenanigans and you're out of there. Okay?'

'Fine. But Adam should be doing this, right?'

'Don't start me...' She walked over to the gate and thumped it. The steel resonated, emitting a huge sound.

The small door set into the gate opened a tiny fraction and a head peered out. Cosmo, frowning at them. 'Oh! Hey, guys.' His frown turned into a smile. 'You decided to pay me a visit, huh?' He disappeared and the gate opened wide. 'Mark, right?'

Through the gap, the camp seemed a lot more like the pamphlet. Wooden chalets from an Alpine ski resort. A few people hung around, laughing.

A speaker played, but it was like someone was reading scripture. Mark recognised it – *The Satanic Bible* by Anton LaVey. Libertarianism dressed up in religion.

So they were Satanists, taking the left-hand path.

Cosmo beamed at them like he had two new pets. 'Are you guys here to enlist? Or to help prepare? Or just to get a massage?'

Mark raised his hands. 'I just want to speak to Kay.'

'Kay?' Cosmo frowned. 'Maybe she was one of the unworthy.'

The *unworthy*? Mark tried to calm himself down with a deep breath. 'Did anyone called—'

'Are you willing, brother?' Cosmo was staring at him with the bright eyes of a zealot.

'I'm not willing, no. Was Kay—'

'Why are you here, if you're not willing?'

Olivia shot Mark a shut-up glare. 'We're here because we gather Mr Campbell's daughter came here. Kay Campbell.'

Cosmo pursed his lips, then a frown flickered across his forehead. 'If she was here, I don't remember her. As I said, it's possible that she wasn't worthy.'

'What does that mean?'

'That she wasn't willing.'

'To do what?'

Cosmo clicked his fingers. 'Follow me.' Without checking if that was okay, he led them across the dirt paths to a large wooden building and opened the front door.

'Swear to God...' Olivia muttered as they followed.

The gates shut behind them with a clang. Two faces peered down at them from a sentry tower.

Mark walked on, following them inside a giant hall. Rows of tables and chairs, with a kitchen in the corner, two people cooking up a curry that smelled of coconut and coriander.

Josh Urquhart was in the middle of a group, discussing Satan only knew what with Cosmo. He spotted them and walked over, thrusting out his fist. 'Mark, isn't it?'

'It is.' Mark bumped his fist again. 'I—'

'I need to meditate.' Cosmo walked over to a stack of mats and sat down on the top of them in the lotus position.

Olivia touched Mark's arm, her glare warning him to stay back. 'Need to speak to Kay Campbell.'

Urquhart pursed his lips. 'Outside.' He marched off out of the room, arms swaying like he was on the drill ground.

Mark saw no choice but to follow him back out into the sunshine.

Urquhart leaned against a wide fence, running from the big building over to the chalets a few hundred metres away. The land beyond must have been at least forty acres, surrounded by the same tall fence with the occasional guard tower, but they seemed unmanned. Whatever they were preparing for, they had fields to protect, with smaller fences latticing the land into different crops. Kale in two of them, potatoes in another. Mark didn't recognise the others.

'Sorry,' said Urquhart, 'but when Cosmo needs to meditate, he really needs to. So we all clear out. Anyhoo. Is this the girl you asked me about in the tearoom?'

Mark nodded. 'My daughter, Kay. Aye.'

'If she's here, she's either in the kitchen or she's out there.' Urquhart pointed at the people working in the fields. 'We all take our turn. Back-breaking work, but it's good for the soul.' He waved to the fields behind the big house, where a few long polytunnels rustled in the breeze. 'Growing soft fruit over there. Peppers and onions and chillies too. All the veg you can eat and more from the fields. Our asparagus is great this year. Beans of all sorts. Only thing we can't grow is coconuts, but we've got a few thousand gallons of milk all stored up here. Last us a long time.' He waved at the far side. 'Oats are due late August, so we're just weeding the fields now. Enough porridge for two years.'

Olivia said, 'Seems like you're preparing for the end of the world.'

Urquhart smiled. 'We believe in being self-sustainable.'

Olivia looked around. 'Don't see any wind turbines.'

'Got all the energy we need from underground streams. Ground source heating too. And massive batteries.' Urquhart gestured towards some earthworks behind the chalets, some JCBs piling mud up. 'Building a big underground place for growing mushrooms. Plan is to scale up to a commercial enterprise over time.'

'That not against your ideals?'

Urquhart shook his head. 'Do what thou wilt shall be the whole of the law.'

'So you are Satanists?'

'It's not a crime. We're not doing anything illegal here.'

'What *are* you doing?'

'We're an independent group, unaffiliated with the Temple of Satan or any other LaVeyan Satanist organisation. We're just... us?'

'Right.' Olivia gave him a polite smile, but her eyes showed she knew this was getting nowhere. 'This isn't answering the question of Kay's whereabouts.'

Urquhart waved across the fields. 'Can you see her?'

Mark was screwing up his eyes, but the truth was, he couldn't. Nobody would even remotely pass for his kid. 'I don't, no.'

'Then she's not here, then.'

'Well, that doesn't strictly follow.' Olivia thumbed behind them. 'Cosmo seems to think you might've spoken to her?'

'Cosmo...' Urquhart shook his head. 'Look. We are a community. People come to us for help, so we get a lot of waifs and strays coming here.'

'Woah, woah.' Olivia raised her hands. 'Children?'

'No, no. God no.' Urquhart raised a shoulder. 'People come to us for help, so we get a lot of society's disenfranchised coming here looking for answers, a new way. They hitch a ride up on a lorry bound for Wick or Thurso, get out at Helmsdale and walk the rest. It's seventeen miles by road, but a fit person can do that in five hours. Maybe six if the wind's against them. We always check their ages. Couple came in the last week, but a Kay wasn't among them.'

'Could someone else have spoken to her?'

'Nope. Just me who deals with the rabble.'

'Cosmo answered the—'

'Yeah, Cosmo's a bit too keen to spread his word. I'll have words with him about it.'

Mark asked, 'Is he in charge here?'

'He's our saviour, yes.'

Olivia said, 'I'm asking you, one last time, is she here?'

'She's not. And I'm a busy man, so I need to get on.'

'Just let us speak to her and we'll get out of your hair.'

'I would if she was here. I suggest you take your macho man here and go annoy somebody else.' Urquhart nudged Mark in the chest, sending him tumbling backwards. The fence helped him stay upright.

Mark felt his heart pounding, the anger burning away. 'You want me to batter the truth out of you?'

'Don't make me laugh.'

Olivia blocked Urquhart's beefy arm from hitting Mark, then twisted it around and pinned him against the fence. 'Sir. We're just asking you some questions. One last time, did Kay Campbell visit here?'

Urquhart laughed again. 'You should go.'

'His daughter's missing and it sounds like she was here. Now, one way or another you're going to help me, because, so help me God, I'll—'

'You'll what?' Urquhart whistled.

Two of his colleagues emerged from the big building. Shirtless and ripped, they were even bigger than Urquhart.

Olivia let him go, then tugged Mark back. 'Come on. It's not worth it.'

'Of course it is!' Mark jabbed a finger in the air towards Urquhart. 'He knows where Kay is!'

'Listen to your friend.' Urquhart glared at Mark. 'Go.'

'Nope.' Mark folded his arms. 'Because I've got the situation where a young woman visits a bunch of Satanists and disappears off the face of the Earth. Now, all of that could easily be explained by, say, you telling me why she was here. Or you could show us inside these chalets.'

'It's private property. And she's not here.'

'But she was.' Olivia narrowed her eyes. 'Right?'

Urquhart licked his lips. 'Persistent little thing, aren't you?'

'Well, we can speak some more about this down at the station in Inverness.'

Urquhart folded his beefy arms. 'You're a cop?'

'DS Olivia Blackman.' She held out her warrant card. 'I get it, though. The powers-that-be take a dim view of you and your politics. You aren't happy with a cop snooping around. Whatever's going on here, I don't care. I just want to find his daughter. That's it.'

'All we're doing is living our lives without the shackles of society. We don't sacrifice goats or virgins here. You can see how peaceful it is, right?'

'Aye, but I could get a big squad of cops over here like that.' Olivia clicked her fingers. 'Not sure we'll like what we find. Not sure your waifs and strays here will like being found. So, I'll let you choose. Here or Inverness. Either way, you're telling me the truth.'

'Fine.' Urquhart snorted. 'It's possible she was here. Girl came here on Wednesday, pretending she was into Satanism. Didn't catch her name. Cosmo spoke to her solo, but I overheard her asking about stuff.'

'Stuff?'

'Aye. Got it in her head that we were connected to devil worshippers who lived around here hundreds of years ago. Child abuse. Ritual sacrifice. You name it. That's pure *evil*.' Urquhart waved over to the fields. 'There are ruins of old croft houses. Heard it said they abused their own children. They're not true Satanists. Deserved everything that happened to them.' He spat on the dirt. 'True Satanism is a rejection of a hierarchy. Anarchy, but that just means equality, not chaos. We follow a strict code based on a collective spirit driven by personal liberty, but if you perpetrate an aggressive act against another person, you're putting a barrier between you and them. There's no consent, no freedom, no liberty.'

Starting to feel like the smoke you got from above a fire.

Olivia turned to Urquhart. 'What did you do with her?'

'Nothing. I got her to leave.'

'You know where she went?'

Urquhart pointed back to the gate. 'That way. Down the lane towards the village.' He tugged at his long beard. 'Actually, one of the things she'd been asking about is how she could speak to Lady Ruthven.'

Olivia frowned. 'Why?'

'Don't know. Cosmo and I have had some dealings with the good lady over the years. Gather she got her number out of Cosmo.'

31

The sun was now hiding behind a cloud, giving the village a sense of gloom and decay.

Olivia shot out the far end, heading towards the loch. 'What do you think?'

Took Mark a beat to realise she meant about the camp. 'About that lot? Well, good luck to them. I just wish people would tell us the truth when we ask them.'

'Mark. I know you're upset about Kay, but when I said you need to let me lead, I meant it. I don't need you getting all punchy.'

Mark had that burning deep in his guts, like something was gnawing to get out. 'I'm not a violent man.'

'No, but your mouth doesn't so much write cheques your body can't cash as do contactless antagonism.'

'Right.' He tried to swallow down the anger, but it stuck in his throat. 'Liv, Kay was there. If her absence was innocent, why lie about it?'

'That's not your job, Mark. It's not mine either, but Adam's... Leave it to us. Okay?' Olivia pulled into the small parking bay across from Ruthven Castle, three spaces separated by half-logs, though there weren't any trees left anywhere nearby to source them. Lumbering big four-by-fours filled the two other spaces, one looking like it had just rolled off the forecourt, the other dark green paint, rusted, splattered with mud, seeming as old as the castle itself.

The castle was a formidable building, looking as if it had been hewn from the rock of the island in the loch. The square central section rose four storeys high with wisps of blue smoke climbing from two of the many chimneys. When they'd arrived the previous night, the castle had glowed with some ancient grandness, but up close it seemed more like a ruin.

Mark got out first but had to reach back into the car for his coat.

'Are you going to behave in there?' she asked.

'Maybe.'

'Mark, maybe you should leave this to me. Get back to the book you've avoided for five years, but now have a sudden urge to finish.'

Mark felt a fluttering in his chest, a tightening he really didn't like. He hadn't told Olivia the full extent of his troubles – he knew how she'd react and a big part of him still wanted to protect her from Vic Hebden, even if she was a big, scary cop. 'Okay. I'll let you lead. Sorry.' His voice sounded thin and shaky.

Olivia guided him from the car over to the castle to a wooden bridge spanning the gap between the island and the mainland, wide enough for two vehicles to get across at the same time, but maybe not sturdy enough. She tugged on a rope and bells pealed out into the afternoon air, broken and out of tune, like a distorted church sound.

The gate opened and a giant loomed there, easily seven foot, slowly scanning them.

Mark smiled at him. 'Hi, wondering if we could speak to Lady Ruthven.'

'Why, of course.' The giant spoke in French-accented English. 'You are the famous author, yes?'

'Hardly famous.'

'Well, it's a pleasure to meet you, hardly famous author.' He held out a shovel-sized hand. 'Löic Cabaye.' His surname was a phonetic explosion, Ca-ba-yay.

'Mark Campbell.' He shook the hand, expecting it to be crushed, but it was like a lover's caress. Up close, Löic smelled of lavender and the ocean. 'This is Olivia Blackman.'

'A pleasure.' Löic took her hand in his. 'Now, follow me.' He walked off into the castle. 'Was your journey a pleasure?'

'It was fine.' Olivia was giving Mark some serious side eye. 'What the hell?'

'Search me,' said Mark.

'It's a beautiful time of the year.' Löic walked across a courtyard, past another two four-by-fours, maybe ten years old but which had seen a lot of miles, with mud caking the wheels.

And Adam's car.

Mark raced to catch up with Löic, just as he turned onto a path under a blossoming laburnum tree, its yellow fronds hanging low. 'Is Adam Mathieson here?'

'Oui.'

Not a lick of wind inside the walls, despite being on a body of water. And the mist blocked out the sun. At one point, the house and its grounds would've been grand, but now it was slightly overgrown with wild roses and long grasses. Thick moss covered the flagstones. Other than the plants, there were no signs of life here; no birds, no insects.

'Just upstairs.' Löic stopped under the central tower and opened a door, then ducked as he entered.

Mark followed him into a long corridor with rooms off both sides. Another passageway led under the stone steps, which ascended into the heavens. A gleaming chandelier lit up the gloom. They climbed the stairs, but they didn't seem to head up as much as around something.

Löic opened the door to a much shorter corridor, then walked over a tartan carpet covering bare stone. 'May I fetch you some coffee? Tea?'

'I'm good.'

'Same.'

'You will regret it. My coffee is legendary.' Löic opened a door and stepped away, gesturing for them to enter.

Inside, the ceiling was at least four metres high. A large fireplace, a well-laid fire sat unlit. One stag's head on the walls, which were lined with oak panelling that needed varnishing.

Two settees sat across from each other, Adam in one, looking like he was shrinking into the upholstery. He stood up and cleared his throat.

A woman sat in an armchair in the bay window looking across the loch, a long purple dress gathered over her shoes. She rose to her feet with regal grace, almost to the same height as Mark. Mid-forties but seeming younger. Red hair flowing in long spiralling curls. Thin, with pale skin, the sort that would burn easily in the sun. She held out a hand to shake, her nails painted green, matching her piercing eyes. 'Lady Elizabeth Ruthven.' Her voice was strong and rich, but guttural Glasgow. Could almost smell the Clyde on her words, rather than the Spey.

Mark dipped his head like he was meeting the Queen. He didn't know why he did that, it just sort of happened. 'Mark Campbell.'

'DS Olivia Blackman.' Her warrant card was flipped out and held in Elizabeth's face. 'Need to ask you a few questions.'

Elizabeth looked at her sidelong. 'Of course. Adam here was just telling me all about it.' She smiled at Adam. 'Hell of a business, Mr Campbell.' She frowned, then sat on a sofa and patted the chair next to her, her prominent cheeks curving up to meet her eyes. 'Come on, have a seat.'

Mark took the armchair in the window, looking across the castle grounds to the sprawling vista of the loch and the rising hills either side of the glen. The waters were perfectly still. 'Which loch is that?'

'Loch an Ruathair. Loch Ruthven to the locals.'

'Where the family name comes from, I presume? An Anglicisation of the Gaelic?'

'Search me.' She leaned back against the opposite arm, running a hand through her hair. 'I mean... I didn't grow up here.

Just inherited the place, you know? My granny, who I knew as Peggy Thomas, turned out to be Margaret Ruthven. Some wee posh lassie who'd got knocked up by a shepherd called John. She got kicked out and they fled to Govan. He worked in the ship-yards, they lived a life together, raised three kids. Then seventy years later, I got a call. Her brother died, aged a hundred. No heirs on his side and I was the only living relative, so I got saddled with a massive castle.'

Olivia rolled her eyes. 'Must be such a hassle.'

'You've no idea.' Elizabeth shook her head. 'I'd been working in Guyana, building schools and teaching the locals. Wish I could go back to that, I tell you.'

Löic reappeared, carrying a tray with four frozen glasses and a pitcher of water, the ice cubes chinking as he walked. He set them down, then started the fire, striking a long match and placing it against some newspaper.

Mark was already roasting. He spotted a few biscuits on the plate and his stomach rumbled. He grabbed one and wolfed it down.

'Cheers, Löic. That's all.' Elizabeth waited until the door clicked shut and shifted her gaze between the three of them. 'He's good, but I'd rather do it all myself. Cared for Peggy's brother in his dying days, so I can't bring myself to fire him. What can I do, eh?' She clapped her hands. 'Now. Adam was saying, you're looking for Mark's daughter. Kay Campbell.'

Olivia nodded. 'Josh Urquhart believes she might've been in touch with you.'

'Does he now.' Elizabeth stuck her tongue in her cheek. 'Some boy, that.' She picked up a diary from the table between them and opened it at the marked place. 'Right, aye. Some wee lassie called Kay called us, looking to arrange an interview on behalf of some author she was working for.' She blushed. 'Have to say, I'm awfully flattered to have been asked. And I was pure disappointed when she didn't turn up.'

Olivia gave her a steely look. 'When was this appointment?'

Elizabeth flicked back a few pages. 'Wednesday afternoon at

four. I waited until half past, but I had to bugger off, didn't I? The ceilidh won't organise itself. Royal pain, I tell you, so it is.'

Another entry to the timeline, stretching forward into the day before Mark discovered her disappearance. The day after she'd fled the hotel in Inverness.

Mark wiped biscuit crumbs from around his mouth. 'You're sure she didn't show?'

'Calling me a liar?' Elizabeth rested the book on the table and picked up her glass, water droplets sliding down the side. Then laughed. 'Sorry, just winding you up. Löic answers the door, but he didn't tell me if she'd been.' She set the glass back down without drinking any. 'Anyway. I googled her to check up on you. You would *not* believe the number of gold diggers who call in here. Wasting their time, I tell you. All the gold in this place is long gone.' She chuckled. 'You're the author, eh?'

Mark took a sip of water. 'That's right.'

'A book about the Highland Clearances, right?'

'Aye. Did she say anything over the phone?'

'Well, just that she wanted to know about my family's history in it.' Elizabeth inspected something on her dress. 'That whole sorry thing is a right saga. I know all about it. Before Guyana, I was a schoolteacher down in Pollockshields. History. And when I moved here, I learnt the hard way myself not to talk about it. It's still a right sore topic. Not just with the crofters, eh? Turns out my family lost a ton of land around that time. All we have left is this bloody castle.' She smiled, then settled back and sipped her water. 'Almost like someone had it in for my ancestors. Probably deserved it.'

Mark topped up his water from the pitcher. 'Any idea why they lost it?'

'There's tons of documentation in the archive downstairs. Interesting reading, when it's not sitting in a foot of water. If what I read is even half true, we were the good guys. Owned thousands of acres around here, but we didn't kick people off the land. And the village helped to support this castle. Spared them the tragedies others inflicted. If you go along to the next glen and see Rosal

Township, they removed them, burning their homes over a couple of nights. '

'So how did you lose your land. Forcibly?'

'Nope.' Her expression soured. 'Legally.' She stared at Mark, her gaze intense. '*Lawyers*, eh?' The searing intensity vanished as quickly as it appeared. 'This whole glen was split between two large clans, all documented in a settlement dating back to the dim and distant, which allowed the land to be taken over by the other if certain conditions were met. And they were, but only on our side. All my family retained was this castle. We lost the rest.'

'What were those conditions?'

'Buggered if I know. The archive is missing a copy of it and I've not got the money to pay some lawyer to look into it for me. From what I gather, our clan was deemed legally responsible for the *Laird of Wedale* disaster.'

The piece of shiny that Kay had chased after.

'You owned that boat?'

'Nope.'

'Who did?'

'The Turnbulls. Lowland clan from Selkirk, down in the Borders. Wedale is this funny wee bit between Selkirk and Edinburgh. Stayed in this funky wee bothy in Stow-in-Wedale with a lad many a year ago. The owner was... Well. Anyway. The Turnbulls made money from sheep farming down there. They bought land up here, next to ours and took over all the legal shite. That contract.'

'So the Turnbull clan were the main benefactors of your demise?'

'Aye. Thing is, from what I've read, instead of torching the land like others did, we both offered the crofters we couldn't directly employ the opportunity to ferry down to the port of Leith aboard that boat, where they could work in the Turnbull's estates and mills in the Borders. Good, honest work. Then the tragedy happened and, as they were all members of our clan and under our protection, we lost our land too.'

Mark felt that gnawing in his stomach again. 'Kay was asking about this specifically?'

'Are you deaf? She didn't turn up.'

'No, but she asked you about it. Right?'

'Right, aye.' She finished her glass. 'Thing is, I can spot a grifter a mile off, and she seemed to think she had something.'

Adam tilted his head to the side. 'What kind of something?'

'I mean, it could be something relating to the land dispute, but it could just be how she'd hook my interest and get an in, if you know what I mean. And she had solid bona fides, so I agreed to meet. But she did mention that she would be speaking to William Turnbull just before she met me. Like she was trying to play us off against each other.'

Another item on the timeline, maybe.

But they needed to see if she made that meeting with William Turnbull.

32

The wind started picking up as soon as they left Ruthven Castle, heading away from the village and deep into the hills. A long plain, with bare moorland on both sides. No signs of any wildlife or even roaming sheep. Just sheer emptiness.

Olivia pulled in at the passing place to let a four-by-four hammer past towards the village. 'Like a bat out of hell...' She set off again. 'You okay there, Mark?'

He cradled the oh-shit handle above the door and focused on the view across the barren moorland towards the distant mountains. 'Trying to figure out what's going on here.'

'What, how someone who sounds like that owns a place like that?'

'That's a bit unkind.'

'I get paid to be unkind, Mark. Being suspicious is a good thing in my line of work.'

'Sure, but you're judging her.'

'No, I'm not. And you can talk. The number of times Kay picked you up on your less-than-woke statements...'

'I'm quite right-on.'

'Sure you are. Sure.'

Mark shook his head. 'I don't get why she's vanished between these meetings on Wednesday.'

'Right, but... We need to get to the bottom of this. Trouble is, it feels like we're just... I don't know, unpicking things so gradually. And I just don't know who to trust.'

A sprawling country estate lurked a few miles along the road, nestled in the arms of a mountain, surrounded by native trees rather than the kind of Norwegian pines some rock stars invested in back in the Eighties.

Mark said, 'I've dealt with enough toffs and aristocrats over the years to have heard the full range of excuses for what amounts to tax avoidance or evasion. Just being custodians of tradition. All that nonsense. If Kay's been looking into some theory about the mass murder of locals that actually holds water, then this Turnbull might want to protect more than his reputation. I've heard of people being stripped of their lands and titles when new evidence emerges. In this day and age, the courts tend to side *against* the landowners.'

'That sounds like bullshit to me.'

'Happened over on Skye. Also down in Galloway last year. The locals were handed the land they rented. This country's changing, Liv.'

'Not fast enough, though.' She rattled over a cattle grid, then pulled up at a T-junction. 'Which way?'

A Forestry Commission sign read 'Rosal Township'.

Mark hopped out of the car and walked towards a corrugated iron church standing alone, opposite a cemetery with barely ten gravestones. He swivelled around through a circle, taking in the full sweep of the glen.

Olivia wound down her window. 'What's up, pussycat?'

'Rosal Township. Elizabeth Ruthven mentioned it. Site of one of the worst atrocities in the Clearances.' Mark barely had the words. His mouth was dry. 'My book is set here.' He waved up at the hillside, where only a few small cottages remained, all spread out. 'Used to be seventy houses up there. The crofters lived a hard life, sure, but it was theirs. But the landowner had other plans.

Sheep farming would get much more bang for his buck than from their rents. So he asked them to move to the coast. Learn fishing, kelp farming. Worse land over there, of course, and we saw what it was like at Badbea. So the villagers refused and stood their ground. But he got his men to burn them out. Torched all the houses one night. Over *two and hundred fifty* people. Men, women, children, the elderly. Their cattle, their hens. All driven out by shepherds and their dogs, forced to walk the hard miles to the coast.'

Olivia got out and the wind hammered at her hair, shaking it free of the clasp.

Mark looked around the empty landscape. 'There'd probably be ten thousand souls by now if that hadn't happened.'

She exhaled slowly. 'See what you mean about narrative. Brings it all home, eh?'

Mark had been writing about it. Unreal characters doing unreal things. But it was real now. Too real.

Jane, the daughter of one of those families.

William, the son of the perpetrator of the atrocity.

The torment these people had gone through for avarice and greed.

Olivia asked, 'Remember Kay doing her history essay on this?'

Mark nodded. 'One of the reasons I knew she'd do a good job for me. She really cared about what happened. She was in tears about a story just like this. Couldn't believe people could do this to other human beings. Nothing like visiting the place, is there?'

'Nope.'

Mark stormed back to the car, like he was pushed on by the ghosts of those who'd lost out here, their story hidden to the mists of time. Forget about artistry or the threat hanging over his head.

This was a story that needed to be written.

A story that needed to be read.

33

For once, Olivia slowed to cross a cattle grid. 'Dubhan toinneamh tairbh.' Excellent pronunciation of the Scots Gaelic. 'Any idea what that means?'

Mark let go of the handle he'd white-knuckled all the way over. 'I think it means "the bull's twisted hoof".'

'Correct. Know why?'

'Probably some Victorian reclaiming of tribal history.'

'Pretty much.' She pulled in to a wide drive and trundled across the pebbles, parking between a collection of four-by-fours. Adam was already here. Again. 'Story goes that a bull twisted his hoof when he was a calf but grew up to sire many prizewinning heifers.'

Mark got out into the rain spiralling in the wind. 'You got into history recently?'

'Had a lot of spare time, haven't I?' She'd re-clasped her hair somehow. 'And I've been up here a lot seeing my folks.'

'Right. Including Adam?'

'Worked a case with him.' She didn't look at Mark. 'Prostitution and people trafficking ring that ran all across Scotland. Centred around Dundee, but it went down to Edinburgh and

Glasgow. Surprisingly many victims come from up here. Adam leant me a few books about the Clearances.'

'Thought he was all about pirates and mutants?'

'He's got hidden depths.' Olivia crunched across the drive ahead of Mark.

He dawdled behind her.

'Dubhan toinneamh tairbh' had the alternative name of Turnbull House. A much smaller building than Ruthven Castle, with just one wing, but it stood in lush grounds full of roses, birch and winding paths of pebbles leading through a verdant lawn. A large walled garden sat at the back, with mature fruit trees poking over the top.

A grinding noise shrieked out, rising in pitch and tempo. Sounded like it came from a set of farm buildings. A group of men in overalls hung around outside. Six or seven four-by-fours were parked at odd angles, like they'd arrived in a hurry.

Olivia set off towards them, warrant card at the ready. 'Lads, I'm looking for Adam Mathieson.'

A red-nosed man stepped away from an angle grinder wheel still spinning. He was like a scarecrow, his yellow beard and hair like straw. And his clothes were packed close to stretching. Green tweed jacket, pink shirt and deep red trousers. He walked over with an outstretched hand. 'Ah, this'll be her, then, Adam.' The sort of accent that betrayed a boarding school education, and somewhere way down south.

Adam was more focused on the angle grinder than anyone else.

'Detective Sergeant Olivia Blackman.' Olivia gave him a stern police officer's stare and thumped Mark on the arm. 'This is Mark Campbell.'

John Rennie was amongst the crowd around the angle grinder, studiously avoiding Mark's gaze. Mark could walk over and act all friendly like in the hotel bar last night, but that coyness...

Hmmm.

Adam left Rennie and walked over to Turnbull. 'Let's have that word now, eh?'

'Come on, then.' Turnbull marched across the gravel towards the house, swinging his arms. 'Let's chat over a wee dram.' He took them through a side door that opened straight onto a staircase, charging up without kicking off his mucky boots. He led into a study with two windows both overlooking the walled garden at the back, and gestured at a pair of matching leather settees, one of those design classics with dimples all over and not much of a back.

Mark couldn't remember the name of the sofa and it was bugging him.

'Please, have a seat.' Turnbull opened up a drinks cabinet and took out three tumblers. 'Sorry, I've nothing less than twenty-five years aged.'

Adam smiled at him. 'I'm driving, Bill. And on duty.'

Olivia folded her arms. 'Same with me.'

'Heathens.' Turnbull was holding out the glass of smoky whisky in front of Mark's face. 'Can I tempt you?'

'Thanks, but no.' Mark sucked deep. 'Smells good, though.'

'It's braw, so it is.' Turnbull's accent jutted up against the words. He collapsed into the matching settee and sipped at his drink. 'Bought the distillery last year. Distressed asset and all that. Storerooms full of whisky barrels going back to the year dot. Rebranded it as the Dark Horse distillery and the stuff's now flying off the shelves.'

A pair of dogs waddled in and lay at Turnbull's feet, both settling into deep sleeps in seconds.

'A little birdie tells me you've been speaking to someone we're looking for,' said Adam. 'Kay Campbell.'

'Ah.' Turnbull looked away. 'Aye, she was here. She's... She's a little witch is what she is.'

Olivia's eyebrows shot up. 'Don't hold back, why don't you?'

'I'm serious.' Turnbull got up. The dogs both stared at him, then rested their heads back down on the rug. His hand was shaking. 'The little harlot called me up on Wednesday morning, accusing me of covering over an atrocity.'

Mark locked eyes with Olivia and guessed they were thinking the same thing. Another item on Kay's timeline. 'When was this?'

'Mid-morning.' Turnbull turned back against the windowsill and cradled his whisky, curling in towards his chest. Like the bull with the twisted hoof. 'But that witch called me up and asked to speak about it. I refused, naturally, but she said she had some people on the record discussing a matter pertaining to my ancestry. So I asked her to come here, see what she's got.'

Mark got a flutter of butterfly wings in his stomach. 'And did she?'

'Well, aye. Wednesday lunchtime. A car dropped her at the gate and she walked right in. Sat in this very room. Drank my coffee. And accused me—' His voice cracked. The shaking got worse. 'Accused me of being complicit in an atrocity.'

'What atrocity would that be?'

'The *Laird of Wedale* disaster.' Turnbull sank the whisky in one go and slammed the glass down on a console table. He stormed back over to his whisky decanter and tipped out another dram. 'Accusing my ancestors of...' He rocked forward, setting off from the window and walked over to the grandfather clock near the door. 'Burning homes, forcing people from their livelihoods. It was a *disgrace*.'

Mark held his fiery gaze. 'You saying there's nothing in it?'

'Of course there is.' Turnbull stared out of the window and slid a good inch of whisky down his throat. 'The sheer suffering that whole class of people were responsible for. The Marquis of Sutherland and his ilk, sending people to the coast without a hope of being able to survive. Well, the Ruthvens cleared their glen of eighty lives. Families, farmers, people. Moved them to Helmsdale, where they boarded the *Laird of Wedale*, bound for Leith and a new life in the Southern Uplands. Minutes after launching, she sank into the depths. It's a tragedy my ancestors bear as much as hers.' He raised the glass but held it over his lips without drinking. 'Because the Turnbull clan spanned the Highlands and the Southern Uplands, so we could—'

'You mean the Borders?'

'Don't call it that. It's undignified. The Southern Uplands, please.' Turnbull twisted his mouth into a grimace. 'My ancestors offered these people a better life down by the Tweed. Our estates, our factories, our farms. These folk were members of *her* clan. *Her* tribe. Not mine. But we lost those poor souls too. While the whole thing clearly caused a lot of unrest, pain and a lingering resentment.' He gripped his glass tight. 'And... And...' He sipped whisky with shaking hands. 'And your daughter came in here... She... She said *we* killed them to gain the Ruthvens' land! How dare she!?' He slammed the glass down and whisky sprayed up his sleeve. 'There's nothing in it! *Nothing!*' He sipped what remained of his drink.

'So you're saying the Ruthvens cleared members of their own clan to the coast, but you offered some of them a new life down in the Bor—' Mark raised a hand. 'Southern Uplands, but they were lost at sea.'

'It's what happened, son.'

'But your ancestors gained this land?'

Turnbull narrowed his eyes. 'What are you trying to say?'

'When we spoke to Lady Ruthven, she suggested your ancestors took this land—'

'Enough!' Turnbull shot to his feet and pointed at the door. 'Get the hell out of here!'

Adam raised his hands. 'Come on, Mark didn't—'

'Listen to me. The three of you.' Turnbull snorted. 'My ancestors took ownership of this land from the Ruthven family by entirely legal means. A sole survivor clause, insisting the Laird maintained peace and prosperity of the land and its people. They were irresponsible landlords, clearing their own clansmen out to the coast. We tried to save them, but we couldn't.'

Mark shared a long look with Olivia, but he had no idea what card to play next.

Turnbull slid his glass onto a side table, then checked his pocket watch. 'I'm afraid we've run out of time. I have another appointment which I can't be late for.'

34

As Olivia drove, Mark watched the countryside shoot past. A male pheasant perched on a wall, watching something in a field. He wished he could be that bird. To live that simple life, just focusing on your next meal. Seemed like bliss.

Then again, the poor bastard would probably be shot by a management consultant from London under John Rennie's tutelage.

Still, that immediate death... It was probably better than the constant stress. The ever-present fear.

Olivia rounded a bend and slowed to a halt.

The road was filled with cows of all colours. Three farmers, all on quads, shooting around the herd, trying to ferry them into the field opposite where half of them were still loitering.

The cows had a different idea and set off towards Mark and Olivia.

She slammed the gearbox into reverse and shot off back the way, wrapping her arm around Mark's headrest, then stopped and put the car in neutral, leaning on the wheel to watch. 'Let's go crazy, eh?'

The lead quad moved fast, like a fish swimming in a loch. The farmer was standing on his pedals, giving little adjustments to push the cattle back down the lane.

'God, remember when we took Kay to that farm down by Ayr?'

Mark smiled. 'That open day thing. She got to feed the pigs and sit with the cattle.'

'The day she became a vegetarian.'

'Wish I had her strength of will.'

'She's a great kid, Mark.' Olivia let out a sigh. 'What's going on in that bonce of yours?'

'Well, I think you should drive slower and keep an eye on where—'

'I meant about Turnbull.'

Mark blew air up his face. 'Hard to tell.' And it was.

Olivia said, 'Turnbull had an explosive temper.'

Mark frowned. 'You're thinking Kay could've set that off?'

'Seems like she did. He was fuming.'

'You don't think he did something to her, though?'

'Don't have anything pointing to it now.'

'You honestly think her digging into the distant past made him want to kill her?'

'No, but scare her off? Sure.'

'But why?'

'Maybe there's something in a historic rout of Satanists in Strathruthven?' She shrugged. 'But if there was, it's been so successfully covered up that there's not even a whisper of it. Thing with conspiracies is people aren't very good at cover-ups. Think about the number of people involved in a mass murder like that. For none of them to have a deathbed confession?'

'True.' Mark shut his eyes, stinging from the bright sky. 'I got myself into trouble with the research for that last book.'

'*Break the Chain?*'

'Right. You were living in Glasgow, I was in Edinburgh. That month where I was in America? Well, I wasn't.'

'You lying twat. You joined a *cult* and didn't tell me?'

'Right. Aye. Plan was to live through it like the character in the book. But one of them found out. Made me, like they'd say in a spy thriller. I promised I'd keep quiet about it. I did it to protect you, Liv.'

'And obviously writing a bestselling novel about it is keeping quiet?'

'Aye, well.' Mark reopened his eyes but they were still sore. Everything was smoky and blurry. 'The Edinburgh police investigated the cult. I had to turn over my research, wouldn't let me publish the novel until the case was done. They convicted the leader. Luckily I didn't even have to stand in court to testify. Got so many of the members to give evidence.'

Olivia waved a hand at the cows, still messing about on the road. 'You should've told me.'

'Didn't want to trouble you. Or risk your safety.'

'Jesus Christ,' she whispered. 'You joined a cult and hid it from me?'

'You saw the fall out, Liv.'

'No. I just heard about the sales. The advance for the next book. Then watched you spend it.'

'Liv, it wasn't just me who wasn't available. You were always too busy to listen.'

'Mark, if they were threatening you? You should've told me.'

'I can handle myself.'

'Really?'

He looked away. He checked the wing mirror. Behind them, the road was blocked by a column of cars, mostly the giant four-by-fours that seemed to be the default up here. In six months, this road would be covered in snow or, worse, black ice, so it made sense.

The oldest farmer swung his quad around and drove the last cow into the field, then waved them on.

Olivia put the car back in gear and slid into the space vacated by the cows, rounding them with ease. She floored it, squealing past with a wave, then shot past a camper van pulled into a passing place.

Mark watched the countryside change from the barren land

managed by Turnbull's men to the lush green lands around Ruthven and its fertile loch.

Olivia pulled up outside the hotel.

Mark hadn't noticed them arriving.

She got out and waved at Adam, leaning against his car. 'Hey.'

Olivia walked over. 'What happened back there?'

Adam shrugged. 'Should've warned you about Bill's temper. Clearly Kay set that off. Never seen him that shade of purple before.'

Mark got a stabbing fear. 'You think he could've done something to her?' The knife was twisting in his chest. 'I thought you said she'd run off.'

'I never assume anything, Mark.' Adam sighed. 'I just thought it was most likely.'

'But now?'

'Still the same. Kay found something, right? And she seems to have confronted at least Bill with some kind of conspiracy theory... Maybe he's threatened her, or maybe his anger was enough to scare her into running off.' Adam scowled. 'Or maybe he took her somewhere to keep her quiet.'

Olivia was frowning. 'Mm, maybe.'

'You don't buy it, Libby?'

'Seems a bit far-fetched to me, that's all.'

'Seriously. The more we dig into this, Libby, the more I think she's got herself caught up in something. Poked the wrong nest and got stung for her trouble.'

It all clicked into place really well.

Christ.

Mark collapsed back against Adam's car.

Adam clapped Mark's arm. 'Come on, it's not that bad.'

'Really? You're saying—'

'We're just spit-balling here, Mark. It's what cops do. Run the scenarios. It's hard to know what happened to her when we've still got so many unanswered questions. But what jumps out at me is why did she leave her car at the station? Who did she stay with on Tuesday night?'

Olivia was nodding. 'I might head down to the station in Inverness. Go through some more of those CCTV hits.'

Adam nodded. 'Sounds wise.'

She stared hard at Mark. 'I'll see you in the morning. I'll call if anything comes up, okay?'

The way they'd been talking, Mark hoped nothing would.

35

Mark put his key in the lock and opened the door. The room was baking. That morning's thick mist had lost out to a bright sky, lighting up some guests outside, sharing a bottle of white wine on the patio, but turning his room into a sauna.

He collapsed into the chair, exhausted, and stared at the laptop screen until the pixels revealed themselves. Tiny dots that gave the illusion of a document.

Kay had been in this village, met some people, but was now missing.

It started to hit him. The truth he'd tried to deny or at least push to the back of his mind.

Kay was in trouble.

Even worse trouble than he was.

Leaving her car in Kinbrace, with a second phone in the glove box. Not checking out of her B&B in Inverness, instead vanishing into thin air. Hell, not being seen since Wednesday afternoon.

He still had no idea where Kay was.

He needed to find her. Needed to find out what had happened to her.

Was she okay?

Did someone have her?

Was she dead?

The walls felt so tightly packed they'd crush him. A panic attack tickled at the edges of his vision, making it start to blur.

He concentrated on his breathing and tried to keep calm. Deep breaths. Ignore the stars and dots in his vision. Ignore it all.

Ignore the fact his fucking daughter might be dead.

Calm down. Organise your thoughts.

No way. No way can wee Kay be dead.

He reached for his notebook and opened it. But his hand was a claw and he couldn't pick up his pen.

Magic...

He huffed out a deep breath then got hold of it.

Right.

He scribbled in his notebook.

Evidence for her being okay:
1) Her laptop is still missing.
2) Previous with running away.

It wasn't a lot.

Evidence for ~~her dea~~ the alternative:
1) Her laptop is still missing.
2) Stirring the pot in Strathruthven.
3) Elizabeth Ruthven.
4) William Turnbull.
5) Josh and his Satanists.
6) Raymond the Blacksmith.
7) Maybe others.
8) Someone had dropped her off.
9) Hebden.

Shit.

Hebden.

Vic Hebden might have her. Mark had missed three payments. Was due a hell of a lot more.

And he knew about Kay. Hell, Mark had used their shared fatherhood as a way of persuading him to lend the money.

Shit, that was it.

Mark shot to his feet, knowing he needed to do stuff. To stop being so passive. Find his daughter. He picked up his mobile from the dressing table and hit dial, but Cath bounced the call.

Charming.

He gave her a few seconds to reply, then he hit dial again. Same, but he got a text back:

Not heard from Kay. You okay?

He hit reply:

Fine. Nothing to worry about. Mx

He hit send and sat back.

Lying bastard.

His phone rang.

Not Cath, but Fiona.

He hit answer. 'Hey, what's up?'

'Hey, I'm just waiting to start my gym class so I thought I'd see how your book was going?'

'It's mostly fine.'

'You need any editing help before it goes to Hamish?'

'No.'

She paused. 'Mark, what's up?'

'Nothing's up.'

'Come on, Mark. That was your chance to either say you don't need editing, especially from me, or joke that I must be desperate for the money.'

'It's...' Ice crawled down his spine. 'Because I'm scared. Kay's missing and I've no idea where she is.'

'Jesus, Mark. Are you okay?'

'I'm fine. Just... She's probably run away. She'll get in touch soon.'

'Have you gone to the cops?'

'I have done. I'm up in the Highlands now, seeing if I can find her.'

'You think Hebden's got her?'

Mark sighed. 'The thought has crossed my mind.'

'Listen, Kay called me last week. Asked her favourite aunt about your debt.'

'My debt? What? Why didn't you tell me?'

'Helps if you answer your phone, dickhead.'

'Right. Sorry. I've been busy. What did you tell her?'

'Nothing. She asked how much, but I didn't say, or to who. But she knows you're in trouble, Mark.'

'Aye, she forced it out of me.'

Fiona laughed. 'She's good at that. Maybe she's done something about it, though.'

Fuck.

'Come on, girls, let's get our blood pumping!'

'Sorry, Mark, I really need to go.' And she went.

Mark slumped back in the chair.

Hard hope jutted up against fear. Why the hell would she want to know how much he owed?

Someone knocked at the door.

Olivia?

He walked over and opened it wide.

A big lump of a man stood there, fists pressed into his hips. 'Mr Hebden would like a word. Down in the restaurant.'

36

'Lovely bit of scran, this.' Vic Hebden arranged his fork and knife on the plate, alongside the full portion of peas he'd left. All that was left of the steak was a thin strip of fat and smears of blood. He chewed the last of the crispy chips that soaked up the juice. 'Please, Mr Campbell, have a seat.'

Mark felt that surging, like he was going to be sick, going to throw up all over the plate. The last thing he wanted to do was sit opposite Hebden, but it felt like someone had removed all the bones from his legs, so he complied.

He felt a trickle of sweat slide down his spine.

How the hell had Vic found him?

Was he going to get his legs broken?

Vic tilted his head to the side. 'You okay?'

'Hardly.' Mark ran his hands through his hair. He tasted bile at the back of his throat. 'Listen, I've agreed with my editor to—'

'Spare me the details. The days of you and I being acquaintances are long gone. You've let me down, Mr Campbell. It breaks my heart. So I'll keep this formal. Will you get me my money by next Friday?'

'I will.'

'Then that's all I'm interested in, Mr Campbell. Now, I'd much rather you were a good customer, someone who paid when they were supposed to. It's a lot of money I've loaned you. But you let me down.'

Mark had to swallow it down. 'I will have it by next Friday.'

Vic pinched his lips. 'Five o'clock, Mr Campbell. Outside your flat.' He lifted his arm and stretched it out. 'I'll be waiting for you.'

Mark nodded. 'I won't be able to get the full amount out in one go.'

'That's fine. You can get it out on Wednesday, Thursday and Friday.'

'No, I mean—'

'Okay, I see what you mean.' A hissing sigh escaped Vic's lips. 'Well. Friday, Saturday, Sunday is good with me.' He dug his pinkie fingernail into his teeth, then swallowed down a lump of meat. 'You're not the first person who thinks they can hide from me in the Highlands, you know?'

'I'm not hiding.'

'I'm very disappointed. Personally disappointed. I lent you that money in good faith. And you try to run.'

'I'm not on the run. Seriously.'

'Pretty hard to get further away from Edinburgh than this place.' Vic tossed his napkin onto his plate and scanned around the dining room, loud with the diners' chatter and early Miles Davis. 'You can't hide from me, Mr Campbell. Anywhere. I've got friends in all the right places. And people who can find *anyone*.'

'I know, but—'

'I've got people on the islands. On the ferries. On all the boats. They all know who's travelling where. And all of the airports. I know where your car is at any time. I know where you *are* at any time.' Vic burped into his fist. 'You can't hide from me.'

'I'm genuinely not trying to.' Mark shut his eyes and wished this wasn't happening. 'I'll hopefully get your money.'

'Hopefully? Come on, Mr Campbell, I don't have any hope left.'

'I will get it.'

'I'm starting to doubt you here. Thing is, if you don't pay, then Bruce and Joe over there—' He flicked his wrist at the door. '—are going to break your legs. You know that. But I'm also going to take your home from you.'

'I can't—'

'I know you own it outright, Mr Campbell. Should've just re-mortgaged it instead of coming to me. But it gives us something to play with here. If you don't pay me those instalments by Friday, then you'll sign over the deeds to me and we'll be quits.'

With broken legs and no home.

Mark exhaled slowly. 'Listen, the reason I'm up here... It's my daughter, Kay. She was staying in Inverness, but she left her hotel room on Tuesday. I'm trying to find her.'

'If my girl did the same that'd break my heart.'

The way Vic was looking away, over at the window and the hotel grounds...

'Do you know anything—'

'No.' Vic leaned forward, narrowing his eyes. 'Let me be clear, Mr Campbell, I'm not responsible for what's happened to Kay.'

'And I'm just supposed to believe you?'

'I'd never target anyone's kids. *Never*. Kay isn't the one being funny with their debt to me. You are. But I can see why you think that. Having leverage over someone without having to spill any blood makes this all so much easier.'

Christ. He had her, didn't he?

Stab him with the steak knife and force him to tell him the truth?

It'd solve a lot of problems, but the big lumps standing guard at the door would be on Mark before he even moved to pick it up.

And you didn't get to where Vic Hebden was in his organisa-tion without being handy. The last thing Mark could be described as was handy.

'Okay. I believe you. Sorry. I *will* get you that money.'

'That's all I want. My money, this time next week. That's it.'

Mark swallowed down a gasp. 'Okay.'

Vic walked around the table and grabbed Mark by both cheeks. 'Now, I've got some business up here, as it happens, so I'll need to love you and leave you. Maybe you should enjoy a nice country stroll.' He slapped his thigh. 'Enjoy these while you still can, eh?'

37

Mark reached for his glass of water, but his hands were shaking so badly he spilled it over the table.

He really needed to get the words to Hamish. Get the money. The alternative...

What the hell was he going to do?

He needed to get up the stairs, get on with writing.

But he also needed to find Kay.

Turnbull seemed to be enraged by her. Then again, would he react in a such a volatile way if he had taken her? Maybe he was a great actor.

Mark tried to kick away from the table but his legs wouldn't let him.

Vic Hebden.

What if he actually had her? He swore that he hadn't, but he knew a lot about Kay. Name, age, university degree. He wasn't a man of violence but his lumps were. Bruce and Joe or whatever they were called.

Surely if he had her, he'd use her as leverage now? Maybe it was just insurance.

Then again, he'd found out that Mark owned that flat outright. Inherited from his mother. How else could he know that?

Either way, Mark needed to take out Vic Hebden. Get him off the board. Not that he'd ever dream of confronting him in person. No, most battles were better fought elsewhere. He got out his phone and called Olivia. Listened to it ringing.

He had to come clean to her, get her to speak to Edinburgh cops about him. Maybe they already had an investigation into Hebden. Maybe Mark would have to wear a wire on a sting. Help them take him down.

Aye. Keep dreaming.

'This is Olivia, please leave a message.'

'Hey, it's Mark.'

I've got friends in all the right places.

People who can find anyone.

I know where you are at any time.

Hebden would have cops on his payroll.

Christ.

'Just, eh, wondered if you, eh, wanted me to order you anything from the menu, but I just remembered you're at your mum's. Cheers. Bye.'

Mark ended the call.

He really couldn't trust anyone. He was on his own.

Magic.

The dining room had been busy when he entered, but now it was only him and a couple. The woman got up to go to the bathroom, muttering something to that effect in German.

Rennie had said Kay'd been sniffing around the hotel. Maybe they'd spoken to her?

No, he needed to focus on what *he* could do, not the police investigation. He needed to write those words. Get that book to Hamish. Get his money. Give it all to Vic Hebden.

Just another day or so's work, then he'd be able to get back to finding Kay.

Besides, Olivia was on it full-time and it was her job. Even after all their shared pain, he could trust her. She loved Kay.

173

Sod it.

Mark got up and his legs were like pâté. He took his time walking over to the door, smiling at the man as he passed.

He pointed at Mark. 'I know you from somewhere.' Heavy German accent.

Mark frowned. 'Not sure.'

The man tilted his head to the side. 'You are a famous movie star.'

'Not with my looks.' But Mark was intrigued. '*Sie sind Deutsch, ja?*'

The man took a bracing sip of wine. 'It's okay, my friend. I speak English.' He held out a hand. 'Friedrich Wanner.'

Mark kept his distance. 'Your English is excellent.'

Friedrich shrugged. 'I work for Bayerische Motoren Werke—BMW—in München and if I didn't speak such good English, I would not have a job.' He dabbed a napkin to his lips. 'I deal with Americans, mostly, but also some English. With the French, for example, we both speak in English.' He laughed. 'My own language is very difficult to learn, but English is a form of German, so we can accept that victory. And Ruthven is twinned with Tutzing, my hometown. It's a village on lake Starnberg in southern Bavaria. In the Alps, so not very different from here.'

'I can imagine.' And Mark could imagine him banging on and on. He needed to get away from this guy. Otherwise, politeness would lead to a lost evening. He got out his mobile and showed him the photo of Kay. 'I was wondering if you'd seen this young woman here?'

Friedrich examined it closely. 'Kay, is it not?'

Mark felt a lump in his throat as he put his phone away. 'She's my daughter. I haven't heard from her in a few days. Did you speak to her?'

'We had dinner with her.' Friedrich frowned. 'Tuesday night, I believe.'

Which contradicted about half a dozen other "facts".

'She was very charming.' Friedrich waved a finger in the air. 'That's how I know you! You are the famous writer, *ja?*'

Kay had been promoting him more than his own publicist. 'I'm a writer, aye, but I'm not exactly famous.'

'Oh, don't do yourself down, my friend. I bought your book.'

Mark batted away the nonsense in his head. 'Thing is, nobody's heard from Kay since Wednesday.'

'You think she has run away?'

'It's possible. The police seem to think so, but I don't believe it.' Mark had that tickle of sweat. His heart was thudding.

'Well, we haven't seen her since then. I wondered if she had checked out.'

'Wait. She was staying here?'

Friedrich frowned, as if rigorously searching his memory. 'I would assume so. She was certainly dining here.' He got to his feet. 'We will be leaving tomorrow, but it was charming to have met you.' He walked off and met his wife by the door.

Leaving Mark alone in the restaurant.

Kay had been in here.

Dining, sure, but maybe staying here too.

Who else was she speaking to?

Why didn't Harris recognise her?

Mark felt a tugging at his arm.

Friedrich was back. 'My wife saw her on Tuesday night. Said she went upstairs.'

Mark felt a surge. He was onto something.

38

A couple of young women stood at the reception desk, blonde-haired, probably Scandinavian, could even be sisters. They looked bored as Harris fussed around with his precious ledger. They looked over at Mark in creepy unison and smiled the same smile.

He kept his distance.

No sign of Vic Hebden, or his bulky assistants.

Mark felt that burning in his throat.

Harris held out the room key to the women, a wide grin filling his face as they both reached for it. He let go and watched them march over to the stairs, then shifted his focus to Mark. 'Now, Mr Campbell, how can I help you?'

'Well, let's start with you telling me the truth.'

Harris kept up the pretence of a smile. 'Excuse me?'

'Kay has been staying here, hasn't she?'

'We've been over this already, sir.' Harris had his eyes shut. 'Your daughter was not a guest of ours.'

Mark felt a slight blush. Confrontation wasn't his strong suit, but when it came to his daughter? All bets were off. 'Okay, but someone saw her go upstairs.'

Harris frowned, opened his eyes, then cleared his throat.

'Well, she might have, I suppose. But—' He slammed his ledger shut. 'Oh flipping Christ, has she been stealing?'

'I didn't say—'

'Christ, Christ, flipping Christ!' Harris reached down and retrieved another ledger, then flicked through it. 'Good heavens, that explains it.'

'Explains what?'

'Things have been going missing here. Expensive things. We pride ourselves on a genuine silver service in the restaurant, but it's become somewhat challenging when you've lost several items of silver.'

Mark didn't give a shit about his cutlery. 'If she's been upstairs here, I—'

'Leave me alone!'

Mark stepped back, arms folded, looking around the grand entrance hall. 'This place intrigues me. Big, with a decent-sized staff. Well-maintained. Thing is, though, I've only seen three rooms occupied out of, what, twenty? Twenty-five? Be interesting to see how much is going through your books.'

Harris looked up at him. 'What are you talking about?'

'Very easy to run a money laundering organisation here. Stick a few grand a day through the books. Cops in Inverness or Wick are probably never in this glen, never even know how quiet this place is.' Mark held his gaze. 'Now, I'm working with police officers, so—'

'Are you *threatening* me?'

'Who said anything about threatening?'

'Sir, I appreciate your concern at finding your daughter, but if she went upstairs, it was without my knowledge. And we have many more guests than you have accounted for.'

'Look, I just want to know what's happened to her. That's it.'

Harris huffed out a sigh. 'If she was as irritating and persistent as you, Mr Campbell, I'm sure everyone she spoke to will recall it vividly.' He held Mark's gaze for a few seconds, then looked away. 'Now, I've passed on your comments to Janek and he's refusing to—'

'Who's Janek?'

'Our chef.' Harris rolled his eyes. 'Polish gentleman. The man who cooked your excellent steak this evening.'

'That wasn't mine.'

'No? Well, it was charged to your room.'

Hebden... 'What comments were those?'

'Your fellow guest says it was overcooked, when it was ordered as rare.'

'That steak is nothing to do with—'

'Come with me!' Before Mark could argue, Harris was storming through reception towards the restaurant area, then into a swinging door.

Mark followed him through the kitchen door and it was roasting in there. How could anyone work in here?

But Janek was doing just that. A big brute, the heels of both palms pressing sliced haggis into a sizzling pan, the meaty aroma filling the thick air. He sang along to a dance remix of some old country tune blasting out of the tiny speakers on the wall, then glanced over at Harris. 'Sorry, man, but I was there when Krista took his order.' His accent was strong, but less Warsaw and more Wishaw. 'This bell end was arguing about his salmon salad, so I came out to show the packet. The boy *definitely* ordered a well-done ribeye.'

'Mr Campbell is refusing to—'

'That little twat can ram it!' Janek picked up a potato masher and drove it deep into a pan. 'Want me to have a word with him?'

'He's right here.' Ever the coward, Harris stepped aside and beckoned to Mark.

'Was your steak not to your taste?'

The sweat got worse, big droplets falling from Mark's forehead like Glasgow rain. 'No, I just didn't order it.'

Janek looked over at Harris. 'That's right. The boy who did was much smaller. Almost as wee as you.' He bellowed out a laugh then drained a pan with a flurry of steam.

'Well, somebody has to pay for the steak!'

'Not like your accounts are real.' Janek laughed again.

Harris grabbed his wrist. 'Shut up. It's not funny.'

Janek pulled his hand free. 'I'm just winding you up. Jesus, you need to keep the heid.'

Harris dusted himself off, then wiped his forehead. Full Highland dress in that heat must be ten times worse. 'Mr Campbell, I'm going to have to charge it to your room. I'm sure a famous author like you can afford to pay for a steak.' He marched off out of there.

Mark made to follow.

Janek blocked his path. 'Aha, so you're the author.'

'Excuse me?' Mark tilted his head to the side. 'Have you spoken to Kay?'

'Right. Tuesday night. Nice girl. But a heartbreaker.'

'She break yours, big guy?'

Janek laughed, then tossed his tattie masher into the sink with a loud clank. 'A woman can make her feelings known, can't she?'

'How did she do that to you?'

'She spurned my advances. She break your heart too? Or are you the man who broke hers?'

'I'm her dad.'

Janek looked him up and down. 'Well, that explains a lot.'

Mark wanted to know what, but he wanted to know her location much more. 'Kay was working for me.'

'So she said.' Janek reached into the frying pan and flipped the haggis slices over with his bare fingers, then pressed down again. His hands were like shovels. 'She was super excited to work for you. And to help you get back on the horse.'

Mark tried not to dwell on the impact his chaos had on her life. Not that he'd seen much of her in the last five years. Seeing him slaving away on his books when he was married to Cath, then not doing anything after he got together with Olivia... Fair to say he had fallen off the horse. Typical Kay, putting others' needs first. 'You spoke to her on Tuesday, right?'

'Must be, aye.'

'Did she stay in the hotel?'

'No, but she was in for dinner a couple of times.'

'Alone?'

'That I saw.' Janek wiped a towel across his sweating brow. 'But I'm in here all the time, eh? If I'm out front, something's gone very wrong with someone's meal, you know?'

'Like tonight's salmon salad?'

'Aye, exactly. Look, I chatted to her in the bar before my shift. She was sitting with the cleaners. I've got a room on the top floor, next to theirs. And those girls can drink, believe.'

'So you had a drink with Kay?'

'Just a couple through in the bar. The lassies cleared off, leaving us on our own. But she had this look in her eye. And the way she held my hand, it was better than sex with anyone else.'

Aye, and Mark really didn't need to hear that. 'Did you take Kay up to your room, then?'

Janek nodded slowly. 'Just twice, man.'

Mark clenched his fists. 'To have sex with her?'

'I wish. Once to drop off her bag.'

Mark didn't know whether to believe it or not. 'And the other?'

'Finish in here at ten.' Janek looked over at the clock on the wall. 'She was waiting outside, needing to collect her bag.'

'This was Tuesday?'

'No. Wednesday. At ten.'

Another entry on the timeline, way later than the other ones.

Just possible Janek had been the last person to see her. Had she fled because of him? Or did he have something to do with her disappearance?

'You said you had a relationship with her?'

'No, pal.'

'But she broke your heart?'

'I kind of exaggerated a bit.'

Mark didn't believe a word of it. Everything contradicted itself, at least a couple of times over. 'You didn't pick her up in Inverness, did you?'

Janek shook his head. 'Don't have a car.'

'Out here? Seriously?'

'That walk to Kinbrace to get the train is brutal in the middle of winter. Did it a few times to see my brother in hospital in Dundee.' Janek shrugged. 'The truth is, I am a good guy. I'm not trying to shag every lassie that comes in here, unlike Harris. Kay asked me to store her bag there while she spoke to this guy. She called him a sex pest. "A filthy degenerate" were her words.'

Mark felt the blood rush up to his head, down to his fists.

'She said he got her to go to his cottage on Tuesday night. Then wouldn't let her leave. Locked the door. That's all she told me. She was in tears when I gave her that bag back.' Janek picked the first haggis slice and slid it onto a serving plate stuffed with a bright orange pile of neeps. He spooned out mashed potato with an ice cream scoop and placed a perfect ball between the haggis and the turnip, then rang a bell. 'I offered to take her to the police station.'

'Is that where she went?'

Janek shrugged. 'Sorry, but she said she'd sort it out herself.'

'She mention this sex pest's name?'

'No.'

'But you've got a good idea who it is, don't you?'

39

In the lounge, the door to the patio was open to the summer's evening out there, insects and birds flying around, the flowers in full bloom, and a dog which trudged right on inside and up to the bar and started lapping at a water bowl on the floor, then scurried off back into the garden.

And there he was, holding court at the bar with Raymond Shearer the blacksmith and a couple of older men. One hand in his pocket, the other clutching a pint of amber beer.

John Rennie's eyes kept going to the screen behind the bar, where a football match was kicking off.

Trapping Kay in his cottage.

Dirty bastard.

Dirty, lying bastard.

Mark walked over to them, his fists tight balls of power. 'Need a word, John.'

Rennie was focusing on the telly, just an impish grin on his face. 'Is that France playing?'

Shearer looked at Mark, then clapped Rennie on the arm. 'I'll let you know how the M1 performs for me, John. See you.' He trudged out of the bar with the other two men.

Leaving Mark and Rennie alone.

Mark tried to make eye contact, but he was no contest for the screen. 'I said I wanted a word, John.'

Rennie frowned. 'I think it's Russia, actually... Against... Who knows? I'm more of a rugby man. God's sport, am I right?' He raised a finger at the barman. 'Can I get you a drink, Mark?'

'If you're going to tell me the truth, then sure.'

Rennie nodded at the barman. 'Pint of the same for him.' He took a table close to the bar, sitting in the seat with the view of the telly. 'Bastard of a day.'

Mark sat opposite, glad to be pointing away from the screen, though it'd be nice if someone looked at you when you accused them of rape. Or kidnapping. 'I gather you—'

'Thought I was going to get away with a nice quiet morning, but I had a school trip up from Inverness today. Then a flock of sheep escaped from their field on the way over to Kinbrace.'

The barman deposited two pints on their table.

'Magic, cheers.' Mark didn't drink any of the beer, just let it sit there.

Rennie knocked back the rest of his first beer. 'Had to get out with my tranq gun. Get a lot of wild dogs here. It's usually domestic breeds gone feral. They can be desperate animals and they'll bite your throat as soon as you look at them.'

'That's a cheery thought.'

'Of course, it's muggins here that has to hunt them down. I tranquillise them and take them down to Inverness. A royal pain in the arse, but all part of the job.' Rennie pulled his pint glass over and took the head off. 'Had a load of management consultants from London up on some team-bonding thing this afternoon.' He bellowed with laugher. 'They're away back to Inverness with a brace of pheasants for their troubles.'

Mark waited for Rennie to look him in the eyes. 'That why you blanked me at the farm?'

Rennie licked his lips, staring into space then locked eyes with Mark again. 'Bill Turnbull can be a bit funny about us speaking to people.'

'Sure it's just that?'

'Bill likes to be in control of the truth, or at least his version of it.'

Mark took a drink of the local ale, which seemed to bite back. 'Wondered if you'd show your face in here tonight.'

Rennie sipped his beer, eyes on the telly. 'Why, what am I supposed to have done?'

'Might be good for your soul if you told me.'

'Eh? This about your kid?'

Mark pushed his glass away.

'Referee!' Rennie raised his arms in the air. 'Must be tough for you, Mark.'

'Well, it'll be a good idea to rehearse what you're going to say to the cops.'

Rennie looked over at him. 'Eh?'

'Heard you spent a fair amount of time with her.'

'Been over that, son.'

'We have, aye. Thing is, you forgot to mention inviting her back to your cottage.'

Rennie stared at Mark for a few seconds, then threw the rest of his pint down his neck. 'Can't linger around tonight. Just that drink with the boys and that's it for me. Early start tomorrow.' He got up.

Mark gestured at his seat. 'Stay.'

'Sorry, son, but—'

Mark grabbed his arm. 'You trapped her in your cottage, you lying bastard.'

Rennie stayed on his feet. 'That didn't happen.'

'No?'

'No. Never happened.'

'Sure about that?'

'Sure.'

'When we spoke yesterday, you didn't mention inviting her to your cottage. Why would that be?'

'You're not a cop.'

'My ex-wife is.'

Rennie looked around the room. 'Don't see her here.'

'This is your chance to tell me what happened, John. Just you and me.'

'Fine...' Rennie waved at the barman. 'Usual whisky, Tam. Stick it on his room.'

Tam the barman went over to the whisky shelf, poured a glass, and brought it over.

'Cheers.' Rennie gave him a silent toast, then at Mark. 'Very good of you, son.'

Tam returned the thirty-year-old Macallan to the shelf behind the bar.

'Now, I've bought you a very expensive whisky, John, so you're going to repay me with some honesty.'

Rennie swirled the whisky around his glass, then sucked in the aroma. 'What do you know about the Ruthven family during the Clearances?'

'I don't give a shit about that. I want to know what you did to Kay.'

Rennie sighed. 'The reason Kay was in my cottage was—'

'So you admit it?'

'She was there. That lassie wanted to talk about some documentation I could... acquire for her.'

'Sounds like shite to me.'

Rennie took a sip of his whisky and grimaced like he'd licked a thistle. 'That's the ticket.' He wiped his lips, his gaze now entirely devoted to Mark. 'It's not shite, son. You might've heard how the Ruthvens kept their title, kept their castle, but the land passed to the Turnbulls. Because of the *Laird of Wedale* disaster and an ancient feudal settlement. If anything happened to either of their clansfolk, a death of more than fifty men, then either clan lost their claim on their land. Your daughter got wind of the fact that Bill Turnbull's family archive had a document that proved the disaster never happened.'

That conspiracy theory again.

And Kay had succumbed to it.

Mark was shaking. 'Go on?'

'Well. Wednesday morning, Bill was out and he'd left the door unlocked. I took the only surviving copy.'

'Do you still have it?'

'Still do, aye.' Rennie winced. 'Bill's not been away since, so I've not had the chance.'

'Still doesn't explain why you locked the door to your cottage.'

Rennie hissed, 'Because that document's worth fifty grand to me.'

'Fifty grand? What are you talking about?'

'The reason I shut the door was Kay needed to check it's valid.'

'Why her?'

Rennie frowned. 'She's an expert, right?'

'She's a first-year student. How does she know anything?'

'Well.' Rennie took another sip of the whisky and raised an eyebrow. 'If that was the real deal, then it'd be worth a lot of money to Lady Ruthven.'

'What was the document?'

'Years back, I got wind of there being an official investigation into the disaster. This was it. Way Kay explained it, Turnbull's people killed the villagers and buried them in a mass grave, then sank the boat themselves. When the boat went down, Turnbull's ancestor conjured up proof that they were all aboard. Tickets and luggage and the only body floating to the surface. According to the terms of the settlements, those deaths were the responsibility of the Clan Ruthven. They died, so they lost the land.'

It could explain Kay's errand. Maybe.

Mark got up. 'I'll see what the police say about it.'

'Son, it's the truth. Why would I lie?'

Fire was surging through Mark's body. 'Because you raped and killed my daughter?'

'No! No way!'

Mark held his gaze until Rennie looked away. 'Kay was at your cottage on Wednesday night. You locked the door. And that's the last time anyone saw her. Lot of places around here you could bury a body and nobody would find it for *years*. Especially a man in your trade, with access to the kind of four-by-fours that could drive up a cliff face.'

'Son, you don't know what you're talking about. I showed her the document, she inspected it, took a copy, then she left. That's the truth. That's it. That's all that happened.'

'Then where did she go?'

'I've no idea.'

'None?'

'None.' Rennie was about to sink more of his whisky, but just put the glass back on the table. 'I've nothing to hide, Mark. I just need that cash.'

'No? Because stealing a document to sell to someone who was going to blackmail your boss sounds a lot like you've got something to hide.'

'She wasn't going to blackmail Bill.' Rennie took a drink of his whisky and raised his eyebrows. 'She was going to sell it to Ruthven.'

'Why do you think that?'

'Because...' Rennie shook his glass, spraying the brown liquid around almost to the lip. 'When I was feeding my sourdough on Wednesday, I might've seen her heading out to the castle.'

40

Mark could've driven to the castle, but instead they walked. Only half a mile and it was a fair night, with the sweet tang of honeysuckle catching the breeze.

Rennie veered off at the end of the village's high street. 'Well, I'll see you around.'

Mark grabbed his sleeve. 'You're coming with me.'

'I'm not welcome there unless I'm delivering livestock.'

'Livestock?'

Rennie grimaced. 'I drop a sheep off at the castle every other week.'

'You're joking?'

'God's honest truth.' Rennie shook his head. 'She's got her own butchery, one of her sons-in-law is a butcher by trade. Had to take two this week, just after I saw you lot at Bill's this afternoon.'

'Must be for the ceilidh.'

'Right, right.' Rennie side eyed Mark. 'What did the good lady have to say for herself?'

'What do you mean?'

'Well, I gather you were asking questions.'

'Kay was supposed to go there on Wednesday afternoon, but she didn't show. Reason I was over speaking to your boss was Elizabeth Ruthven told me Turnbull was the last to speak to Kay. Now it turns out you were the last to see her. At your cottage.'

'Right. Listen, I spoke to her at Bill's. She recognised me. And I told her about the settlement. She knew how much she could get for it.'

'How?'

'Spoke to the good lady, I gather.'

Mark was sick of people lying to his face.

Rennie tried to walk off. 'See you.'

Mark tugged him back towards him. 'Seriously, you're coming with me.'

'No, son. I'm not.' Rennie shook free of Mark's grip. 'Now, I've been a help, so kindly bugger off.' He walked up a path to pretty much the last cottage in the village and unlocked a door.

'Can I at least see this document?' asked Mark.

'What document?' Rennie skipped inside and slammed the door. A deadlock slid shut.

Magic.

Was he telling the truth?

Mark didn't know.

But if Rennie *was* telling the truth, then Kay had information that Elizabeth Ruthven wanted. Proof that Turnbull's ancestors had killed all those crofters, buried them, and they were complicit in the cover-up.

If it was true, Turnbull had a lot to lose and Ruthven a lot to gain.

Sod it, he had to see what she was hiding.

Mark set off, walking past the actual last building, an old concrete telephone exchange that seemed derelict, and hit the short road to the loch, sticking to the grass verge.

The castle was silhouetted by the low sun, almost like it was holding on to it at the top of the central tower. Tomorrow was midsummer's night – maybe the sun would be enslaved then.

Mark got out his phone. A text from an unknown number:

Remember our agreement, chief. Honour it.

Vic Hebden's burner.

Mark had tried trusting Olivia and Adam. Tried it all the official way, but he needed to do this himself. Confront Elizabeth Ruthven, see what she had to say.

Maybe not confront, so much as wheedle and cajole. But he had a theory, something to put to the test.

As if by magic, a message popped up from Olivia:

Feeling any better?

Sod it.

Mark hit dial.

Olivia answered with a yawn. 'Hey, you okay?' Sounded like the din of a party in the background.

'Aye, fine. Are you in the pub?'

'My cousin's.'

'Oh, right.'

'Good news is I've finally got one of Adam's numpties to run Kay's phone records now and we've started calling around.'

'Anything?'

'Not yet, but it's a start.'

Mark didn't know how to say it. 'I've got an update on Kay's movements. She was in the hotel at half ten on Wednesday night.'

'Right.' Sounded like Olivia was rubbing her eyes. 'Is it true?'

'Two sources now. It's possible she went to speak to Elizabeth Ruthven.'

Mark was aware he was leaving out so much of the truth himself now.

'Okay, let's head there tomorrow, aye?'

Mark stepped back against the hedge to let a hulking four-by-four past. 'I'll let you know how it goes.'

'Mark, seriously. Wait until tomorrow, then we'll both go.'

'Catch you later.' Mark ended the call and walked on towards the castle.

41

The dining room in Ruthven Castle had seen better days and must have seen grander occasions than a writer visiting to ask about his daughter.

It was at the opposite end of the second floor from the drawing room they'd been in that afternoon. The walls were plastered on only two sides, with the remaining two showing exposed stone, but the large settlement cracks meant it didn't have the shabby chic of an Edinburgh-style bar. A fire crackled in its grate beside them, flooding Mark with heat he didn't need. The large picture windows overlooked the garden and the castle's shadows lengthened across the lawn.

Below, the courtyard milled with workmen, lugging scaffolding and flight cases around.

'Sorry about the racket.' Elizabeth sat at the head of a long table, and wore a short black dress, hugging her lithe figure. 'Can't hear myself think in here. The ceilidh's always last minute. Gets on my ti— nerves.' She sliced the lamb cutlet with a steak knife, then put a piece in her mouth and chewed, her eyes locked onto his. 'Hope you don't mind me eating, but it's been a hell of a day. You'll be coming tomorrow night, eh?'

'To the ceilidh?' Mark sat at the opposite end of the long table, which felt like it was in another postcode. 'I'll probably be gone home. And I'm not much of a dancer.'

'Oh, come on. Bet you can boogie.'

'I really can't.'

'Two left feet, eh?' She dabbed at her lips with a napkin. 'Sure I can't feed you?'

'No, I ate earlier.' And he couldn't face the prospect of food.

'Man, you should taste this lamb. It's delicious. *Sure* I can't tempt you?'

'No, I just wanted to ask—'

'Löic!' She cut off a slice of the lamb, dipped it in mint sauce and held it out to Mark. 'Please. I insist.'

Mark stared at the lump of meat on the fork. One of Rennie's animals dropped off every week? 'I'm vegan.'

She rolled her eyes. 'One of them, eh? Can't chuck a bottle of ginger in Glasgow without hitting ten vegans.' She took a drink of wine from her large goblet. 'Löic's an amazing chef. And Clare's husband, Paul, worked as a butcher in the Ashworth's next to Ibrox.'

'Who's Clare?'

Elizabeth held a small forkful of the meat in front of her mouth. 'My daughter. You met her in the hotel bar last night.'

The woman he thought was Kay? But she was Northern Irish. Wasn't she?

'You don't look old enough to have a daughter in her twenties.' Mark blushed as he said it.

'I've got three daughters. The all live here with me. And their useless husbands...'

Seemed strange. All of them living in a gloomy old castle.

'What happened to their father?'

Elizabeth chewed another sliver of lamb. 'Davie worked on the rigs. Died before I inherited this place.' She put her knife and fork down on the plate together, then leaned forward, the deep cleavage showing through her tight dress. 'How's your book going?'

Mark was aware his eyes betrayed him. He needed to take control here, stop her dominating him. 'I want to know if—'

'Forgot to say, I found a copy in the library. *Break the Chain?* My grannie's brother must've bought it just before he popped his clogs. Looks like a great read, have to say.'

'Thanks.'

'Will you sign it for me?'

'Aye, sure.' Mark scratched the back of his neck. 'Listen. Did Kay turn up here on Wednesday night?'

She frowned. 'Why would you think that?'

'I heard she set off for here, that's all.'

'Well, if she did, she never turned up.' Elizabeth took a big drink of wine. 'Forgot to say. After you left, I asked my children if they'd met her. Clare told me someone called Kay had been drinking with her and Paul in the village hotel.' Her forehead twitched. 'She was asking questions about a certain someone.'

'Who'd that be?'

'I'm sure your friend, Mr Rennie, would know.'

'Bill Turnbull?'

Löic lumbered into the room, accompanied by a dog.

Big, red-furred and panting, its hungry eyes trained on her almost-empty plate. It could be a littermate to the one he'd seen outside his room but had no malice in its eyes. Up close, it looked like a greyhound that had been hitting the weights.

'Come here, Bess.' She grabbed the dog and hugged it close. 'She's a big softie.' She reached over and drained her glass.

Löic started clearing the table.

She frowned at him. 'Löic, I'll do that.'

'Please, I insist.' He stacked both of her plates together, then lumbered over and stoked the fire one-handed. He shoved another log on, then left the room.

The last thing Mark needed was that fire to be any hotter. It was melting in there. 'I'll cut to the chase. Did Kay talk to you about a document?'

'A document?'

'Proof that some events that occurred a long time ago didn't happen the way people think they did.'

'You're talking like—' She sighed. 'John Rennie, right? Watch yourself with that one.' A grimace tightened her face. 'John's got some fanciful ideas.'

'So Kay never discussed it with you?'

'Will you listen to me?' Elizabeth flared her nostrils. 'She never turned up.'

'What about when she phoned?'

'You're a persistent bugger, aren't you?'

'If one of your daughters was missing, I'm sure you'd be the same.'

'True. Except for Janice.' She laughed, then tipped more wine into her glass. 'Your kid might've mentioned something. "A document that might be of some use to you." Her words, which she used to reel me in. Intrigued, so I agree to meet her. She didn't turn up. And that's it.'

'Kay definitely didn't turn up here on Wednesday night?'

'No!' Though her lips were twitching. 'Wait a sec, though.' She clicked her fingers. 'Löic, can you fetch that bag?'

If the bag was Kay's, could it lead to her whereabouts?

'Löic found a bag on the jetty down to the loch on Thursday morning.'

'Here's the thing.' Mark rested on his elbows. 'I'm finding it a bit weird how she's got this document, which could lead to you overturning the loss of your lands, and then she goes missing.'

Elizabeth laughed, eyes wide. 'You've got some balls coming in here and saying I've kidnapped your kid!'

'I'm not saying that at all. Just that—'

'Oh. Right. You think Bill Turnbull's got something to do with this?'

'Do you?'

'No secret that Bill and I don't see eye to eye. Doesn't like a scumbag like me running a place like this.' She held up her hands. 'Still, we're trying to put that behind us. Bill's the guest of honour at the ceilidh tomorrow night.'

Löic lumbered back into the room, carrying a laptop bag that his giant paws made seem like a smartphone purse. He ran his hand across it. 'This is one of my top three fabrics.'

Mark took it off him and had no idea what the other two could be. It was a sleek navy that looked natural but felt artificial. He opened the zips and got out the device.

A MacBook with a sticker in the middle that read 'Megustalations'. Mark had no idea what the phrase meant, but he remembered Kay getting it through the post.

A little flutter of relief in his stomach, followed by a rumble of fear.

On Wednesday night, she'd collected her bag from Janek's room, then headed here.

Löic had found her laptop by the castle the following morning.

What happened to her?

Mark needed to get back to his room and dig into Kay's computer.

Forget about her words, he just wanted to find her.

He got to his feet. 'This is hers. Thank you.'

Elizabeth put a hand to her mouth. 'I hope it helps you find her.'

42

The countryside glowed in that spooky mid blue, not quite day but not night either. The birds hung around, crowing in the empty fields.

How had it got so late?

It started to rain.

Magic.

Mark pulled up his shirt collar and hurried through the worsening downpour, tucking the laptop case under his arm. At least that way it might get a little bit more protection than the flimsy case.

Up ahead, the village was a blur of faint lights. The fields on either side were already flooding at the edges, dotting the road with puddles.

A four-by-four slammed through the rain towards him and he darted to the side, onto the grass verge. When it passed, he stepped right in a puddle and slipped over. Mud splashed over his shoes and up his legs.

He shook as much mud from his foot as he could, sliding a big load towards the hedge, then stepped back onto the wet road and squelched towards the village, wishing he'd driven.

A howl came from behind him.

Mark hurried his pace.

Another howl, much closer.

Was it gaining on him? He didn't know, but he sped up anyway.

Answering calls came from another field, ahead of him and to the side.

He couldn't tell how far away they were, but his breathing was getting harder with each step. The rain was sluicing down his face, covering his mouth. At least his trousers and shoes were now pretty much clear of mud.

A dog howled in front of him this time.

He stopped dead, squinting through the rain, but struggling to see anything. His glasses were covered in drops, so he took them off, but that didn't help any. He rubbed the lenses and put them back on. Within seconds, they were dotted with rain again.

Three overlapping howls came from in front of him.

Mark's chest tightened and his heart stung. Another panic attack. Or an actual heart attack.

Dying in a country lane, miles from a hospital.

Such a stupid death.

Such a pointless death.

Maybe better than the fate Vic Hebden had in store for him, but he'd rather take his chances with that.

He needed to get back to the hotel, take sanctuary in his room.

Mark stopped, trying to see the dogs.

The wind picked up and blew the rain at his face, almost horizontal.

A dog emerged from the gloom, its fur bright orange, eyes glowing, almost smiling at him.

A long howl came from behind.

He turned back towards the castle. Two dogs blocked the way, standing in the middle of the road, their green eyes glowing.

He was surrounded.

He needed to get past them and get on to the village.

The wind buffeted him.

The dog in front of him turned and set off towards the settlement.

This was his chance.

Mark started running after it, pushing against the wind, thighs starting to burn, tasting blood at the back of his throat.

Something shot across the path ahead.

Mark stopped, toppling forward until he braced himself against the hedge. The barbs bit into his palms.

A yelp came from the side and the dog cowered by a gate, tail between its legs.

Mark seized the opportunity to put some distance between himself and the animal, powering on along the lane. He glanced behind him, heart pounding, and saw the dog trotting towards him, racing on the grass verge alongside the road, its feet double the speed of his own, slapping against the tarmac.

The wind worsened as the dog closed on him. Lights shone behind it, strobing through the rain. Bright, making it hard to see.

Mark ran on, acid burning in his legs, his heart feeling like it was going to explode.

The dog sped up, eating up the ground between them.

He ducked his head and shot through an open gate into a field.

The dog hadn't followed, but his feet were sloshing through ankle-deep mud.

Something clamped around his ankle.

Mark tumbled forward, landing on the dirt. His glasses flew off and landed in the dirt.

The dog chewed at his ankle, its jaw like a vice. Felt like it was trying to snap his foot off.

Mark kicked out, trying to shake it off, but it was gripping tight.

Then it let go.

He rolled over and grabbed his glasses, putting them on. He saw sky, heavy rain teeming down towards him.

The dog stepped towards him.

A gunshot rang out.

The dog stumbled and fell, over to the side.

Mark scrambled away from it, then rolled and got to his knees. He stood up and walked over to the edge of the field.

He slipped in the mud. His face hit the grass and he tasted damp earth.

An angry growl came from just behind him.

Another shot.

Then another.

He got up again, then splashed over to the gate and leaned against it.

No sounds, just the rain hitting the road. Gentle, almost soothing.

Mark twisted around a full three-sixty.

Another two dogs lay off to the side of the road, breathing slowly and heavily. Another streaked past him, heading towards the castle, but slowing with each step.

A man marched through the driving rain, a rifle resting on his shoulder. John Rennie, grinning. 'Evening, Mr Campbell.'

'Thanks.' Mark rubbed at his ankle, but the dog didn't seem to have broken the skin. Just enough to send him flying. 'You saved me.'

'Heard a load of howling.' Rennie crouched down next to the nearest dog and put a finger against its neck. 'These buggers come out in the rain, for some reason.'

Mark stepped closer. 'You killed it?'

'No, she's just sleeping.' Rennie stood up. 'Tranquilliser darts, but there's nothing tranquil about these animals.' He inserted another dart into his gun. 'I'll get these buggers down to Inverness first thing tomorrow.' He looked around at the other one, lying by the side of the road, then watched as the third drunkenly fell over. Rennie shook his head. 'Three of them. It's getting worse.'

'There were more.'

Rennie narrowed his eyes. 'Sure about that?'

Mark wasn't, but he'd heard three calls from ahead and another two behind. 'Another two. At least.'

'Christ.' Rennie reached into his jacket pocket for another pair of darts, then loaded them into his gun. 'Josh Urquhart told me he's seen a few up that way. Had a bit of a stramash here a few years back when one of their lot disappeared. He blamed it on the dogs, but we never found his body.'

'Just like Kay.'

'Mark, you get yourself back to the hotel. I'll see you in the bar. Mine's a Macallan, okay?'

'Sure.'

Rennie's eyes widened. 'Ah, shite.'

Bright lights blared through the haze.

Three dogs ran towards him, fangs bared.

'Go!' Rennie took aim and fired another round.

The lead dog skidded, falling head over heels.

The second slowed, but it swerved around Rennie's second shot.

Rennie looked over at Mark, eyes wide. 'Run!'

Mark didn't need to be told twice. He sprinted towards the village, his feet thundering against the road. He kept glancing behind him – no sign of the dog or Rennie in the heavy rain.

The village appeared in heavy judders, the long row of buildings lit up in the gloom, and Mark didn't slow until he was standing outside the hotel, doubled over, catching his breath.

Shearer the blacksmith waved as he left the church up ahead.

The general store glowed through the damp gloom.

Back towards the castle, lights burned through the misty rain.

He heard a throaty roar, some howls, then nothing.

Mark got out his phone to call Rennie.

But his phone wasn't in his pocket.

And he didn't have Kay's laptop.

43

Mark wrapped his shaking hands around the whisky glass and threw the dram down his throat. It burnt the sides, but it felt good. A layer of cotton wool around his head, shielding him from what had just happened. He sat in the corner, at a table with a view across the back lawn, cast in the damp twilight.

The only movement out there was crows swooping around in the aftermath of the rain.

No sign of the dogs.

Mark checked his watch. Ten minutes since he'd seen Rennie, since he'd been told to run, told to meet in the bar. And he had. Easily the furthest and fastest he'd run since school. He was shivering from cold, exertion and fear.

He should get out of his wet clothes, step into the shower and try to block it all out, but his nerves were shot.

If John hadn't intervened when he did, that dog would've gone for his throat.

He'd been so stupid going there on his own.

The bar door opened and Mark shot to his feet.

Raymond Shearer sloped in, shoulders hunched. He gave Mark a nod and sat down at a table. The church minister followed him in and sat opposite. Shearer chucked the dominoes onto the table and waved a hand over at Tam the barman.

Mark sat back down.

The only thing to do was follow John's orders. Wait it out. He'd turn up.

But what were those lights? A car? A torch? A fucking flying saucer?

Feral dogs, strange lights. What the hell was happening here? Was he losing his mind?

Probably.

He walked over to the payphone and he was buggered if he knew Olivia's mobile number. Shite. It was all stored on his phone. Everything was.

Tam the barman delivered two pints to Shearer's table, then meandered over to Mark. 'Can I get you another drink, sir?'

Mark stared at his empty glass. A pint of whisky wouldn't be enough.

Should he get another, though? Drinking to cope with acute stress was a cliché. Right? But did he care?

No.

No more booze, though.

He needed Kay's laptop. Needed to find her.

Rennie was the last person to see Kay. Okay so he'd lied, but he'd seen Kay leaving the village.

That laptop had all the clues.

Mark needed to get that machine.

He'd give Rennie another five minutes, then go look for him. Take a torch, wear that thick waterproof jacket.

The rain was off now, maybe he'd be able to find his phone too. Must be buried in the mud.

Magic.

'I'm good, thanks.' Mark handed Tam his empty glass and walked over to Shearer's table.

The blacksmith gave Mark a friendly nod. 'Evening, son.' He continued with the game. 'You watching the WWDC keynote tomorrow?'

'The what?'

'The Apple keynote.' Shearer shook his head. 'Never mind.'

Mark asked, 'Have either of you seen John Rennie tonight?'

Shearer frowned then laid out a domino. 'Not since earlier, son, when you were hounding the poor lad.'

Hardly hounding him...

Especially when Mark thought Rennie had been extremely inappropriate with his daughter. Not that he had any evidence to the contrary.

'Either of you got a phone number for him?' he asked.

They both shook their heads, more focused on their game than anything else.

'No need to have a phone up here.' Shearer placed a tile but didn't seem too happy with it. 'I rely on word of mouth. Everyone pops in here or Maggie's or my workshop once a week anyway. And nothing ever happens in Strathruthven.' He frowned at him now. 'You look like you've seen a ghost.'

'If you see or hear from John, tell him I was here.'

Shearer took a big drink of beer, soaking his beard with foam like it was bread dunked in cullen skink. 'Sure thing, son.'

Mark walked off through the door, then out into reception. Nobody in there, let alone John Rennie.

Maybe Rennie had just gone home instead of coming here.

But that shout... Those dogs. Those lights.

No, Mark needed to find him.

He stepped out into the warm night and plipped the locks on his car. He got in and drove off along the soggy high street, taking it slowly, keeping his eyes open for any sign of John Rennie. Any sign of those feral dogs. Anyone who might've seen him.

The church was dark, but the shop was still open. Empty, save for the bored kid behind the till, chewing away and staring at his phone. Maybe he'd seen something, but maybe not.

A four-by-four shot up from behind him, flashing lights, and doing way more than Mark's ten miles an hour.

He pulled in to let it past.

Rennie's cottage sat in darkness, set back from the road. The old telephone exchange lumbered next to it, lit up for no apparent reason.

Sod it.

Mark got out into the last gasps of the rain, now reduced to some thin drops hitting the soaked pavement. The wind had abated. He trudged up the pebble path and knocked on the door.

The cottage must've been done up recently, with a new front door and surround. Fresh screws yet to rust, smooth paint yet to flake. Curtains drawn on both sides, no sign of any lights on behind them. No sounds, except for the constant crowing.

Mark knocked again, but it was clear Rennie wasn't in. His hope that he'd gone home instead of to the hotel bar was seeming a forlorn one. He walked back to the gate and tried to look for a way around to the back garden.

The telephone exchange butted up against a stone wall about six foot from the cottage, but the tall fence didn't have a gate. The cottage leaned against its neighbour on the other side, meaning the only way to the back garden was through the house.

There must be a way in at the back.

Mark set off along the main road. The telephone exchange still seemed to be in operation, whirring and clicking, but it didn't look like anyone had been inside for years. The car park was big enough for ten, but empty, the tarmac all cracked and covered in weeds. Just a big puddle, really.

Mark rounded the building and got onto the path at the back, leading along the cottages towards the shop's rear entrance, which jutted out. The houses at the far end of town doubled up, with a well-lit paved street running between them, but this side was just one deep and only a soggy path.

John's cottage had eight-foot walls guarding the rear. And if there was one thing Mark couldn't do, it was climb.

Nothing ventured...

He tried the gate and it creaked open.

Magic.

The garden was like stepping into a show home. A tidy lawn, edged with planters filled with a few crops. Potatoes, the whisper of carrots and the balls of onions. In the middle was a wide patio set into a pebble bed filled with rattan furniture, dripping wet. A weeping pear and a birch sat either side of the stout back door.

Mark crunched over the path and tried the door.

Locked.

He peered in through the windows. A high-end kitchen, dark grey units, plain black worktop with a loaf of bread cooling on a wire rack. Oak dining table and chairs. Whisky bottle sitting on the counter.

No sign of anyone in there, alive or dead.

Mark trudged back down the path, but his shoes felt more like flippers, and splashed around back to the high street.

Another four-by-four shot past, but the windows were blackened.

Christ, who was in there? Still a while until the shooting season opened. Maybe some celebrities were in town for the ceilidh, though he couldn't imagine rappers doing the Gay Gordons.

Mark got in the car and drove off in the wake of the four-by-four.

The rain had cleared now, but the visibility was still low.

Mark scanned the dark road, trying to spot where his altercation happened. Where the dog attacked him. It all bled into one, just a single-track road with beech hedges on both sides. The occasional gate.

No sleeping dogs, no dead ghillies.

He reached the fork, where the road split between the local path around the loch and the road up to Reay on the far north coast.

The castle was lit up in the gloaming, set against a backdrop of the rugged hills and brutal rainclouds. The gate was shut and unwelcoming.

Mark got out and crossed the bridge, then pulled the bell. Aside from the lights in Ruthven, you could be forgiven for thinking you were a hundred miles from civilisation. The loch seemed swollen and heavy, like it was going to give birth soon. Just the splashing, the calls of the birds and the wind.

Nobody answered. All the activity an hour earlier and it looked like nobody was in now.

Mark walked back over the bridge to his car and got in.

What now?

He'd driven from the village to the castle and hadn't seen anything.

This area was miles and miles of empty fields, and miles and miles of loch. It'd take a lot of people a lot of time to scour that ground.

He started on a quick U-turn that wasn't so quick and took seven points to get around, but at least he was driving back up the road, taking it very, very carefully.

He was attacked next to the road, wasn't he?

On the verge. He went into a field, which must be where he'd lost the phone and laptop.

A flash of colour.

Mark got out and shone his torch over the ground, the damp grass covered with broken branches.

Nothing.

He aimed the light back towards the village. No sign of—

There.

Mark walked over and crouched next to it. A tranquilliser dart, with a fluffy red tail.

Rennie had shot and missed a dog. This must be that dart.

He turned and walked towards the village, training his torch across the ground, aided by his headlights.

An open gate at an intersection between two fields. No sheep or cattle, just grass and some wildflowers, bright yellows and pale blues in the vivid green.

A muddy path ran through.

Maybe the mud was his trail. Or Rennie's.

Mark shone his torch across it, finding some shapes that could've been footprints. Human and canine, probably, but they'd already been defaced by the rain until they were just lumps of earth.

He pointed at the grass verge, pressed flat into the shape of chunky tyres. He wasn't sure if that was recent, but he'd seen some lights.

All those four-by-fours coming through the village...

He didn't hear any engine sounds, but the rain was heavy. Slapping off the mud.

He looked across the dark fields. He could walk through the fields for hours searching for John Rennie, but he had no idea if he was even out there.

Maybe he was upstairs in the bath.

Or on his way down to Inverness, with his trailer filled with those dogs, ready for rehoming.

The rain was hitting hard again and it needed someone better than Mark to find John Rennie.

He needed to leave it until morning. Until Olivia and Adam came here.

He trudged over to the gate, wet mud slapping off his shoes, then he hit a dry patch.

Christ, there it was. Mark's phone sat in a puddle.

He grabbed it and wiped the dirt off enough to see the screen. It seemed okay, just caked in mud. The battery was almost empty.

A missed call and three texts, all from Olivia.

Aye, he needed to leave that until the morning.

44

The window rattled, shaking so hard it might collapse into the room and shower Mark with a thousand shards of glass.

He screwed his eyes shut, trying to ignore the maelstrom brewing out there. Trying to focus on the words. They weren't coming anywhere near fast enough, though he'd managed to write some good stuff from the perspective of the chief crofter, John. His daughter went missing and he blamed it on the clan patriarch.

It channelled a lot of rage and the words just flowed out of him.

But not just that, he also managed to include some of the history of the disaster. Real life.

He was exhausted. While he had another week to get Vic Hebden his money, Hamish Archibald was a sneaky bugger. Mark would have to stay on top of him to get the payment.

It'd be so much easier if he had Kay's laptop.

God, if he had her.

Mark took off his glasses and pinched his nose, then looked out of the window. No sign of a woman or a dog.

He'd definitely seen a woman out there, hidden in the trees.

Could it have been Kay?

He had no idea.

All he knew was he'd lost her laptop. The one thing he had on her last movements.

Rennie...

What he'd been cooking up with her. Stealing a document and trying to sell it to Ruthven. Or blackmailing Turnbull.

He didn't have to think too hard about why she was doing it. She knew he was in debt—had been asking Fiona and God knows who else—and, somehow, she'd stumbled upon this opportunity to make a ton of cash.

To repay his debt.

Christ.

Typical Kay.

Putting others ahead of her. Jumping into the deep end.

The walls closed in around him. His breathing increased, unsteady and uneven. Felt like his chest was going to explode.

Panic attack.

Mark pulled his eyelids shut, fighting against himself and his fear, but his body stopped responding, no longer trusting him. His breathing was out of control, his mouth taking in air that his lungs had no hope of processing.

He felt like he was in a tiny box, a metre square. Then smaller, squeezing him tight.

Focus.

He tried to focus on what he could control. His breathing, because he was close to hyperventilating.

He opened his eyes, then got up and stumbled around the room, looking for anything to help, anything solid to cling to, all the time fighting his body's natural instinct to close down.

A paper bag lay on the desk, still with a sandwich wrapper in it. Mark shook it out, his head light, small dots in his vision.

Dizzy.

He breathed in, squashing the bag, as slowly as he could, then out again.

The walls moved away from him and his vision started to clear.

He checked his heart rate on his watch and it was back under a hundred.

Control.

A woman stood on the lawn, in the shade of the tree. Her ringlets seemed dark brown in the low light.

Kay!

Mark cupped his hands on the window, desperate to get a better view. He blinked and the figure disappeared behind the tree.

He was sure it was her. Same as the previous night. Hiding among the foliage.

Mark went out into the corridor, making sure that he had his key, then raced down the stairs and headed through the dark restaurant, out into the garden.

He pressed his face against the glass.

No sign of Kay.

He twisted the key in the lock and opened the door.

The twilight was silent, like something sucked up all the sound like a sponge. A twig dropped from a branch without a sound. Not even a single crow call. The wind was gone too.

He stepped out onto the patio and took a few steps across the lawn.

Something shifted at the edge. Green eyes focused on him. The dog stepped onto the lawn and barked.

Sinews of muscle rippled under the shaggy red coat. No body fat. Claws digging into the mud at the edge of the lawn. It opened its mouth, revealing sharp teeth, strong enough to snap bones.

Was it one of the pack who chased him?

Mark stood there, transfixed by the creature.

The dog stood there too, mouth clamped shut, tail between its legs.

Submissive.

That was good.

It was a stray Scottish deerhound. Just needed to be fed.

Didn't it?

Mark stared hard at it until it looked away. He was in charge now, he was alpha. He teased his way forward over the grass, hand out.

The dog growled at him, low and harsh, but more a warning than a threat. It tilted its head to the side.

Mark crept forward again, focusing on the dog's every movement. The slight wag in the tail, the tongue hanging out of its mouth, all the time ready to shoot back to the door.

The dog yelped and trotted towards him. It brushed its head against his leg.

Mark kneeled down and stroked the dog, slowly, his fingers fighting against the damp fur. Poor thing had been out in the rain all night. He scratched it behind the ears and it tilted its neck to the other side now. The dog's eyes rolled back.

'You're not so bad, are you?' Mark laughed and kept stroking, kept scratching. For a stray, it seemed pretty clean, cleaner than most family pets he'd seen.

The faint brush of a car in the distance. The background noise of crows rose up again.

He looked around the garden, to where the figure had been. Two nights in a row now. The moonlight caught the spot perfectly, making it glow.

Nobody there, just his tired brain playing tricks on him. Seeing what he wanted to see.

Mark got up slowly. 'I need to go back inside, okay?' He backed away from the dog, then stepped inside the conservatory.

The dog followed him and was trying to come inside. Probably used to it, even expecting it. That water bowl in the bar. Scraps in the restaurant or from Janek's kitchen.

'Poor soul.' Mark kneeled down again and stroked its head. 'I'm sorry, but I just can't let you in. Not until later.'

The dog bared its teeth at him.

Mark jumped back, slammed the door and fumbled with the key until it locked.

The dog snarled and snapped at him.

The panic attack crept back, blurring the edges of his vision.

Mark raced back up to his room, feet hammering up the clattering steps, and wrestled his door open.

Aye, he was losing his mind.

45

Mark groaned as the daylight hit his face. He reached over and checked his watch, charging beside his bed. 6.49am.

His ankle ached like something had bitten it.

The dog.

Christ.

Approaching that one outside had been really stupid, especially after what happened. Even if it wasn't a member of the pack that chased him, it was still a wild animal. It almost turned on him. Could've had his throat.

Idiot.

Bloody idiot.

He got up and headed straight to the bathroom, pouring himself a glass of water and downing it in one. Still felt thirsty, so he drank another. He went back through with another glass of water and sat down at the desk.

He needed to finish this book.

No, he needed to find Kay.

He was sure it had been her standing on the lawn, under the tree.

But how could it have been? Why was she there? Why didn't

she speak to him?

Mark threw on some clothes, put his feet into his trainers, still damp. He could only see the dog snapping at him. Giant teeth, hungry. And the other one, pressing him down, going for his throat. He stumbled to his feet, left the room and raced down the steps two at a time. Reception was busier than he'd seen, but he had a clear run at the desk.

'Mr Campbell.' Harris sashayed his way over. 'How can I help?'

Mark leaned against the desk. The only thing holding him up. He felt like he'd died during the night. 'Have any of your other guests mentioned a woman in the garden last night?'

Harris folded his arms across his chest. 'Not to my knowledge, but it is rather early.'

Mark chanced a look at his reflection and, aye, he looked like a demon was eating his soul. 'Do you mind if I have a look outside?'

'We don't open that door until we start serving breakfast at seven.'

'It's five to.'

Harris peered down his nose at him. 'Well, if you insist.' He glanced over at his assistant. 'Agnieska, can you hold the fort for a few minutes, please?' He led Mark through the dining room. 'Do you think the woman you saw might be this Ms Campbell you've been searching for?'

Mark scratched at his neck. 'Not sure.'

Harris opened the conservatory door with a tut. 'I need to have a word with *her* for not leaving the keys in overnight.' He opened it and stepped out.

Mark followed him onto the patio and the crisp, cool air. The air was heavy with a hundred different plant perfumes, alive with birds and insects. Didn't feel like the same place as during the night.

He felt his vision blur and fought to control it.

Sod it, he stormed over the soaking grass towards the tree.

The soil was damp, but no footprints, human or otherwise.

'Oh, for crying out loud!' Harris was standing by the gate to the back lane, scowling at his feet. 'That flipping *dog*!'

The only footprint Mark could see was in the middle of a giant dog turd in the middle of the lawn. And the remainder on Harris's shoes.

'Sodding hell!' Harris rubbed his foot on the grass, then stepped inside. He hopped on one foot across the carpet, clutching his soiled loafer at arm's reach. 'Agnieska!' He made it into reception. 'I'll be a moment, but please call Mr Turnbull and arrange for the canine pest controller to come around, please? THANK YOU!' He hopped off behind his curtain.

Agnieska waited until Harris slammed the office door, struggling to hide her amusement. She pointed towards the bar. 'A friend of yours is waiting.'

Rennie?

Mark charged through to the bar, relief surging in his stomach.

Rennie was alive and well. Probably sucking on a thirty-year-old MacAllan for breakfast.

Adam was behind the counter, trying to pour himself a pint but just getting a blast of foam. He wore snow camouflage combat trousers and a too-cool-for-school rock band T-shirt. He looked over with a slack grin. 'Marky Mark.'

Shite.

'Surprised to see you here this early.'

Adam put the pint glass into a sink. 'Someone stole a load of animal feed from Turnbull overnight. Seven hundred kilos of free-range hen feed.' He gave a flash of his eyebrows. 'And your missus is worried about you.'

'Olivia?'

'Unless you've got another wife, champ.'

'You do know we're divorced, right?'

'Right, aye, but still. Once married, always married. Or something. Sure that's a phrase. Anyhoo, Libby in the station last night, asking if I thought you were okay.' Adam vaulted over the barrier with grace that belied his age. 'Are you okay, Mark?'

'I'm fine.'

'Sure about that?'

'Completely.'

'Well, Libby's worried about the pressure you're putting yourself under. Kept trying to call you, but you weren't answering.'

Mark looked away again, through the window to the lawn. The German couple were already out there, sipping coffees on the patio. Agnieska was on the lawn, clearing up the dog mess. 'I lost my phone.'

Adam frowned at him. 'What happened?'

'Just lost it.'

'Bloody hell, Mark. You went to the castle, didn't you?'

'Castle?'

'Libby told me you were determined to go. She advised you to wait. Kept calling you.'

Mark stared at him just as hard as Adam was staring at him. 'Okay, so I did. Lady Ruthven gave me Kay's laptop.' He had to look away. 'But I lost it.'

'You lost *that* as well as your phone? What the hell's going on?'

'I must've dropped them when the dogs chased me.'

'*Dogs?*' Adam screwed up his face. 'Mark, you've gone mental, haven't you?'

'No!' Mark waved his arm around the bar. 'You've seen that big thing in here, right? It's like something out of *The Howling*. There was a whole group of them chasing me. They're *massive*.'

Adam roared with laughter. 'So you were hunted by a pack of werewolves?'

Mark glared at him. 'I'm being serious here.'

'Oh great, so you *do* think they're werewolves.' Adam laughed, but his eyes were ice cold. 'Jesus, Mark. Libby's right. You are cracking up. It'll be lesbian vampires next.'

Mark stared at the wood on the table top.

He wasn't okay. Not sleeping, racing up against the hard brick wall of a deadline that wouldn't shift. Owing money to someone who was going to break him, physically and financially.

And his daughter was missing.

How could anyone be okay with that?

He needed to talk to someone about this. Covering it over was getting nowhere.

Mark sat down at a table and swallowed, then pointed through the door to the garden. 'I think I saw Kay last night. Outside, hiding behind the tree.'

Adam's eyes widened. 'Mark, can you tell me where you're sourcing the magic mushrooms? Hallucinogens are all well and good, but I don't think you should be taking them in your state.'

'I'm serious. She was hiding under a tree. I went out and a dog emerged from the bushes. Same breed as the ones that chased me last night. One of them almost...'

But he couldn't speak any more. The lump in his throat was like he'd swallowed a grapefruit.

'I thought you were supposed to be an intellectual, Mark. Wild dogs trying to kill you? Dude!' Adam raised his hands, palms out. Mischief twinkled in his eyes. 'This is all a smokescreen, isn't it? You just happening to stroll over at that great big castle on your own of an evening is entirely innocent, eh?'

'Shut up.'

'Mark, you need to level with me. Are you shagging Lady Ruthven?'

'No!' Mark pushed up to standing, fists clenched. 'Of course I'm not. You were the one visiting her yesterday. Sure that's innocent?'

'Mark. I was there asking her about your kid.' Adam rested a hand on his arm. 'I'm trying to help, okay? I know it's hard. Can't imagine what you're going through. And I know you think I'm a dick, but—'

'I don't.'

'You do. Admit it. But I'm trying, okay? Trying to find your kid. That's all. That's all that's going on.'

Mark slumped back in the chair. 'Those dogs... John Rennie tranquillised a few of them. I was supposed to meet him in here afterwards, but he didn't show. I checked here, then drove out to the castle. No sign of him anywhere, but I did find my phone.'

'Then we need to find him.' Adam set off back towards reception. 'Let's see where Libby's got to.'

46

Adam led along the high street, talking into his phone as they walked. 'Come on, Libby, it'll be fun.' He laughed. 'Somebody's got to, eh?' Another laugh. 'Aye, he's with me.' He held out his phone.

Mark took it off him and the screen showed an old photo of Olivia as a teenager, looking coquettish and cool. Her hair a few shades darker, with vampish makeup.

Adam must've scanned that from a print and applied it to her contact entry.

Jesus.

Mark put the phone to his ear. 'Liv, it's Mark. Where—'

'At the police station in Brora. Kay made some calls to someone here.'

'Oh. Thank you. Anything on Kay?'

'No. And that's worrying me. But I'll do everything I can. Okay?'

'Thank you, Liv.'

'Why haven't you been answering your phone, Mark?'

'I dropped it in a field last night. Lost it.'

'Really. Because last time we spoke, you were heading to the castle to speak to Lady Ruthven.'

'Right. I went there and got Kay's laptop. But I've lost the bloody thing.'

'Mark... I told you to wait.'

'Sorry, I thought—'

'Don't think. Let Adam do that for you, please. He knows the local area; he knows John Rennie. Something feels off about this whole thing, help him find it.'

'Will do.' Mark handed the phone back to Adam. 'Here.'

He took it. 'Aye?' He laughed. 'I'll kick it for you.' Another laugh. 'Aye, I'll keep you updated.' He tossed it in the air, then pocketed it. 'Well, you better hope that laptop turns up.'

Mark ignored it and walked up to Rennie's front door, giving it a hard knock. Place seemed just as empty as the previous night. And no answer. 'Can you get in here?'

Adam looked back along the high street, forehead creased. 'It's a grey area.' He ran a hand down his face. 'If John's lying dead in his bed, I'd be okay. But if he's not? I've broken and entered. Without justifiable cause.'

'Even if he was chased by a pack of wild dogs?'

'Like I said, grey area. Assuming there even are any dogs.'

A lorry was causing chaos this side of the hotel, probably a delivery for Harris. Or...

Mark charged off in its direction.

Ruthven General Store was open. Sheets of that yellow stuff in the window, not that there was anything that would fade in direct sunlight, just some months-old magazines and cans of energy drink. Not even raspberry and cheddar WakeyWakey.

Inside, a couple of locals stopped talking to eye up Mark. Both male, both in their forties. One went behind the till and stuffed his thumbs into the hoops on his beltless jeans. He wore a black-and-white polo shirt that made him look like a giant barcode. 'Looking for anything in particular, sir?'

Mark stepped inside. 'Do either of you know John Rennie?'

'Who doesn't know that loonie? Comes in to get his paper first thing every day.' Barcode scowled at Mark. 'Why, who's asking? You a cop?'

'Just a friend. Wondering if he's got his paper this morning, that's all.'

'Well, no. He hasn't been in. Dickhead owes me fifty quid in dues, so I'll batter his arse when I catch up with him.'

Adam rested his hands on his hips. 'When did you last see him?'

'You sound like he owes *you* money or you're trying to score drugs off the felly.'

Adam frowned. 'Does he deal drugs?'

'Not that I know. Why are you so keen?'

'Mark here was supposed to meet him last night.'

'Well, John works over at Turnbull's. Might be worth asking him if he's seen him?'

'Good idea.' Adam left the shop. 'They haven't seen him, Mark.' He fixed him with a tight stare. 'You're looking for your keys where the light is rather than where you dropped them.' He patted Mark's arm. 'Come on, let's go see where you dropped the keys.' He crossed the road and got into his Subaru.

Mark followed him over and got in. 'I went there last night, so I'm—'

'Aye, but Libby asked me to scour it again with you.' Adam turned the ignition and The Zeroes burst out of the speakers. That really annoying single. Not what Mark had expected. Adam adjusted the volume up, then drove off down the lane running towards the castle, the car rocking as he navigated the potholes. He kept it at grandfather speed, leaning forward and visually scouring the fields on both sides.

Mark kept his eyes on the road, trying to spot where he'd last seen Rennie. There, that gate just up ahead. 'That's where I saw him.'

Adam pulled in, then killed the engine and, mercifully, the music.

Mark got out and the air was already warm from the bright sun. The mud from last night's downpour had dried to a thick cake. His chase the previous night hadn't got him very far at all, just a few hundred metres away from Ruthven Castle, looming over the loch, glowing in the early morning light. The sun was already high above the hills behind.

'What the hell's this?' Adam snapped on a blue plastic glove and crouched down, then held something up. A long needle with a fluffy tail like a kid's doll. 'A tranquilliser dart?'

'I found one last night too. Rennie shot one and missed the dog.'

Adam got to his feet and stuffed the dart into a bag. 'Was it in human or wolf form?'

'Seriously.'

'Sorry.' Adam popped the dart into a bag. 'But a couple of things stick out. If you found one and I've found one, then he's missed *twice*. And if he managed to hit any of the others, then those darts are only good for a few hours at the most. Need to get the dog into a cage quick smart.'

Mark spotted some footprints leading through a field, heading away from the gate. Big enough to be Rennie's boots but faded with the rain, so hard to tell for sure. He followed them, but soon lost them in the quagmire.

He got a flash of Rennie being pulled apart by wild dogs. His body lying somewhere, bleeding out.

'What's this?' Adam was over in the middle of the field now, staring into a patch of grass. He raised up a tranquilliser gun, clanking and clattering, and still loaded with a dart. 'Well, well. He's dumped this and bombed it. Question is, where did he go? And did the dogs catch him?'

'What do you think?'

Adam inspected the rifle. 'I think we need to talk to his boss.'

47

A manservant showed Mark and Adam into the same room as the previous afternoon.

William Turnbull sat in the same armchair, head stuck in a large document. He raised a finger but didn't look up. 'Just one minute.'

While the day was much brighter, this room felt colder and more sinister, the flickering fire casting long shadows across the parquet floor. Through the window, the garden seemed less lush and more overgrown.

Two dogs lay at his feet, not so different from the sort that had plagued Mark the previous night.

Mark stopped on the threshold, his chest tight, his hands trembling.

He could see the dog, charging through the rain after him. Growling. Snarling. Biting his leg.

But these were pets, asleep at their master's feet. Didn't look like they'd be attacking anyone anytime soon.

Mark sat opposite and cleaned his glasses on his T-shirt. They still didn't sit quite right after all that chasing around in the rain. Must've bent the legs when he fell.

Turnbull put aside the document and took off his own glasses, folding them and putting them in his shirt pocket. 'Gentlemen, it's a frantic time just now, so this must be brief. You getting anywhere?'

Adam was standing by the fire and gave a polite smile. 'It's not about that, Bill.'

'Oh?'

'Listen, I've got some lads out searching for your hen feed, but that van seems to have vanished off the face of the Earth.'

'Just bloody bought the thing too. Archie and young Jack will be scarred for years by six buggers with guns holding them up.'

'We're doing all we can. Promise.' Adam took the chair next to Mark. 'Anyway. John Rennie works for you, right?'

Turnbull nodded, though his face filled with a dark expression. 'You think John's involved?'

'No, no. Just wondering if he's turned up for work today?'

His temper was fizzing like the fresh log on the fire. 'I'm not the sort to keep a sheet of paper on my desk with everyone's start time and then religiously check it.'

Adam smiled wide, like he was trying to disarm him. 'Not implying you are, Bill. Just need a word with him.'

'Well, he should be here by now.' Turnbull picked up an industrial-looking mobile phone and held it to his ear. Where modern smartphones were thin and sleek, this was like a clapped-out tractor, its dark blue case inches thick. 'Hi Dougal.' He paused. 'Aye, I'm sure it has. If you could arrange to see that it's fixed ahead of the ceilidh tonight, then... Aye. Listen. Has John turned up today? Rennie. If you could, thanks. No? Any idea where he is? If you could. Obviously after you've fixed the signage. Okay, thanks, bye.' He ended the call and looked over at Adam. 'John hasn't turned up today.'

Mark ran a hand through his hair. Kay missing, now Rennie. 'He does work a Saturday, aye?'

'At this time of year? God aye.' Turnbull glowered. 'Unlike most farms in the area, I've got a sizeable arable crop and it's getting harder and harder to source quality labourers who're prepared to work the hours necessary for a good harvest. And

John's one of the very best.' He shifted his gaze over to Adam. 'You think something's happened to him?'

'Potentially.' Adam was standing tall but it was hard to project professionalism wearing a T-shirt that read 'I Am Less Than Nothing'. He hefted up the tranquilliser gun and tossed it over, the rifle rattling as Turnbull caught it. 'Found this in a field this morning. Is it his?'

Turnbull inspected the weapon, turning it over and over. 'Well, it's technically mine, but aye.' He leaned down and scratched behind the ears of one of his dogs. 'He uses this gun for catching the occasional stray.'

'Mark saw him last night, chasing off some wild dogs.'

'We're plagued by the buggers.' He raised a hand. 'All in accordance with guidelines set down by both the SSPCA and the local council. It's something I ask him to do for me when he's got a spare moment. We usually put it down to holidaymakers losing their dogs, which then go feral.'

'But those would be labradoodles and what have you.' Mark sat forward. 'The ones I saw were deerhounds.' He pointed at the animals at Turnbull's feet. 'Like yours.'

'Ah, well, Misty and Rosie here are Irish *wolf*hounds, you see. An extinct breed that was restarted by breeding some Highland dogs with Great Danes. They're a much bigger breed than a deerhound. Much more trainable.'

'And who's doing the trai—'

Adam cut in, 'Do you know anyone with a pack of wolfhounds, Highland or Irish?'

'What goes on behind closed gates, eh?' Turnbull laughed, then it turned into a grimace. 'Listen. John Rennie is an extremely experienced dog handler. He will be fine.'

'Regardless of his experience, Bill, his number might be up.'

The manservant returned with a tray laden with a silver service.

Adam's phone rang. 'Better take this.' He put it to his ear and walked out of the room. 'Boss, aye.'

The servant poured out a cup for Mark. 'Milk, sir?'

'Please.' Mark waited then took the cup and sat back in the armchair.

The last time he'd seen Rennie, he'd...

Been charged by three dogs. He took one down, missed another and the other dogs...

One thought dug into his mind:

It could've been me.

That slavering dog would've bitten out his throat.

Rennie had saved him.

And now he was, what, dead? Or missing?

What if that's what happened to Kay too?

Adam's voice echoed in the hallway, but Mark couldn't pick out the words.

Mark sipped his coffee. Far too weak. 'John seems like a good guy. Anyone he's particularly close to?'

'A few friends in the village, but John lives a solitary life. No wife or kids.' Turnbull gave a wry chuckle. 'Certainly none that I'm aware of.'

'What about family?'

'His sister used to stay in a cottage on my estate, but she lives with her daughter over in Canada now.' Turnbull picked up his phone and thumbed the keys. 'It turns out this machine, for all its good sides, doesn't have her number stored on it.'

Mark drank more coffee. 'Shame.'

'Is there any word on your daughter?'

'Nope. Still hasn't surfaced.' Mark grimaced. 'Starting to wonder if she will. Been a few days since she was last seen. And John Rennie going missing too. Makes you think, eh?'

Turnbull rested his cup on the side table. 'Quite.'

'Thing I can't get out of my head is why anyone would target Kay. All I can think of is she was asking the wrong people the wrong questions. And they didn't take too kindly to it.'

'Mm.'

Aye, he wasn't getting anything out of him. 'Shame about your hen feed. That what your guys were making with the angle grinder?'

'I wish.' Turnbull laughed. 'No, that was a grinder-mixer. We use it to create animal feed from—' He smiled. 'You lowlanders probably don't want to know.'

'I can imagine.'

'It's for cattle. Hen feed is from grain. Have to get that brought up in the van.'

Mark held his gaze for a few seconds. 'I've been digging into the *Laird of Wedale* and—'

'This again.' Turnbull looked ready to up and leave. 'Like I told you yesterday, there's nothing in it. *Nothing.*'

'What if there was?'

'There's nothing!' Turnbull flicked a dismissive hand towards Mark. 'Sitting there, drinking my coffee and accusing my ancestors of ridding our lands by murdering people...'

'I'm not saying anything like that.'

'No, but she did. Sat there. Saying our shepherds butchered our clansmen. Buried them in a mass grave!'

'Did she have proof?'

'Of course not! Because it's bullshit!' Turnbull cracked his cup down on the saucer, spilling coffee onto the side table. 'We tried to give honest folk a new life down in the Southern Uplands. What happened on that boat was a tragedy my ancestors have taken to their graves. But they weren't *our* responsibility.'

Mark connected a couple of dots, though. The document Kay got from Rennie, stolen from the Turnbull family archive, if it proved the atrocity happened that way... 'I appreciate this is digging up old history, but this is a chance to absolve your ancestors of any lingering guilt. If there was a possibility—'

'It's a *myth* and I won't have anyone come in here, dredging it all up! My father thought he'd put an end to it once and for all. Back in the Sixties, some cavalier *pseudoscientist* wrote about how the Clan Turnbull could've been responsible for that ghastly act.'

The book Séan had sold Mark, surely. Which he hadn't read.

'Well, it stinks. There's no evidence of any mass grave and it's an insult to the memory of those lost in a tragedy.'

'What if a document proved—'

'A document?' Turnbull shot to his feet. 'What do you know about any documents?'

Mark tried to keep his voice level. 'A document that proved a cover-up of this murder, in collusion—'

'Is this what your bloody book's about? Eh? Printing lies about my family? Because if it is, I'll see you in court.'

'I'm just saying. If there's a—'

'Get out!' Turnbull pointed to the door. 'You're as bad as your daughter! Get the fuck out of my house, you lying bastard!'

Mark stayed sitting, even reached for his coffee. 'Seems like you've been triggered by—'

'*Triggered?*' Turnbull walked over and grabbed Rennie's dart gun. 'I'll show you triggered!' He hurled it across the room. It slammed into the wall above Mark's head, dislodging a deer head. 'Accusing my family of being murderers? Who the fuck do you think you are?'

'The truth will come out.'

Turnbull gritted his teeth and pointed at the door again. 'Get! Out!'

48

Mark waited in the sunshine, crouching in the shade of a tall hedge, a million thoughts whirring through his brain.

Turnbull was looking down from his drawing room window, sipping coffee, scowling at him.

Aye, there was a man with skeletons in his closet.

Had Mark been a daft bastard in accusing him?

Sod it, he had a friendly neighbourhood police officer with him. And one down in Brora.

Though he couldn't see Adam. Or his car.

Stuck miles from Ruthven. Just a long, winding lane through the back end of beyond. Might be fifteen miles back to the village.

A dirty van pulled up and men in overalls hopped out, then lugged bags of equipment into some farm buildings. Within seconds, the angle grinder, or whatever Turnbull called it, whirred up to a screech.

Christ, was that where Kay was? Turned into pig feed?

Something crunched across the gravel towards Mark. Then a roar, accompanied by the skank of the Zeroes.

Adam was behind the wheel of his Subaru. A man out of time. He stopped and reached over to open the door.

Mark got in and didn't have his belt plugged in until Adam had hit sixty along the single-track road. 'Everything okay?' he asked.

'Not really. Boss isn't happy. Two missing persons in the same village... That's suspicious as hell. My DI's threatening to head up from Inverness to supervise. Last thing I need. Could hear him cracking his knuckles down the phone line at having something to do other than those robberies. So he wants me to report to Tain.'

'Why Tain?'

'That's where Turnbull's van went missing.' Adam slowed to take a nasty bend. 'Bill say anything after I left?'

'Not really.' Mark stared out of the window at the small river trailing the road a few hundred yards away. 'Just talked about coffee.'

'Coffee?'

'He's not a fan of tea.'

'Right. Didn't mention anything about Rennie?'

'Not to me.'

Adam reached over to turn the air conditioning up. 'Rennie might be dead. You know that, right?'

It hit Mark in the face like a sledgehammer. 'So I could be the last person to see him alive?'

'Except for his killer, aye.' Adam glanced over as he took a sharp turning. 'Assuming it wasn't a werewolf.'

Mark tried to laugh it off, but it didn't work. 'Last night, I was cornered and one of those dogs was going for me. John Rennie rescued me. The dogs were the same breed as Turnbull's, more or less.'

'All of them?'

'I think so.'

'Right, so Irish wolfhounds.' Adam slalomed around a bend. 'Quite a trainable dog, if you get them young. I need to speak to whoever owns any around here.'

The lights.

Headlights or torches. Maybe what Mark had seen was

whoever owned the pack, whoever trained them to kill, watching them attack Mark. When Rennie intervened, they went after him.

'This is messed up.' Mark ran a hand through his soaking hair, slick from sweat. 'You seem to know him.'

'Turnbull? Let's just say I've had dealings with him over the years. If anyone knows what's going on here, it's him.'

'Thing is.' Mark took a deep breath, trying to decide whether to tell the truth. Sod it. 'I asked Turnbull about that document and he lost his shit. Threw the gun at the wall. Asked me to leave.'

'That'll be why I didn't get let back in, then.' The corner of Adam's mouth turned up into a sly grin. 'Thought you just talked about coffee?'

'Well, no. It was mostly about that document.'

'Libby told me all about it, so there's no need to repeat it.' Adam looked over right on the crest of another bend he was taking way too fast. 'You believe it?'

Mark shrugged. 'Until I've seen it for myself, I can't say. If it's what Rennie seemed to think, then Turnbull would lose all this land.'

They crested over a hill and looked down on Strathruthven, the glen spreading out wide, trapped between two hill ranges.

Adam asked, 'You think Turnbull's ancestors committed that atrocity?'

'I'm not a legal expert, but I've seen cases where land had changed hands because of ancient ancestral feuds. Rennie told me he took that document. Surely killing him is...' He had a cold sweat up his back. 'Is that enough to kill over?'

Adam shrugged. 'Time we had a little look inside Rennie's cottage, eh?'

'Aren't you due back in Tain?'

'Boss drives like my old man. He'll think I'll be ages getting back down there. Take me hardly any time in this bad boy.' He reached over and turned up the music.

49

Mark stood outside the telephone exchange, the machinery clattering away in the morning sun. He checked his phone, but there was nothing from Olivia.

The lorry from earlier was still in the village, but was now trundling along the high street, heading towards the castle.

Mark had to turn away to avoid the blast of bitter diesel fumes. 'What's the plan? Smash in a window?'

'I've got ways and means.' Adam walked up the cottage's front path.

The door opened and Olivia stepped out. 'Heard you invoking the Ways And Means Act, eh?'

Adam stood there like a wee boy caught with his hand in the biscuit tin. 'You got a warrant or something?'

'Not quite, but the trace on Rennie's mobile showed a last-known location of inside this house. I got us approval to search from your DI.'

'So let's search it.'

Olivia pushed him inside, then jabbed a finger at Mark. 'Stay there.'

'Come on, Liv.'

'Cops only.' Olivia was glaring at him. 'You can't help yourself, can you?'

'Me? What?'

'Adam told me you got chucked out of Turnbull's.'

'I did nothing!'

'Mm.'

'I just asked him some questions, Liv. That's it.'

'Mark, that's not your job. Adam and I are taking time out to help you find your daughter. Neither of us have to get involved, you know? And you getting stuck in isn't making things easier.'

And she was right. Mark was up shit creek and forget about a paddle, he didn't have a canoe.

'Now, you can bottle all this shite up, or you can talk to me. What's going on?'

'Nothing, I swear.'

'And if they don't believe me now...'

She disappeared inside but hadn't closed the door.

Mark stayed outside. He peered through the window. A poky wee hallway, cream walls and oatmeal carpet. Chintzy landscape paintings. Immaculate, like a show home, not a ghillie's bachelor pad. The place was very expensively done up, probably by William Turnbull rather than John Rennie, unless the ghillie game was more lucrative than Mark imagined. A neat row of shoes and boots over by the door, something for any occasion.

Adam patted her arm, then clumped up the stairs.

Mark switched to the living room window. The rest of the floor was an open plan living room space, with a door through to the kitchen Mark had peered into last night. A curtain flapped in the breeze by the back door.

Trouble with old cottages was the windows let in bugger all light, even at this time of year.

Olivia flicked the switch on the wall and the spotlights glittered into life.

The resting loaf of bread was now on a wooden bread board, with the heel cut off. In the middle of the kitchen table, a whisky glass sat next to a bottle of Talisker, both half empty.

Someone had been here.

Rennie?

A chair was kicked over in the corner.

Footprints led over from the door, muddy, dotted with red.

Olivia opened a door and went through another door.

Holy hell, Kay's laptop bag was resting against the front floor, smeared in mud. Both of them had missed it.

What should he do?

He should give it to Adam or Olivia, get their police forensics guys to work away at it.

But...

It was technically *his* laptop. He'd paid for it, he'd set it up for Kay. Knew the password, assuming she hadn't changed it. And if it could lead him to finding her?

No, he had to hand it over.

But if she'd been taken by Vic Hebden, maybe there was some clue on it?

Assuming it survived all that rain and mud, he could get the machine back to the hotel, power it up and check what she had. Quick and easy. A surface check.

Then hand it over and let the cops do their deep searches.

Right?

Mark opened the door wider, grabbed the laptop bag and stepped back out to the front of the cottage.

Nobody on the street, no second-floor windows overlooking him, so he dropped the laptop in the middle of a bush.

The door opened and Olivia shouted, 'Adam!'

A floorboard creaked upstairs.

'Found these.' Olivia stepped out of the bathroom carrying some muddy clothes in gloved hands. 'Shower's been used too.'

She wasn't looking at Mark, though. He'd got away with it.

'So he's been here?' Adam hopped down the stairs and walked over to her. 'His bed hasn't been slept in.'

'I've got something.' Mark stayed outside, but pointed at the table. 'Last night, I had a look through the window. The bread was intact, no whisky glass. I think he's come back, had a whisky, a slice of bread, then...' He shrugged. 'Then someone came in? Attacked him?'

'Stay there.' Adam crept over to the door, avoiding the muddy prints, and tried the door. 'Thing's locked.' He frowned at Olivia. 'How did *you* get in?'

Olivia waved over to the front door. 'Found some keys under a cheeky little gnome.'

Mark hadn't seen one. He hoped it was far enough away from the bush he'd stashed the laptop in.

Adam looked around the room. 'So he's been kidnapped, right?'

'Looks that way.' Olivia walked over to the door. 'So. He got back here, bleeding over the tiles. Thought he'd locked the door behind him. Had a whisky, bit of a snack, then got in the shower. Came through, but someone was here. Think they broke in?'

Adam scowled. 'Could be someone he knew. If a mate came to your door like that, you'd be cool, right?' His gaze swept around the room like a bird of prey shooting between targets. 'I mean, you'd be a bit annoyed at that time of night, but what I mean is, if I was wearing a balaclava, you'd lose your shit and try to hide. Or cause a scene. But all we've got is an upturned chair. Right?'

Mark said, 'There's not exactly a lot of furniture in there.'

'True. Okay, we need to get out of here.' Adam led through, opened the front door and stepped outside. He waited for Olivia to come out then shut it. 'That's looking like a crime scene, Libby. No body, but still. I'm not happy about it.'

'Agreed.' She stared off towards the castle. 'Better report this to your boss.'

'Heading to see him down in Tain. There's a lad in the village coming over to guard the place.'

Mark tried to avoid looking into the middle of the bush. Or anywhere near it. 'Who could've done it, though?'

Olivia said, 'You're still thinking Turnbull, aye?'

Mark frowned. 'Still?'

'Well, aye,' said Adam. 'He owns a lot of land around here.

Plenty spaces to hide, say, stolen lorries like I've been investigating.'

'Why would he...' Mark thumbed at the cottage. 'Do that, though?'

'Word is Turnbull's involved with some crooked people. And John Rennie's notoriously loose-lipped, especially with members of our profession. Maybe Turnbull got wind of that. Maybe he's taken him?'

Olivia checked her watch. 'Christ, I really need to hoof it.' She stormed off down the path and swung around, making an 'I'll phone you' gesture with her hand to Adam, then ran over the road towards her car.

All Mark could think of was that Rennie had been abducted, taken from his home.

Because of a document.

Because of his daughter.

Finding Rennie meant finding Kay.

And maybe she was right, maybe he did need to be honest for once in his life.

He followed Olivia over and stopped her reversing.

She wound down the window. 'You want to get run over?'

'There's something I need to tell you.'

50

Olivia looked up at the bright blue sky, releasing a deep breath. 'Let me get this straight. You borrowed money from a loan shark to pay for our divorce? And now he's going to take your house and break your legs unless you pay him back?'

'No, I don't think it.' Mark kept his arms folded. 'He will.'

'You get worse, you really do.' She pushed his chest, hard enough that he wobbled. 'Why didn't you tell me?'

'Because... Because I can't...'

'What's his name?'

'Liv, I can't tell you that. I'm worried he has Kay. And you being you, you'll head down there, cause trouble.' Mark felt that lump in his throat again, but it was like a melon now. He swallowed it down, though his throat felt all tight and sore. 'And I'll never hear from Kay again.'

'Jesus Christ.' She looked over at the hotel. 'And he was in there?'

'Correct.'

'Mark, if he has her, surely he'd have let you know. Use it as another threat against you.'

Mark took off his glasses and pinched his nose. 'I wish I could believe that, Liv. I really do.'

'Mark, how did he find you?'

'Said he's got eyes everywhere. Ferries. Hotels. You name it.'

'That's total bollocks.'

'Knows where I am all the time. Knows where my car is. Liv, that means he's got cops on his payroll!'

'No, it doesn't.' She set off across the street to the hotel. 'Come on.'

Mark glanced back at the bush, at Kay's laptop bag. He should tell Olivia.

But instead, he followed her.

She was crouching behind Mark's car, feeling under the wheel trim. She pulled out a device. 'He planted a tracker on your car, Mark.' She went around the rest of it, back to where she started. 'I've removed it for you and it doesn't look like there's any more.' She got to her feet. 'You of all people shouldn't believe in magic. If someone knows where you are, it's because they've stuck something on your car or hacked your phone.' She held out a hand. 'Give.'

Mark unlocked his mobile and passed it over.

She tapped some text in, then waited. 'Your phone's clear.'

'That was quick.'

'Those models are totally locked down. Very hard to hack it.' She passed it back. 'Who was it?'

Should he tell her?

Really, he had no choice. And he felt a little bit freer now.

'Vic Hebden.'

Her eyes bulged. 'You're even more stupid than I thought. How?'

'I bumped into him in a casino and one thing led to another.' Mark was sweating again. 'Tell me he's not got Kay.'

'Unlike you, I don't lie.' She got out her own phone and put it to her ear. 'Adam, does the name Vic Hebden mean anything to you?' A sour expression filled her face. 'Interesting. Who do I need to speak— Oh, I know him. Sure. Okay, I'll catch you later.'

She ended the call and pocketed her phone. 'Well, Hebden's on their radar up here. A known associate of William Turnbull.'

'Shite.'

'Must be why he's up here.' She sighed. 'Thank you for eventually telling me, I suppose.' Another sigh, even bigger. 'Right. I'm heading to Inverness to speak to Adam's mate. This could be part of that robbery spree. Where will you be?'

'You mean I'm not invited?'

She patted his shoulder. 'Mark, I think this is getting more serious than I realised, so I need you to keep at arm's reach. Okay?'

He glanced over to the cottage. 'Fair enough. I'll get my head down in my hotel room. Do some writing. Maybe even finish the chunk I'm on, go through it all and send it off to Fiona.'

'Well, good luck with it.' She got in her car and started the engine, then drove off with a wave.

Mark walked over to the hotel entrance, watching her leave the village.

He looked at the cottage. A beanpole cop was talking to Adam outside, then they went in.

Mark ran over the road and reached into the bush.

Still there.

He grabbed the laptop bag and hotfooted it over to the hotel, keeping an eye on the road.

Barcode the shopkeeper was outside, sucking on his vape stick, but was more engrossed in his phone than Mark's antics.

Mark slipped inside reception and stopped by the desk. He rang the bell, eager to get upstairs.

A bustle came from the bar area, loud chattering. The gossip of a village on a Saturday morning.

Mark had no idea why.

'Ah, Mr Campbell.' Harris scurried through from the bar, rubbing his hands on his kilt. 'Sorry, but your room's being cleaned just now. Would it be okay for you to wait ten minutes?'

No, it wouldn't.

He needed to get up the stairs, power up the laptop and find out what Kay had been working on.

Any clues as to her whereabouts.

See if Rennie's story about a mystical document bore any fruit.

See if she'd been in contact with Vic Hebden.

But he smiled and said, 'Sure, that's fine.' He glanced over at the bar, just as Raymond Shearer wandered through. 'Busy today.'

'Double-edged sword,' said Harris. 'A lot of early drams and toasts before the ceilidh tonight at the castle. And we're so understaffed that muggins here has to serve teas and coffees himself. Myself. Anyway, can I fetch you a pot?'

'Sure. Coffee would be great. Thanks. And no rush.' Mark followed him through, busy as a writers' conference hotel bar at three in the morning and the faces were just as red, the raised voices echoing around the space.

Be a surprise if any of them made it to the Gay Gordons, let alone the Dashing White Sergeants.

Mark found the only free table, over in the corner, surrounded by a banquette. He slid around it, then rested the laptop bag on the wood.

'Mr Campbell.'

Mark expected to see Harris with his coffee.

Vic Hebden stood there, clutching a whisky glass, misery in his eyes. 'How the devil are you?'

'I'm fine.' Mark sat back in the seat, feet tapping. 'You still here?'

'Me? Oh aye. Enjoying a nice wee whisky.' Vic slid in next to Mark. 'That you getting my money?'

A bead of sweat slid down Mark's spine. 'I'm trying to.'

'Good man.' Vic splashed the whisky down his throat. 'I read your last one on the way up here. Bit far-fetched, wasn't it?'

'What, the cult? That was pretty much what happened to me.'

'Aye, sure thing.' Vic laughed. 'Just make sure you keep your fiction on the page.' He slapped Mark's back. 'Now, less chatty chatty, more typey typey.' He slid out and walked over to the crowd by the bar.

Mark gripped the edge of the table and tried to stabilise himself.

Christ.

He blinked hard a few times, trying to push the panic attack away. Felt like his chest was being hit by a hammer.

Focus.

He took out Kay's laptop and opened it.

Nothing happened.

He pressed the power button. Again, nothing happened.

Magic.

It had worked last night, but now it was, what? Broken? Or just out of charge.

He searched through the bag for a cable.

Bingo.

Not too much of a stretch from the power socket, so he plugged it in, then pressed the button again.

Nothing.

Magic. Just bloody magic.

Shearer walked over and stared at the machine like it was from the future. 'You okay there, son?'

Mark held the power button down now, but still nothing happened. Just a blank screen. Not blank, just black. Nothing. Empty, no light coming from it. 'Thing's bloody broken and I'm on a tight deadline.'

'Trouble with technology, eh?' Shearer clutched a half-empty pint glass in his hand, tilted against his body like someone might try to steal it. 'Oh, you've got the M1 model. Fancy that myself, but I'm holding for the new Pro.'

'Right, right.' Fuck's sake. Mark had stolen a laptop, lied to the police and now this berk was going to bore him to death. 'Any idea how to fix it?'

Shearer pressed the button and waited. 'It's goosed.' He sipped more beer. 'Laddie down in Inversnecky fixed mine for me last time it went the bonk.'

Mark pinched his eyes. 'Why do people call it that?'

'The bonk? No idea, son.'

'No, Inversnecky.'

'Oh, right. Well. I think it's some kind of joke at their expense. No idea why. Doesn't make me laugh.'

'Right. Well, I'll have a think about that. Cheers.'

'Sure thing.' Shearer tapped his temple and walked over to the throng where he collected a fresh pint from Tam the barman.

Mark tried holding down the power button again, but the thing was dead.

He should call Olivia, hand over the laptop. She'd barely be ten miles away by now. She'd know someone in Inverness who could get it working, or at least recover the data.

He tried calling her.

'This is Olivia, please leave a message.'

Magic.

Aye, he should head down there and hand it over, make sure it was prioritised.

51

Mark had lost count of how many bridges he'd driven over on the way down. Seemed to be one every five miles and a few more than he'd spotted on the drive up on Thursday. This one was so low, so close to the water, he felt like he would get submerged. The river was maybe a mile wide now and the land beyond swelled up like a green slug. The Black Isle. So he was going over the Cromarty Firth, not too far from Inverness.

His phone blasted out:

Liv calling...

He hit the answer button.

'Mark?' It sounded like she was in a wind tunnel and about a mile from the microphone.

'Hey, what's up?'

'I'm—' A burst of static. '—at okay?'

'Sorry, you're breaking up.'

Loud static. '—hear me?'

'I'll call you back.' Mark hung up and redialled.

'This is Olivia, please leave a message.'

Magic.

The one time he needed her, she—

His phone blasted out again. He hit answer and her voice filled the car.

'Sorry, reception's crap here, but I should be fine now. What's up?'

'Keep thinking about that laptop. Kay's one. If we got it, how—'

'Have you got it?'

'I'm just wondering if we had it, how long it'd take.'

Her sigh rattled the speaker. 'Well, I've been asking here and there'd be nobody available to analyse her laptop until Monday. You saw how much hassle it was getting the phones done and that's trivial.'

'So, what, sending it down to Glasgow?'

'Sure. And that's assuming they'd start work on it when they receive it. Might be quicker getting Titch up here or driving it down. Bottom, we'd be looking at a few days.'

Days he didn't have.

'Okay, that's what I was thinking.'

'Mark, *have* you got it?'

'No, it's just when we get it. If I find it. Knowing what to do with it.'

'Mm. Well, you let me know if it turns up.' Click and she was gone.

He was closing on the Kessock Bridge now. He hadn't been up this far in years, only staying just short of it in Inverness at Olivia's parents. Seeing it again, twice in almost as many days...

The road was really quiet.

Fuck it.

He stuck on his hazards and pulled in, blocking a lane. He checked it was clear, then got out and raced across the carriageway, then hopped the barrier into the central reservation. Had to wait for a lorry and a queue of cars, then he got across to the strut.

A car horn blared as he shuffled over the second barrier.

Ahead, the Moray Firth cut into the landscape, the trees and rising hills.

Down below, the brown water foamed.

Where his dad died.

The patch of water he'd tumbled into, seeing no other way out. Separated from his kid, with no hope.

All his life, Mark hadn't been able to see why he'd thought that. Why he'd seen suicide as his only option.

But now. The pain of not knowing where Kay was, maybe that was like Dad knowing where Mark was, but knowing he'd never see him again.

They'd tar him as a child molester. Lock him up with the worst of society, while somebody else raised his son.

If only he'd waited another week.

Instead, Mark had been raised by his mum and his gran, growing up in Edinburgh. Miles away from here, a totally different life.

His life would've been so different if he'd stayed at Boleskine. Living in a cult, sure, but sometimes ignorance really was bliss.

Writing a novel about it was supposed to help him process, when in reality it had triggered him.

Staying with James Colliston and his group, he saw what people got out of it. He saw the evil Colliston did, helped take him down.

And it had cost him being able to write again.

He'd frozen, lost himself in alcohol. Pushed away his wife, his daughter. Been so fucking selfish.

He hadn't been there for Kay, just like his old man hadn't been there for him.

A lorry horn blared out behind him. Traffic filed past his car.

He needed to focus on Kay. And only her. Make sure she was okay.

He needed to find her, show her he loved her. Be the dad she needed.

Whatever had happened to Kay, it was because of him. Sending her up here on her own. Okay, so she was acting the big girl, studying at Glasgow, living in a flat. But she was still his little girl. And his selfishness had put her in danger.

He should've written that book years ago. Paid his debts, not taken a loan from Vic Hebden.

Mark needed to get into the laptop and now. Not in a few days.

Now.

He needed to do this himself.

Mark blew a kiss into the air. 'I love you, Dad.'

52

Mark managed to get a parking space opposite the computer repair shop. Deep in Inverness's Old Town, which made it sound all sophisticated, like it was in the south of France or northern Italy. No, it was just the bit that wasn't all roundabouts and what the Americans would call strip malls.

He got out and the castle loomed over him, not some classic ruin with a deep ancestral past, just a Victorian-era military building.

Christ, who was he kidding?

The site was fascinating, with castles dating back into the mists of time. He remembered a lecture at university on it, how Malcolm III lived up there, about how Mary Queen of Scots was refused entry.

He tried to get Kay's laptop bag out of the boot, but it was jammed in place, pressed between the side of the car and the box of shite, mostly filled with stuff from his old home with Olivia that he'd not even taken into his flat and yet he'd driven up to the Highlands with. He shifted the box over. One sharp tug and he loosened the bag enough to get it out.

Jesus, he hoped Shearer's guy could get something off it. Some notes, some clues.

He wrapped the bag around his chest, keeping a tight grip on it, and walked along the street, passing bars, cafés and shops on both sides. An Oxfam bookshop with a couple of Highland Clearances paperbacks in the window. The shopping arcade with *Avartagh's Esoterica* was over the road, wedged between a whisky cellar and a café.

People. Cars. Buses. Taxis.

Civilisation.

Life.

The bell tinkled as he entered Snecky Bytes. A tiny wee place but crammed full of gaming PCs with monitors bigger than most TVs. Bizarre. The huge workbench was manned by a chubby man, fiddling with the back of an open mobile phone. He wore a Zeroes T-shirt, but the cover of their first album was twisted into a weird shape by his massive gut. 'Good morning, sir. I will be but a moment.' His fingertips were dyed a weird orange. Some tangerine-coloured crumbs were on his shirt. Wotsits, probably. Or some obscure skin condition. His tongue slapped over his lips, still working away. 'I'm Dennis. How can I help?'

Mark rested Kay's bag on the desk. 'My daughter's laptop's not switching on. Her university dissertation. The back-up failed and some of the files didn't transfer over to the cloud.'

'Well, let's have a look, shall we?' Dennis pawed at the bag and liberated the machine. He opened it, pressed the power button, then adjusted his mass, his seat creaking and grinding. Clicked his tongue a few times. 'You might be shit out of luck, pal. Firstly, that's water damage. Has it been left outside or dropped in a body of water?'

Shite.

All that... Lying to Olivia... All for a broken laptop?

'Not that I know of.'

Dennis smirked. 'Or that she told you, am I right?'

'Got it in one.' Mark grinned a 'kids, eh?' grin. 'Can you extract the data from the drive?'

'Well, that's my second point.' Dennis closed the machine and inspected it from all angles. 'Thing is, these days, most laptops encrypt the drives by default.'

'What does that mean?'

Dennis looked at him like he was five years old. 'What's stored on the device is gibberish, basically. When you read anything from it, there's a little chip that deciphers the gibberish into useful stuff. But only for you. It's to avoid any third parties getting at the data on the machine.'

Aye, and that would be terrible...

Dennis smirked. 'Third parties like me, for example. Do you know the password?'

'I do, aye.' Mark wrote it on a Post-It pad, then tapped the laptop. 'Can you fix it?'

'Hmm.' Dennis licked his lips. 'The issue is the power supply has suffered water damage. You might be a lucky boy. It's possible I can repair it and recover the data.'

'How long?'

'It's going to take me a few days. Peak tourist season and I'm backed up with phones and laptops.'

'I haven't got a few days. Kay hasn't. My daughter. She needs to finish it and get it to her lecturer on Monday.'

'Know how many people use that line?' Dennis sat back. 'If you've not got the time, then you might have the next best thing.'

'What would that be?'

'Money. Double the rate for same-day service.'

'Fine. Deal.'

'Then it'll be ready by five.' Dennis clicked his orange fingers and pointed at Mark. 'Be here or be square.'

53

The waiter brought Mark's croissant over. 'Can I get you anything else, sir?'

'No, thanks.' He had a seat in the window, overlooking the damp street. He wolfed down the pastry in a few bites and wanted to get another. Maybe a pain au chocolat. The muffins looked good. Or maybe he should get something healthy, like the muesli bowl.

His leg was jogging and he got out his phone. Still nothing from Dennis. Nothing from anyone.

He opened the lid of his coffee and sucked in the steam. Seemed strong, hopefully strong enough to kick his brain into gear. He stuck the lid back on and left the café, carrying his laptop and his coffee back into the thriving library.

Mostly parents and kids getting their Saturday treats, but a few amateur historians in the archives.

Mark found his chair was still empty, so went back to his book, a contemporary account of the Clearances. Hardest part of the next chunk of his novel was making Jamie's father as little like the Duke of Sutherland as possible, while still basing the landowner character on him.

And as little like William Turnbull's ancestor.

He scanned through the text, getting some nice background on his hunting practises and how he actually married off some of his daughters.

That would be a great tension between Jamie and Margaret, maybe even trying to get his son to marry Elizabeth Ruthven's ancestor.

Shite.

Her ancestor was a Margaret. He needed to change that. Isobel. Martha. Agnes. Marion. Ann.

Go with Ann.

Aye, it had something to it.

But the storyline had the same Machiavellian logic that would lead Jamie to executing the crofters...

And lo and behold, the *Laird of Wedale* got a mention. But just a passing glimpse into the tragedy.

He flicked back to the index and it didn't have an entry. But there were some entries for the Ruthven clan.

The first section confirmed the story of losing their estate in 1822. The land for miles and miles around the castle, including the banks of the loch, but excluding the castle itself and the village, which passed on to the tenants.

The second reference showed the annual ceilidh dated back to the time when the family owned the village. Used to be held in what became the hotel, a village hall later expanded and extended, but moved to the castle in the Sixties. Probably at the peak of Elizabeth's great-uncle's powers.

None of the other three references mentioned the land passing from the Ruthvens to the Turnbull clan.

As for Satanism in the Highlands?

Well, nothing. Not even a flicker.

And nothing about John Rennie's document, the supposed proof of a cover-up.

If the truth behind what happened to the passengers aboard the *Laird of Wedale* was really a mass murder, then why was there no evidence?

The only thing Mark had was the ruined Catholic church,

supposedly taken over by devil worshippers, destroyed and left as a monument. Ancient folk tales, curses on the land and stuff like that.

He needed something real and tangible, but he was struggling to find it. He flicked through the pages, idly, his trained eyes scanning for it.

And there it was. Two maps.

The Strathruthven glen, from Forsinard down to Kinbrace, filling the whole valley.

The left page was from 1795, with dividing lines cutting around the loch, giving a small sliver to the Turnbulls, showing "Dubhan toinneamh tairbh". Where Turnbull House was situated now.

The right page was from 1827, with the map inverted. Aside from Ruthven Castle and some land in the village, the entire glen was Turnbull land now.

The legend read:

Before and after the 1822 Strathruthven Settlement

No detail of the actual settlement, nothing in the index.

But surely that was the document Rennie had stolen for Kay. Wasn't it?

Oh, what was this?

The papers were sealed in accordance with the investigation into the *Laird of Wedale* disaster.

Sealed papers, early in the rein of George IV. A chaotic time, for sure. A lot more smoke, but was it enough fire?

And that was much more likely to be what was hidden away in the Turnbull family archive.

Mark took a drink of coffee, then headed through to the library's microfiche. Luckily it was in the same layout as the National Library in Edinburgh, otherwise he'd have to ask for help. And there was nobody around.

He found a terminal and plugged in his search criteria.

Bingo.

Nowadays, the document would be redacted, with black marks covering words, phrases and whole paragraphs, but this one just had a simple note.

The contents of this document are classified top secret.

So there had to be something in it.

He searched the results and found another reference a few pages on.

The residents of Old Ruthven formed the bulk of the contingent lost to the North Sea aboard the *Laird of Wedale*.

Old Ruthven?

The name tickled at his brain. Had he heard of the place? He got out his phone and typed it into the Google Maps app.

A pin dropped down a road about two miles from Ruthven. He tapped on the street view and got a brass plaque mounted on a stone next to some trees. No road, no sign of any old crofts there. Not even the stone outlines like at Badbea or Rosal, just empty land.

But it seemed familiar.

Mark zoomed the map out. Christ, it was the camp. Where Urquhart and Cosmo lived.

Children of the Future.

Even had a website. An Instagram account. A TikTok account.

Looked like they were renting some land from Turnbull.

Mark's phone blasted out in his hand.

He got a glare from the old man next to him.

Adam calling...

Mark jolted upright and left the archive room. He stopped at the point furthest from the room, but where he could still keep an eye on his stuff, then answered the phone. 'Hey, you okay?'

'Gather you're not in your hotel room, Mark? Fed up with the countryside already?'

'No, I've come down to Inverness for a change of scene.'

'Right.'

'Doing some research. Need to clear my head.'

'Well, the thing is, we need a word with you.'

We?

Mark swallowed hard. 'Okay, how about getting something to eat when I finish here?'

'No, Mark. A word in the police station.'

54

Mark drove along the road, warehouses and factories on both sides, feeling like someone was prodding his back with an electrical wire.

Inverness police station was on the way back towards the A9 and the road north. Back to Ruthven. Or south, home.

Neither diction could stop Mark from thinking the worst, that the reason he'd been called to the station was because they'd found Kay.

Dead.

He had to pull in.

The station sat opposite a train yard that just happened to have a lorry carrying a train carriage making a royal mess of pulling out onto the road.

Mark punched the steering wheel.

Again.

And again.

A dull pain erupted in his palm, like he'd really hurt himself.

So he did it again.

The pain was like a cold shower, snapping him out of it.

Don't assume the worst.

Hard not to...

Mark called Olivia but she bounced the call.

Magic, magic, magic.

The lorry hopped up onto the opposite pavement. Definitely going to bend the barrier. Definitely.

He shut his eyes. His Kay... How could she be dead? It was all down to him. All on him. Every last part of it.

He reopened his eyes and realised he was crying. He wiped the tears away and blew his nose.

Fuck.

What a fucking mess.

The lorry managed to scrape past the barrier and hopped down onto the road, then shunted off along it. No train yards nearby. No trains nearby, really.

Still, Mark squeezed past and powered along the road.

The police station was a big Nineties building at the far reaches of an industrial estate that could've been a council gym or swimming pool. No left turn straight in, so he had to take the long way around the square plot, then swung into the car park.

Two spaces free, either side of Adam's car.

Mark parked and killed the engine, then got out into the afternoon.

Butterflies flapped in his stomach.

A shudder rose up from his thighs.

Fuck.

'Mark.' Olivia got out of a car. Hands on hips. Jaw clenched. Eyes frosty.

Mark walked over, trying to hide his fear behind a smile. 'What's going on?' His voice was a squeak.

'What are you doing down here, Mark?' she asked.

'That stuff with the dogs and John Rennie spooked me a bit. I needed normality. Where's Kay'

Olivia rolled her eyes. 'I know when you're lying, Mark. Your lips move.' Her eyes narrowed. 'Tell me why you're really here.'

'Is Kay dead?'

'What?' Olivia scowled. 'What are you talking about?'

Mark shifted his gaze between them. 'I thought... You called me here, to... um, tell me she was dead?'

'No.' Olivia ran a hand down her face. 'We haven't found her.'

'Thank fuck.' Mark collapsed back against his car.

'Jesus, are you okay?'

'I thought she... Fuck.' Mark sighed. 'I'm down here because I needed to do some research. I'm basing a character on the Duke of Sutherland. I found out some stuff about what Kay's been looking into, then Adam called and...'

Olivia folded her arms. 'Mark, I've made some calls about Vic Hebden. You know how much trouble you're in?'

He couldn't look at her. 'I am completely aware of how fucked I am, aye.'

'Hebden is a very smart guy. Keeps the more violent stuff at arm's reach, but there's a massive file on him down in Edinburgh. We can prosecute him, Mark, but you need to open up to us.'

'Liv... I can't.'

'Why not?'

'As I'm finding out, Vic and his guys are nasty men. The truth is, I'm worried about who'll get caught in the crossfire.'

'I can handle myself.'

'I suspect Kay thought that too. I'm worried Vic's got her.'

Olivia laughed. 'Mark, she's a student. I'm a cop.'

'Even so, I just can't.'

'What's going on?' Adam appeared from behind the parked cars, charging towards them. He'd changed from his casual wear into a suit and tie. 'Come on, guys. Let's do this inside, shall we?'

55

'And here we go, guys.' Adam held the door to a grotty little cupboard. A big table, four seats. Mirror on the wall. Camera in the corner.

A police interview room.

And Adam was acting all serious, for once. Shite.

Mark barged in, leaving them outside.

Adam let Olivia go first, but she stayed by the door. 'Need to use the loo.' She walked off along the corridor.

Leaving him alone with Adam. Magic.

The room stank of a mixture of mould and bleach, but the mould was winning. The hum of an air conditioning unit, the quiet padding of footsteps in the corridor, words being spoken elsewhere, but the words themselves inaudible.

Mark tossed his glasses onto the table. His eyes were encrusted with dried tears. 'Way to make this feel like an interrogation.'

Adam sat down, leaning back and lifting the front two legs of his chair off the floor. 'This is just questions.'

Mark couldn't hold his gaze for long. 'Do I need a lawyer?'

'Only if you've done something wrong, Mark.'

Mark didn't have an answer.

'You've got a choice, Mark. Insist on getting a lawyer and this goes on tape and on paper.'

'If all you want to do is scare me, then well done.' Mark clapped his hands slowly. Hopefully slowly enough to really annoy Adam. But he had that stabbing fear in his side. 'What do you owe her?'

'Owe who?'

Mark placed his hands on the table, carefully. 'The reason you're helping us look for Kay is you owe Liv. You said it was something big.'

Adam sat back and ran a hand over his shaved head. 'Why are you so interested?'

'Mark.' Adam drummed his thumbs on the table like he was in a pipe band. 'Why do you think you're here?'

'Vic Hebden?'

'Guess again.'

Mark frowned. 'Kay?'

Adam tapped his nose and pointed at Mark. 'There you go. We treat Missing Persons cases very seriously up here. Not a lot of people live in the Highlands and a few too many of them go missing, proportionally. Kay running away is one thing, but her and John Rennie both disappearing in the same week? That's got the brass up here rattled. You ask me? Two people missing from the same time and place... They've run off together.'

'What?'

'My boss wants me to cover off foul play, but let's be serious, she's been going from one older man to another this entire case Mark.'

Mark scraped his chair back and shot to his feet. 'What the hell are you—'

'Sit.'

'No! You're saying she's been—'

'Mark.' Adam opened up his notebook and flattened it on the table top. 'The reason you're here is because people representing James McNab have phoned up the Chief Constable to complain about you.'

Mark sat down, but his veins were like power lines. 'Who's James McNab?'

'The rock star. The singer in the Zeroes. Owns Boleskine House near Inverness. You spoke to him and—'

'*I* spoke to him?'

'Two days ago. Outside his gatehouse.'

'That was him?'

'Right. You got him all irate, enough to complain about your presence on his property.'

Mark threw his arms up in the air and glared at him. 'But I was looking for Kay!'

'Doesn't excuse you squaring up to him.'

'I didn't!'

'Mark.' Adam smacked his hand off the table. 'You did. Libby saw it.'

Mark nibbled at his thumbnail.

'I spoke to him myself.' Adam leaned forward. 'Told me Kay had been in touch with him. She used your name. Had a wee chat, then left. Trouble is, she broke in about an hour later.'

Mark felt a jolt in his neck. 'She *broke* in?'

'There's a police report.' Adam thumped a document down on the desk. 'She got inside Boleskine House, or what's left of it.'

Mark picked up his glasses and put them back on. 'Come on. That's *nothing* to do with me.'

'True.' Adam flicked through the pages. 'But Kay stole some books that belonged to Aleister Crowley.'

That'll be how she managed to persuade them she was a Satanist, then.

Mark sighed. 'So you're interviewing me here because she stole some books?'

'I'll call Mr McNab back and have a word. Apologise on your behalf.'

'That's very noble of you. Thanks.' Mark struggled to hide the sarcasm.

'Mark, I know you grew up there. Member of a cult based there. Got taken into care. Your dad committed suicide because of it. A whole mess. I read a few chapters of the book about it. No mutants, pirates or zombies, just evil human beings.' Adam jotted something down. 'Did Kay know about this?'

'Seemed like she did, but I didn't tell her.'

Adam shut his notebook. 'Anyway. Onto John Rennie.' He drummed his fingernails this time, the same insistent rhythm. 'One of my colleagues spoke to the local dog pounds in the area. There are some private ones dotted around the Highlands and SSPCA centres in Inverness and Thurso. Spoken to all of them, but only Inverness know about Rennie. They told us he's taken dogs down, but not since last summer.'

Mark frowned. 'Bill Turnbull said he's been rescuing loads of dogs. What's he been doing with them?'

'That's the thing. We just don't know. Him not taking them where he's supposed to seems mighty fishy to me.'

Mark sat back and folded his arms. 'What do you think he's been doing?'

'No idea.'

'Okay. Is that us?'

'Almost.' Adam raised a finger. 'Just a quick one, then you can go.' He turned the page and ran a finger down it. 'Ah, yes. Talk to me about the laptop?'

'What laptop?'

'The one belonging to Kay.'

'And I told you, Lady Ruthven gave me it, but I lost it in the field.'

'You told me that, aye.' Adam leaned forward. 'But you didn't tell me you found it in Rennie's cottage this morning.'

'What?' Mark swallowed. 'That's nonsense!'

'Mark, because of what's happened to Kay and John Rennie, I've got people doing door-to-doors in Ruthven.' Adam sucked air across his teeth. 'The shopkeeper saw you taking something from a bush, then you ran across the road carrying a bag. A laptop bag. Just after Olivia drove off. Then you were seen with it in the hotel bar.'

'Crap.'

'Is that you fessing up?' asked Adam. 'Because I hope for your sake that it is.'

Mark had a big choice here. Own up, or double down. But it wasn't much of a decision, was it? 'I needed that laptop.'

'So you just took it?'

Mark gave him a nod.

'You needed it that badly that you didn't tell me or Olivia that you'd found it?'

Mark stared at the desk, shaking his head. He swept his gaze between them. 'I called Liv, spoke to her, but—'

'But you lied. Why?'

'You both know why.'

Adam gave him a cold stare. 'Enlighten us.'

'Because it's...' Mark didn't have a good explanation. He was desperate and he'd gone off on his own. 'As far as I can tell, Kay had been cooking something up with John Rennie. Something related to a government cover-up of an atrocity masked as a disaster. Possibly doing it for Ruthven, possibly blackmailing Turnbull.' Probably doing it because her father's a fucking idiot. 'That laptop might lead to what's happened to them both.'

Adam scraped back his chair and stood. 'Need to have a word with DI Emery and Libby.'

'Her name is Olivia,' said Mark. 'Or Liv. Not Libby.'

Adam frowned. 'Eh?'

'You heard me. What's going on between you two?'

Adam laughed. 'You've got a cheek, mate. I'm in here helping you on my day off.'

'Why? What's in it for you?'

'I'm an old friend of hers. A cop in the Highlands, where *your* daughter went missing. And we're doing this for Kay, not you.'

Mark didn't have anything for that.

Adam was scratching the stubble on his chin, loudly and really annoying. 'You nicked that laptop, Mark. Why?'

'Seemed like a good idea.'

'Lying to the police is a good idea?'

'Adam, I'm desperate. I need to find my daughter. Finding out what she's been working on might lead to that.'

'And?'

'And what?'

'Well, what has she been working on?'

Mark looked away.

Adam was on his feet. 'Jesus Christ, man. Talk to me! Let me help you!'

'Her laptop's in the computer shop. Data recovery job.'

Adam leaned on the table and sprayed rancid breath over him. 'We've got forensics officers who can do that.'

'I thought this would be much quicker.'

It sounded pathetic. Trivial. Selfish.

Because it was.

Mark stared at Adam. 'I'm sorry. I shouldn't have done that.'

Adam sat down again. 'This looks really bad, you know? You took evidence from Rennie's cottage, Mark! That place is a crime scene!' He stabbed a finger in the air. 'For all I know, you could've followed Rennie back to his cottage, knocked on the door, got inside, attacked him, stashed the laptop, then told me all that crap when I turned up.'

'Why would I do any of that?' Mark held his gaze. 'Listen to me. I'd much rather be finding my daughter or working on my bloody book than being down here trying to get that laptop fixed. But the thing's broken! Possibly from the rain last night, or possibly from something else. And I'm trying to get it fixed!'

'Right.' Adam couldn't look at him. 'You've become very close to Lady Ruthven, haven't you?'

'What? Of course not.'

'You visited there last night.'

'Rennie told me Kay might've visited there on Wednesday night, that's all.'

He was whining. He sounded pathetic.

Grab hold of yourself!

'Adam, this whole thing is freaking me out and I know I'm

acting erratically. I was completely in the wrong to take the laptop.'

'Get over yourself, Mark.' Adam looked at him like he was a pathetic child. 'Always about you...Let me get this straight, you think Kay's laptop has a document proving the *Laird of Wedale* disaster was perpetrated by the Turnbulls to get the Ruthven land and that it was covered up by the *government*?'

'Right. Rennie stole it from Turnbull. The way these things work is, if there was proof, then Turnbull would lose the title to the whole land and it'd return to Elizabeth Ruthven.'

Adam frowned. 'You've seen this document?'

'No, but I found some corroborating evidence in the library.' Mark opened up his laptop bag and got out a photocopy of the maps. 'Where I was when you called me. There definitely was a transfer of land from the Ruthvens to the Turnbulls.'

Adam snatched up the document and inspected it. 'Anything else?'

Mark passed over another photocopy. 'The government did an investigation into it, but the report was top secret. Still might be.'

'Back in a sec.' Adam got up and left the room.

Olivia stood in the doorway, hands on hips. She walked over and thumped Mark's shoulder, a bit too hard to be playful. 'Dickhead.'

'Liv, I'm just trying to find her. Please understand.'

Olivia paced around the room. 'Always doing stuff on your own. Causing chaos. You're such a selfish prick.'

'I know. Believe me, I know. But I just want to find my daughter. That's it.'

'Mark. What's happened has been bad, but it's not because you trusted someone. Maybe Kay stumbled on something people want to stay covered up. I just wish you'd talk to me about it.'

'I try, but—'

'But you're a dickhead.'

'Right. I am. And that's no excuse.'

'And Vic Hebden? Seriously? You know how many operations we've got open on him?'

'I'm sorry for—'

'Stealing evidence?'

Mark swallowed. 'Aye. I'm really sorry.'

She gave him that glower again. Made him look away. 'Mark, you should've given the laptop to Adam or me and let us do our jobs.'

'That'll take days! You told me that yourself! My fucking daughter is missing and I—'

'Mark, whatever cowboy you've given it to might ruin Kay's computer.'

'It's already ruined. Water damage.'

'*We* can recover data from it. Can he?'

The realisation was hitting him hard, like a loan shark kneecapping him.

Olivia walked over to the door and opened it.

Adam was standing outside, messing with his phone. He gave her a nod and took his seat again. 'Okay, here's the deal.' His gaze shot between them. 'I've persuaded the DI to go easy on you for the laptop thing, but there's to be no more tea-leafing, okay?'

Mark nodded. 'Okay.'

Adam slapped his arm. 'Mark, you better hope this laptop is working.'

56

Adam whirred back into the space behind Mark, way too close to Mark's car.

Mark got out of his car, pressing against the side to avoid the passing bus. 'That was too close!'

Adam ignored him. 'Right, sunshine, let's see what your magician has found.' He hopped up onto the high kerb and entered the computer shop.

Olivia followed, but stopped in the doorway, prodding Mark in the chest. 'Let him lead here, okay?'

'No arguments from me.'

'I'm serious. Let him deal with this.' She entered the shop, leaving Mark out in the hot sun. Thumping down now, a late flurry. He pushed through the door and got a dull mechanical squawk.

'Not without the customer's express approval, sir.' Dennis the computer geek sat behind the desk, hands resting on the top of his belly. Eyes closed. 'I have a strict confidentiality agreement that I won't breach except where I'm legally required.' He held out a hand, eyes still closed. 'I need a warrant, sir.'

Adam thumbed at Mark. 'The customer's here.'

Dennis opened his eyes. 'Ah, well.' He smiled wide. 'I'm not finished, but if you can get this big palooka to let me do my job, I'll have it done in a jiffy.'

'Fine.' Adam gestured at the innards of the machine in front of him. 'Fill your boots.' He got out his phone, checked the screen and grimaced. 'Duty calls. Back in a sec.' He left the shop with another blast of the broken buzzer.

Mark tilted his head to the side and walked over, perching on the edge of a desk. The machine behind him played a game in silky smooth resolution.

Olivia couldn't keep her eyes off it.

He wanted to talk to her, to try to explain to her what the hell was going on inside his head.

But he couldn't.

'And we're in!' Dennis clicked his fingers.

Mark walked over to the window and waved at Adam. Leaning against his car, talking on the phone. No reaction, so Mark thumped the glass. Adam looked at him and Mark raised his thumb, then he walked over to the desk.

'I'm fricking *awesome*.' Dennis sat back and rested his hands on his belly again. 'Thing was practically empty. New machine, or new to the user, so that's to be expected.' He swivelled his tablet around for Mark to see. 'Which of these files do you wish me to extract?'

Mark scanned through the directory, though it was a bloody pigsty, just all the files in one place. But it actually seemed to be book research, with documents like "Ruthven clan history" and "Turnbull southern uplands mills". Scans of the same stuff Mark found at the library. Interview transcripts with Josh Urquhart, William Turnbull and people all the way up the coast. Some text scraped from Mhairi the barmaid's Facebook page. And at least six names Mark didn't recognise.

One file was called "Rennie scan".

The document Kay had obtained from Rennie?

Probably.

Mark reached over and clicked on it. A photo scan of an old document filled the screen, several pages worth. He skimmed it –

seemed to back up what he'd found at the library, but listed the parcels of land in detail. Legal conditions. Names, dates. Signatures. The condition for the transfer of title. And Old Ruthven was mentioned. Names of the dead listed.

'Well, well, well.' Adam's head was stuck between Mark and Olivia. 'This what you want?'

'Not sure.' Mark flinched and got out of the way. There was another file, entitled "Rennie scan 2".

Mark reached over.

And got his hand slapped away by Dennis. 'Not until you pay for it.'

Mark reached into his wallet and dropped a hundred quid on the desk. 'There you go.'

'Another fifty pounds.'

'We agreed a hundred quid.'

'And the recovered data needs to go onto some hardware. A USB drive or a DVD, for instance?'

'Fifty quid for a *DVD*?'

'It's my time, as much as anything.'

'Can't you just email me them?'

'I can, but it's a WeTransfer job, so I'll have to charge the same amount.'

'Christ.' Mark sighed but dropped the additional cash on the desk. 'There you go. Put it on a USB stick.'

'Excellent choice, my friend. Excellent choice.' He plugged one into the side, then started clicking around.

Mark opened the file and it was supporting documentation for the original.

Evidence.

Proof.

The smoking gun was testimony from two Turnbull shepherds, confirming that they perpetrated the crimes, murdering eighty people and burying them in a mass grave, then scuttling the boat at Helmsdale.

Mark felt dizzy, like he might fall over at any moment.

This was exactly what Ruthven would need to recover her

land. A hundred grand was chump change to how much she stood to gain from it.

Olivia smiled at Dennis. 'Do you know where these files entitled "Rennie scan" came from?'

'The user's hard drive.'

'No. I mean, was it scanned on the machine or did it come from a phone or something?'

'Okay, well. It wasn't scanned using the machine. I'm extracting her emails and messages as we speak.' Dennis's fingers danced across the keyboard. 'And there we go. Whoever Kay Campbell really is, she emailed one John Rennie seventeen times.'

Olivia winced. 'I thought we'd run her emails.'

'This is kaykay156369 at pumpmail dot com.'

'Shite, that's a burner, right?'

'Correctamundo.' Dennis tapped the monitor in front of him. His fingers were now stained green, like he'd switched from Wotsits to wasabi peas. 'Well, the last email was about "that document". They arranged to meet at his cottage to scan it. He appears to have been the one who scanned it and emailed her it. These files will be but a moment. But...' He licked his lips. 'What does this have to do with her essay?'

'It's about the Highland Clearances.'

'I see.' But Dennis didn't seem to.

'Thanks, though.' Mark walked back over to the corner, where a gaming machine seemed to be having a fit, flashing a maze at a stupidly fast speed. 'Okay, so they met, emailed, she got a scan of the document from him. But it wasn't in his cottage, was it?'

'You didn't nick it?' Olivia raised an eyebrow at Mark. 'Well, I didn't see it, no. Adam would've mentioned it. And Rennie was a neat freak. Not a thing out of place. I mean, when you're that tidy it's all about storage, right? A place for everything and everything in its place. Could be cupboards we didn't find. Or he could've put it back in Turnbull's safe afterwards.'

Mark shook his head. 'He said he hadn't.'

'But John Rennie isn't exactly reliable, is he?'

She had a point.

Mark walked over to the desk. 'See these emails, do they mention anything about where the document actually is?'

'She's talking a lot about how much debt her dad is in. Worries about how he'll get out of it.'

'Shite.' Mark collapsed back against the wall. She *was* doing this for him. Speaking to Olivia, speaking to Fiona, now John. She'd been trying to get him out of the hole.

He'd totally fucked up.

He only wanted her to be happy, but her over-generous nature had made her devalue her own worth to the point where his selfishness was the only thing being nurtured.

What an arsehole he was.

Mark looked at Olivia. 'She asked you about it, didn't she?'

'Your debt? I told her I had no idea, Mark. And I didn't.'

Dennis tapped the screen. 'Do you want me to extract the emails here between her and Séan?'

'*John.*'

'Nope.' Dennis rested his hands on his belly again. 'I meant precisely what I said. There are emails between your daughter and John, but these are between her and Séan. It's Gaelic for John, hence the confusion.'

'What are you talking about?' Olivia snatched the laptop out of his green-tinged fingers. 'Oh no, not my baby...' She looked at Mark. 'There's a ton of emails between Kay and Séan Avartagh.'

Mark scowled at her, then it clicked. 'The freaky guy in the shop?'

'Him.' She sighed, then looked out of the window at Adam. 'Looks like they'd been working on something together. And had been in love. Or at least *he* was.'

57

Adam thumped the window and stepped back. 'Half past three on a Saturday and his shop's shut. Not even a schoolkid manning the place.'

Not a good sign.

But there was a light on inside.

The street was busy with shoppers. Olivia was in her car, on the phone to someone. Dennis was shuttering his shop early, probably eager to spend the money he'd practically stolen from Mark.

Being in touch with Kay was one thing, he knew that, but those emails…

'Séan!' Adam rattled the door. 'You there?'

Séan Avartagh had been in love with Kay, that was clear. So many declarations.

> "My goddess, I long to worship you."
> "I desire to drink you in again."

Without any explicit reciprocation from her.

Adam laughed. 'What flavour of dickhead tries to get his leg over by talking like a seventeenth century dandy?'

'That's my daughter.' Still, it made Mark's stomach pitch and roll. How little he knew about her life. Maybe Kay had been teasing Séan, leading him on. And she'd got what she wanted out of it – a lead to John Rennie and his document, who had been so kind as to deliver it.

Adam shook the door again. 'Not another missing person.'

The light flickered inside. A figure appeared through a doorway at the back of the shop. Séan perched on a high stool, next to a stack of old books, and started writing in a ledger with a fountain pen. At his feet was one of those massive army surplus holdalls.

Adam thumped again, then waved, gesturing to be let in. He hit the door again.

Séan looked around and his shoulders sagged. He walked over to the door, avoiding eye contact as he undid the locks and opened the door to a crack. 'Adam.' He pinched the bridge of his nose. 'I thought it was another bunch of kids attacking the shop.'

'Eh?'

'Freaky bookshop owner is an easy target.' Séan stared at his fingernails, then back at Adam. 'What's up?'

'Need a word, pal.'

'I'm in the middle of a stock check.' Séan kept a tight grip on the door. 'Been putting it off for months. Accountant needs it first thing on Monday.'

'This'll only take a couple of minutes.'

Séan swallowed hard. 'Adam, I've got a meeting with him now. I need to go.'

'Your accountant? On a Saturday night?'

'I'm busy the rest of the time.'

'Just a couple of minutes, Séan. That's it.'

'Right, come on in then.' Séan walked over to the counter and took his seat again.

Adam followed him over, tilting his head at Mark. 'Show him.'

Mark got his laptop out of his bag and opened up the emails between Séan and Kay, then put it down on the counter.

Séan shifted his gaze between them. 'What is this?'

'What does it look like?' Adam got in his face. 'It's proof of you lying to us, Séan. Lying to *me*. You told us Kay was a customer, but that's where the truth ended.' He gestured at the laptop screen. 'Seems to be more than that. A whole lot more.'

Séan looked like he was going to smash the laptop into a thousand pieces. He said nothing, though.

'I hate it when people lie to me, Séan.' Adam sucked in a deep breath. 'Especially when it's to my face. So you've got a very simple choice here. Come with me to the station and talk. Or tell us it all now, then I take you to the station and you talk.'

'But I've not done anything!'

'Séan, you were involved in a romantic liaison with the missing person I asked you about. That's doing something. And it's also lying.'

Séan stared at the counter, his long nail scratching at the wood, a fearful expression cutting across his face. 'You should leave.'

'Leave?' Adam laughed. 'I'm going nowhere until you speak. Or I'm taking you in.'

Séan stared right at him. 'I'm a vampire and I need to drink.'

Adam threw his head back and bellowed with laughter. 'Right, that's it. You're coming with me.' He reached for Séan's arm.

Séan launched himself at Adam, teeth bared, aiming them at his neck. The pair went down in a heap, then rolled behind a bookshelf.

Séan's stool clattered over and landed on Mark's foot. Pain roared up his leg.

Séan was now on top, elbow wrapped around Adam's throat, his free hand pushing him down. He moved his teeth towards Adam's neck.

Mark jerked into action, grabbing the stool and swinging it through the air.

It missed Séan by inches but did make him let go of Adam. He scurried back against a bookshelf, glaring at Mark with animal menace. He hissed.

Mark walked over to him. 'What the hell have you done with my daughter?'

Séan jerked forward and bit Mark's wrist.

Felt like he'd put his arm down on a lit barbecue again.

He fell back against the counter, then the bookshop spun around and he landed on his side.

Séan jumped on him, pinning him down. Stronger and heavier than he looked. 'You'll do!' He reached over to Mark's neck.

Mark clawed at Séan's wrists, trying to push him away. 'Help!'

All Mark saw was a stool swinging through the air, then Séan tumbled over.

He looked up.

Adam was standing over Séan, ready to crash the stool down.

The door rattled open. 'Adam, I can't get hold—' Olivia. 'What the fuck?' She raced over and tackled Adam, knocking him off Séan. She twisted Séan's arm round his back and pushed him face first to the shop floor. Books fell from shelves all over her, bouncing on her shoulders.

Mark raced into the tumbling maelstrom and helped her out.

Leaving Séan under a pile of books.

Adam sat up, rubbing at his wrist. 'Bastard broke the skin.'

Mark checked his wrist, expecting gushing blood, but found just toothmarks. Human toothmarks.

Adam was on his feet now, rubbing at his throat. 'Jesus Christ, am I going to turn into a vampire?'

Mark pulled some books out of the way and helped Olivia get Séan upright. He grabbed him by the throat and pressed him against the empty bookcase. 'Where is she? Where the fuck is Kay?'

'You should get out of here! My blood lust is—'

'You're not a vampire!' Mark tightened his grip. 'What have you done with Kay?'

Séan gurgled and Mark let his grip slacken off a touch. 'You've been warned, friend.' But his accent was slipping into a broad Midwest one with a Southern twang.

Mark let go. 'You're American?'

'I'm from the old country!' A cod Irish accent now. Séan bared his teeth, sharpened probably artificially so. Probably. 'You should let me go. I'll have no control over what I do!'

Olivia was rifling around in the drawers under the till. She held out a card. 'Bradley Irwin Schultz from Columbus, Ohio.'

'My name is Séan Avartagh! I'm a vampire!'

'Quit it, *Brad.*' Adam lifted him up like he was a toddler and perched him back on the stool and pinned his biceps down on the counter, leaning over him. 'You got lucky when you surprised me. That won't happen again. Now, you're going to stop lying to us. The truth. Now.'

'Okay, so I'm freaking out about how I bit you and sucked your blood and yet you're still standing!'

'Séan. *Brad.*' Adam grabbed his shoulders. 'You're not a vampire.'

Séan nodded, like the use of his real name was the only thing stopping turning his bookshop into an abattoir. 'I will feast upon all three of you.'

'Séan...'

'I can survive for months at a time without drinking human blood.' Séan tried to raise his arms.

Adam pinned them down. 'Quit it.'

'I buy pig blood from the butcher.'

Adam let him go. 'Jesus Christ.'

'It's just like black pudding.'

'Black pudding is cooked!'

'Same difference.'

'You're going to talk.' Adam put his face right next to Séan's. 'First, let's hear why Bradley Irwin Schultz is living in Inverness under the name Séan Avartagh.'

Séan pursed his lips. 'My grandfather was born in Donegal. Went over to the States on a boat, but he'd been bitten and infected. He's passed vampirism down through the family.'

'So you are Brad Schultz?'

'I was born that, yes, but it's not my name now.'

'Okay.' Adam cracked his knuckles. 'Séan, I want to know about you and Kay Campbell.'

'Adam, I can't talk to you about this.'

'Why not?'

'Because they'll kill me.'

'Who will?'

Séan shook his head.

'Okay, so how did you meet her?'

'Meet who?'

'Séan, Séan, Séan... Don't even think about denying it. We've got a ton of emails between the pair of you. So, I want the truth about Kay. All of it. Now.'

'She came into my shop one morning two weeks ago.' Séan bowed his head. 'She was into the occult history of the Highlands. The dark side. Like, *really* into it. The people. The glens. The rivers. The hills. That whole area, but Strathruthven especially. And I had something for her. Sold her a few books on the topic. Kay was fascinated with the *Laird of Wedale*, kept asking me about it. And... Well, you've got those emails. You know it was more than just her being a customer. We went on a couple of dates. I picked her up from Inverness on Sunday and took her to Helmsdale and Ruthven to show her where it all happened.'

'Where what happened?'

'The disaster.'

'Did you stay in the hotel with her?'

'No, sir.'

'But you visited that hotel with her?'

'We spoke to this dude in the bar of the village hotel. Rennie. John Rennie.' Séan dragged his teeth across his forefinger like he was checking they could still cut flesh. 'Kay asked him a few questions and... you know that phrase about the walls having ears?' He trained his eyes on Mark. 'Well, he asked us to meet him at his cottage. So we went over there and he told us about his boss, William Turnbull, and how he had a morbid fascination about what happened to his ancestors' boat. The *Laird of Wedale*. A whole section of his family archive related to documentation about the disaster. And Mr Rennie seemed to think the disaster hadn't happened the way it was supposed to.'

'In what way?'

'That there was a government cover-up. Rennie told us the truth. The way he described it, the document proved the Turnbulls perpetrated the atrocity, including the cover-up involving the sinking of their boat, which was of course insured. About how Lady Ruthven could get her land back from William Turnbull.'

Mark could just see Rennie standing in the bar, cupping a whisky in his hand, talking all the shite of the day to whoever was listening. Just so long as he got another drink and fed them what they wanted to hear.

Adam raised a bushy eyebrow. 'Of course, you've seen the document?'

'No. Rennie was very cagey about that. He'd have to steal it. He was more interested in negotiating the right price for it.'

'He was blackmailing you?'

'No, it was just a business agreement. He wanted fifty thousand for it.'

'Did Kay have that money?'

Séan shook his head. 'It's not like that. She wanted fifty thousand too.'

So Kay knew that'd cover Mark's debt to Hebden. How? A guess? Had Fiona blabbed?

And Christ, she was doing this for *him*.

Fucking hell.

'It's why Kay wanted to speak to Lady Ruthven. I waited for her outside Turnbull's, then dropped her outside the castle on Wednesday lunchtime.' Séan's shrug extended to his hands, open wide. 'And that seems to be the last anyone's heard from her.'

'Trouble is, it's not the last.' Adam put his hands in his pockets. 'She was seen in the hotel bar that night. Left about half past ten.'

'I'll bow to your superior knowledge, Adam.'

'You seem pretty sure that's the last anyone's heard from her, though.'

Séan nibbled at his fingernail.

'You don't seem to mind?'

'Kay broke it off with me.' He huffed like a spurned teenager. 'I took her to the goddamn castle, yeah? On Wednesday afternoon. And she ditched me outside. Said it wasn't love. Man, she'd been using me.'

'She didn't show up.'

'That's a lie. As far as I know, she was there. Saw her go in. No idea what was said. But something must've happened.'

Adam was on his feet now, hands on hips. 'Why didn't Rennie speak to her himself?'

'You'll have to ask him that.'

'I would, but Mr Rennie is missing too.'

'Oh my god.' Séan tugged at his ponytail. 'Shit. I'd bet the farm on Turnbull having something to do with their disappearances, then.'

Adam stood over Séan, staring down at him. 'Go on?'

'If Kay sold that document to Ruthven, Turnbull stands to lose his land. There's no document without Rennie getting it out of his archive. Easy to spot it going missing.'

'Okay, I need to understand the timeline here, Séan. It seems like she went straight from the hotel to Rennie's to see the document on Wednesday night.'

'Okay, that's after I saw her. Problem is, she got the scans on Tuesday night.'

Adam looked at Mark, then back at Séan. 'Excuse me?'

'Here's what happened. She spoke to Rennie on Tuesday in the tea room. Found out about the document. She got it from him on Tuesday night. She stayed in his cottage.'

'She said he was a sex pest?'

Séan shook his head, all matter of fact. 'Not that she told me. Perfect gentleman.'

'We heard she—'

'Thing about Kay?' Séan smiled. 'She knows how to play people. Like Janek, right? She stashed her laptop with him because he's got a safe in his room. Used to be a bank vault, so it's really hard to get into.'

'Why did she have to use it?'

'Her laptop had the document on it. And she definitely thought people were after her. Wouldn't say who. They called her on her burner, threatening her. So she ditched the phone and her car in Kinbrace.'

'Why?'

'Well, because I had mine, so she'd still be mobile, but she thought the police were following her so didn't want to be trackable.'

Adam scowled at him. 'The *police* were after her?'

'I mean, someone was. It's why she left her phone in Inverness. She'd been to the police in Inverness, about a threat she'd received to stop looking into this stuff. But she thought they seemed to be in league with whoever was threatening her. She got paranoid they'd be able to track her, hence ditching her phone, hence ditching her car. She got a call from someone on the burner. I don't know who it was, but it was a threat. Made her more determined, though. And she had a second burner.'

'So she was going to see Ruthven with a copy of the document?'

Séan nodded. 'She'd have used that sex pest story to get Rennie out of the picture. Keep all the money for herself.'

'Well.' Adam got out his phone and put it to his ear. 'Aye, he's talking. Sure thing.' He put the phone away then walked over to them. He smacked Mark's arm. 'Thanks for your help with this. We'll find out what happened.'

Mark deflated. 'You're acting like they're dead.'

'No, Mark. That's not where my head's at.' Adam exhaled deeply. 'The DI's just got a warrant to search this place and interview this bugger under caution.' He looked over at Séan. 'You got a lawyer?'

He frowned. 'Sure. Why?'

'Call them now, saves us time at the station.'

'What have I done?'

'Money laundering.'

Séan deflated, like he was going to fall off his stool.

Adam squeezed Mark's bicep. 'You look like you've been bitten by a vampire. Get back to the hotel, get your head down. Get some food too. There's a cracking chippy in Golspie.'

58

'Surprised they let the name stand.' Mark pointed a chip back to the sign for Campbell's Lane, then popped it in his mouth and chewed as he walked. Not enough salt, but just about perfectly done. Crispy on the outside, fluffy in the middle. And absolutely melting hot, made him breathe out molten air. 'Then again, they've got a statue to the Duke of Sutherland on the hill up there, so who knows.'

The sky behind it was a sheet of granite now, but the statue overlooking the small town was all lit up by the sunlight trained on the beach.

Olivia hopped down onto the sand and sat on the wall. She opened her box, having the patience to wait before getting stuck in. 'Starving.'

'Me too.' Mark joined her and shut the lid of his fish supper to protect it from the seagulls wheeling above them. He pulled out the two cans of juice from his pocket, resting them between them, then reopened his box and tore off a big chunk of fish. His mouth was watering.

'Used to come here all the time when I was wee.' She pointed up ahead at the beach, a wide vista of golden sand curving around the bay, set against the backdrop of hills and inland clouds. 'A bit of a drive up from Inverness, but so worth it.'

'You okay, Liv?'

'Not really.' She blew air out of her mouth like it was on fire.

'I'm sorry.'

She frowned at him, eyes narrow. 'What for?'

'This is all a mess of my making. I should've put that book to bed a long time ago. When we were together. Then Kay wouldn't have come up here and got into this. She's... She's doing this for me. Selling it to Ruthven for fifty grand. Christ.'

'Is that how much you owe Hebden?'

Mark looked away. 'Well, it'll clear my immediate debts. I feel like such a fucking idiot.'

'That's because you are. But Kay's a good kid. She's so generous. Don't know where she gets that from.'

'Her mother.'

'Right. Must be. But Kay's like you in a lot of ways. Like on my birthday two years ago, when she was staying with us and she got up super early to bake a cake so I could take it into work and not have to buy doughnuts for the office.'

Mark laughed. 'I forgot about that.'

'She is a great kid.' She took her time finishing chewing a chip. 'Have faith in Adam.'

He swallowed down his chunk of fish. 'I'm trying to.'

She opened her can with a pineapple-scented spray. 'Why are you looking at me like that?'

'It's just...' Mark knew he shouldn't say it but sod it. 'What's going on between you two?'

Olivia scowled at him. 'What are you talking about?'

'It's like you've rekindled some old romance.'

'With *Adam*?'

'No, with the dude who fixed Kay's laptop.' She rolled her eyes. 'Of course, I mean Adam. He's calling you. You're calling him. I'm just putting two and two together.'

Olivia laughed. 'That was a *long* time ago.'

'And that's not a denial.'

'It's really none of your business, Mark.'

'What about before you divorced me?'

'No!'

'Seriously?'

'There's *nothing* going on, Mark. *Nothing.*'

Mark didn't know whether to believe it or not. He stared into his box, his fish all eaten. Just chips left. He took a drink but struggled to swallow it down.

She looked back at him. 'Me and *Adam*? Really?'

'He seems to know a lot about you.'

'I could say the same about your female friends. Like Fiona.'

'I went to uni with her. She's my agent.'

'Same deal, Mark. Adam's a friend. If you must know, Adam and I went out for six months in our last year at school. And he broke my heart. I caught him snogging someone in the year below us. And that was it. I must have a thing for dickheads. Didn't speak to him for ten years until I was a cop. Thing is, after Adam left the army, he applied for direct entry to the Highlands and Islands force, as was. He was ex-Military Police, so it seemed like a good fit. Trouble is, they rejected him. Someone from our schooldays made an allegation against him. They got done for drugs, said Adam was involved.'

'And was he?'

'No. But some people have long memories and can't wait to exact revenge.'

'And you backed him up?'

'That's why he owes me. And big time. I cashed in the chips on this, got him to help you find Kay. Help *us.*'

Mark ran a hand down his face. 'I don't know what to say.'

'You could start with "thank you". And you could tell the truth. No more bullshit, no more lying. Just the truth. From now on. And try to respect people, Mark.'

He exhaled slowly. 'On my way down here, I stopped at the Kessock Bridge. Stopped *on* it. Where my dad jumped off. And it made me realise how selfish I've been. I'm just the same as him.

My distance has made her grow up without a dad. I hope I find her.'

'Kay loves you, you know? Despite you being a total bell end, Kay really loves you.'

Mark felt that lump in his throat. Even the chip grease couldn't ease it down.

'But you're right. You are a selfish prick, Mark. Always have been.'

He sat there, all deflated. 'Why did you marry me if I'm a selfish prick and a total bell end?'

'I literally have no idea.'

'There must've been something.'

'Okay, you're actually a decent person, but you're damaged. I thought I could fix you. But nobody can.'

'Damaged?'

'The way you treat people. It's... It's transactional. It's all about what you can gain from them. You've neglected your daughter, you've ruined our marriage. Ruined two marriages.'

'Almost bankrupted myself too.'

'Still about you.'

'I know, but... After what I lived through, do you blame me?'

'Aye. I do, Mark. It's one thing to be traumatised by your childhood when you're twenty. You're *forty-three*. Stop letting it fuck up your life. Get help. Counselling, therapy, meds. Whatever. Focus on what *you* can do. You fix the future by controlling the present and learning from the past.'

Mark had no idea what to say. The wind chucked a blast of grit at him. 'I am such a selfish prick. I have been so focused on myself, on my own bullshit. I have tried to ignore it all. Blot it out. And it's just got me into such a bad situation. I'm done with it all, Liv. I can't keep doing this to people. To you, to Kay. Christ, even to Cath.'

She sat there, drinking her juice.

'When I was driving to the police station in Inverness, after Adam called me, I thought she was dead.'

'What?'

'Adam wouldn't tell me over the phone. Just expected one of those moments like in a TV show. You know?'

'Right. I get it.'

'Liv, if we find her... I'm going to be the best dad. Make up for all the shit I've put her through.'

'She's a good kid, Mark. Despite you.'

'Must be to Cath's credit.'

'No. You might've been a selfish prick, but you were a fun dad. You took her to the zoo. Ice skating on Princess Street Gardens.'

'It's Princes Street.'

'Mark!'

'Sorry. Force of habit.'

Olivia took his hand, as greasy as hers. 'I loved you, despite how annoying you can be. I would've had a child with you.' A tear slid down her cheek. 'If I could. Kay was the closest I could get to that.'

Mark reached over but she flinched away.

Still, his head felt lighter than it had in years, like it contained a lot less bullshit and noise and pain than it had for the last... God, he couldn't remember. 'And you're right. You and him, it's none of my business.'

She stared at him, deep into his eyes, for the first time in years.

He held her gaze, then had to look away.

Olivia's phone blared out. She shuffled away and checked it. 'Adam, what's up?' She frowned. 'Still in Golspie, why?' She stared at Mark. 'Okay, then, see you in Ruthven.'

59

Ruthven village rolled by under the sodium glare – the white streetlights of Edinburgh hadn't made it this far north. Mark slowed as he passed the hotel, but no sign of Adam's car in the car park. Olivia pulled into the last space, so Mark had to settle for one on the high street, just past the shop.

There.

Adam was leaning against his car. Black suit, white shirt, like someone out of a gangster film.

Olivia was already walking over to him, hands in pockets.

Mark pulled up alongside him and got out just as the rain started. Thin dots, but the sort that would soon turn into a heavy downpour. 'You got here quick.'

Adam reached into a blue plastic bag and pulled out a samosa, attacking the packaging like it was an Invernessian vampire. 'That motor flies like shit off a shovel.' He looked north towards the granite sky, slowly chewing. 'Took a bit of persuading to get Séan to open up again. But, assuming it's true and assuming we can back it all up, Emery thinks we can do him for money laundering.'

Olivia nodded at Mark. 'I told you.'

'Too much money going through that shop?' asked Mark.

'Right. Exactly that.' Adam brushed crumbs from his jacket.

'Known him a few years now. Get my comics from there. He recommends some freaky stuff. Mad, crazy, gonzo shit, but really good. Feel a bit daft for not spotting the obvious, but you live and learn, eh?'

Mark asked, 'Who's he laundering the money for?'

'Won't say. Just keeps asking to get out of there.'

'Daft twat shouldn't have attacked a police officer.' Olivia frowned. 'What are we doing here?'

Adam pointed over towards the telephone exchange. 'Got a warrant to search Rennie's cottage.'

It was dark inside.

Mark frowned at him. 'What do you hope to find?'

'That's the magic of what we call a dunt, Mark. Just never know what you're going to uncover.' Adam grinned wide. 'But Séan's phone records from the shop show a few calls to John Rennie. Seems like they *were* cooking something up with Kay. Thing is, my guys are all down in Tain looking into this robbery, so I'm meeting a bunch of locals, but they're coming down from Thurso...' He smiled at Olivia. 'Wondered if a big city DS might want to show a country rube how it's done?'

Olivia held out her hand. 'Lead on, MacDuff.'

'You know it's "lay on" and not "lead on", right? Means to attack.'

'Whatever. This is your territory, so this is your dunt.'

'Alrighty.' Adam clicked his fingers and strolled along the street. 'How was your fish supper?'

'Better than your samosa,' said Olivia.

'Don't doubt it.' Adam stopped dead. 'Shite.' He held out a hand to block Mark. 'Wait.'

The door was open to a crack.

Adam pushed the door wide. 'Shug? You here?'

'Great.' Olivia reached into her pocket and got out one of those blue gloves, then pulled it on and opened the front door. 'Mark, stay there. It's already a potential crime scene.'

'Even though I was in there earlier?'

'Even so. You can't come in.' She stepped inside. 'I mean it. Stay right there.'

Mark raised his hands. 'Staying.' He stepped to the side and peered through the front window.

And saw a trail of destruction. Not that Rennie had many possessions, but they were all over the floor. His sofa and armchair were tipped right over. All the drawers from a dresser were upended, reams of paperwork fanning out across the carpet.

The beanpole cop was lying by the doorway. Eyes closed, blood leaking from a wound in his head.

Adam stepped into the room, catching Mark's eye through the glass and scowling. He came back out, phone to his ear. 'This is a bloody disaster.' He shook his head. 'Aye, need an ambulance and two squad cars to Ruthven.' He nodded. 'That's great.'

Inside, Olivia was squatting by a safe, previously hidden behind a side table. Hanging open and emptied.

Mark winced. 'Must've been after that document.'

'Must've found it too.' Adam gritted his teeth. 'If Turnbull spotted the document was missing, he'd go after Rennie to get it back. Torture him to get the safe code.'

Mark couldn't argue with the logic. 'So, what's the plan? Get him into custody?'

'Slow down, man.' Adam smiled. 'No, we need hard evidence first.'

The front door opened again and Olivia joined them. 'My money's on Elizabeth Ruthven. Found this inside.' She pulled out an evidence bag, containing something blue and plasticky. 'Know anyone with a triple XL glove size?'

60

The car park was full, with vehicles lining the road in all directions, including around the loch.

Ruthven Castle loomed over them, the front of the building lit up with flaming torches, flickering in the wind, but redundant in the bright evening. The steel clouds had been blown away by the strong gale that cut up the glen like a knife gutting fish. The loch level was low and the nearby water was filled with floating lanterns burning something perfumed.

Löic stood guard like a sentry.

Behind him, the front door was wide open with a crowd gathered in the courtyard. Women in their best gowns and tallest heels, which they'd surely kick off for the dance. Some men in jackets, jeans and shoes, but most wore kilts, with that rugged rugby-style top.

Mark got out of Olivia's car on the lochside.

Adam strolled over from his, parked on the road from the village. 'That big monster of hers is ex-military, knows his stuff. Would stake my mortgage on it being him who tossed Rennie's place.'

'Surely people would've spotted him?' Mark swallowed hard. 'A seven-foot giant kind of sticks out like a sore thumb.' He shook his head, but his frazzled brain was struggling to process it all. 'Still doesn't make sense to me. Ruthven stood to gain from that document. Why would she—?'

'Simple, Mark.' Adam smirked at them. 'This thing she was cooking up with Kay and Rennie, say she did agree to pay them fifty grand each for that document. Well, she doesn't have that kind of cash.' He held up his phone. 'I did some digging into her finances. She's brassic. And all of her money is going to be needed for legal work, right?' He switched his gaze between them, eyebrows raised. 'What we know is Kay was on her way to the castle, with a scan of the document. Ruthven knew what it said, but more importantly what the original represented. She'd want that original. When you went blundering in there last night, Mark, she finally knew where it was. In Rennie's cottage. So she sent Löic around there to toss the place and retrieve the document. Saved herself a hundred grand.'

Aye, Mark couldn't argue with that. 'So where are they?'

'While you two were driving over, I got the boss to drill into Séan, back in Inverness. He obviously wants us to find Kay. Said if Ruthven has her, she's probably being held downstairs.'

'Why would he know?'

'Thing is, Séan's had dealings with the good Lady recently. She sold him a lot of her own family history. Books, documents, a load of Viking shite. But one book is a history of the castle, built back in the dim and distant. He's going to do a print run of it, so he knows it inside out. And it's got plans of the place. Looks like what can only be described as a torture chamber in the basement.'

Mark's stomach clenched and a gasp escaped his lips. It gave him hope. Hope that Kay was alive. That he could save her.

But the thought of her being held down there...?

Olivia rolled her eyes. 'So you're going to knock on the door and ask if she's kidnapped Kay and is holding her in her torture dungeon?' She laughed. 'Good luck with that.'

Adam grinned at her. 'Libby, to root around, all we need is suspicion that something's happened to Mark's kid in there. If we find anything, then I can get a warrant and forensics team to do the doings. And what better time to recce the castle than during the ceilidh. So, let's go in there and find out if Kay's downstairs.'

'See, this is what I was saying. We can't keep using the Ways And Means Act Brackets Scotland Close Brackets. Adam, you can't just go poking around. You need grounds, probable cause, reasonable suspicion. Do this by the book for once, aye? Me and Mark can go in as private persons who have tickets. Then, if we have reasonable suspicion, bingo.'

Adam sucked in a deep breath. 'Okay, fine. I'll keep an eye on the incomers.'

'Then let's do this.' Mark crossed the road and stepped over the bridge. This plan just had to work, didn't it? Because he had nothing else.

Löic bowed. 'Bonsoir, mon ami.' He was wearing white tie, not a kilt in sight.

Mark smiled at him. 'Sorry, we don't have tickets, but—'

Löic pressed a finger to Mark's lips. 'We took the liberty of adding some to your hotel room.' He beamed at Olivia. 'Go on in!'

'Thank you.' Olivia gave her warmest smile instead of her police officer's glare. 'Will you be dancing?'

'Not with my hip.' Löic waved them off.

Olivia led, weaving through the crowd outside, then into the main hall. 'What a creepy bastard.'

Two floors high, the ballroom occupied much of the central tower and was decorated in the same style as the rest of the castle, but to a much higher standard. Or at least they'd papered over the settlement cracks. The dance floor was big enough for a hundred people to throw themselves around, though barely twenty were inside just now.

Mark stopped at a table with a view of a makeshift bar, the wooden top all wrapped up in fairy lights, then took a seat facing it and scanned around the room.

A door opened. Seemed to lead to the staircase he'd gone up the previous evening. Another one was double width, with some caterers working away behind.

Leaving that final one over in the corner.

Mark said, 'I'm guessing that's the one to the basement?'

Olivia nodded. 'Must be.'

Harris carried a tray over to their table. 'Here are your complimentary drinks.' He set down a glass of red wine and one of white. He smiled then cleared off.

Olivia sniffed her glass of *vino regurgito*. 'Christ, I could've done with that on my chips.'

A guy in his twenties with a shaved head started tapping the microphone. The band's drummer, judging by the sticks he clutched. He grinned at the room, waiting for silence. And got none, so he thumped the mic with his sticks and got his shush. 'Ladies and gentlemen! Sincere thanks go to every one of you for attending tonight.' He toasted them with a whisky. 'Sláinte!' Then necked it.

A cry rang out in response, 'Dheagh shlàinte!'

The room was much busier now, with at least a hundred in there.

The drummer laughed. 'As you know, the Ruthven midsummer ceilidh's one of the highlights of the Highlands' social calendar and has been held every year in this very hall since the early nineteenth century, replacing the historic gathering in the old village. It's become a family tradition to let you into our home and celebrate our culture as part of an ancient festival that predates the clans.' He paused then grimaced, biting his lip. 'I'm sure you'd all love to know that I could talk for at least another hour on the topic, but I won't. Instead I'm going to sit down at the drums and start playing so you lot can start dancing.'

A loud cheer went up.

The drummer took a deep breath, then held up his empty. 'But first, please raise your glass in a toast to my mother-in-law, Lady Elizabeth Ruthven. This is her family's tradition, after all.' He grinned at someone in the crowd beneath him. 'Before we get down to some Gay Gordons, here's to Elizabeth!'

The audience echoed the last two words and lifted their glasses to their lips.

Elizabeth mounted the stage. She rested her fists on her hips that tightened her purple dress. Her red hair hung about her shoulders in tight ringlets. 'Thanks, Paul. And thanks to all for attending! First, a cheers to Mr Harris and his team at the Ruthven Arms for their catering and staffing.' She stopped and raised a glass of wine. 'Brilliant work as ever, though a haggis got loose in the kitchen.'

Laughter roared around them.

'Anyway. After the first set of dances, there'll be a choice of haggis, neaps and tatties, or stovies with oatcakes.' She grinned at Mark. 'And aye, Mr Campbell, there are vegan options too, but you all know I like a bit of meat.'

A group of lads at the entrance were sharing leery comments. One of them raised his eyebrows and stuck his tongue in his cheek.

'The food was so kindly provided by William Turnbull.' She raised her glass. 'Thanks, Bill!'

Turnbull was at the front, turning to wave at the audience.

'As you're guest of honour this year, I'd like to bury the hatchet, though not in your neck for once!'

A ripple of laughter went around the room, but it seemed less than she expected.

'Anyway, enough of this nonsense.' Elizabeth downed her glass and smashed it on the table. 'Let's have a wee boogie!' She jumped down to the dance floor, her dress pluming around her.

The drummer hit a snare roll like a machine gun, then started playing a fast disco beat, like he was in some hipster band from Glasgow. He spoke into the microphone attached to his small drum kit. 'Ladies and gentlemen, find a partner for our first dance, *The Gay Gordons!*'

Mark was on his feet. 'Right, what's the plan?'

Olivia pointed over at the staircase. 'Löic's guarding the door now. Adam thinks it leads to the basement.' She picked up her wine glass and necked it. 'Let's blend in.'

'Dancing?' Mark shook his head. 'No way.'

'Yes, sir, I can boogie.' Olivia grinned. 'And you're boogying with me.' She grabbed Mark by the wrist and led him into the space at the edge of the dance floor, then spun around, ready for him to hold her hands in front and on top.

Elizabeth stood before them, arms wrapped up and held by a man a bit shorter than her.

Vic Hebden turned around and winked at Mark. 'Evening, Mr Campbell. Didn't know you were a vegan?'

61

Mark was out of breath, sweat soaking through his shirt. Feet stamping on the wooden floors, trying to keep upright as he clung on to Elizabeth.

Next to them, Vic Hebden swung Olivia around and around.

Mark couldn't remember the name of the dance.

Elizabeth turned to face him, cheeks full of colour, eyes alive with mischief.

They were at the head of a group, the lead man and woman, then they had to cut around the back where he met up with Elizabeth again. As much as he could make an arse of even *The Gay Gordon*, Mark could actually manage some of the harder dances. Their complex rhythms and shifting focus kept him on his toes. Literally.

No sign of Löic loitering over by the door.

The coast was clear.

Elizabeth clasped Mark's hand tight and cupped his buttock, then nuzzled his neck, her teeth nibbling at his throat.

What the hell?

The drums and bass cut out, then the accordion player did a little run, a long wheezing end to the song.

They all stopped to applaud.

Mark broke off from Elizabeth's embrace and tried to leave.

'You're no' getting away that quickly.' Elizabeth stood there, hands on his hips, eyes trained on him. 'Another dance? Or...?'

'Sorry, but I need to go to the toilet.'

She frowned. 'You want me to...?'

'On my own.'

'Listen, if you want to brush me off, then just say.'

'Okay, I'm—'

'Here we go.' Raymond Shearer stepped in to take Elizabeth's hand. 'I'm having the next dance, Lizzie.'

Elizabeth didn't look too pleased.

Mark needed to keep her sweet. After all, it was her castle they were going to snoop around. 'I will be back.' He pecked her on the cheek, then walked off towards Olivia.

'Jesus, Mark, she was practically throwing herself at you.'

'Well, I didn't catch her.' Mark gritted his teeth. 'Where's Hebden?'

'Off to snort another line of coke.' Olivia sighed. 'Getting high off his own supply. That guy is so close to the edge he doesn't need any pushing.'

'Well, at least she's off the board now.'

Elizabeth stood next to Shearer, but only had eyes for Mark. Furious ones.

'Thank you, ladies and gents.' The drummer adjusted his microphone. 'Up next, the *Dashing White Sergeant!*'

A series of groans, but the crowd got into the new formation.

Shearer was like an octopus attacking Elizabeth, his hands everywhere. Bill Turnbull finished off their threesome.

'Come on.' Olivia set off towards the door.

Vic Hebden was blocking the way, rubbing his nostrils. 'You can sure cut some rug, Mr Campbell.' He leaned in close. 'Though I'm surprised you're here and not writing that book of yours.'

'There's a ceilidh scene in the book, so I thought—'

'Sure there is. Might even read it.'

The music started up again, then feet thumped off the floor.

295

Vic walked off, still rubbing at his nose, and grabbed a woman who Mark took to be one of Elizabeth's daughters.

'Right, let's go.' Mark took Olivia's hand and led her around the dance floor.

She checked back. 'Someone could trap us down there.'

Mark didn't see any other choice. 'I'm doing it.' He opened the door, then slipped through into a long corridor illuminated by a series of flaming torches, each one giving a fair blast of heat as they walked along.

Olivia overtook him and opened the door at the end and shone her phone's torch inside. 'Bingo.' She set off down some steps, fear etched her face as she led down the winding staircase into the dark, their footsteps cannoning off the walls.

To the torture chamber.

Thumping footsteps came from above them. They were under the dance floor.

Mark slipped on a step, catching himself on the rail. 'Christ, the steps are soaking. Must be below the level of the loch now.'

'That means we're on the right path, then.' Olivia opened the door at the bottom and swivelled her phone around the room.

A cavernous chamber carved out of the rock. Several doors, only one was ajar.

Mark crept towards the open door, his own torchlight dancing around, and nudged it open.

Cages lined the walls on both sides.

Medical equipment sat in the corner. Tubes and pumps. No clues as to what they were for.

Löic spun around and his eyes widened. 'What the hell are you doing here?'

Mark turned and ran away from him.

Up ahead, Olivia stumbled back but the door swung open wide.

Elizabeth Ruthven stepped through the door. 'This isn't the toilet, Mr Campbell.'

62

Feet still thumped away upstairs, almost in time to the music.

Ruthven focused on Mark, her gaze searing into him. 'Sneaking around my home while I have guests?' she shouted, her voice bouncing off the bare walls. She snarled at them. 'The cops are on their way.'

'Good.' Mark held her gaze. 'She's a police officer.'

Fury burnt in Elizabeth's eyes. 'You won't get away with this.'

'*We* won't?' shouted Mark. '*You*'re the one abducting people and restraining them in your dungeon.'

'A *dungeon*? What are you talking about?'

'You've got Kay. You killed Rennie.'

'You pair of numpties. This was a spirit cellar for the village distillery. There's nobody here.' She gestured. 'Go on, son. Have a look.'

Mark kept a wary gaze on Löic, then entered the cell. Empty. Just the equipment, which admittedly could also actually be used in the distillation of spirits.

Shite.

Mark felt like someone had hit him in the side of the head. 'What... Where is she?'

'Who?'

'My daughter.'

'You thought I'd kidnapped your lassie and kept her down here?'

Mark didn't have the words. Everything felt upside down. He was *sure* Kay was there. She had to be.

Because... he didn't know where she was.

The door upstairs opened again, accompanied by the din of thudding of feet. Someone clattered down the stairs. Paul the drummer walked in.

Mark saw no choice but to explain it all. 'John last saw Kay on her way here on Wednesday night. She was coming here to speak to you about that document.'

'Aye, and I told you. She never turned up.'

'But you know about the document. And you found her laptop outside. And John Rennie went missing last night.'

'Jesus Christ. You're a special kind of stupid, aren't you?' Elizabeth shook her head. 'How about you explain it like I'm five?'

'Your family lost all that land because they were blamed for an atrocity. All you've got left is your heritage, this castle and your title. But Kay told you that she had proof the Turnbulls had done it, not your family. You could get all that land back.' He walked over to stand next to Elizabeth. 'There's a document that proves Richard Turnbull got his men to murder all those clansmen, then bury the bodies in a mass grave. How he faked it with the *Laird of Wedale* disaster.'

'This is bollocks. Absolute bullshit. My family lost our land fair and square.'

'You're giving up way too easy.'

'It's an interesting story, Mark, but unless you have proof it is just a passage in a fiction tale, like the kind you write.'

'I don't believe that. You knew about the document but you didn't know where it was. Until I told you John Rennie stole it from Turnbull's archive. His house has been tossed. A professional job too. Even got into his safe.' Mark focused on Elizabeth. 'Did you take it?

'Mark, I have no grudge against anyone. And I just don't care. See if I had my way, I'd be able to sell this place and get my money, then get on with doing something with my life. Instead, I'm trapped here, having to look after this place. It's a nightmare!'

'Even if you could get your land back?'

She was glaring at him. 'I don't give a shite about that. Seriously. I just don't. This place is a bind. If I could sell, I would, but nobody wants to take a place this riddled with damp and mould.'

'Look, Kay spoke to you last week. You promised her fifty grand for the document, fifty to Rennie.'

'I don't have that kind of money to give anyone. And I told you, she never showed up here on Wednesday afternoon.'

'She came on Wednesday *night*, though. It's why I was here last night. John Rennie saved my life and now he's missing.'

Elizabeth waved at the door. 'You want to know what happened to John Rennie? Where he is?'

Mark nodded. 'Please.'

'He's in hospital in Inverness.'

'What?' Mark fell back against the wall. 'But he was here. Last night?'

'Aye. We heard dogs outside, snarling and barking. Then engines. Then a scream. Löic caught the attack on the castle's CCTV. Rennie ran here but got pushed back towards the village by two four-by-fours. He went outside, fired into the air. The cars disappeared and the dogs ran off. But we couldn't find Rennie.'

Löic grimaced. 'Later, we drove to his home and found him in the kitchen. Bleeding and battered.'

Elizabeth said, 'Worse than if he'd been in a Glasgow nightclub, I tell you. Boy was lucky to survive. But he'd managed to get back, drank some whisky and eat a slice of *bread*. He was passed out and was going to bleed out. Me and Löic tended to him, but he wasn't having any of it. Woke up and started slapping our hands away. He blacked out and we drove him down to the hospital in Inverness.'

Mark looked at Olivia and got a shrug. 'Sorry, but you could've—'

'Could've what? Told *you*? Why?' Elizabeth shook her head. 'Finding someone you know bleeding to death in their kitchen's a wee bit stressful. And I've got a ceilidh on, in case you hadn't noticed.'

Mark tried to process it, tried to see if it made any sense. Trouble was, too much of it did.

Maybe car headlights explained the mysterious lights he'd seen. And maybe he had an explanation for how they were attacked. And maybe why. But not who.

'Do you know who it was out there?'

'If I did, they'd be sitting on a sword right now.'

'Was it the same people who took Kay?'

'I've told you, Mark, she didn't come here!'

Paul frowned. 'Was this Wednesday night?'

Mark looked over at him. 'Aye, why?'

'Well, I heard the bell ring downstairs. Be about eleven o'clock? I was slicing up a sheep at the time, everyone else had gone to bed. By the time I got out there, there was nobody there. Thought it was the wind or those wee sods in the village. But I heard a noise from over by the far bank of the loch.' He pointed out of the window, looking over the water. 'At the time, I put it down to those wild dogs chasing a deer, but it might've been the same dogs and men as last night.'

Elizabeth asked, 'You think they were chasing Kay?'

'It's possible.' Paul cleared his throat. 'Ask me, only one guy around here who has that many men and dogs.'

Elizabeth raised her eyebrows at Paul. 'Well, let's go and have a wee word with that arsehole, then.'

'Eh, that's the problem.' Paul scratched his neck. 'Turnbull's already left.'

63

Paul led Mark and Olivia back through the ceilidh hall, still thumping away with someone else behind the drum kit, then into a side room.

A tiny wee cupboard under the stairs, but big enough for all three of them. A huge screen hung off a stone wall, segmented into six different video feeds. Three different angles of the ceilidh, one just inside the entrance and two looking across the loch towards the village.

Paul leaned over and played with the controls.

Onscreen, the ceilidh dancers went into reverse, then resumed an earlier dance. Mark and Olivia were front and centre, next to Elizabeth and Vic Hebden.

Paul whizzed it forward, then let it run.

At the bottom of the screen, Turnbull pecked a young woman on the cheek then walked off, undoing his bowtie as he slipped off the edge of the screen.

Paul pointed at another segment, showing the castle entrance over the wooden bridge, then clicked his fingers just as Turnbull appeared, talking on his phone as he walked across the bridge and got into a tall Range Rover, then disappeared towards the village.

Mark paused it. 'How long's the ceilidh supposed to last?'

Paul checked his watch. 'At least another hour.'

Olivia just rolled her shoulders. 'So why is Turnbull leaving then?'

'I've no idea.'

The door opened and Elizabeth stepped in. The room was definitely too small for four. 'Youse got anything?'

'He's left, aye,' said Paul.

'Right.' Elizabeth was staring hard at Mark. 'You thinking he's got your daughter?'

'I do.' Mark had that tingling on his back, like spiders were crawling up his spine. 'When we visited, Turnbull called Kay a witch. He was seething about her. I went around, asking the same questions. Stands to reason he set his dogs on me last night. And Rennie saved me. Turnbull's going to lose his land because of what Kay found. What Rennie had stolen.' He shut his eyes. 'And I visited him this morning. Told him I knew about the document. Magic...'

Elizabeth looked at her mobile phone like she wanted to smash it. 'Well, I tried calling him but he's not answering.'

Olivia snatched it out of her grasp, then read it. 'I'll get a trace on that number.' She stepped back out and the door shut again, leaving just the three of them.

Mark focused on the display. Something stuck out to him.

A car's indicators were on.

He leaned over and hit play.

Sure enough, a Subaru pulled off, following at a distance.

Adam.

Mark didn't know what to make of it. Maybe he suspected Turnbull and was keeping it from them. Still, he didn't know what Turnbull slipping off like that meant. 'Can you play it back earlier?'

'Sure.' Paul wound the video a bit further back, past Adam getting turfed out by Harris, then Turnbull's exit. 'There?'

'No, to Wednesday night?'

'Why would—' Paul nodded. 'Right, got you.' He hit a few keys and the display changed.

And there she was.

Kay.

Mark's daughter.

Alive and well. Breathing.

Ringing the bell and looking around. Time stamped 22:49.

She checked her watch, then trudged off back towards the village.

Then nothing.

Five minutes later, she was running back down the road, right up to the door. She rang the bell again and looked back towards the village, panic in her eyes. She dropped the laptop and stepped off the side of the bridge, then disappeared.

Mark looked over at Elizabeth. 'You knew it was her laptop, didn't you?'

'I haven't seen this.' She was shaking her head. 'If Bill's taken her...'

Olivia opened the door but didn't step back in. 'Right, I've just called in a favour with a mate. Turnbull's mobile's been off for the last two hours, last-known location was here.'

Aye, and that didn't look dodgy.

Olivia's phone rang. She answered it and walked away from them. 'Hey, Doug. You got him?'

Mark stood up straight, but he wanted to collapse into a ball. He'd no idea where Kay was.

Olivia came back over. 'Rennie *is* in hospital.' She put the phone down on the desk, angled to point up.

John Rennie was on screen, head against the pillow. His skin was pale and he seemed to have aged a decade in the hours since Mark had last seen him. It was only when he opened his eyes that Mark realised it was a video call.

Mark crouched in front of the screen. 'You okay?'

'Do I look it?' His voice was slow, slurry. 'I could have been *killed* after I saved *you*!' He coughed and it sounded like a lung had come up.

Mark swallowed hard, but his throat was tight. 'Who attacked you, John? Wild dogs?'

303

'No. It was dogs, but they weren't wild.' Rennie frowned. 'They were trained, had their masters guiding them. Lots of whistles and some advanced tracking tactics. Couldn't see much in the rain, but there were... Headlights and military torches. I got overrun by the buggers. Someone must've hit me with a tranq dart because I woke up in here. That big bugger Löic was outside, said he'd saved me, said Lady Ruthven got him to drive me here, but I don't know whether to believe him.'

'John, we think it's the truth.' Olivia joined Mark in a crouch. 'You'd got home, had some bread and some whisky, but you'd passed out. They saved your life. Sounds like someone sent dogs and men out after you, John. Why?'

'Well, I've got one idea.' Rennie swallowed. 'But...' He frowned. 'They went after you, Mark, not me.'

Mark frowned. 'Because I had Kay's laptop?'

'The laptop.' Rennie coughed. 'I found a bag in a field, then took it back with me. I think?'

Olivia leaned forward. 'John, the document you took from Turnbull. Where did you put it?'

'I'm not telling you.'

'In your safe?'

'I'm old, but not stupid. I kept a copy in the safe but the original's with a friend.'

'Raymond Shearer?'

'Good guess.'

'Did anyone else know the combination to the safe?'

'Shite... I rent the place off Bill. Don't know how to change the code myself.'

Shite.

Olivia asked, 'Did you give Kay a scan?'

'Aye, took a photo of it and emailed her.'

'When?'

'Tuesday night. Lassie was worried about people being after her. And with good reason, though I thought she'd just hoofed it myself. Until they came after me. But I let her stay in my spare room. Nowhere else to go.' He coughed. 'Thing is, Kay had other proof too. Some lassie up in Wick told her about a mass grave dating back to the Clearances. Hundreds of bodies there.'

And Mark knew exactly where. 'Old Ruthven? The Children of the Future site?'

'Right, right. And I told her all about it. Somehow Kay got in there. That Séan guy used to be a member.'

'You're sure about that?'

Rennie nodded. 'Might still be. She was only there a few hours but she told me she found the site. Next thing I know she's arranging a meeting with Ruthven, then turning up to blackmail Bill Turnbull.'

'She *blackmailed* him?' asked Olivia.

'If that document was worth a hundred grand to Ruthven, then imagine what it must be worth to him. And your kid was desperate. Wanted money for some debts.'

And Mark knew whose debts he was talking about.

Rennie coughed again. 'She told Bill she had it, wanted two hundred grand for it or she'd go public with it. By then, I just wanted to get it back in the safe, but I think Bill suspected me.'

'What did Kay do?'

'Well, she was pissed off with me. I told you I saw her heading back to the castle.'

'Okay, thanks.' Olivia picked up the phone.

'Just a sec.' Mark took the phone. 'John, did she go to the castle?'

'Aye. Twice, that I know of. Spoke to the good lady in the afternoon, and she wasn't interested. But she went back at night, trying to persuade her.'

'Okay, thanks.' Olivia took the phone off Mark and stood. 'Hand the phone back to Doug, please.'

A grizzled copper filled the screen, his face way too close, giving a view right up his nose. 'That do you?'

'For now. Stay with him, please.'

'Aye, sure.' The screen went blank.

Olivia looked over at Mark. 'What are you thinking?'

'We need to get over there, Liv. To Turnbull's farm.' Mark

stormed out of the room, then out of the castle, over the bridge and back towards his car. He opened the door, but Olivia stopped him getting in. 'What are you playing at, Liv?'

'Stop.'

'Stop? What the—'

'Mark, I've seen you like this before. You're going to rush off there and confront him. You need me and Adam there to make this official.'

'Come on, then. I'm not stopping you. And I don't see him here, do you?'

'Stop me if you think that you've heard this one before...'

Mark sighed. 'I wish you'd stop doing that.'

'Look, this is Adam's case.'

'Aye, and I've given him a chance. It's time to do it my way.'

'Just give me a second, okay?' Olivia put her phone to her ear. 'Bloody hell.' She paused. 'Adam, call me. Cheers.' She hung up.

Mark said, 'Well, that's your second up.'

Olivia looked like she was going to throw the phone right at him. Almost immediately, it rang. She answered it and walked away.

'Hey.' Elizabeth Ruthven was there, shivering in her flimsy dress. 'You know you arseholes were trespassing in my home, right?'

Mark opened the door to Olivia's car.

Elizabeth batted at his arm. 'Here, I'm talking to you!'

Mark turned to her. 'Listen, the document is with Raymond Shearer.'

'What?'

'The original. You can get your family's land back. Tell him John Rennie said it's okay.'

'What do you want out of it?'

'Just my daughter.'

Elizabeth smiled at him. 'Thank you.'

Olivia was charging towards him, eyes wide. 'Mark, Adam's phone's still on. Last-known location is the Children of the Future camp.'

64

Olivia drove through the darkening glen with the confidence of someone who took that route every day. A trundling VW camper van loomed just at the crest of the bend. She was already overtaking it by the time they hit the straight, then took her eye off the road to glance at Mark. 'The sound of silence over there.'

Mark looked away, watching the dark countryside roll past. 'What's there to say?' He looked across the glen in what he hoped was the direction of the compound.

'Confession's good for the soul.'

'Right.' He blew out a lungful of air, knowing she was right, knowing how so many of his problems were because he'd kept worries and fears to himself. 'I was thinking how John Rennie said Kay was doing this for financial reasons. The money she was trying to get out of Ruthven, that's all because of me. All the time Cath and I were together, raising her, Kay saw my stupid, careless attitude to money, but she hasn't seen the deep shite it's got me into, so she's just repeating my mistakes...'

'There's only so much blaming yourself I can listen to, Mark. You're a selfish twat, aye, but you do have good qualities.'

'You're not welcome at this pity party, Liv.'

She laughed. 'Mark, we're going to get her back. Okay?' She slowed as they neared the compound and pulled in, just along the lane from the entrance, then killed the engine and let it cruise until they silently came to a halt.

Mark opened his door and listened. The evening was still warm, but the stiff breeze carried no sounds from inside the compound.

The place had a different feel about it at night, with football stadium floodlights shining down. You'd be able to see it from the air. Maybe they had supplies parachuted in – a plane wouldn't have to land, could give any number of innocent explanations to flight control for its trip.

He asked, 'We're waiting for your back-up to arrive?'

'Right.' Olivia checked her phone. 'Still about ten minutes away.' She frowned, looking into the woods opposite. 'Is that... Is that Adam's car?'

Mark had to squint to see it. Sure enough, a Subaru was hidden by the branches.

Olivia's phone rang out. She waved for him to shut the door, then answered it, setting the mobile down on the dashboard.

Another video call, a gruff face filling the screen. A monster of a man. Thick dark hair. Blue jumper, indigo jeans tucked into ankle-height black boots. He snorted with each breath, regular like the beat of a drum. 'Sergeant, your text message was a bit opaque. Care to elucidate?' Must be DI Chris Emery, Adam's boss.

Olivia glowered at him. 'Are you with Séan Avartagh now?'

'He's down the hall, why?'

'Because...' She sighed. 'It looks like Bill Turnbull might be behind this whole thing. The disappearances, maybe more. But he's gone to the Children of the Future camp. And I can't figure out why.'

'Well, it's probably because they're behind all these bloody robberies up here.'

Olivia jerked back in her chair. 'What?'

Emery narrowed his eyes. 'Didn't Adam tell you?'

'No. We've been busy.'

'Right, well. Can I speak to him?'

'Adam's gone rogue. He's... Gone into the camp.'

'Oh, Christ, he'll get himself killed. Listen, we've been working them for two years now and that lot came up in conjunction with it a few times, but they always had alibis. We didn't connect Turnbull until laughing boy in there started talking. But then he just as quickly stopped.'

'Why?'

'That's the weird thing. He was shouting and screaming to get let out. Said he'd do anything if we let him go, started singing about this, that and the other thing, but half an hour ago, he just shut up. Said he wants a deal now.'

'Weird.'

'There's no chance of him getting out without any time served. He's been laundering tens of thousands for them, but that's all we've got on him. As it stands, there's really not going to be any deal on the table, just a long sentence for him.'

'What's he said?'

'They're libertarians, anarchists, drop-outs, slackers, whatever. Pretending they're Satanists. Kind of implying the laundering is for them but won't be explicit.'

'I need to speak to him.'

'This going to help me?'

'I think so.'

'Fine.' Emery was strolling along the corridor, the video skipping and weaving. 'Here we go.' He seemed to open a door, then it went all blurry.

The shot solidified. The room glowed through the screen, the fluorescent light flickering above the table and chairs, all bolted to the floor. The same table and chairs Mark had been interviewed in an hour or so ago. Séan sat at the end, head in his hands.

Olivia leaned forward, resting her arm on the steering wheel. 'Séan, can you hear me?'

He didn't answer.

'Séan, I need you to—'

Séan held up his hand. 'I'm not giving you anything else until I know I'm okay.' He sat back and folded his arms. 'Legally okay.'

Olivia picked up the phone and pulled it towards her face. 'Séan, we think the Children of the Future have Kay.'

His mouth hung open. 'Shit.'

Mark frowned at Olivia, but she was ignoring him. That seemed like a bit of a stretch, but the most likely explanation.

And he could see what she was playing at.

Séan didn't look too sure about anything now. He stared up at the ceiling. 'The reason I'm laundering money is...' He sighed. 'The Children of the Future are preparing for the end of the world.'

Emery snorted twice in quick succession. 'They're preppers?'

'We prefer the term "Collapsitarian". Because society is collapsing. The tragedy of the commons writ large.'

'You said "we".' Olivia asked, 'You're a believer?'

'Big time. The world is ending, anyone can see that.' Séan stroked his throat. 'I was doing a postgrad in behavioural economics at the University of Southwark. Met some people through a mutual friend. People like me who saw the end of the world coming. The real deal. Gave up my postgrad, moved up from London.'

'What was the catch?'

Séan winced. 'We tried and failed. We really tried. We stopped roads getting built. Oil pipelines. But we've also got wind-farms approved. Vertical farms. Solar farms. But it's not enough. Nowhere near enough.'

'And you needed to raise money, didn't you?'

'Right. And I didn't have enough capital, even with my inheritance. So I bought that shop and I needed to turn it into a gold-mine. Which I did. Pretended I got orders from all across the country. All over the world.'

Emery snorted. 'Now that sounds like money laundering to me.'

Séan raised his hands.

Mark could see him clamming up here. He got Olivia to angle the phone so he was in the frame too. 'What's the money for?'

Séan stared hard at the screen. They'd definitely lost him. But he asked, 'Have you heard of Ayn Rand?'

Mark nodded, glad that Séan hadn't cut them off yet. 'Russian author, moved to America as a child. Wrote *Atlas Shrugged* and *The Fountainhead*.'

'Go on?'

'Developed a cod philosophy called objectivism, which is... It's screw the little man. Rich people are the only important ones and civilisation will collapse if they leave.'

'Right, right.' Séan blew out a deep breath. 'You know how many members of the US Congress cite Rand as an influence? Who live their lives by that philosophy? I stopped counting when I hit a hundred. Silicon Valley CEOs too. Bankers. Industrialists. You name it. They're leading this planet into an apocalypse. *Deliberately*. They don't care because they'll ride it out in Hawaii or New Zealand, where they're all buying up land right now.'

'That's what you're doing?' asked Emery. 'Buying up land to—'

'No, but that's what they've forced us to do. We know the world is going to collapse, sure, but we want to wake up in a new world where it's all fresh and ready for a good life. A new nature.'

'But the collapse is like *Mad Max*, right? Society crumbles. Anarchy. You're talking about nuclear war.'

'The Doomsday Clock is the closest to midnight it's ever been. Nuclear war's almost an inevitability now. Thing is, Scotland's pretty safe. Faslane's the only target because of the nuclear subs based there, but that's down in the Clyde, over two hundred and fifty miles away from here, so we're far away from the blast radius. The dominant wind would blow anything over to Scandinavia, so the land up here would be unaffected.'

Emery asked, 'So you're just going to sit there singing kumbaya while the nukes land?'

'Very funny. No. We're building a bunker.'

Emery shouted, 'A *bunker*?'

311

'A survival bunker.'

Mark realised he'd seen it. 'The mushroom facility?'

'Right, exactly that. Pretended it was an underground mushroom facility. Used to live near one, places was massive, so you can see why they go away with it.'

'So they just built it here?'

'Nope. Imported it from Texas or Colorado as farm equipment. Some corrupt port employees waved it through without an inspection. Then shipped it up in pieces so you didn't notice. Military-grade equipment, designed by the government and sold by people who really don't like the government. That thing could operate on *Mars*. Cost four million just for the parts.'

'Hence needing the money,' said Emery. 'Because you needed money to pay for everything? The engineering, the digging, the construction. That'll be millions too, on top of the parts. That's why you've been laundering money for them.'

'Right, right. Not just me. The hotel in the village too. A lot of businesses up here. It's big enough for three hundred people to live comfortably, but we're only taking about forty. Recycles water and stores enough food to live underground for at least twenty years, to see out the coming chaos. Hydroponics to grow fruit and vegetables. Sunlamps for vitamin D, backed up with supplements. But we need other crops too. Oats, wheat, barley. All milled and frozen.'

'Hence the robberies. Mills. Lorries. A load of hen food last night. That was your lot?'

Séan bared his teeth, but in a grimace rather than a threat. 'Right. But Josh has...' He sighed. 'Josh Urquhart is behind it all.'

'Not Cosmo?' asked Emery.

'No. Cosmo's his puppet. Josh has taken it over. He charges for access to Cosmo. His main thing has been selling entry to the bunker. To rich people. People who agree that the end of the world is coming.'

'Like who?'

'I don't know.'

'Come on, Séan. I need more than this.'

'I don't know.'

'Bill Turnbull?'

'Who?'

'Right. You, my lad, are in deep, deep shite here.' Emery sighed. 'Is Kay in there?'

'That'd be my guess. She pissed off a lot of people. Asking too many questions.'

'We need in that camp to see if that's where Kay is.' A big hand reached forward and clamped onto Séan's arm. 'And you're going to help us. So let's pack your bags and drive north, shall we?'

Séan winced. 'It's not as simple as that. Like that old song said, tonight's the night.'

'Neil Young?' asked Mark.

'No, Rod Stewart.'

'What do you mean?'

'The reason I wanted out of here. The reason I gave up trying. They're going into the bunker tonight. You won't be able to get inside. It's already too late. We can't get there in time.'

65

'I don't believe him.' Mark got out of the car, into the warm air.

'Are you sure it's because you don't want to?' Olivia joined him, walking around the car until she could grab hold of him. Not for affection, just to stop him doing something stupid. 'Mark, if they go into that bunker tonight, if Kay's in there with them? You'll never see her again. Well, not for twenty years.'

'That's great, Liv.' But she was right. Denying it was empty hope. Hoping against hope. And hope was something he struggled with. 'If Kay's inside... Tonight is their end game?'

'Apocalyptic cults always have an end game,' said Olivia. 'You of all people should know that.'

'I guess. But they're always wrong. Each fresh prediction is a test of the faith for their followers. A new message from God or the universe or whatever gives them another date to look forward to.' He looked at her. 'You don't honestly believe they'll go in tonight, do you?'

'Maybe.' She shrugged. 'Séan seemed desperate to get away so he could go in with them. Maybe when he realised he couldn't get there in time, he started stalling until they went inside. One last contribution and then he's done.'

Mark shook his head again. He couldn't believe it. He had to hope. 'Every second counts here, Liv. We can't wait for your backup to arrive. You and me. Now. Let's do this.'

She looked back down the road, then checked her phone. 'Okay.'

Mark walked towards the camp, acting all casual, then stopped outside the main gate and sucked in a deep breath. He knocked on the gate.

Maybe they were too late. Maybe they'd headed inside the vault already, waiting out the non-existent apocalypse.

Maybe Kay wasn't even here.

Maybe like Josh said, she had been, but had left.

But maybe he had her and had been a lying piece of shit.

The gates slid open and Cosmo popped his head out. He nodded at Mark. 'You come to recant your sins, friend?'

So much for charging access to the big man. But Mark saw the dazed look in his eyes, the pupils like black saucers. Aye, he was on something.

'We want in,' said Mark. 'We can pay.'

The door opened wide and another couple of cohorts were alongside Cosmo. Big brutes, bigger than the two the previous time they'd visited.

Cosmo stepped back into the compound and the gate started to slide shut. 'Sorry, man. All full up today.'

Mark lurched forward and tried stopping the gate from shutting, but he felt some serious power there and couldn't do anything. 'Please, guys. We're having... the worst day. Just let us in. We've got money. We know what's happening tonight and we can't face any longer outside.'

The door stopped.

'Money's no use to us.' Cosmo appraised Olivia like he was at a cattle auction, licking his lips. 'But we need people to repopulate the planet.'

Olivia said, 'Please. We know what's happening. We know what's going to happen. Just let us in.'

'And what is going to happen?'

'You're preparing for the collapse, right?'

'Completely. Stock markets, lawyers, big tech. Everything has been ruined by them. Everything. We just want to live our lives, but other people are screwing it up for us. Make it all *their* way, man, squeezing *us* out. They're weak, man, weak! It's time to reclaim the world for us, the real people!'

Mark was nodding along with Cosmo's words as he scanned the place, looking for his daughter, looking for any clues that his daughter had been there or was still here. 'I'm sick of being told what to do. They think they own us.'

'Damn right. Damn right! They tell us what to do. When to do it. Where. Who with. But they don't say why, do they? They never say why. But they know the reason and they just won't share it. Well, screw them, man. The climate crisis will split people in half. Those who can escape, and those who can't. They'll fight over water, food, land. The system's been rotting forever and the collapse is happening now, man. Right in front of our eyes! Droughts in the Pacific Northwest. Wildfires in the Arctic. Bond yields are down. Inflation is up. Markets are rising so much they're going to collapse hard. Everything's a bubble. People are throwing money at cryptocurrencies like *they* can protect them from crippling inflation. The concentration of wealth to not even the one percent but, like, fifty people worldwide. The system's completely broken, man. It's going to collapse very, very soon, but we're going to escape.'

Mark could start to see the appeal of the man, even through the drug haze. He'd seemed like a lumbering fool, but once he got going, there was a truth to his words. No conspiracy theories, just reflecting reality. And he spoke with the calm, reassuring voice of a teacher rather than a zealot.

And he was clearly starting to trust Mark and Olivia.

'And you're escaping tonight?' Mark used Cosmo's own language to gain trust.

'Damn right.' Cosmo narrowed his eyes at them, then sucked in a deep breath. 'What do you think, chaps?'

The bigger lump grunted.

The other one lifted a shoulder.

Cosmo swivelled around and entered the compound. 'Let's see what Josh has to say about it.'

Mark followed Olivia into the compound.

The gates clattered shut behind them.

Locked in.

But this had been way easier than Mark expected.

Too easy? Maybe, but as long as he found Kay, everything would be fine.

Cosmo led them away from the friendly building, the happy place where they'd been cooking vegan food yesterday, where Cosmo had been meditating, towards a gap between some piles of farm crates. A long tunnel, lined with corrugated steel on both sides, wide enough for two cars to drive through, and blocked off with a steel door at the end.

Cosmo banged on it, twice in quick succession, then a pause, then three times. A hatch in the door opened and Cosmo ushered them through. 'You like what we've done with the place?'

'Impressive.' Mark looked around.

A wide-open space, as big as a football pitch and just as flood-lit, lined with tall crates on all sides. Another set of gates presumably led to the fields. Farm machinery sat around, an old combine harvester and a couple of tractors. A long row of wooden housing was lit up in the night. An articulated lorry was parked over at the side; the Ashworth's signage was still there, but the contents had been removed.

An ancient sign hanging from a pole read 'Old Ruthven', black text on a white background.

This is where Kay had been, where she'd found her evidence.

Right in the middle, a small building was out of place. A blur of sheer black, like it was carved from onyx. A blue light lanced around the sides of a door, pulsing to a hidden rhythm. The sort of thing you saw in a CGI-intense film.

Cosmo walked over to it. 'We're going underground tonight, man. Twenty years, then we'll re-emerge into the world, after it's collapsed. When it's ready to come back. And we'll be ready for it all. An army of us. And half of that army won't even be born, man. Think of how cool it'll be growing up down there.'

'Super cool.' Olivia peered behind him. 'It looks really advanced.'

Cosmo wheeled around. 'You haven't even seen inside this bad boy. This is a top-of-the-line bunker, shipped over from the States. Took months to get here, but here it is. Solar power up here, but if that isn't practical, we've got ground-source heating, and even hydro from the underground rivers. A bleeding-edge capacitor to act as a massive battery. We'll *never* run out of power.'

'Bet it took a long time to dig it out?'

'A *long* time, man.'

'I know what you found.'

Cosmo laughed. 'Mushrooms?'

'No, a mass grave.'

Cosmo's eyes went wide. 'How did you...?' He swallowed. 'Pit was full of bones. Human bones. Some arseholes killed and buried their own.'

'Who does that?'

'I'll tell you who.' Cosmo waved his hand in the direction of the village sign. '*They* do. The landowners, man. It's not new; this has been happening for hundreds of years. The powerful take what they want. What happened here, I've no idea.'

'I do,' said Mark. 'The crofters who lived here were said to have been taken aboard some boat, but they were killed and buried here. Butchered, so the landowner could make more money from sheep farming. And this is what you're talking about. People are out for themselves. Taking what they can.'

'Well, that's...' Cosmo looked up at the sky. 'That makes me sick.'

Mark asked, 'But you're going to live in that grave for twenty years?'

'It's the perfect spot, man. The soil was *so* easy to dislodge.' Cosmo pointed towards the fields next to the housing. 'We moved the bodies to new graves over there. All respectfully reinterred.

The people who rule the world don't care about us, man. They just don't care.'

'Must've cost a lot to do this.'

'We've got rich backers. And the beauty of it is, they think this is for them.' Cosmo tapped his nose. 'It's not. They think they can come up here when the shit hits the fan and go down into *their* bunker. Well, tough luck. This is our bunker and we're going when I say we go. Tonight. And they *can't* get in. This is bomb-proof. Nuclear-bomb-proof.'

Mark had that flickering of hope in his stomach. They weren't too late. 'Can we come with you?'

Cosmo pointed at Olivia. 'You most definitely are coming on this journey. We need strong women like you. *Fertile* women.' He pulled out a knife and placed it against Mark's throat. 'But you, well, we have a use for you.'

The cold steel bit into Mark's skin.

Olivia's mouth hung open. 'No!'

Mark raised his hands, but Cosmo's goons grabbed his wrists. 'Don't do this.'

'You think we don't know who you are?' Cosmo sliced the knife hard across Mark's throat, nicking his skin. His whole body screamed out. 'Of course you can come play with us. Every sport needs a ball!'

A trail of blood ran down Mark's neck to his shirt. 'Please, I just want my daughter. That's all.'

'Who's that?'

Mark struggled to speak. 'Kay. Is she here?'

'Oh yeah, man. She's down there, waiting.' Cosmo let the knife go a touch. 'Or is she? You'll never know.'

'Please. Let me inside.'

'No, my friend. That won't happen. See, this is midsummer's night. The sun and the moon align with the Earth and we need to harness that perfect harmony. The universe demands a sacrifice and it's going to be you. He helped me see.'

'Who did?'

'My best friend.' Cosmo grabbed Mark in a tight embrace,

squeezing his arms around his chest and throat. He could feel the life drain out of him. 'Go to sleep, pumpkin.' He lifted Mark clean off his feet.

Mark tried kicking, but his feet just windmilled.

The blade dug into his throat.

Mark's eyes closed.

He'd failed. Kay had been taken and was going to spend twenty years at the mercy of Cosmo and Josh and whoever else was in here.

Lover, not a fighter.

No.

In the distance, blue lights flashed.

Backup had arrived.

Mark needed to fight.

He needed to fight for his daughter.

Mark jerked his head backwards and crashed it into Cosmo's nose.

Cosmo let go and Mark fell to the ground, landing on his knees. He put his fingers to his throat, but there was only a sliver of blood, not the river he'd expected. Just a bad shaving cut.

Cosmo was up, though, and had the knife.

Olivia grabbed hold of Cosmo from behind. She snatched the knife out of his hand and pressed it against his throat. 'Guys, if you come for me, I will kill him.'

The two goons looked at each other, then shrugged.

Olivia used her free hand to reach for her phone, then put it to her ear. 'In you come.'

A rumble came from behind them. Then a loud crash.

Mark inspected the building. Hard to make out a door in the sheer blackness of the cabin. 'Liv, if Kay's down there, we need to—'

Two big cops ran through the tunnel.

'Hey!' Olivia waved at Cosmo's goons. 'Lock down this area.' Then to Mark: 'Let's do this.' She let go of Cosmo. 'Nice and slowly does it, there's a good boy. You're going to get us downstairs.'

Cosmo was shaking his head. 'I'm going nowhere.'

'I'll kill you if you don't.' She pricked Cosmo's forehead above his bloody nose. 'That's just a taste.' She grabbed his T-shirt and pressed the blade against Cosmo's back. 'Where is Kay?'

'I've no idea.'

She held the knife against his throat. 'Tell me the fucking truth.'

'Fuck off.'

Olivia grabbed his ear and cut the knife into it.

Cosmo screamed. 'Okay, okay!'

She pulled the knife away. 'Where is she?'

'Downstairs. I'll show you.' Cosmo let her walk him over to the entrance and tapped in a code on an almost-invisible keypad.

Mark caught the numbers—8008135.

The door opened, accompanied with a swooshing sound like in a sci-fi TV show.

Cosmo stepped over the threshold, then Olivia followed him inside.

Mark inspected the door but, really, nothing would move it. The thing was *solid*.

The room was barely as big as an Edinburgh box room, just two doors, marked 'Staircase 1' and 'Staircase 2'. Separate flights heading down. Redundancy, Mark guessed.

Cosmo jerked forward, landing on the floor. He grabbed something, rolled, and swung at Olivia's legs.

The blade clattered off the floor.

She buckled and collapsed against Mark, screaming.

He struggled to hold her up, she caught him off-balance and they went down.

Cosmo was on his feet now, brandishing a baseball bat.

Olivia rolled to the side and scooped up the knife, then drove it into Cosmo's leg.

He dropped the bat and fell back against a control panel set into the wall. He pressed a button and grinned. 'Welcome to the future.'

A siren blared out and a timer appeared above the bunker door.

10:00

09:59

09:58

66

Mark watched the door slowly close.

The counter ticked down.

They'd let Cosmo do that.

Mark said, 'I've got ten minutes to find Kay.'

Olivia pulled the knife out of Cosmo's thigh and pressed it against his neck. 'What happens after ten minutes?'

'That door locks for twenty years.'

Mark crouched down in front of Cosmo. 'Where is Kay?'

'Why should I tell you?'

Olivia let the knife go. 'Because you're going to come outside with us. Right now. You'll go to prison. You won't be in here with your people.'

Cosmo looked at her, fear in his eyes. Genuine fear. 'You can't do that. I need to be here with my people. Please.'

'Okay, that can happen, but you need to show us where Kay is.'

'Second floor down.'

'Thank you.' She waved outside at one of the waiting cops. 'Come on in.'

Mark didn't want to hang around. He set a timer, matching the countdown, and walked over to the door marked 'Staircase 1'.

Heavy, like a fire door, which you'd expect in a survivalist bunker. He checked the timer before he entered. The stairs zig-zagged down and back, to just under the door they'd entered. Another fire door.

Mark eased it open and peered out.

Unlike the cramped room upstairs, this was a wide-open space. A few doors at the sides led to glass-windowed offices, with another two pairs of doors for the dual staircase system. It seemed like a control room, but it was empty. No people, just computer screens everywhere, showing status reports.

Battery: 100%
Life support: Good
Hydro: Optimal
Sunlamp: Day Cycle

No power button. Or controls. No obvious way of cancelling the timer.

But no wailing klaxons or flashing lights either. A silent alarm, like in a bank.

They were expecting a midnight entry, but there was still over an hour to go.

And Cosmo wasn't down there. You can't enter the survival bunker without your leader.

'There's a map.' Mark pointed at a screen at the side. On the right was a selector for floors. 'There are ten floors here!' He felt his guts flutter. 'We'll never find her!'

'Need you to stay calm, Mark.' Olivia tapped the control for the second floor. 'Cosmo said she was there.'

'He's a lying bastard, though.'

'No, he's not. That's the one thing he's not. Look.'

The screen filled with a map of the space. It was big, with sixteen small rooms leading off a central corridor.

No clues as to what was where. Or who.

Or if Kay was even here. Or Adam.

Mark charged off towards the stairs.

Olivia tugged him back again, this time stopping him. 'Wait.'

'Wait?' He glanced at the display. 8:48. 'We don't have the time to wait!'

'Mark, you don't know what's down there. Or who is. We need a plan.'

'I need to do something, Liv. I need to find Kay!'

'That door is shutting and you won't get out for twenty years. Assuming you survive.'

Mark stared at the numbers counting down.

8:37.

8:36.

8:35.

She was right.

Olivia pressed buttons on the control system and the display switched to a CCTV view. 'There. See?'

And Mark could.

Magic.

The main area downstairs was a rec room, with five big lumps, even bigger than Cosmo, all sitting around playing cards.

What a way to spend twenty years.

'We can take them, Liv.'

'No, Mark. We can't. Not alone.'

'What about getting those cops outside in here to help?'

'We could, but this will turn into a hostage situation very quickly. All the bozos downstairs need to do is wait for ten minutes to be up.'

'Seven minutes, fifty-nine.'

'Pedant.' Olivia walked off towards the staircase. 'I'm going to distract them. You get down the other staircase. Find her, Mark.' She opened the door and disappeared.

Jesus.

She was... She was going to sacrifice herself?

7:42

Shite, he needed to shift.

Mark walked over to the door next to the one they'd emerged

from and crept down the stairs. At the bottom, he nudged the fire door and peeked out.

The space was smaller, with more rooms leading off. Bedrooms, supposedly.

The goons were still there. One threw down his cards. 'Ah, shit, I'm out.' London accent.

'Well, I'll raise you twenty, Josh.'

Josh Urquhart was there.

Magic.

'Bill, Bill, Bill. That's rich talk.'

'I'm a very rich man.'

'True enough.'

Mark had to squint to make him out, but it was Bill Turnbull. He hadn't seen him on the CCTV.

Behind them, he could only see fourteen doors. Supposed to be sixteen. Maybe the plans and the execution were different, with a couple of rooms bolted together. A suite for Cosmo, maybe.

Mark checked his watch. Hard to remember how far out it was, but the timer would be just over seven minutes now.

Why weren't these guys reacting to it? Just sitting and playing cards?

Maybe they expected Cosmo's guys upstairs to be running things. Maybe thought it was going to be at midnight and were just waiting out the time until then. So maybe they just didn't know. Or care.

An alarm blared out from some hidden speakers.

'Fire detected in Stairwell Two, upper section.'

Josh Urquhart shot into action and raced over to the other staircase, the one leading down. Turnbull followed him, but the others headed over to the other stairs up to the control room.

Mark would have to cross that bridge when it came to it.

Right now, he had a free run, so he raced over to the bedrooms. He peered into the first door.

An unmade bed.

The second door was a double-width room, like a hotel suite when his publisher used to pay for such things.

He opened the third door.

Bingo.

Kay lay on a bed, staring into space.

Mark felt like he'd turned to jelly. The tension all sucked out of his body.

No, he wasn't done.

This wasn't over.

He walked over and shook her. 'Are you okay?'

Her head lolled forward.

She was out of her skull on something.

But she was alive.

'Don't move.' Cold metal pressed against his neck. 'I was worried you'd miss the party. But here you are, with an hour to go.'

67

Mark stayed perfectly still. He didn't know who it was. No tell-tale smells. No aftershave or cigarettes. 'I'm taking her out of here with me.'

'No, you're not.' The man leaned in close enough that Mark could taste the spearmint on his breath. 'She's staying here with us. For a very long time.'

Mark swivelled around to see him.

Adam.

Pointing a gun at him.

Shite.

'What the hell, Adam?'

'What, you're surprised? You're really that stupid? Of course we needed someone on the inside. Why do you think the investigations all went dead? How much money do you think I put through that pub? Can't believe you and Libby didn't think I'd tossed Rennie's place.'

'I don't give a shit about all of that. Kay's leaving with me.'

'I've got a gun to you, Mark. How exactly are you in control here?'

'Let us go.'

'No. And that's the end of it.'

'You know—'

'Shh.' Adam pressed his gun to Mark's lips, grinning wide. 'This will be so much fun, Mark. Down in this bunker for twenty years. Raising a new generation while the world burns.'

'The timer is already running.'

Adam frowned. 'No it's not.'

'Cosmo started it five minutes ago. You should check.'

'God no.' Adam licked his lips. 'Fuck it. Who cares if it's early?'

'You. You were the cop she went to.'

'No, Mark. But I found out she'd gone to someone. Managed to take the case under my remit.'

'You threatened her?'

'No. I picked her up on Sunday morning, tried to show her the truth. But she's a sly one. Took us so long to figure out she had a copy of that document. Dropped off the radar. Took us ages to find her after she left her two phones.'

Mark stared at Kay on the bed. Her mouth hanging open. 'What have you done to her?'

'Me? Nothing.' Adam laughed. 'Honest. She's just a piece of meat to me.'

That was it.

Mark ducked left then, and when he saw Adam lurch that way, he crashed his elbow into his face. He dropped the gun on Mark's foot and stumbled backwards, his nose a bloody mess.

Mark grabbed him by the throat and pinned him against the wall. 'You don't come after me! You don't come after my kid!' He crouched down and picked up the gun, then pressed it into Adam's mouth. 'She's not a piece of meat!'

Sounded like he said, 'Please.'

'I know what I'm doing with a gun, Adam. I've fired more than you.'

Adam punched Mark in the stomach.

The gun went off, deafening him.

Adam grabbed Mark by the throat and pushed him against the wall.

Mark choked as the fist tightened around his windpipe. Scratching at the hand around his throat, struggling to breathe, lungs burning.

He gave up, ready for whatever happened to him.

The grip released and Mark fell to his knees.

Adam toppled forward, groaning. He landed on Mark, his body almost crushing him.

Mark pushed him off and scrambled away.

Kay was kneeling on the bed, clutching a metal tube. She fell back, dropping it onto the floor, the clatter drilling into Mark's skull.

He shot over to the bed. 'Are you okay?'

'Just keep them away from me.'

'Always.'

'Dad, what the hell's going on?'

'No time, Kay. We need to get out of here.' Mark picked up the gun and shoved it in his pocket. 'Are you able to walk?'

She tumbled back onto the bed, then collapsed down onto the floor.

Shite.

Mark felt like he'd fallen down a flight of stairs.

'Okay, baby girl.' He scooped her up in his arms, still so light, and carried her back into the rec area.

No sign of Olivia, just the cards and the drinks fizzing away on the table.

Mark carried her over to the stairs and shouldered through the door. He had to take it slow climbing, but soon was at the top door, ready for the control room.

He checked his watch. Somehow, they still had four minutes to go. He opened the door to a crack, just wide enough to see through.

The control room was empty, despite the two goons who'd headed up.

No sign of Olivia up here, though.

Shite.

What the hell should he do?

He had to get her upstairs and out. Then he had to go back down to find Olivia. With the two cops up there, they'd be able to cover the area in a minute. Enough time.

But was it?

Shite, if Olivia got stuck in here?

With *them*?

Focus. No, he needed to get Kay out first, so he carried her over to the next stair door and stepped over the threshold, limping, the crushed glass feeling in his foot getting worse as he started climbing the stairs.

Whatever the hell Adam had done to him was really fucking sore.

He planted his right foot on the landing, then his left onto first step of the second flight, bracing himself to carry her up.

Josh Urquhart was standing at the top, pointing a gun at Olivia. 'Nice move.'

Didn't look like he'd seen Mark, so he stepped back and rested Kay down, but she was unable to stand up so he helped her settle on the floor. He glanced at his watch. Three minutes. He raced up the steps, stopping just short of Urquhart, then got out the gun, grabbing the barrel.

'Olivia, you're a smart cookie, setting a fire in the kitchens to distract us.'

Olivia said, 'We're walking out of that door.'

Urquhart laughed. 'That's not going to—'

Mark cracked the gun off his skull and Urquhart went down.

Olivia lashed out with her foot, cracking him in the balls.

'Hey, that's enough.' Mark grabbed her hand. 'Need some help with Kay.' He led her back down the stairs, clutching her hand tight.

'You found her?'

At the landing, he stepped around and stopped dead.

Adam was pointing a knife at Kay's throat. 'Need to try harder than that, chief.'

Mark raised his gun. 'Let her go.'

'Or what? You'll shoot? Hoping I don't cut her throat first? Good one.'

Olivia was standing there, mouth hanging open. 'What the fuck?'

'Sorry, Liv, but business is business.' Adam focused on Mark. 'Kay's here because of you, my friend.'

'What are you talking about?'

Adam smiled. 'When the famous Mark Campbell's daughter posted on her socials, saying she was in the Highlands, it was too tempting to resist. I asked someone to find her, but it turned out she'd been here, had spoken to Cosmo. I mean, talk about it falling into your lap, eh? All I had to do was hunt her down. We got her on Wednesday night. And I knew you'd come calling.'

Mark didn't have the words.

Just a crunching pain in his foot, a gun and an arsehole holding his daughter hostage.

'Adam, please. Let us go.'

'No, Mark. You don't get it, do you? You're here because I want you to be here.'

The gun felt slick in his hand. Mark couldn't fire without Adam cutting her throat first. 'You're going to kill me?'

'That's the idea, yes.' Adam shook his knife but pressed it back before Mark could fire. 'It won't be with this, though. No, we'll take our time making you pay, Mark. Months, I think. You'll be begging me to stop.'

'Why me? What have I done to you?'

'You don't remember me, do you?'

'Should I?'

'*Break the Chain* was based on your time in a religious organisation, right?'

'A cult, aye.'

'It wasn't a cult.' Adam snarled. 'I was a member.'

Olivia was shaking her head. 'What are you talking about?'

Adam ignored her. 'We met, Mark. One time, with Mr Colliston.'

Jim Colliston. The cult leader. Mark met him a few times,

gathering evidence on him, building a character who he covered in the novel. But he couldn't remember Adam. And he would have done.

'Adam, I uncovered some horrific abuse at Colliston's hands. The kind my parents were accused of when I was a kid. But it was *real*. The police investigated them. They arrested him, prosecuted him. They put him away for life, Adam. Colliston raped women and children.'

'Bullshit!' Adam pushed Kay against the wall and she went down. Then he put the knife against Mark's forehead. 'He was innocent! He was murdered in prison because of you!'

'Well, if he didn't personally abuse those kids, he knew all about it. Turned a blind eye to it. Lied to cover it up. And that's the best case.'

'He was framed, Mark. I was going to take over! You jeopardised my life-saving work!'

'So you joined a new cult? Lying to people about how the world is going to end?'

'It's ending, Mark. And it's already started...'

Mark caught a glance of his watch. Less than a minute now.

Adam's talking was running the clock down.

He had to do something!

'Mark, even if the world doesn't end, there'll be no consequences to me murdering you. I won't face any prosecution. So I can take my time torturing you, then savouring your death. By the time that door opens in twenty years—' He tilted his knife hand up. '—you will—'

Mark surged towards him and pinned Adam against the wall. He grabbed his wrist and clattered it off the light switch, driving his bone against the brass cylinder. Adam squealed and dropped the knife.

Son of a bitch was going to kill him, trap his daughter down here for twenty years and—

He slammed Adam's head back against the wall, then kicked him in the stomach.

Olivia grabbed his arm. 'We need to go!'

Mark's watch read:

00:36

He picked Kay up again, then carried her up the stairs.

Olivia was up ahead.

Mark stepped into the entrance room.

The door was warning that it was going to shut.

00:30

Olivia ran ahead of him. 'Hurry!'

'I'm trying!' Mark stumbled and almost let Kay go. He threw her out of the door, then stepped outside himself.

'Mr Campbell.' Vic Hebden was standing there, his goons aiming a gun at Kay. 'Care to enlighten me as to what's going on here?'

Mark was dizzy, like he could flop over at any point. He didn't have the gun. He must've dropped it. 'You followed us?'

Vic nodded. 'Saw you shooting off, so we decided to follow you. See if you were stupid enough to think you could run from me.' He pointed behind Mark. 'It's raining, so let's have a chat inside your wee house there.'

Stall him.

The time would run out.

The door would shut and lock.

'That's nothing to do—'

'Mr Campbell, get inside!' Vic pushed Mark back inside.

'You don't understand.' Mark was metres from the door now. 'They're going to—'

'Oh, I know what's going on here, Mr Campbell. Bill Turnbull explained it all to me, the whole scheme. Can't say I'm interested. Rather enjoy the real world. Have to say, heading down here for twenty years to avoid me is a bit of an over-reaction.'

'I'm not. I...'

'All I wanted was to help you, Mark. You've really upset me. And I really don't like doing this, but here goes.' He trained the gun down and to the side.

Sound burst Mark's ears. Something sliced at his ankle, burning pain shooting up his leg.

Mark went down, clutching his ankle. Blood pooled in his hands.

Vic had shot him.

Fucking shot him!

Vic pointed the gun at him. 'I'm a man of my word, Mr Campbell. You shouldn't have pushed things like you have.'

'The timer's almost up, Vic. We'll be stuck in here.'

'What?' Vic peered behind him. 'Oh fuu—'

Mark lashed out, cracking his fist into Vic's skull, then driving it into the console.

Vic went down, head buried in his hands.

Mark kicked him in the face and pushed him. He rolled away, disappearing down the staircase.

00:05

00:04

00:03

Mark shot towards the door and squeezed through the gap.

Back into the warm air outside.

The door clicked shut with a hiss.

68

Mark sat back in the ambulance and his ankle screamed out. He felt like he'd lost a leg. 'I'll be able to walk again?'

'You big jessie.' The female paramedic put the cap back on the bottle. 'It's a through and through wound. You'll be fine.'

'Really?'

'Aye!' She patted his knee. 'Make sure you get to casualty soon, though. Like, tonight.'

So Mark did and he couldn't put weight down. Felt like someone had sawn off his foot. 'Ow!'

'Oh, aye. You'll have a bugger of a bruise for a week or so. Don't be surprised if your foot looks like a big aubergine. You should worry if it starts to look like a big courgette, though.' She held out a cane. 'This might help until you get to casualty.'

Mark took it and managed to get some weight on it, then let out a deep breath. 'Thank you.'

'Aye, well, you should be thanking me for the tetanus shot.'

'Tetanus?'

'For the dog bite.'

'It bit me?'

'Well, I assume it's a dog unless you're into some deep kinks.'

She laughed. 'Aye, you were bitten. Not badly, but you don't want to catch God knows what else from it.'

Magic.

'Can I go?'

'Aye, on you go. But you could do with some sleep, son. Your eyes are like golf balls.'

'Thank you.' Mark stepped down from the ambulance into the compound. The walking stick was a godsend.

All glowing in the harsh police lights. Must be half of Police Scotland out, searching everything. Didn't seem to be achieving much. Most of the attention was centred around the pair of fire engines over by the bunker. A wailing sound burst out into the night, like they were sawing open a gateway to hell.

Which they pretty much were. And it would be just as impossible to get in.

Olivia was standing at the next ambulance over, checking her phone. She frowned at him. 'You okay?'

'I'll live, just about.' Mark hobbled over, but his leg was tickling a bit. Felt better than it had in days, though. That stick was going to take some getting used to. 'How's she doing?'

Inside the ambulance, Kay was hooked up to drips and machines. And sound asleep. Seemed a lot younger than nineteen.

His wee girl.

Thank God.

Mark felt his heart melt. 'All the shite she's been through, just because of who her dad is. What I did...'

'She's going to be okay, Mark.' Olivia stepped back as the paramedic hopped out and slammed the door. 'No physical harm.'

Mark scratched at his chin. 'Just psychological trauma. Three nights spent down in that place, whacked up on whatever.'

Olivia looked over to the bunker. 'Better than twenty years.'

Another hell demon shrieked out and sparks lit up the night.

'How hard are those things to open?' he asked.

'That door is seven tonnes. Designed to survive a nuclear

blast.' She looked over at Mark with tears in her eyes. 'Bottom line, they're in there until they want to come out.'

Mark leaned back against a pallet. 'Is Cosmo in custody?'

She nodded. 'He's not speaking yet, but he will. Not that it'll get the door open.'

Something tickled at Mark's brain. 'They said something about underground rivers?'

'Aye, there's a river system under there, which we could divert, dam or just poison, but the water filtration system uses cutting-edge sterilisation techniques. And they've got twenty-five-thousand-gallon tanks, enough to last a bloody long time.'

Mark took off his glasses and blew on the lenses. 'So they're going to escape justice?'

'Hardly.' She grimaced. 'We're setting up a camera pointing at the entrance. Soon as there's any signs of life, we'll be on them.'

'I'm really sorry, Liv. Adam—'

'You saved me and Kay, Mark.'

Mark nodded. 'Did you have any idea that Adam was involved?'

'Emery had a suspicion but... I thought it was bullshit. Be careful who you trust, eh?' She sucked in a deep breath. Maybe she was in love with Adam, or maybe just because he was an old friend, but she seemed broken by the news. 'Anyway, you're off the hook to your loan shark?'

Mark realised he was. Free. Untethered. A lot of money richer. Or less in debt. 'Still, I quite like the idea of finishing that book. Getting on with a new one too. God knows this wee trip has given me enough ideas for a trilogy.' He yawned into his fist. 'But I need my bed first. Bet I'm going to have some horrific dreams about being stuck in a bunker with Adam and Vic Hebden.'

69

One step at a time. Up, shuffle, up, shuffle. Ignore the pain.

Mark finished climbing the stairs and opened the door, then entered the flat. He rested the box of shite in his office, ready to be unpacked whenever he could be arsed. He dumped his laptop case down and hung his jacket up on the back of the door.

Nowhere near enough sleep and the longest drive in the world. Still, at least casualty had confirmed the paramedic's assessment. Just a through-and-through. The drugs were mostly excellent until they weren't, then he felt terrible, like he had the 'flu. Everything ached, especially his shoulders and neck. *Especially* his foot, but at least that was a dull numbness.

Sweat everywhere. Carrying boxes upstairs with a walking stick... Aye, he was an idiot. But that stuff belonged up here, not down in his boot.

And it was good to be home.

Something rumbled in his pocket. He got out his phone – an email from Fiona. He opened it and read.

Mark —

I've spoken to Hamish and he's happy with new direction, especially the mass grave and the boat disaster. Spooky as hell. Oh and the crofter's daughter being kidnapped by a religious cult? He loves it, sees it as a real tie-in to Break the Chain. Instead of those words, he wants a revised synopsis by Wednesday to get you some cash by Friday.

Hope that works.

Love,

Fi xxx

Funny how those kisses got added when she saw money in him. The prospect of another few books too, plus this one having a massive new hook.

And he didn't have the same urgent need to deliver.

All of that was tomorrow's work. A synopsis by Wednesday was child's play. A few hours' work to craft a hundred words. Maybe two, just to be on the safe side.

His phone rang in his hand.

Cath calling...

Mark had that sour milk taste in his mouth as he answered it. 'Hey, what's up?'

'Just wanted to see how Kay's doing?'

'She's okay.'

'Wondering when we can see her?'

Mark opened the kitchen door.

Kay was leaning against the sink, cradled by Olivia, arm around her shoulder, letting her rest her head.

God, it was so good seeing her.

And they really were like mother and daughter.

'Well, we've just got back from Inverness,' said Mark. 'Doctor gave her the all-clear, but she's going to need some counselling, which I'll pay for.'

'That's very generous of you, Mr Moneybags.'

'Least I could do. How about I bring her round to yours tomorrow?'

'Sounds good to me.' Cath paused. 'I got a text saying she wants to stay with you for a bit?'

Mark felt his throat tighten. 'That's right.' His voice was at least an octave too high. 'I think we both need the company.'

'Good. Well, we're out in the evening, so if you could make it before eleven that'd be smashing.'

Mark didn't want to ask. Just wanted to take each second as it came. 'I'll see you tomorrow, Cath.' He ended the call and sat at the kitchen table.

He needed to sleep for another two days.

But his head was still too full. If he closed his eyes, he didn't know what he'd see. Last night's dreams were weird and terrifying in equal measure. He didn't know what tonight's would bring.

'Well.' He had no idea why he said that. 'I need to clear my head. Who wants some coffee?'

'That'd be great, Dad.'

Olivia smiled. 'I'll have a cup before I get on the road home.'

'Cool.' Mark filled the kettle and flicked it on. At least Past Mark had left the cafetière out on the counter.

Because he'd run out of coffee beans on Thursday.

Magic.

'Just a sec.' Mark grabbed his keys and his wallet.

Kay followed him into the hallway. 'Dad, what's up?'

'Can't make coffee if I don't have any. And I'm not drinking *tea*.'

Kay wrapped him in a hug. 'Thanks, Dad. You saved me.'

He let himself fall into it. 'It wasn't entirely down to me.'

'Just take it, Dad.' She broke off then kissed him on the cheek. Seconds later, she was back in the kitchen, pawing at her phone.

Some things never change.

Mark grabbed the cane, left the flat and walked down the stairs as fast as he could. His foot screamed as he stepped out into Edinburgh's cool air.

He wanted to walk up to the Waitrose on Morningside Road,

treat the girls to something special. After all, Kay was safe. Try and walk off some of the pain. But his foot...

No. Olivia deserved the best. For what she'd done, and for...

Aye, Waitrose it was.

He walked towards Bruntsfield Road. Maybe catch a cab up there.

A car door opened and a man mountain stepped out, blocking Mark's path.

'Sorry,' Mark said, 'I just need to get past?'

'No you don't.'

The back door opened and a wee guy got out. Barely five foot. Designer suit and styled hair like he'd just come from a modelling shoot. Late forties, though, with flecks of silver in his stubble and hard lines around his eyes. 'Mr Campbell.' He thrust out a hand. 'Jonathan Burston. How the devil are you?'

Mark kept his hand by his side. 'Sorry, I don't know who you are?'

'Ah, well, there you go. That's the problem. See, Victor Hebden works for me and I haven't heard from him in a while.' He sniffed. 'You wouldn't happen to know anything about that, would you?'

Aye, he's locked in a survival bunker in the Highlands for the next two decades. 'Sorry, no. Haven't heard from him in a while myself.'

'Well, it's just that he's due a princely sum from yourself, so I would've thought he'd have been in touch.'

'Hang on.' Mark frowned. 'I settled that debt with him.'

'Did you?'

'I paid cash, aye.'

'Don't lie to me, Mr Campbell.' Burston nodded at the beefcake. 'I want paid. Now.'

Just fucking magic.

The guy reached for him.

Mark slashed out with the cane, belting him in the nose. Mark twisted to the side and lashed the cane against his knee.

The big lump tumbled forward.

Mark raised the cane, pointing at Burston. 'That debt is repaid. You hear me?'

Burston narrowed his eyes at him. 'I can see your position.' He sniffed, then helped his goon to his feet. 'Come on, Prentice, let's get out of here.'

Mark stood there, fizzing with energy as he watched them drive off back towards the city centre.

Aye, they'd be back. But they'd know what he was capable of.

And, more importantly, Mark would too.

Afterword

This is one of those books that... Well, it's been a tough one. A really tough one.

During the Covid-19 pandemic, I suffered a heart condition called Atrial Flutter, a type of arrythmia that sidelined me while the world was opening up between waves, before we had vaccines. (My ticker has now been ticking perfectly in time for almost eighteen months at the time of writing, thankfully.) I had early doses of the vaccine, so I felt safe in getting back to all that travel that I love, that I'd missed at the tail end of 2020.

One of the locations I longed to revisit was the far north of the Scottish Highlands. While they really start around about Perth, the true Highlands—at least to me—is the bit north of Inverness. Sparsely populated on the coasts, desolate and beautiful in the inland glens. I spent a few days up that way, working my way through the locations in this book at Midsummer, just like Mark does in the book.

Some of the locations are made up. There's no village of Ruthven and the glen of Strathruthven isn't really called that. If you take the A897 from Kinbrace to Forsinard, you'll pass Loch an Ruathair on your left. That's where the village and the castle are.

But all of the other places are real. Badbea and Rosal Township are very spooky places, you can almost feel the terror that was inflicted there. I hope in a small way that this book can at least make people aware of what happened during that time.

Finally, I have this affliction where I need to made good on failed projects. The nucleus of this book is in SHOT THROUGH THE HEART, a vampire thriller I published back in 2013. Nobody bought it, so I unpublished it. But I loved the location, the characters and it kept gnawing away at me. In 2021, I grew weary of writing so many police procedurals, so I wanted to do something different and decided to redevelop it into a psychological thriller. This book is about 90% different from that and it would've been a lot easier to just write it from scratch. But I feel a sense of closure now, and I hope this new book doesn't make me full of regret all over again!

Thanks to James Mackay and Al Guthrie for the development editing work, to John Rickards for the copy editing, to Mare Bate for the proofing, and to you know who for all the moral support through a hugely difficult time in my life.

Thank you too, for buying and reading this book. I hope it was worth it.

Cheers,
Ed James
Scottish Borders, March 2022

About Ed James

Ed James writes crime-fiction novels, primarily the DI Simon Fenchurch series, set on the gritty streets of East London featuring a detective with little to lose. His Scott Cullen series features a young Edinburgh detective constable investigating crimes from the bottom rung of the career ladder he's desperate to climb.

Formerly an IT project manager, Ed began writing on planes, trains and automobiles to fill his weekly commute to London. He now writes full-time and lives in the Scottish Borders, with his girlfriend and a menagerie of rescued animals.

Other Books By Ed James

SCOTT CULLEN MYSTERIES SERIES

Eight novels featuring a detective eager to climb the career ladder, covering Edinburgh and its surrounding counties, and further across Scotland.

1. GHOST IN THE MACHINE
2. DEVIL IN THE DETAIL
3. FIRE IN THE BLOOD
4. STAB IN THE DARK
5. COPS & ROBBERS
6. LIARS & THIEVES
7. COWBOYS & INDIANS
8. HEROES & VILLAINS

CULLEN & BAIN SERIES

Six novellas spinning off from the main Cullen series covering the events of the global pandemic in 2020.

1. CITY OF THE DEAD
2. WORLD'S END
3. HELL'S KITCHEN
4. GORE GLEN
5. DEAD IN THE WATER
6. THE LAST DROP

CRAIG HUNTER SERIES

A spin-off series from the Cullen series, with Hunter first featuring in the fifth book, starring an ex-squaddie cop struggling with PTSD, investigating crimes in Scotland and further afield.

1. MISSING
2. HUNTED
3. THE BLACK ISLE

DS VICKY DODDS SERIES

Gritty crime novels set in Dundee and Tayside, featuring a DS juggling being a cop and a single mother.

1. BLOOD & GUTS
2. TOOTH & CLAW
3. FLESH & BLOOD
4. SKIN & BONE

DI SIMON FENCHURCH SERIES

Set in East London, will Fenchurch ever find what happened to his daughter, missing for the last ten years?

1. THE HOPE THAT KILLS
2. WORTH KILLING FOR
3. WHAT DOESN'T KILL YOU
4. IN FOR THE KILL
5. KILL WITH KINDNESS
6. KILL THE MESSENGER
7. DEAD MAN'S SHOES
8. A HILL TO DIE ON
9. THE LAST THING TO DIE (December 2022)

Other Books

Other crime novels, with Senseless set in southern England, and the other three set in Seattle, Washington.

- SENSELESS
- TELL ME LIES
- GONE IN SECONDS

- BEFORE SHE WAKES

By signing up to my mailing list, you'll get access to **free, exclusive** content and be up-to-speed with all of my releases:

https://geni.us/EJmailD2

Printed in Great Britain
by Amazon